NOVA FANNUM

NOVA FANNUM

D. Brian Shafer

 Unless otherwise identified, Scripture quotations are from the King James Version. Please note that Destiny Image's publishing style capitalizes certain pronouns in Scripture that refer to the Father, Son, and Holy Spirit, and may differ from some publishers' styles. Take note that the name satan and related names are not capitalized. We choose not to acknowledge him, even to the point of violating grammatical rules.

Destiny Image Fiction an imprint of
DESTINY IMAGE® PUBLISHERS, INC.
P.O. Box 310, Shippensburg, PA 17257-0310

"Speaking to the Purposes of God for this Generation and for the Generations to Come."

This book and all other Destiny Image, Revival Press, Mercy Place, Fresh Bread, Destiny Image Fiction, and Treasure House books are available at Christian bookstores and distributors worldwide.

For a U.S. bookstore nearest you, call
1-800-722-6774.

For more information on foreign distributors, call
717-532-3040.

Or reach us on the Internet:
www.destinyimage.com.

ISBN 10: 0-7684-2429-1

ISBN 13: 978-0-7684-2429-4

For Worldwide Distribution, Printed in the U.S.A.

1 2 3 4 5 6 7 8 9 10 11 / 09 08 07

Acknowledgments

I have always been an enormous fan of a good book that features a struggling young hero pitted against a determined and capable villain where everything is at stake. In *Nova Fannum*, I hope I have captured that thrilling conflict of good vs. evil in an entertaining and inspiring way. Many thanks to some folks who encouraged me along the way: John Rayburn and Sam Drake, for great input and edits; Dave Knapp and Rob Ewens, for their prayerful support; and finally, to my wife, Lori, for letting me hide out and write; and my kids, Kiersten, Breelin, and Ethan, whose names are found in some form in characters featured in the book. Next year—Disneyworld! I love you all!

Part I

HUMUS

Chapter 1

Two Visitors

JEFFREY JEFFORD hated gathering wood for the fire. No matter how carefully he placed the sticks in the cart he always managed to get stuck or bitten or otherwise assaulted in some woody fashion. He pulled a splinter out of his thumb and threw the offending branch down. He was decidedly not a woodsman like his grandfather. And that was just fine with him.

It was a typically chilly evening in Humus, and the thick fog created the usual sense of suffocation. Jeffrey waited for spring with great impatience when this, his least favorite chore, would melt away with the last bit of snow. He looked up at the two stars that had recently begun rising in the north. He hoped they brought with them a bright future. But for now, it was cold. Winters in Humus seemed so long. Still, what was an inn in the dead of winter without an inviting fire?

Upon arriving back at the Trout and Truffles with his cartload of dead branches, Jeffrey heard unfamiliar voices and laughter coming from inside. His heart jumped with excitement at the thought of a patron *finally* bringing some commerce to the inn.

Perhaps their luck was changing! He was taken aback, however, when he walked in and his eyes met two of the strangest figures he had ever seen in conversation with his father.

"Ah, there is my boy now," said Malcolm, indicating that Jeffrey should come and meet his guests. The men sat at the table in the common room, where they had been drinking some of the inn's better ale. The room was hazy with pipe tobacco. There was also a sickly sweet aroma. Was it lilac? Jeffrey remembered such a fragrance the spring before when his great aunt had brought his mother, Cornelia, a basket of freshly cut flowers for her birthday. The room had a hint of cheap lilac cologne.

The strangers were a dramatic contrast to the room's cheery interior, like a bearskin rug in the middle of a grand ballroom. There was a little fellow, more mouse than man, with a longish nose and little black dots for eyes. He had noticeably round ears and a spindly mustache that added to his rodent-like appearance. Or perhaps weasel? And he had no eyebrows. He was very pale and didn't look up at Jeffrey until the boy reached the table.

The other man, a large fellow with a dark green frock coat and a rather long-shaped head, stood as Jeffrey came into the room. He grinned a toothy hello and stood to offer his hand. Jeffrey quickly dropped the firewood in the box and took the man's hand. The man was quite affable, with a strong handshake and a cheery demeanor. His salt-and-pepper hair belied his real age, but what stood out most in Jeffrey's mind was the leather patch over his right eye.

"How are you, young Jefford?" he bellowed. "My name is Jack. My, you're a healthy one. And nice looking too, just like your father." He looked enthusiastically at Malcolm.

Jeffrey was becoming a fine looking young man. He'd inherited his grandfather's good sense and his family's good looks. He had the Jefford hair (blond) the Jefford nose (straight) and the Jefford eyes (gray). He was above average in height and decidedly a sensible Jefford in his demeanor.

"Thank you, sir," said Jeffrey, looking over at the other fellow.

"Oh, and this is Finius, my comrade."

"There, there my lad," said Finius, who finally looked up from his ale, flashing hideous yellow teeth that looked like beeswax. "Smile for uncle."

Jeffrey managed a smile and glanced at his father, bemused.

"These are some gentlemen who stopped by for a bit of warmth and fellowship, Jeffrey. They won't be staying the night so no need to prepare a room."

"Just dropping in, lad," added Jack with a wink of his good eye. "Got a bit of business with your pappy."

"Where's mother?"

"In her room," said Malcolm. "Be sure and look in on her. She's doing a bit better tonight, I think."

SQUAWK!

"Hello Corinth," Jeffrey said, smiling at the raven perched in the corner of the room on a large set of antlers. "Staying out of trouble tonight?"

"Jeffrey! That bird of yours stole Jack's watch chain earlier," said Malcolm. "You better reform him or he'll be looking for a new home."

Jeffrey laughed, "Some birds you just can't reform!"

SQUAWK!

Jeffrey thought about the visitors as he climbed the stairs. Many unusual characters had come and gone in this place since he could remember. After all, the Trout and Truffles had been in the family for several generations. "Long as they pay, Jeffrey," had been his grandfather Kilian's maxim. But there was something more to it this time.

What concerned him were some of his father's old charts and notes he had seen on the table between them. They had obviously been studying them. Jeffrey could only pray that his father was not about to set off on another of his forlorn quests for a trove of hidden wealth. How many times had Cornelia and Jeffrey heard Malcolm speak of this or that opportunity?

"This is the genuine map, my dear. Notice the bloody fingerprint…"

"Only a few more miles and I would have found the entrance…"

"These men have seen the treasure themselves…"

"Cornelia, please do not think me a fool…"

"Dying lips do not lie…"

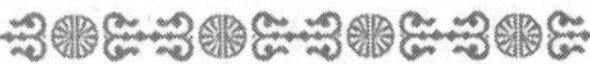

Jeffrey knocked on the door.

"Mother?"

"Come in, Jeff."

The dimly lit room always made Jeffrey uneasy, like he was entering a funeral chamber rather than a bedroom. He shook his head and went about the room lighting lamps. In seconds the light in the room revealed Cornelia Jefford in her bed, her favorite quilt pulled up to her middle. An uneaten plate of food was on the table next to her. Jeffrey looked at the food he had prepared earlier.

"You have to eat," he said. "You know you won't get better if you're not eating."

She smiled. "Those men still here?" she asked, sitting up a bit.

"Yeah," Jeffrey answered, coaxing some broth to his mother's mouth. "They have the old charts and maps out. Probably just reliving some past treasure scheme."

"Or reviving one," Cornelia answered wearily, sipping the broth. "You know your father. He'll not be kept by this inn."

Jeffrey nodded. "And what about you, mother? Are you kept by this inn?"

She smiled. "My family is the greatest treasure I will ever have," she said, looking vacantly into the air. She glanced at Jeffrey. "Love is the greatest treasure, Jeffrey." Jeffrey nodded in agreement, though he secretly felt that love *and* a bit of treasure would be nice too. "But I knew when I met him that his passion was not in a family but a family fortune," Cornelia continued. "I thought he would outgrow it. Your grandfather tried to shape him into a respectable innkeeper but..."

"I know," said Jeffrey, who had heard the story a hundred times. "It didn't take."

"Not at all," she said. "He had been bitten by the treasure bug while a little boy. Some prospectors or treasure hunters or some such wanderers had stayed here with their talk of vast hoards of dwarfish gold hidden in a secret cave on the other side of the Groggy Way. Your father caught the fever and it never left him."

"Poor grandpa Killian," Jeffrey said.

"While he was alive, your father was on a leash," she said. "But when he died, your father inherited the inn and was freed from your grandfather's constant admonitions to keep the inn in its grand tradition." She looked up at Jeffrey. "So your father spent the money that all of the Jeffords before him had saved on equipment and maps and lanterns and this and that."

She snickered, "Once he bought a length of rope so long that it almost filled the stable! He thought he was headed to Neria—

some underground kingdom of legend. 'Very deep place, Cornelia,' he assured me." Her smile turned into a sigh. "So as I watched the money slowly disappearing, I set aside the meager income the inn produced just in case Malcolm should finally run through everything we had. We had quite a tidy sum at one time."

"Mother, why didn't you just tell him 'no more!' and be done with it?"

She sighed. "Because I loved him—even in all his silliness," she said. "I wanted to take you and walk out on him so many times. But somehow I couldn't bring myself to dash what was, after his family, the second great love of his life. And so I listened to his pipe dreams, looked into his gray eyes and loved him all the more. And still do. Besides, perhaps he is simply helping these men out by pointing them out something on the map."

Jeffrey could only hope this was the case as muffled laughter drifted into her room from downstairs. Corinth's loud chatter also resounded. Jeffrey smiled. "Well, mother, you just can't reform some birds."

And that was how it went the next night as well. The men sat up late at the table in the great room, poring over the frayed map, smoking pungent pipes all the while making merry and encouraging each other on some sort of grand, albeit up until now undisclosed, prospect. Jack was always accompanied by Finius the weasel, as Jeffrey now thought of him, whose gnarled yellow teeth made him wince whenever the old man smiled and cooed, "There, there, little fellow. Smile for uncle!"

Cornelia and Jeffrey tried to warn Malcolm that there was something suspicious about these two—even more so than the others—but he wouldn't hear of it. As for Jeffrey, who considered himself an expert in reading people because he had seen so many characters during the inn's livelier days, he had concocted a complete case history of the pair. He decided that they were fugitives from a mental asylum who gained the confidence of innkeepers, murdering whole families in their beds and stealing their gold. From that night forward, he slept with a knife under his pillow. Of course, Malcolm continued to shrug off their pleas for caution.

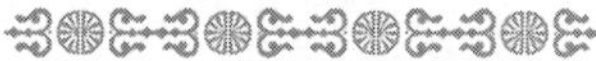

"Eccentric, perhaps," Malcolm assured them after the two had left for the night. "Maybe even more so than the others, but I am gleaning right now, my dears. Have no cares! These bizarre sorts of characters who hang out in dreary taverns and smuggler's dens are just the type of people who would *have* such information."

"At least get some proof this time," Cornelia said wearily. "I would like to leave something for our son!"

"And so I shall," said Malcolm, as he followed his wife up the stairs. "But they seem to be hiding an amazing story, Cornelia. There's something to this. I believe they have an important secret—one that could make us very wealthy indeed!"

Malcolm stopped halfway up the stairs as Cornelia turned around to confront him. Standing there, hands on her hips, she might have been the fiery young woman he had married all those years ago. It was as if her recent illness had never occurred. He couldn't help but smile at the woman who had been the belle of Aurora. She was still beautiful, and quite shapely, with dark hair cascading down past her shoulders. "Don't you want to be a great lady with servants and all the things I want for you and Jeffrey?" Malcolm asked.

"I don't want wealth, Malcolm," Cornelia said. "I want a sensible husband who does not go chasing after every one-eyed scoundrel with a map. Do you realize how much you have wasted on such trivia? Why, Jeffrey and I hardly know you anymore, you're gone so often. And what about your son's inheritance? And your promise?"

"I promise my dear," said Malcolm. "This will be the last time." And he meant it.

She looked at him, not seeing the pleading husband on the stairs whose erratic notions were bringing them to ruin. For the moment, she saw the young man she had fallen in love with—the rascal who'd talked of castles in the sky and pots of gold at rainbows' ends. She gazed intently, seeing the handsome young Jefford whose wild schemes seemed so charming, back then.

She thought of Malcolm's father, Killian, scowling at his dreamer of a son, telling him he had better learn the business of running an inn or end up in the poorhouse. And she thought of their son, Jeffrey, asleep upstairs, and wondered about his future. She looked deeply into Malcolm's eyes, and she melted.

"I love you," she said, finally turning and walking up the stairs. "Somehow I still love you." And she meant it.

The very next night, after Jeffrey had gone to his room, Jack and Finius came in for what was becoming their usual late-night visit. Jack had apparently been drinking quite heavily—more so than usual. When he asked for another draft of ale, Malcolm, though not as sensible a Jefford as *his* father, thought of Cornelia's hunch, and became suspicious that perhaps these two were more interested in ale than adventure. Three nights of this was quite enough.

"Before I pour I would finally like to hear this fantastic story," Malcolm said.

The two men looked at each other.

"It isn't that I don't trust you…"

At first Jack seemed incensed at such a suggestion, glancing over at Finius, whose face was vacant as usual. He pulled on his lower lip for a moment, stared at Malcolm and chuckled. Then, with a triumphant smile, he reached into an inner pocket in his vest, pulled out a folded paper and carefully laid it out on the table.

It was ancient looking and curled at the edges—like many of the other maps that had been brought into this house to be authenticated and hopefully purchased or otherwise validated by Malcolm. This one had obviously been in a fire at some point. Malcolm sighed at the sight of yet another map and looked up at Jack. He felt a tinge of sorrow for his Cornelia who had married such a fool. He hoped she wasn't listening.

"I suspected you would require some proof," Jack said proudly. "And I decided that tonight would be the night!"

Malcolm looked at the document against the dark brown table. "A map," he sighed.

"A very special map, I'm told," Jack said, slurring his drunken words and looking about him as if to make sure they were quite alone. Finius likewise looked about. Jack kept his hand on the map as if not quite ready to completely reveal it to Malcolm's doubtful expression. When he finally lifted his hand, Malcolm examined the map looking for signs of forgery.

"Quite old," Jack assured him.

"I'm sure it is very old," said Malcolm, now looking at the clock as much as the map. "But I've seen older."

"Very rare. One of great value," Jack continued. "The blood of thousands on it, to be sure. Why, I was that close to losing my life when I acquired it. How do you suppose I got this?" He lifted up his patch, plucked out a cheaply made glass eye and plopped it down on the table with a thud. Jack laughed heartily and after a moment, fixed the eye back into place. He always enjoyed the effect of such a demonstration on unsuspecting people. Finius slammed his hand down on the table in delight, as if he was seeing this spectacle for the very first time. Malcolm smirked, and ignoring the eye, examined the map further.

"So what do you think?" asked Jack, puffing away on his pipe.

Never one to turn down an opportunity to reveal his great knowledge of such things, Malcolm pointed out the more interesting features on the old parchment. After a few minutes he began speaking as if giving a lecture at the Academy. "I must admit it is unlike any map that I have ever seen," he began. "This is obviously the Tellit Sound—the hooked tip of Bloodswain Bay gives it away. Not much detail in the north. Humus, to be sure, but as if mapped by someone who had never fully explored the interior. And of course, the coastal south is completely impenetrable because the southern half of Humus is nothing but high, treacherous cliffs and rocky shoals."

He pointed to a spot on the map. "Edenshore is not even noted. And I believe this is southern Humus and possibly Mount Ereth marked here. Its peak sometimes emerges from the fog—a great friend to mapmakers in that foggy mist that skirts our southern borders. But this…"

"Yes?" asked Jack, watching Malcolm's eyes studying the map.

"This other land south of the mountains," he said, brushing the map. "It doesn't exist on any known maps. Here on the other side of the mountains. And look at this city! It must be enormous! If only we knew the meaning of this strange writing!"

Malcolm turned the map so that Jack could see the inscriptions to which he referred. It was indeed marked with strange writings, and in a language that he had never before encountered. It also seemed a bit thicker than most maps he had seen—certainly thicker than the usual maps that promised hidden wealth and secret treasures.

"I saw that scribbling myself," said Jack. "But nobody could tell me what it meant. Only that it was somehow connected to untold wealth."

"There have always been legends of a great city or some such thing beyond the mountainous border in the south," Jack said, wondering aloud. "Seems impossible, although the great Laramor claimed to have seen the other side just before he died."

He looked at Jack, the gleam of a hunter in his eyes. "But what if..."

Malcolm looked once more at the writing and shook his head doubtfully when he suddenly turned, as if he heard something. Glancing toward the stairway, he began wracking his mind, mumbling to himself.

"Well, we had hoped you might be able to decipher this," said Jack, scanning Malcolm for a hint of what he was thinking. "I mean what with your knowledge of such things."

Malcolm looked up at Jack with a wide-eyed stare.

"What is it, Jefford?" Jack asked, reading the intent countenance Malcolm was displaying. "Something familiar to you, perhaps?"

"Yes, as a matter of fact," said Malcolm, triumphantly. "I know that I have seen that writing before."

"Perhaps your f-f-f-father was f-f-f-familiar with it?" offered Finius.

Jack scowled at Finius fiercely.

"My father!" Malcolm said loudly. "That's it! Excuse me gentlemen!"

He disappeared up the stairs. Jack and Finius looked at each other hopefully as the noise of a closet door or dresser drawer could be heard being opened and shut. A minute later Malcolm bounded down the stairs, just clearing Roxanne the cat who was moving across the room. The cat dodged his boots, yowling angrily. Corinth squawked from his perch on the elk antlers. Malcolm sat back down and produced a small black pouch. He took out a large gold coin and plopped it on the table.

The coin—more medallion in size—did indeed have the same strange writing as on the map. There was also a beautiful sword engraved on it. Malcolm watched for the men's reaction.

"By the Great Ones!" said Finius, staring at the coin triumphantly. "So you do have it?"

Jack glared menacingly at Finius who cowed into his chair.

"Yes," said Malcolm, looking at the two men. "As you apparently suspected. So it's the coin you are after. Well done, tracking it down."

"Well, there's a bit more to it than that," Jack began uncomfortably.

Malcolm, flush with the excitement of connecting his coin with the map ignored Jack and carefully compared the writing. No doubt about it, they had distinct, identical points of comparison. They were both written in the same unknown language. He handed the coin to Jack, who held it nervously and then put it down on the table.

"You'd best explain yourself," said Malcolm.

Jack looked uncomfortable for a moment and then grinned a guilty smile.

"You knew somehow that it was in my possession," Malcolm said.

"Let's just say I suspected it," said Jack. "I'm afraid I was never one for subtlety. Your deduction proves that we have found not only the coin, but the right person to join us on a great adventure. Your reputation for knowledge of such things goes far beyond this little inn. And as to the other, yes I was informed that this coin, once my very own, might now be in your possession."

Malcolm poured himself a fresh drink and, for the first time since meeting these two seedy characters, thought that perhaps there was something more to all of this. Maybe this is the opportunity of a lifetime—the very thing that had eluded him all these years and made him seem just a dreamer in the eyes of many of friends and family.

"So the coin was once yours? This is all very interesting," said Malcolm, shaking himself from his thoughts. "A strange coin and a map—both with the same, unknown markings. Obviously they have some connection."

He looked at Jack squarely.

"And exactly how did you come by them?"

Jack smiled. "As I said, the blood of thousands is on it. Let's just leave it at that. For now"

Finius snickered under his breath.

Malcolm extended his hand to take the coin back. Jack held on to it a moment more before giving it back. "A strange coin, an old map, blood of thousands? I've heard all sorts of stories, my would-be partner. I need to know exactly what this is all about before I sink one eden into it."

Jack smiled at the man, and wagged his finger at him. "You are much more of a sensible man than people give you credit for, Jefford," he said tapping his head, amused by Malcolm's increasingly suspicious attitude. "That is a good thing. I tell you what. Let Finius pour, let this dear lady serve, and I'll give you something very substantial to think about."

He leaned in once more as he packed his pipe. "But beware. Like this coin, certain knowledge carries with it a heavy price and grievous responsibilities."

"D-d-drink up gentlemen!" blurted Finius, emptying the ale into the three cups.

Chapter 2

A Tell-Tale Coin

BEFORE Jack was able to begin his story, Cornelia, who was feeling better, brought fresh rolls and meat to the men, who still made her uneasy with their patronizing compliments. After the brief meal, the men sat around making small conversation about nothing in particular until it was painfully obvious that Jack wasn't going to talk business while the lady of the house was within earshot.

"I'm off to bed, gentlemen," she finally said, catching her husband's dismissive look for the third time. "If you'll excuse me."

Jack stood up and bowed with the elegance of a grand duke. Finius did likewise.

"Until we meet again, dear lady," purred Jack magnificently.

Cornelia nodded politely and caught a glimpse of Finius' crooked teeth as he grinned at her and nodded enthusiastically.

"Thank you, sirs," she replied. "Goodnight, Malcolm."

"Goodnight love," he answered.

When Jack was fully convinced that Cornelia had retired, he lit his pipe, took a long drink of the ale and said. "You must know,

Malcolm, I have not always been the pitiful figure you see before you. I had a great trade ahead of me at one time."

He puffed away on the cheap tobacco and looked up past Malcolm's shoulders, pointing with his pipe. "Handsome bit of weaponry there," he said.

Malcolm didn't have to turn around to know that Jack was pointing at the sword that hung over his mantel. The two had been glancing at it from time to time ever since they first arrived. He'd wondered when it would come up in conversation.

"A family heirloom," said Malcolm casually.

"A S-S-Sauren relic," said Finius offhandedly.

Jack looked at Finius with a vicious scowl and then back at Malcolm. Finius excused his interruption and added, "I mean to say, it has all the markings of a royal weapon of Sauren c-c-craftsmanship."

"My friend here is something of an antiquarian," Jack offered, as if to excuse Finius' rare lucidity. "Though you would not now it to look at him, Finius is an eclectic scholar of sorts and whenever he runs across certain items of an obscure nature he becomes quite enthusiastic. Comes in handy in this sort of work."

Finius' countenance fell once more back into his flagon.

"How unfortunate his knowledge does not extend to the writing on the map," said Malcolm. "But he's quite right. It is a Sauren piece. You have a good eye, Finius. An ancestor of mine took it off the Sauren king in the Black Water Wars."

"Ah yes," said Jack. "The Black Water Wars. That certainly made an end to Sauren ambitions, didn't it? They never recovered. I hear now that there are only a few remnants of that once proud race."

"So I've heard."

"But evoking their dread memory comes in handy dealing with children at bedtime," Jack continued. "Many's the night my pap told me that if I got out of bed a Sauren might be waiting to snatch me up and take me to their haunted mountain Sabrek. Let me tell you, I stayed in my bed in terror of Sauren eyes watching me all night long!"

"Much of our history is connected with that war," Malcolm continued. "Our clothes, our family crest..."

"The story is that Sir William Jefford, my ancestor, was a mercenary who had been rescued by a flock of ravens. The Saurens were hot on his heels when the black birds led the perishing troops he was commanding to fresh water. That sign of the ravens so encouraged the troops that the battle turned to their advantage. The black-feathered cap and the black clothes have been a family tradition ever since."

"Ah yes, the hero of Aurora," said Jack.

He laughed at Malcolm's obvious surprise.

"You think because I am the man you see before you that I have never been educated?" Jack said. "Sir William Jefford, Hero of Aurora, and awarded the sword that he had taken off the slain body of the Sauren king. I understand that he even ordered the Sauren bodies burned with sulphur so that they might not come back to life."

He glanced at Malcolm and whispered.

"As Sauren bodies are said to do."

"Nonsense," said Malcolm. "So the sword has hung above every Jefford mantel since the battle. And the ravens were not forgotten either—a raven feather is featured in the Jefford family crest above the sword and inscribed with the Jefford' family motto "Nunquam saepenumero siccus," which means "Never again thirsty."

"Yes a magnificent trophy. May I?" asked Jack, reaching his hands out toward the sword.

"Of course," said Malcolm, a bit hesitant but well aware of his own dagger tucked neatly in his boot. "I'll fetch it down."

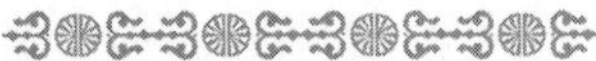

Knowing that Malcolm was not as sensible as some Jeffords, Cornelia took not to her bed but to her curiosity, and positioned herself in a pantry which had a common wall with the great room. From this vantage she was able to hear every word that was spoken. Listening to the men from the pantry, she sat in horror awaiting what she was sure to be the sound of the Sauren sword crashing down upon Malcolm's unsuspecting skull. She was looking for some sort of weapon herself when she was aware of someone else in the pantry with her.

"Jeffrey!" she whispered. "What are you doing here?"

"I don't know," said Jeffrey. "I just don't trust them, mother."

Cornelia pulled the boy close to her and said that he must be very quiet. Together they listened to the remainder of the conversation.

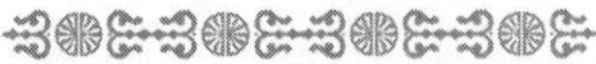

Jack handled the ancient sword as if it were made of glass. He showed it to Finius who looked but did not touch. On the tip of the scabbard was a roughly-cut green stone, a large emerald which shown like green fire in the room's firelight.

"The Saurens always had a fondness for precious stones as I recall," said Jack, nearly drooling at the sight of the stone. "Five magnificent emeralds were set in the crown which has since disappeared. Perhaps we should go after the remaining treasure one day as well!" he laughed.

Malcolm only smiled as if amused. Jack handed the sword back to him.

"You certainly are well-informed on your Sauren history," said Malcolm, as he returned the sword to its place above the mantle.

"Not at all, sir," said Jack. "I am merely well-informed on precious stones!"

Finius burst out in laughter and Jack joined in. They carried on like this for several seconds. Malcolm only looked on, thinking of his family upstairs and how he subjected them to the company of such louts. They were certainly strange ducks. But after all, they were treasure hunters and eccentric by nature. At least that was the benefit of the doubt Malcolm was allowing them at that moment.

"Is that the only Sauren article you have?" asked Jack, as he poured himself another ale. "Have you any other items?"

"That's all I have," said Malcolm firmly.

"But s-s-s-surely not!" began Finius, who yelped in pain as Jack delivered a harsh kick to his shin that startled Malcolm and almost overturned the table.

"Shut your gob, Finius!" said Jack, almost growling. "You insult our host. If he says he has no other Sauren relic then the matter is settled."

Malcolm was getting quite fed up with them by now. After all, these men were drinking some of his best ale, had taken advantage of his wife's hospitality, and now they were also wasting his time prying into his family business. He intended to disclose nothing more.

"That matter may be settled," Malcolm finally sputtered. "But the matter of this coin or medal or medallion or whatever it is and our conversation these many nights still remains a mystery. Now either give me reason to throw you two out and never lay eyes on you again, or give me reason to throw in with you on this venture. But do so now! My patience is behind me."

Finius looked up at Jack with a startled expression.

"Ah, forgive us," said Jack turning quite red in the face and looking very uncomfortable, sort of like a cat caught with a wet paw around a fish bowl. "Our minds are so cluttered with this and that treasure and legend after all these years. What with the conversation about the Black Water Wars and the sword and all. Finius naturally thought of the Five Stones of the Sauren crown which most certainly would have been on the head of the one bearing this sword in battle. It seemed possible that your revered ancestor might have picked up the crown as well." He stopped long enough to see if there was any reaction from Malcolm at the mention of the five stones and the crown. Seeing none he sniffed and continued.

"It is a mania, Jefford—an absolute mania!" he said, slapping the table with his hand. "This hunt for legendary treasure will be the death of me! The glowing rocks at Newbury; hoards of elfish gold in the canyons of Yor-Bel; stores of gems in the Stawshaw Mountains; the haunted chasm at Quix, fraudulent maps, unscrupulous guides..." He grasped his head in both hands as if he were experiencing a tremendous headache. "My mind these days is like an unkempt catalog of mythological minutia. It will drive me insane one day. You see—you must forgive me my erratic wanderings."

"Of course," said Malcolm. "Consider the subject closed."

"You're very gracious," sniffed Jack.

"And now, the tale of the coin," prompted Malcolm.

Jack sipped his ale.

"The coin. As I mentioned earlier, Malcolm, I have not always been the broken figure of a man you now see before you. Years of throwing in with all sorts of characters on all sorts of hunts for all sorts of treasure have taken their toll."

He leaned back now, relaxing as he spoke of happier times.

"I always enjoyed traveling. You know—seeing the different people and towns of Humus. I suppose I got it from my father. He was a captain and owner of a trading vessel which took him along the coast and up the rivers of Humus many, many times. I always enjoyed those trips between Aurora and the other great ports and river towns. I was to follow in his place and inherit his ship. I dreamt of owning several ships—a fleet of commercial vessels which would buy me the greatest estate in Humus."

He smiled as if he could smell the salty air once more, and hear the sea birds calling in the distance. His eyes closed and his head cocked back a bit.

"You were saying…"

"Yes," continued Jack. "And so I accompanied my father on his voyages and as you can imagine we ran across some very interesting characters. The stories I could tell! Well sir, on one voyage—the ship's last as it turned out—we took on a strange little man whose coin this was."

"You got the coin from him?" repeated Malcolm.

Jack nodded and continued. "He was an old man, wearing a well-worn, dark-blue robe that draped down to his ankles. Rather like a monk or some sort of holy man as I have seen in the north. He also wore a dark cowl with a symbol of a sword upon it—much like the sword on that coin. He was quite polite, albeit a bit odd, and mainly kept to himself. He spoke our language but with a bit of an accent that I did not recognize.

"He came aboard at Syndarton and was taking the journey with us to the southlands near Squall Bay where we were to unload a cargo of dried herbs, spices, and oils. We took on all sorts of passengers from time to time and as far as my father was concerned, he was a paying customer and I was to leave him be.

"I suppose he took a liking to me—maybe because I was just a boy. He knew I liked a good story because I listened to the crew's rather embellished yarns of their adventures. Well sir, one evening after a fine sunset, the old man said he had a story he wished to tell me. Said he thought I might believe him and would appreciate what he had to say. I was thrilled at the prospect of a fresh tale.

"And so my father and I and the old man sat by ourselves and he told us that he came from another land, beyond the reach of this world—a land of great wealth and mystery and beauty and power! He filled my head with descriptions of a great city that defied my imagination. A land of magic and strange creatures and bizarre inventions. He talked of going back to this land of his. Said he knew of a special passage. 'Through the waters' he would say. But first he had something he must do in Humus—a sacred mission that he must complete."

Jack knocked the dottle out of his pipe against the table leg and continued as he refilled the bowl. He pointed the pipe stem at Malcolm as he continued.

"Now there have long been such stories of lands on the other side of the misty sea—through the waters, as he put it. But my father and I had never encountered anyone who claimed to have actually come from the other side of the watery mist over to Humus! You can imagine the ridicule that the poor man would have suffered that evening from the sailors if he had shared this with them."

"A man from the other side?" Malcolm interrupted, looking at the strange map. "I have been on the sea where the mist begins and I must say I find it hard to believe that anything exists beyond that murky shroud—legend of such places or not. I know of a few men who entered the clouds determined to see what lay beyond its shroud—but they never returned. Yet it is indicated on the map."

"Hmm," snorted Jack, as he continued. "Of course we didn't believe him. Later on, my father, who had taken to the old man, spoke to him on the deck as they looked toward the misty horizon. I stood next to my father, pretending not to listen. The old man, Dontel by name, said that he had come to Humus in search of his brothers. Apparently he had a lead on one of them and had something he must give to him. He became weepy as he spoke. "My father tried to calm the poor man down, but Dontel was determined to complete his mission in Humus, and then get back to his country. Eager to prove that he was speaking the truth, he showed my father the gold coin with the strange inscription."

Malcolm pulled the coin out of his breast pocket and looked at it.

"Yes," said Jack, lighting his pipe. "That very coin. Dontel told my father that he would soon be dead and must find his brother in time. He said that the coin is sacred and that there are more of them. He then showed us a map—this map—and explained that if we helped him, he would guide us to his brother and pay us handsomely. You see, the old fellow was almost blind and desperately needed to confide in someone. Then he took out the map to show us a passageway to his land."

"Sounds as if he was deluded," said Malcolm.

"Perhaps," said Jack, puffing on his pipe. "The story gets rather murky for me here because an alarm suddenly rang out when a fire was discovered in the hold!"

"A fire?" Malcolm exclaimed, sitting up.

"A lantern had fallen over below and the cargo burned very quickly. Probably a drunken seaman. The crew dashed about madly trying to find the source of the flames but with all that herbal oil in the hold, flames seemed to be breaking forth everywhere. In the meantime, poor old Dontel was pointing at an unseen demon who he claimed was setting fire to the ship. He was invoking his gods, I suppose.

"Well sir, there was a great explosion and a large nail pierced my eye. It was horrible, Malcolm. Seamen running about in confusion, people screaming in agony. The ship took on a list and we knew it was doomed. My father ordered his chief mate to take care of me and then raced down below to fight the fire. I never saw him again.

"After a moment or two I remember being lifted into the one spare boat and the boat being lowered into the water with a crash. My eye was bleeding and I tied a dirty piece of cloth around it. Beside me was old Dontel, clutching his singed knapsack which he had somehow managed to rescue from the fire before climbing in the boat. The ship went down quickly and every man was lost. I never again saw my father."

Jack paused, taking a large gulp of ale.

"As it turned out, Malcolm, the fire that killed my father and that entire crew also had all but finished the old man. And as he lay dying beside me, he handed me this coin and the map you now see. You see? Parts of the map were scorched by the fire."

Malcolm bent down to examine the paper.

"He made me take a vow to complete his mission," Jack continued. "He told me to find his youngest brother, and in doing so, that I would find something greater than mere wealth."

"Greater than mere wealth?" Malcolm could only utter.

"He said I would find his brother in the mountains near Gillingham and that this coin would be all the introduction I would need." Jack stopped talking for a moment as if he was reliving the terrible event. He looked at Malcolm.

"Did he say nothing else?"

"He died."

Jack stopped talking and took a drink from his half-empty cup.

"And?" Malcolm demanded. "Nothing more about treasure? No details?" Malcolm was both baffled and thrilled at the prospect of a dying man's request, a coin of destiny, and a promise of immortality and wealth. There must be more to the story—more information or clues as to the great mystery that was unfolding.

"He died," continued Jack, pouring himself more ale. "And I made a promise to myself that someday I would find that man's brother and perhaps collect a handsome reward. But as I was quite injured I apparently fainted dead away and drifted for some time before being found by a fishing boat out of Meridianus. I awoke in a drafty barn of a sick ward tended by priests. The coin was no longer in my possession. It had been pilfered in my sickness!"

"What happened after that?" Malcolm demanded.

"The priests tried to raise me as a decent young man," Jack continued. "They educated me in their ways. That is how I learned proper talk, and how to read; but piety was never one of my strengths. One priest in particular, a rather gloomy fellow named Thaddius, always treated me with a bit of contempt and finally brought charges against me to have me expelled from their order. The charges were unfounded, of course."

"Of course," said Malcolm.

"Well and so my life went on. I'm afraid my scandalous and shady career began there as a young man. The story behind the gold coin was slowly forgotten as I learned to live by my wits and my one eye. But I held on to the map, for sentimental reasons, I suppose. The memory of a dying man's wish, maybe. That has been over 40 years ago.

So you see before you what such a life has produced."

"Until..." prompted Malcolm.

"Until several weeks ago when a fantastic event occurred. A holy novice from that order of monks found me in Plodi and announced that he had brought a bequest! I had no idea who would have left anything to me. But what would you think was in the little pouch that this young priest carried?"

"I would say...,"

"Coins!" roared Jack, who had been waiting for such a long time to tell this story again. "The pouch held three gold edens. Turns out that old Thaddius wasn't living up to his vow of poverty. In fact, the scoundrel had taken to stealing from pilgrims and other unfortunates, taking the one or two articles that meant anything to them. It was he who had taken my coin! After he died the priests found not only my coin in his room but many other items taken from others like myself who had passed their way.

"The priests, trying to make amends for their disgraced brother I suppose, took every item they found in Thaddius's room, selling them to various collectors and merchants, trying their best to give something back to those who had been wronged. That is how your family came by the coin, I presume. Bought it off some dealer or something?"

Malcolm acknowledged the question with a quiet nod.

"Or something," he said. "Actually my father bought it from some curio shop and gave it to me when I was young."

"Yes, I know," said Jack with a bit of smugness. "The young priest told me the whole story. Seems that right before he died, Thaddius had gone delirious and confessed to his decades of pilfering. Died screaming at unseen spirits, I was told. All of the other items were catalogued and sold off. Guilty conscience, no doubt. He claimed that the coin was bewitched and had cursed him or some such nonsense. So the priests didn't know quite whether to destroy it or appease it. In the end they blessed it and ordered it immediately returned to me or sold off. Well sir, as they could not find me at the time, and wanted to be rid of the accursed thing, they sold it to a dealer in magical artifacts in Wikkam.

"The young priest told me all this. They got three gold edens for it—which they faithfully held for me until word got to them that I was in the vicinity. I must confess I was quite surprised at it all. And so, I received payment for the coin in gold and in blood—so to speak."

"Blood?"

"Well, Thaddius died on the spot," Jack continued, "babbling about demon spirits that inhabited the coin. That got me to thinking. Now I'm not a religious man, mind you, but I began feeling a sacred obligation to see the map and the coin united once more—and see them both delivered safely to Dontel's brother. So I went straight to Wikkam where the priests had sold the coin and found that the old warlock had recently vanished after having sold his entire stock of artifacts.

"The old lady who was living there told me that she remembered the priests and the coin. Said that a delightful man had purchased it for his son who was a collector of oddities. Remembered who it was too—your father, Killian Jefford."

Jack smiled at Malcolm.

"The name is not unknown in those parts," Jack continued. "Apparently he had really charmed the old girl. Probably trying to get the price down. Anyway she told me all this a couple of weeks ago. I now had a name and a destination and so I decided to approach you. And so here we are."

"So, are we talking about a sacred obligation to see the coin delivered?" asked Malcolm. "Or just a selfish opportunity to collect on the reward."

Jack laughed.

"Maybe a little of both," he said. "Which brings me to the proposition."

"I'm listening," said Malcolm.

"You are something of a legend in, shall we say, more discreet circles. People in our trade tend to stick together and mind our business—if you know what I'm getting at..."

"No, I'm sure I do not," said Malcolm.

"Come now," said Jack, "I have run into many a character—drunk and sober, scoundrel and saint—who knows your name and reputation for going after the stuff of legends. And, what with you having the experience, the means to back us with Killian's good name and fortune and, most importantly, the coin itself, we determined the best course was to unite map with coin, find old Dontel's brother, and..."

He winked at Malcolm. "I hear the inn doesn't pay as well as it once did when kings dined here. Perhaps we might collect on a reward that will let us dine like kings for the remainder of our lives!"

Jack and Finius laughed heartily.

"If the old man's brother is still alive after all this time," said Malcolm doubtfully.

Jack looked at Malcolm, who was still playing with the coin in his hand. "Ah, but that's the game of it, isn't it?" he asked matter-of-factly. "The greatest rewards require the greatest risks." He leaned back in his chair, as smug with his explanation as a man who has just saved his own neck in the docket. He placed his dirty hand on the map that lay before them on the table. "Something greater than mere wealth, my boy," he whispered, pointing to the map. "Think of it. Somewhere in Humus—in this area as of 40 years ago—is an old man with some answers and a vast reward. A sacred mission in a hidden land. Remember, Jefford, a dying man has no reason to lie."

Malcolm was intrigued by the story. Could it be possible? These two had appeared out of nowhere with this fantastic tale. That didn't disqualify them from wanting the finer things in life, did it? Jack and Finius waited for Malcolm's reaction. Finally, he spoke. "Very well," he said, folding up the map. "Though I have my doubts about this other land. I mean—a secret passageway through the mountains? You can't cross those mountains. It's never been done—at least not by anyone who lived to tell about it."

"Laramore did it," offered Jack. "His map indicated a pass."

"Laramore *said* he did it," said Malcolm, "on his deathbed. A dying man wants to be remembered for something. And that pass was never depicted on a map—only mentioned as he died. It was never found again." He paused. "Still..." He looked at the map again, wondering if there really was such a land on the other side of the cloudy shroud. Blast him! He found himself intrigued by the strange writing; compelled by the mysterious coin. He wet his lips and looked squarely at Jack.

"I'll accompany you." Jack beamed and looked at Finius. He started to take Malcolm's hand. "But I'll need the greater percent of the take." Jack was about to protest but Malcolm continued. "Or we can go our separate ways—you with the map, me with the coin. As for me, I have seen enough of the map to have a fairly good understanding of where to begin. The mines and passes around Gillingham are tricky..."

"Fair enough," Jack said after a moment's grim reflection. He wiped his greasy mouth with his sleeve and shrugged.

"And now let us d-d-d-drink to the d-d-d-deal," piped in Finius. He reached for his empty glass. Malcolm gave a sly smile and kept his hand over his glass, preventing Finius from pouring. He looked Jack squarely in the eye.

"Then it is agreed that I will accompany you on the journey and throw my fortune behind its expense. But until we have determined exactly what this business of the coin and map is about, I shall hold the map."

"But..." protested Jack.

"Gentlemen, should this all prove a bust I stand to lose a great deal of money, time, and effort. Good business sense dictates I should retain both coin and map as security for underwriting this quest. After all, the map should never again leave the company of this coin. They belong together. And together they will make a grand addition to my collection should this trip turn out to be fruitless. We don't know if Dontel's brother is even alive."

"He's alive," Jack said. "I can feel it." He winked. "Besides, it's all part of the game, isn't it?"

"Those are my terms," Malcolm said. "The map and the coin."

"Agreed," said Jack resignedly. "You may hold them. But mind you—value them as you would you own life."

"Done!" said Malcolm. "And now Finius, fill the glasses!"

And so they stayed up the remainder of the night puffing on their pipes and making plans for the expedition. They drew up a list of essential supplies, which included a great deal of rope, pack animals, food, lanterns, medicines, and the like. Finally Jack handed Finius the list and looked at Malcolm.

"I will, of course, need money to purchase these items," he said.

"Of course," said Malcolm with some annoyance.

Malcolm excused himself and went to a back room where, behind a false volume of the writings of Aeloram, one of Aurora's great poets, he retrieved a small box. He brought it out to the great room where Jack and Finius eagerly waited. As he opened the box, Finius wiped his drooling mouth with his sleeve. When he produced a strange-looking key, Jack reached out his hand as if to receive it, but Malcolm made a point of tucking it away in his jacket. Finius peered inside the now empty box.

"Is that it?" Jack asked in a tone that betrayed his disappointment. "Is there nothing else?"

"You think I would keep the gold here with all the scoundrels in the woods these days?" He laughed. "This key opens the door to a family vault a half-day's ride from here where I've hidden my father's fortune as well as certain other family heirlooms."

"We shall accompany you," offered Jack.

Malcolm shook his head. "I swore the place to secrecy to my father, as he did his father. I can reveal neither the contents nor the location. Not even the craftiest of villains has ever been able to discover where our vault lies. Meet me back here in one week and I shall have what we need for the venture."

Jack glanced at Finius. He then shrugged and smiled a yellowy smile. "Certainly, my boy," he said. "Family secrets are family secrets." Jack leaned in and with the harsh smell of many days' drink on his breath added, "Just remember, we need gold for the journey, but the coin and map are even more important. Hold them dear."

He leaned back in his chair and puffed once more on his pipe. "Besides, what are a few days' wait compared to what we'll get when we divide the great reward I'm sure Dontel's brother has in store for us!"

His grin disappeared in a blue cloud of acrid smoke.

And so within a week of that fateful meeting, Malcolm stood ready to set out with Jack, Finius, the pack animals, and all the supplies he'd purchased, along with a substantial portion of the fortune he had inherited from his father. Their plan was to head west into the interior of Humus. Malcolm kissed his sobbing wife and young son and promised he would return to them within a few months.

"Malcolm, I don't trust these men," she stammered for what seemed like the hundredth time.

"Neither do I, my dear, but as that scoundrel Jack said, I hold all the cards."

"Then why are you going with them? Perhaps they only mean you harm...to coax your remaining fortune out of you. Perhaps the map is worthless and merely a trick to gain your confidence so they can do you harm. Think of it, dearest. The information they gleaned about you from some priest. It all seems far too convenient. Perhaps the rest of the story—the old man and the coin and the..."

"Keep that old lantern burning for me," he said as he had countless times in the past when going away on one of his expeditions. She nodded, wiping her tears away with her sleeve, knowing this was the part of her husband there was no use fighting.

Then, looking carefully around him, he turned to his son and said, "You mind these for me, Jeffrey." He handed Jeffrey the strange coin, the map, and the key to the vault. "Don't lose them now, my boy. You keep these for me until I come back."

"Aren't you going to need the map on your journey?"

"The map I have safely here," he said, pointing to his head. "I have it committed to memory."

He looked at Cornelia. "These should probably be in the vault."

She nodded.

Looking out the window in the door, he saw Jack waiting with Finius. He looked at the coin as Jeffrey deposited it into his vest. "Don't worry, my dears. If that coin is as important as they say, it might make a good bargaining chip one day. I may need it to make a play. Or perhaps you will."

He looked once more at the two men waiting for him.

"I'll keep them," said Jeffrey.

He had accompanied his father a few days earlier to retrieve the gold for the expedition, and now held in his heart and mind the sacred knowledge of where the Jefford treasure vault was hidden. He would die with that secret, he vowed.

"You are soon to be eighteen, Jeffrey. Not quite a man but certainly no longer a boy. You look after things. Look after your mother."

Malcolm turned and opened the door. Corinth squawked loudly behind him. He turned and winked at the bird and said a final good-bye to his wife and son. Jack and Finius waited at the end of the path. Malcolm stopped for a moment, and after one final look back, headed down the path wearing his black frock and black raven's feathered cap. Jack waved good-bye to Cornelia and Jeffrey, promising to take good care of Malcolm. Finius managed to sputter a weak, "Farewell," and they disappeared into the forest.

Chapter 3

A Stranger

AS Jeffrey lit the old lantern one evening many months later, he looked up at the dark sky and shook his head in disbelief. Every night he looked up to see if there might be a star or a moon breaking through, and every night he was disappointed. What was worse, it was getting dark earlier and earlier in Humus. Only a month before, he was lighting the lantern a full quarter hour later than he was now. He looked at his watch, a beautiful watch in a silver case left to him by his grandfather Killian.

"Only a bit after five in the afternoon," he muttered to himself.

He scanned the forest, looking as far as he could down the Shadberry Way which passed in front of the Trout and Truffles. It was as empty as it was dark. He looked up again at the brooding sky, the ever-present clouds roiling just above the trees, it seemed. How long it had been since he had seen blue sky in the day or stars at night? Since he was a child? He turned and headed back into the house, shutting the door behind him.

THUMP!

"Not again," he fumed.

Jeffrey walked back to the door and opened it. Sure enough, the bronze plaque had fallen off again. He picked it up and, noticing a speck of tarnish, brought it in to the table by the fire to polish it. Sitting himself down, he took out his little polishing cloth and went to work on the bronze.

The front room of the inn was quite comfortably laid out, with a comfy old rocker in front of the cheery fire. Nearby, a table supporting an ornate chess set beckoned anyone interested in a game. Several large pillows were placed around the room for guests to loll about on should they so desire. There was also a nice selection of books in a large case that dominated one wall. Jeffrey had read every book twice, and was into his third reading of several old volumes.

Roxanne the cat had taken her usual place on the yellow pillow near the fireplace, purring contentedly. Corinth perched himself on the elk antlers above the sword over the mantel and chattered noisily. And in a scene which replayed itself every night, Jeffrey sat down with a meal of bread and cheese, polishing the tarnished plaque, studying the chess board (should he ever have the chance to play), reading, or playing his flute, or…

KNOCK! KNOCK! KNOCK!

The sound of someone knocking had become so foreign, that, initially, Jeffrey forgot himself. He jumped so high that he bumped against the table, scattering several of the chess pieces. Roxanne hissed and ran for cover under the rocker. Corinth squawked noisily like a town crier sounding the alarm.

"Perhaps we have a guest," Jeffrey announced, collecting himself. "Hush, you silly animals!" he said, as he hastily threw a fresh log on the fire, put a tea kettle on, and set the chessboard back in order—all in a matter of a few seconds. (Jeffrey was not only sensible but very quick on his feet.) Corinth squawked loudly and flew down to the table. The big black raven deftly moved the white king and queen which Jeffrey had misplaced on the board, then flew back to the safety of his perch.

"Thank you Corinth," said Jeffrey, smirking at the clever bird.

SQUAWK!

Checking himself in the mirror, Jeffrey assumed the role of hospitable innkeeper. Perhaps business was picking up now, he thought to himself. And so with a grand smile on his face, Jeffrey opened the door to what he hoped was the Trout and Truffles' first guest in over a year.

Opening the door with wonderful panache (something Jeffrey had been practicing all of these vacant months) the young innkeeper found himself eye to eye with a gentleman dressed in well-tailored clothing. The stranger held two soft leather bags, one in each hand, and smelled of a very expensive tobacco that Jeffrey remembered from childhood when wealthier guests frequented the inn. The man looked at Jeffrey and Jeffrey looked back at the man—as if sizing each other up in those opening seconds. Collecting himself, Jeffrey welcomed his guest and grandly bid him enter the hospitality of the Trout and Truffles.

The man nodded, grunted a word of thanks and moved into the great room. Seating himself near the welcoming fire, he removed his gloves and scarf, pulled off first one boot and then the other, setting them on the hearth. He kept his two larger cases near him. Jeffrey noted both were monogrammed with the initials, "J.P." Other than these things, he had with him a small knapsack and a few smaller pouches tied about his waist.

"You are very welcome, sir," Jeffrey said. "May I offer you something warm?" The man nodded and Jeffrey brought him some tea and a few little cakes on a tray and set it down before him. He didn't seem very sociable, which was disappointing to Jeffrey as he longed for news from the world outside the Trout and Truffles.

The man settled in quite comfortably and propped his feet near the fire, something that made Roxanne uncomfortable. For a few moments he relished the warmth of the room while sipping the delightful tea and puffing on a long thin pipe. Jeffrey quickly took the man's horse to the small stable, cared for the animal expertly and returned.

Jeffrey, as he'd always done with past guests, studied the man as he sat there. He was probably in his late 50s or early 60s, and was definitely a gentleman of some means. He wore a dark green frock coat with crimson cuffs and expensive crimson-dyed leather boots, which were standing near the fire. Underneath his coat he wore a dark green jacket and vest, with gold buttons and green trousers that had been tucked into his boots before he had slipped them off.

"We haven't had many travelers our way in some time," Jeffrey finally said, breaking the spell of the fire and the tea. He set down some more cakes.

"No, I suspect not," said the stranger, looking up as if roused from a dream. "Then, again, there is not much traveling anywhere these days. Not on these infernal roads anyway. I was sure I would be fallen upon by some thief or other."

"Then you're not from around here?" asked Jeffrey as innocently as he could, knowing that the man was definitely foreign.

"Goodness, no," said the man, looking at the plaque on the table. "Well what's this?" he asked, picking the bronze up. He puffed his pipe and read the plaque commemorating the king's visit, which had made such local history. "Well, well!" he said, puffing away as if very impressed. "To think that I am in the same inn in which a king was once entertained!"

With that he read aloud the plaque:

"Be it known,

The Jefford Inn, known as the Trout and Truffles, did on this day host none other than Adamar XII, King of Aurora, and set before His Majesty an exceptional meal in the form of trout and truffles, which the King enjoyed immensely. His Majesty declares that the Trout and Truffles be, henceforth and forever, deemed a royal favorite.

"Well, well." the man said once more.

Jeffrey couldn't help but feel a burst of pride for the Jefford name and hoped that somehow Killian Jefford was enjoying all of this. The man set the plaque down.

"But there's no date on it, my lad," he said. "What good is a commemoration without a date?"

"Well, the date doesn't really matter," said Jeffrey, annoyed at the question and even more annoyed that he had never really thought about it before. "It happened, and I suppose that is the important thing," he said, clearing the little cake plates.

"Of course there is no proof," continued the man. "You must have proof! First rule of law. Without proof that plaque is as worthless as the nail it hangs on."

Jeffrey, increasingly annoyed, brought the man fresh hot water and a menu of the inn's current fare. He took the plaque back to the kitchen with him. How dare this man come in and try to discredit a great event in Jefford family history? Still, he was the first guest in a very long time so Jeffrey's good business sense dictated he swallow his pride.

"Corroboration," he heard the man saying. "That is the name of the game. Proof and corroboration, my boy! First rule of law!"

"So you know something of the law?" asked Jeffrey, biting his irritation and setting some cheese and bread in front of the man.

"Of course I do," the man said, as he cut a piece of very sharp cheddar from the block. "I am a lawyer, among other things. And what good is a lawyer who doesn't know the law, hmm? Sort of like a fisherman who doesn't understand fish; or a gardener who doesn't understand flowers; or an artist who doesn't understand paint…"

"Or an innkeeper who doesn't understand inns!" Jeffrey chimed in hopefully.

The man thought about that long and hard, as if pondering one of the great mysteries of the universe. He then apparently arrived at a decision and nodded his head very carefully. "I suppose that *could* be," he said, contemplating Jeffrey's question and puffing away on the pipe, "Strictly speaking, of course."

"Hmph!" Jeffrey thought, looking at the man. "Will you be staying the night?" he asked, wanting to move away from the law and back into more familiar territory.

"Those are my plans at present," the man said. "Have you any rooms available?"

"As you can see, the entire inn is at your disposal," Jeffrey said with a bit of embarrassment. "You may have your choice of rooms."

"Well, well," said the lawyer. "That is a dilemma. Let's have a look."

And so Jeffrey led the man up the stairs, and, one by one, opened the door of every room in the inn. And without fail, every time he unlocked a room the man would stick his head in and, peering through the light offered by Jeffrey's lamp, would say,

"Oh yes, this will do nicely!" When they reached the last room at the end of the hallway, and the man again peered into the room and said, "Oh yes, this will do nicely," Jeffrey asked him which room he would like for the night.

"I'll take them all," he said.

"All of them?"

"Well, they *are* available, aren't they?" he asked.

"Of course," said Jeffrey. "It's just that you are…I mean there is only one of you and there are seven rooms. I suppose you are expecting others?"

"Of course not," said the man.

"I mean…I beg your pardon, sir, but may I ask why you want all the rooms?"

"Policy, of course, lad," the man said. "Whenever I travel I do so with a strict obligation to myself and my client that whatever business I undertake be conducted in utmost secrecy and privacy. And so it is that I always take all the rooms in an inn when I am doing business there. That ensures complete privacy," he winked and added, "as well as a generous expense account."

Jeffrey nodded as if it all made sense. But in reality it made little sense to him. Still, if he had a paying customer who wanted to take every room for the night because he wanted to do business at the inn, what difference did it make to the innkeeper? Then it occurred to Jeffrey to inquire as to what the gentlemen would be doing at the inn.

"Business?" asked Jeffrey. "At this inn?"

"Why, yes," said the man. "That is why I am here."

"But business with whom?" asked Jeffrey.

"Why with you, Jeffrey Jefford," said the lawyer, as he indicated Jeffrey should put his belongings in the first room on the right.

"This room will do nicely. Now, how about that trout and truffles? I'm famished!"

Chapter 4

A GAME OF THE MIND

THE clean plate which sat before the lawyer was evidence that trout and truffles was still a favorite with guests. Jeffrey had been so busy with the meal, he hadn't had time to quiz the stranger on the nature of the "business" that brought him to the inn. But now that dinner was finished, he wanted to get down to it.

"Very good, very good," said the man, "and that gooseberry pie was scrumptious. I would say that it was so good that if a king really did come here he might indeed give you such a plaque."

"I assure you, the king *was* here," said Jeffrey, serving coffee.

The man looked over the room with its cheery fire, orange cat, and…now where had that black bird gone off to? He looked about, but there was no sign of Corinth. Jeffrey saw the man looking at the sword.

"Now there is a very interesting bit of work," he said. "Is that a family piece?"

"Yes, it's been in the family for…oh, I suppose for two hundred years or so. It was taken in battle by one of my ancestors. Our guests frequently comment on it."

"How awfully interesting," said the man. "It must be very dear to you."

"Well, yes," said Jeffrey, "I suppose so. It's important to our family. It's even on our crest. I'd thought of taking it to my bedroom but it's always been above our mantle. Tradition, you know."

"Very commendable," said the man, puffing on his pipe.

Jeffrey was a bit curious.

"Are you a dealer as well?"

"Depends," said the man.

Jeffrey reached up and removed the sword from its hanger. Behind it was an outline, where it had protected the wall from the sooty air. Jeffrey turned red. "Been a while since I took it down."

He handed it to the man so he might examine it. The man hesitated a moment, as if deciding whether or not to take it. He looked it over from varying angles, and in different degrees of light without ever taking it from Jeffrey's hands. "Thank you, lad," he said, "very impressive. I have made it a rule not to hold family pieces unless I have purchased them—owing to an accident I once had in the home of a wealthy client. Shattered a priceless vase. Created an absolute phobia for me, you know."

Jeffrey shrugged and placed it back above the mantle.

"Take good care of it my boy," he said, never taking his eyes off it. "And now, down to business."

Jeffrey sat up, feeling a mixture of excitement and nervousness. He had never met a lawyer before, especially not a lawyer who had business with him. He was surprised when the man reached over to the chessboard and slid the game between them.

"Do you prefer black or white?" the man asked, laying a gold watch down on the table next to him.

"I don't think I understand," said Jeffrey, watching the man look over the board as if contemplating his moves already.

"What, you don't understand chess?"

"Well, yes. Chess I understand. But what about the business?"

"Business after chess," the lawyer said. "When engaging in something requiring deep thought, one is better served by tickling one's brain. First rule of law!"

And so they played through most of the night. Jeffrey, more concerned about the lawyer's business than with the chess, quickly ran through his moves. The lawyer, who seemed more concerned about the chess game than the business, took several minutes between moves, sometimes rising and walking around to contemplate the board from various angles. The only interruption to the evening occurred when Jeffrey excused himself to light the lantern outside and take his mother her late-night tea.

About halfway through their fifth game, the lawyer, having just placed Jeffrey's black queen in jeopardy, suddenly pushed the board aside and announced that it was now time for business. Jeffrey looked at the clock on the mantel. It was nearly two in the morning. What sort of lawyer conducted business in such a strange manner?

The man reached into a pouch, drew forth a pair of gold-rimmed spectacles and placed them on top of his head, just over his eyebrows. Then he produced a small black box with a lock on it. Taking a key from his vest pocket, he opened the box and removed a single sheet of paper on which Jeffrey could see something had been written in ink.

"Allow me to introduce myself, he said, extending his hand. "My name is Jasper Pickworth. Perhaps you have heard of me?"

"Yes, of course," said Jeffrey, stretching the truth a bit here.

"Then you also know that in addition to being a collector of rare artifacts, as I mentioned beforehand, I also perform certain delicate legal and other functions which require delicate and articulate disposition. Naturally, I take on only the most exclusive of clients."

"Naturally," said Jeffrey, trying to read the ink through the paper or make out a signature on the bottom of the sheet he had pulled out of his monogrammed case. Jasper lit his pipe once more and set the letter down in front of him. After a few puffs of the pungent tobacco, he winked at Jeffrey and said, "Bit of exciting news coming your way, young Jefford."

"Really? How interesting," Jeffrey said, trying to appear sanguine.

"Yes," said Jasper. "Quite."

The lawyer adjusted himself in his chair, and then, leaning forward, transformed himself from mystery guest at the Trout and Truffles to Jasper Pickworth, Agent Working on Behalf of A Mysterious (and apparently very exclusive) Client. "I have to tell you that I didn't know what to make of the story of an inn in the middle of so bleak a place as this," he began.

"It wasn't always so bleak," replied Jeffrey, looking around the room and remembering the sounds of a once active inn; booming voices from the past; hearty laughter and sweet company.

"And I also have to tell you that I had my doubts about such a name as Trout and Truffles," he continued.

"Well, here you are," said Jeffrey, making a grand sweeping motion of his hands to convince Mr. Pickworth that he was indeed in such a place. Good news or not, the man was indeed taking his (and Jeffrey's) sweet time!

"But my client insisted, and since he secured my services with an embarrassingly large fee as well as a bonus if I should take on the job personally, how could I refuse?"

"How indeed?" Jeffrey replied, asking, "and who is your client?"

"Ah, young Jefford, that is privileged information," he said. "First rule of law!" He lowered the spectacles and picked up the letter. "But this shall clear things up for you nicely, I believe." Jasper cleared his throat and read the letter.

My dearest Jeffrey,

You will of course remember me. You were only a bit younger, but you seemed at the time to take a great interest in me when we came to your father's inn and met with him. I would come near to you and you would give me the grandest smile whenever I called my self 'uncle'....

"Finius! That scoundrel, 'Uncle' indeed!"

"Quiet, now," said Jasper.

Jeffrey's mind raced back to that strange looking man with the misshapen teeth who had peered at him as he stood next to his father so many months ago. But why was he writing after all this time—what happened to his father?

I have hired the honorable Jasper Pickworth, a man of impeccable credentials, to handle this correspondence and trust that, as my agent in this grave matter, he will treat you with the utmost professionalism and according to all of my wishes...

Jasper Pickworth gave a slight nod of the head and flashed his credentials, which were such a blur of seals and documentation that Jeffrey scarcely even saw them. Not wishing to appear ignorant, he nodded in approval. Jasper then continued reading.

I wish to express your father's regrets that he has not communicated with you or your mother since we departed. He is at this time in a place that I cannot disclose in this communication, but rest assured he is alive—at least at the writing of this letter…

"My father!" Jeffrey blurted, "He's alive!"

I am also happy to report that I have forever ended my partnership with that one-eyed lout, Jack, who brought your father's health to near ruin. I present to you a trophy, which I hope will give you as much pleasure as the grief its loss has given my erstwhile comrade…

Jasper took out a small pouch and handed it over to Jeffrey. He looked at the lawyer with an odd expression, then opened the bag and pulled out Jack's glass eye. As he looked at it Jasper continued reading.

This I took one night after overhearing Jack speaking in his sleep about murdering your father and myself and continuing the venture. As you can imagine, after so many months of searching, the thought of being cheated out of it all after having finally made meaningful contact was infuriating.

And so a few nights ago as he lay drunk and snoring as usual, I struck him hard on the head and made plans with your father to abandon Jack and meet old Dontel's brother on our own. Your father and I decided to close the deal ourselves. When Jack awakened and realized what we were doing, he made a thrust at me with a hidden weapon. Due to his hangover (complicated by a blow to the head) he missed me and fell on his knife. Cruel as it might sound, I left him for dead and took his eye for good measure, which I now present to you with my and your father's compliments…

"Another Jefford war trophy," Jasper said, smiling.

After much searching and many gold coins to loosen tongues, we finally met up with an old relic of a man and had a nice long talk. Yes, lad! He knew where to find Dontel's brother! Somewhere in or around the Aethra mines near Gillingham, he said. The old man had been in hiding and was difficult to locate—but locate him we did!

But now some dark and urgent news. We have need of you, Jeffrey. Your father is near death and may not last the week. He begs your forgiveness for not having contacted you all these months, but promises to explain all when you arrive. He is asking for you, dear boy...

Jeffrey looked up at Jasper, who remained impassive.

One more thing: You MUST bring the coin and map your father left in your possession immediately. I trust you still have them? It is his only hope. Without them, we cannot meet Dontel's brother and recover what promises to be an exceptional reward and be able to afford the medical attention needed to save your father's life. I have sent along a map that I have drawn up that will direct you to an inn very unlike yours, but where you shall meet an escort to the house in which I am staying in Gillingham. From here we can continue to Aethra. I also have provided some coins to help you in your journey...

The lawyer opened the case bearing his initials and presented a small box to Jeffrey, who opened it with the key Jasper also provided. Inside were 12 or so gold coins. He picked up one of the coins and examined it.

"Coins again," Jeffrey mused aloud. "It was a coin that began this whole disaster."

"What's that, lad?" asked Pickworth, looking up curiously.

Jeffrey reached inside his shirt and produced the leather case he had fashioned for the coin, hanging by a thong around his neck. Inside rested the coin his father had given him before he left. He held it next to the coins Pickworth had brought. They were just a bit smaller, though the strange inscription clearly gave Jeffrey's coin away. He handed it to Pickworth.

"This coin," Jeffrey said. "Ever seen anything like it?"

Pickworth's hands trembled a bit as he held the coin. He examined it with great interest and then handed it back to Jeffrey. "Very odd," he said. "Quite foreign to me, but obviously of great importance to my client and to your father's recovery. So this is the coin in question?"

Jeffrey nodded. "I have kept it on me ever since my father gave it to me. I never take it off, although my mother wants me to put it in the vault. She almost took it herself once."

"Excellent advice," said the lawyer, gazing at the box. "Always good to keep the family heritage together. My own father gave me this watch." He reached back to the table where his watch had been. It was not there.

"Well, I'll be," the lawyer said. "I know I just put that watch down."

Jeffrey instinctively looked up at Corinth, perched in his usual spot. The bird cocked his head to look at Jeffrey.

"Corinth?" Jeffrey said in the tone one might use with one's naughty child.

The bird responded with a guilty squawk, and flew to the table with the watch. Pickworth was astonished.

"Well! A thieving raven! That might get you in want of a lawyer in a hurry."

"Sorry, Mr. Pickworth," Jeffrey said, shooing the bird back to its perch. "Corinth has an instinct for things that I admire."

"Oh, well, thank you lad," said Pickworth, as he deposited the watch back in his coat. "It is quite an admirable watch." He cleared his throat and resumed his lawyerly demeanor. "Now as to the remainder of the letter…"

And now I must finish this and tend to your ailing father. Pickworth will personally deliver this letter into your hands. Then you must hurry to Gillingham, the town where you will meet the escort to where your father awaits your coming. I will find you there and take you to him. <u>But do not forget the coin!</u> Your father's very life depends upon its arrival.

Good fortune to you, my precious lad.
Ever your 'uncle,'
Finius

The room fell silent for a few moments as Jasper Pickworth finished reading and placed the paper down on the table. He began preparing his pipe for a fresh smoke.

"I am directed by my client to deliver into your hands this map, which he says will direct you to an inn at Roxbury on the edge of the Forlorn Mountains. There you are to meet with an escort who will find you and take you to your father. You may also collect the portion of the treasure that he has deposited with the innkeeper there."

Jasper removed his spectacles, sipped his tea and puffed on his pipe, looking at Jeffrey. He had learned long ago that when one dropped news of such enormity upon someone it was prudent to let it sink in for a while.

"Did you see my father?" Jeffrey asked.

"I only saw my client," he said, puffing away, "and he was quite alone."

"But why didn't Finius come himself?"

"To keep abreast of your father's situation, most likely."

"Then my father really is alive somewhere near Gillingham?"

"That, I do not know," said Jasper, putting away the letter; "but that is what is indicated in the correspondence."

"Peculiar thing that letter," mused Jeffrey.

"Really?" said Jasper, looking over his spectacles, "how so?"

"It's so well written. Almost like it was written by…"

"A lawyer?" Jasper finished, smugly.

"Well, yes," said Jeffrey, "Finius was hardly the articulate type."

"Naturally," agreed Jasper. "That is why he employed me. I wrote the letter for him as he dictated. It must have taken him two hours to sputter forth this story. Of course, I cleaned it up a bit but I believe it speaks to what he was endeavoring to say to you."

"What am I thinking?" Jeffrey suddenly said, standing up. "I must go at once!" He looked about the house mentally packing for the journey to Gillingham. I have to tell my mother! How far is Gillingham, sir? I mean—what do I do?"

Jasper puffed away on his pipe for a moment. He pulled out the map that was provided him by Finius and spread it out on the table. "You mean speaking as an acquaintance, or as your lawyer?" he responded.

"What's the difference?" asked Jeffrey, blinking.

"About three gold edens. You'll find, young Jeffrey, that in the world you are about to encounter, information that comes at no cost may in the end cost you the most. Three of these coins should cover my fee," Jasper said, playing with the coins in the box in front of Jeffrey.

"Take them then," Jeffrey said, "and answer as my lawyer."

Jasper Pickworth took three of the coins and reached into his case. He made out a receipt and signed it and gave it to Jeffrey. He then placed his spectacles back on his head, assuming the role of Jeffrey's lawyer.

"My advice to you, my lad, is to follow the first part of this map, go to Gillingham, and collect what the innkeeper has for you. Finius…er…my client, will have someone meet you there and escort you to your father. You should hire a good horse and travel only by daylight. The inns along the way are not as hospitable as your place, but they are preferable to the inhospitality that the darkness provides these days. Whatever you do, keep to the roads. But my lad, you must go to your father. And as to that coin your father gave you which began this whole thing, you must not delay in bringing it along."

"We can do it!" said Jeffrey. "Right, Corinth?"

Corinth squawked loudly.

"Ahem. Now as to Gillingham..." Jasper began pointing to the map, an old map that Jeffrey recognized as a copy of the famous map by Laramore who had done the most extensive exploration of the interior of Humus ever about 200 years earlier. He had mapped out the central forests of the land apart from a bit around the Forlorn Mountains. Malcolm once owned such a copy. Why Finius boasted that he had just drawn it up puzzled him.

"Here we are, boy," said Jasper. "Your inn is here, on the border of Aurora along the Shadberry Way. This is the Warfield Marsh with the abbot ruins nearby. Have you ever seen them?"

"No," said Jeffrey. "But my father told me about them. He used to play there when he was younger. Said they were haunted. Probably to keep me away."

"I've heard that as well. Seems one of the priests went mad and murdered all the other monks in the dead of night. They found him hanging from the belfry. Anyway, the map tells you to take Shadberry all the way through DuPris and then skirt the mountains. This will take you along the Cheyse River. The road is a bit rough nowadays, but you should be safe as long as you remain on it."

"But didn't you just come up from Gillingham?" Jeffrey asked. "How long did it take you?"

"Two days," said Jasper. "And that was on a good horse, mind you. Have you ever traveled any distance?"

"Not really," said Jeffrey, embarrassed at the smallness of his world.

"I suggest then, that beyond a good horse you also arm yourself," Jasper continued. "Since the darkness has increased there are some rather unfriendly creatures about who are becoming increasingly bold of late."

"Armed?" Jeffrey said. "I have no weapons here. Apart from an old dagger that was given to my grandfather by a guest who was a weapons dealer, I have nothing."

"That is a problem" said Pickworth, furrowing his brow. "Your father really has need of you now. But you mustn't go unarmed and really have no time to visit a shop."

He looked up over the mantel.

"What about that," he said, pointing.

"The Sauren sword?" asked Jeffrey laughing.

"It served William Jefford well," said Jasper earnestly. "You may not run into any trolls or Saurens, but there are other creatures just as dangerous to lone travelers, not to mention the brigands and highwaymen seeking prey along the roads. The sword would give the appearance of a well-armed man. And appearance is half the battle! First rule of law!"

"But you made it here and I saw no weapons," Jeffrey said.

"Ah but I am quite well armed," he said, tapping his head. "I am armed with my wits and ability to speak a dozen languages and dialects. Besides, I never take any unnecessary chances. Something I learned the hard way in a trial one time."

Jeffrey looked at the sword, and thinking about it for a moment, took it down. Jasper watched as the young man darted about the inn, gathering a few meager belongings to take with him on the journey.

"Follow the map," Jeffrey said, finally. "I suppose that's easy enough."

Jasper watched Jeffrey, looking for all the world the very image of a young adventurer, planning aloud as he gathered items. He would leave a note for the baker who came every other week to take Roxanne until he got back. He must also arrange with the baker's wife to take care of his mother. She visited frequently as it was. Corinth, he would take along for company.

"Great Aerath!" the lawyer exclaimed. "It is nearly four! How much do I owe you for the rooms?"

"No charge," Jeffrey smiled. Jasper looked warmly at Jeffrey. He stood up and paced the room a bit, as if thinking about something deeply. Jeffrey was amused at the man who looked as if he were in court arguing a case. Finally, he looked back at Jeffrey.

"You know, boy, I really shouldn't be saying this," said Jasper. "But I have really taken a liking to you." He puffed on his pipe. "I know that the first rule of law is not to become personally involved with your clients—but I can't help it." His eyes began tearing up a bit. "My own father died before I was able to get to him. I was delayed. I can't bide that happening to as nice a lad as you. Besides, you wouldn't know how to negotiate with this blackguard in Roxbury. Why, he is liable to take advantage of such a nice young man."

Pickworth pounded his fist on the table with resolution. "Jeffrey, I would be honored to escort you to Gillingham myself!" A great smile came upon Jeffrey's face. "I know the way, and I know the inn," he said. "I can get you there much more quickly than if you are alone. And besides it will be much safer. I'll chat with this fellow who will take us on to Gillingham and we'll see this thing through together."

"But you were heading on up to Superna," said Jeffrey. "And I'm sure I couldn't afford your fee."

"Nonsense! I wouldn't dream of charging you for this," Jasper said. "Besides, lad, you are about to come into a great deal of wealth. We can talk fees later."

"But you have only one horse," Jeffrey pointed out. "And our horse died last winter."

"Pity," said Jasper, puffing away. "What were you planning to do?"

"Travel on foot, I suppose."

"No time lad, no time."

"Then what am I to do?" Jeffrey demanded.

Jasper smiled a knowing sort of smile. "As it turns out, I have an associate arriving tomorrow with a fresh horse." His face flushed as if caught in an indiscretion. "I had thought to sell it to you as I anticipated your need for a good mount. You know, Jeffrey, when one is accustomed to making a profit in life, one looks for every opportunity. But as I have taken such a fondness for you I shall not charge you for it. It's all yours, my boy!"

"Thank you, sir! It's almost as if it were planned. My luck must be changing!"

Jasper nodded in agreement.

"Horses! Stupid creatures, but necessary. Never liked them since a horse went bad on me once and cost me a fortune. So you see—we shall both have a horse and with any luck we should arrive in Gillingham by the end of the week!"

"You hear that, Corinth?" Jeffrey said, shaking his head in complete confusion. "We're going to see father!"

The raven lighted on Jeffrey's shoulder.

SQUAWK!

"How will I ever repay you, Mr. Pickworth?" asked Jeffrey.

"Seeing you and your father reunited is pay enough," said Jasper, who headed up the stairs for a couple of hours of sleep. "Besides, it makes sense that I should go with you. I know the way. Always take along your lawyer. First rule of law!"

Chapter 5

GILLINGHAM PASSAGE

JEFFREY felt badly for his mother as he prepared to leave. She watched from her bed as he moved about the place, locking shutters, and putting things away. He looked at Roxanne, who meowed loudly. "Now Roxy, don't worry," Jeffrey said soothingly. "You'll be staying with the baker who is very good friends with the butcher, which means some good eating for you!"

MEOW!

"I told you he was alive!" Jeffrey said to his mother.

Cornelia smiled wanly. "You go and get him, Jeffrey," she said. "We'll manage here. Roxanne and I."

"The baker will look in on you as will his wife," Jeffrey continued. "He even promised to come and light the lantern from time to time. Within two weeks, we'll be coming home by that lantern!"

He took something out of his pocket. "Father gave me this coin and made me promise to look after it until he returned,"

Jeffrey said, holding back tears. "I'm going to take it to him and bring him back to us."

Cornelia nodded and took the coin. She held it for a moment—almost caressing it—as if she were holding Malcolm once more. Jeffrey was surprised as she rose from the bed and walked to a small picture that hung on the wall. Removing the picture revealed a hidden door that surprised Jeffrey.

"I never knew about that!" Jeffrey said.

"One of the only secrets I ever kept from your father," she said, as she opened the small wooden door. "I had it put in while he was off on his last journey. But it was only to make sure we were taken care of."

She reached inside and pulled out a small bag. The sound of coins jingled. But before she could hand it to Jeffrey she staggered and dropped the bag to the floor. It burst and gold edens of different sizes went everywhere. She knelt down and began picking up the scattered coins, some of which had rolled under her bed. Jeffrey gently lifted his mother up and helped her back onto the bed, then stooped to recover the remaining coins.

"I want you to take these," she said, holding them out.

"No mother, I have money. See?"

He handed her one of the coins Jasper had brought.

"I'll be fine."

He hugged his mother tenderly one final time. She gave the eden back to Jeffrey. Retrieving her sewing basket from the night stand, and with the dexterity of her younger days, Cornelia sewed Jeffrey's special coin into the lining of his shirt near the neck. This was something she often did for Malcolm whenever he was carrying important documents, as he tended to lose them along the way. She did this now with the strange coin that had started it all so many years ago. She hummed softly as she sewed.

Jeffrey smiled at her, noticing how much older she seemed. He put the remaining coins back in her secret cache. Before he shut the little door, he took the key that his father had given him and tied a leather cord onto it. He carefully lifted the key over his mother's head so that she wore it like a jewel around her neck. "Now you'll always feel father and I nearby," he said tenderly. Jeffrey shut the compartment door and placed the picture back on the wall. He hugged her one last time and promised to return very soon—with his father. He wiped a tear from his eye as he shut her bedroom door.

Jeffrey watched through the little window in the front door as Jasper dealt with a scruffy looking man who delivered the second horse. He had apparently brought him in from Roxbury, only a couple of days' ride away. The horse was a beautiful creature, black except for the white stocking above his right front hoof. Jasper nodded, curtly dismissing the man. As he turned to leave, he peered curiously toward the house, as if trying to see inside. Jeffrey was stunned to see Jasper box him on the ear, point down the Shadberry, and send him off, watching until he disappeared.

Other than the half-day trip to the family vault with his father, Jeffrey had never before been farther from the inn than Crown Point, a mere three miles down the lane. He had never even been to Roxbury, which was the nearest town. His young head churned with feelings at the prospect of the adventure that lay before him. On the one hand, a quest to bring his father home, with treasure to boot! On the other, the melancholy feeling of his ailing mother and the Trout and Truffles Inn, the home he'd never left before.

"Nice looking horse there," said Jasper, knocking his pipe against his boot heel. "He'll get you from here to Aethra, I imagine."

"Who was that man?" Jeffrey asked.

"Oh, just a lout by the name of Clemmons," Jasper answered, taking a bit of tobacco from his pouch and stuffing the bowl of his pipe. "I did some legal work for him once. Saved his worthless neck. He has been indebted to me ever since. I sent him ahead to Roxbury to make arrangements for our night. After that he will join us for the remainder of the journey." Jasper looked up at the sky. Though the sun was up now, it wouldn't get much lighter than this because of the roiling clouds. "This dark sky is infuriating," he said. "I have never seen anything like it." He looked at Jeffrey. "We'd best be off."

"Right," said Jeffrey. "Corinth, come along!"

The raven flew from the antlers above the mantel and landed on Jeffrey's shoulder. The boy gave the bird a bit of meat, which he gulped down quickly. Jeffrey placed his bag on the porch and started to lock the door.

"The sword, boy!" Jasper yelled back from his horse. "The sword!"

"I thought since you were coming along I shouldn't need such a heavy thing," he protested. "I brought along the dagger!" he held it up.

"Nonsense!" said Jasper. "That sword is the mark of a warrior. Why, the very appearance of it will frighten even the boldest of creatures. I told you that these forests are filled with all manner of beasts. The troops stay much closer to their billets these days, leaving the roads to highwaymen and scoundrels. You *do* have the coin, don't you?"

Jeffrey fingered his shirt lining to make sure the coin was still there. Yes, he felt it. He went back inside and took one more look about the inn. He looked up at the mantel and the objects which meant so much to the Jefford family. He took the key from around his neck and hung it on the mantle where his mother would find it—perhaps the sight of the vault key would give her hope. Within a few moments, he emerged with the sword, locked the door, and packed his things on the black horse.

"Good lad," said Jasper, seated on his horse. "Quick good-byes are the best! He reined the horse toward the path in the woods. "We'd best be off. Its two days to Roxbury. We'll stop at Will's Point tonight. Not exactly the finest host in the world but better than being out in the open."

As they turned to leave, Jeffrey stopped and jumped off the horse. Running back to the lantern on the post near the front door, he lit it and looked up at his mother's upstairs window. "For you mama," he whispered. Then he remounted the horse and joined Jasper Pickworth on the Shadberry Way with Corinth on his shoulder chattering merrily.

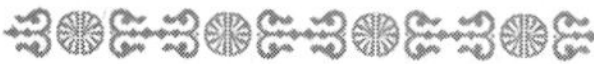

The first few miles of the journey were familiar to Jeffrey. Certain outcrops of rock, or particular trees brought back memories of running through these very woods with his cousins when they came to the inn for a visit. One particular rocky outcrop held the painful memory of a broken arm that he'd suffered climbing it when he was seven. He looked up at the trees which seemed so much smaller than when he was a younger boy. Back then they were giants, forming a towering forest canopy against a sky that was clear and blue.

After a bit, the road became a bit more rugged, with large pinecones tossed about, bits of twigs and branches lying here and there, and weeds breaking through the cobbled surface. An abandoned cart, covered in moss, lay discarded at the side of the path. Killian Jefford would be shocked to see what had become of the once fine highway he'd built decades ago!

"I'm glad my grandfather can't see what has become of the road," Jeffrey said, ducking a low branch.

"Ah yes," said Pickworth, puffing away. "He created this road, didn't he? Named it after the royal family."

"The Shadberry Way," Jeffrey responded proudly. "Grandfather inherited a tidy sum and bet the entire fortune on a road that he cut through the forest and deep into the interior of Aurora, connecting with the main road to Edenshore." Jeffrey recounted how up until that time, the only roads used for commerce between the four major kingdoms in Humus were the coastal roads. The Shadberry Way went down in history as one of the great engineering marvels in Humus, and added considerably to Killian's wealth as he was allowed a percentage of the toll charged by the king of Aurora as his return on the investment. To use the vernacular—he made a killing.

"That's when he established the inn?"

"The Shadberry Way became the most well-traveled and popular route across Humus. So, one day, while making a surveying trip south, my grandfather saw a small encampment of travelers. He said that they were a group of merchants from Meridianus, traveling to Edenshore to buy and sell. He inquired of them, and was told that since this was the midway point on the Shadberry Way, people often stopped in that clearing for the night."

"And so he seized an opportunity," mused the lawyer.

Jeffrey held his finger up proudly as if making a great point. "He also observed something else. There was plenty of fresh water nearby and a natural opening in the woods where a man of enterprise might build an inn and tavern. He could make money coming and going, so to speak," Jeffrey laughed.

"And so Killian Jefford established the family inn where his grandson would later be born," said Pickworth, finishing the story. "Very good. But how did it come to be called Trout and Truffles?"

"Ah, another great Jefford story," beamed Jeffrey. "For originally the place was called Killian's Inn—a comfortably suited, seven-room guesthouse."

As they rode along the once pristine road, Jeffrey explained how, just as with every other business endeavor that Killian engineered, the inn prospered. Its prime situation on the Shadberry Way through the Great Forest and around the bleak Sedgewick Mountains made it the ideal stopover. All manner of guests, of various means, noble and common, human and semi-human, stopped at the inn on their travels across Humus. Killian's Inn, with its seven well-furnished rooms, boasted the cleanest beds and finest food in all of Humus.

"And if there is anything the people of Humus appreciate, it is clean beds and fine food," Jeffrey added.

The inn's reputation for hospitality even won royal patronage after the king's cousin, Sir William, made an unscheduled stop there on his way to a royal wedding. Jeffrey proudly told the story of how William Shadberry loved the cuisine so much, that he returned to the Jefford establishment many times thereafter.

"It was always the same," Jeffrey said. "He would take most of the evening looking over the extensive menu and endless wine list, fussing over what he should eat. But no matter how long he took deciding; or how much he talked about the venison pate' or the roast lamb with basil sauce, he always settled on the inn's specialty. 'Trout and truffles, Killian, my good man,' he would say, and off my grandfather went to prepare it, served with the best wine in the inn.

"As royals in Aurora tend to gossip, word soon got around that the king's own cousin, a very popular fellow, enjoyed the fare and hospitality at Killian's Inn. The reputation of the inn exploded and within a few months, the place was filled with patrons ordering trout and truffles and sleeping on the cleanest beds in Humus."

"But the greatest day in the inn's history—and in Killian's life, to be sure—came when the king himself traveled all the way to Killian's Inn with his cousin, William, just to sample the trout and truffles. Such a moment! Killian nervously set the plate—his finest crockery, to be sure—of food before His Majesty, and all eyes were upon the king as he first sniffed, then nibbled at, then chewed, then swallowed the first morsel of food.

His decision was in the balance for a tense moment or two as everyone waited upon the royal verdict. To Killian's delight—and relief—the King's smile said it all, and on that very day, the plaque you read yesterday evening was placed on the front door with great ceremony. Killian's Inn and Tavern became known forever after as Trout and Truffles. Killian continued this fine tradition for many years before handing the recipes and the reputation down to his son, my father, Malcolm Jefford."

"Wonderful, wonderful, and well told!" Pickworth chuckled. "I don't believe I have heard such a delightful story—true or not."

"Hmph," snorted Jeffrey. "It's true all right."

They stopped for the evening at a run-down establishment called Ethanridge. The host was a veteran of several local skirmishes who wore his medals proudly and spoke about them endlessly. Still, any bed and hearth was welcome to Jeffrey who slept very well that night in spite of strange dreams of Saurens, swords, and truffles.

The next day began very early as they were due in Roxbury that very night. As they rode along, the only noise in the woods was the clop of the horses' hooves and an occasional bird calling in the distance. The trees were becoming increasingly dense as well, hemming Jeffrey and Jasper into a dark, foreboding world. Jeffrey could tell when the road began to slope upward a bit as they neared the foothills of the Forlorn Mountains. Corinth seemed very content to remain perched on Jeffrey's shoulder.

Jasper contentedly smoked his pipe and chattered about this and that trip that he had had on this very road. Jeffrey listened to the man who had quickly become an important part of his life. As they rode along, Jeffrey took the sword out and decided to polish it.

The sword itself was fairly simple in design. It had a beautiful scabbard with a large green emerald at its tip. The haft was wrapped in leather for a secure grip. The hilt was forged with small studs—seven of them—forming a ridge all the way around the guard. There were no markings on the blade except for a strange symbol—a letter of some sort perhaps—which was engraved into its center about half way up, out of which there were bands streaming outward. Beyond that, the only other markings were a few nicks which Jeffrey liked to imagine were from battles the Sauren king had fought. This got him to thinking.

"Mr. Pickworth?"

"Yes, my boy."

"Whatever became of the Saurens and their allies after the battle in which this sword became ours?" he asked. "I mean—where are they now?"

"My, but you do need an education, don't you, lad?"

"I have done quite a bit of reading," Jeffrey protested, "but we have no current books in our library at the inn. Grandfather had no time for such nonsense, and my father was never around to tell me."

"Of course," said Jasper, forgetting himself. "As I told you, I know a fellow who has extensive knowledge of the bizarre and bloody history of Humus—including the very battle of which you speak. Though once a proud race to be reckoned with, the Saurens are reduced to a few relics, supposedly living around Mt. Sobrek. I understand they're mostly occupied with begging and thievery these days."

"Thank you, sir," said Jeffrey. "But as for the werewolves and other creatures?"

"A rarity these days," replied Jasper, nervously. "Best you hear about them later." He pulled his cloak up around his neck, eyes darting into the trees above. "And best not mention those things while we're in the forest."

After several more hours' ride, Jeffrey and Mr. Pickworth arrived at Roxbury, in the foothills of the western mountains. They stayed the night in a small tavern called the Lost Unicorn, run by an old blind woman. The sign hanging above the door depicted a rampant unicorn wearing a blindfold. Jeffrey had never seen one of these creatures, but remembered his grandfather saying he had seen one of the last of them deep in the Kerrigan marshes.

Jeffrey was astonished at the number of people inside—maybe 20 or so—filling the tables and the bar in the dim little place. He didn't even think Roxbury had so many locals. They sat about drinking, playing cards, and otherwise socializing. Some smoked pipes and the cloud hung heavy overhead, casting a dream-like pall over the place. But of all the people in the room, Jeffrey was most amused at the old woman who ran the place. Though blind as a bat, she could spit tobacco juice into a pot with greater accuracy than any seeing man there.

When Jasper and Jeffrey first walked in, the place became quiet for a few seconds. This apparently cued the old woman who called out in a very loud voice, "You looking to sleep or get drunk?"

"A little of both, madam," said Pickworth jokingly.

The old woman laughed harshly.

Pickworth walked over to the bar, introduced himself and made arrangements for the night. The woman ducked behind the bar. When she emerged, she handed a key over. "Second door on the left, and no muddy shoes. I runs a clean place and I don't like my floors tramped all over by dirty boots."

The town itself was little more than a place for a quick stopover at the Lost Unicorn. Jeffrey later learned that there was also a stable where one could purchase or trade a horse and a small shop run by an ex-wizard whose powers had been taken away for some indiscretion which he never made public. A few small houses stood in places where the forest had been crudely cleared away.

After depositing their things in the room, Pickworth and Jeffrey came back downstairs to get a meal. Jasper excused himself to make "further arrangements" and seated himself with a couple of men, one of whom, Jeffrey noticed, was the man who had brought his horse the day before. Jeffrey ate some warm gruel with a piece of bread while Jasper conducted his business. For the tiny population of the town, itself, the tavern drew quite a business in the evening despite its meager bill of fare, so poorly prepared. *We would never serve such a meal at the Trout and Truffles!* Jeffrey thought. Still, this inn was doing a fine business—something that had eluded the Trout and Truffles for some time. Any old light in a dark forest, Jeffrey presumed.

CRASH!

"'Nuff of that!" came a piercing shriek from the old woman. "You treat my establishment wit' respect, now!"

Jeffrey looked across the room where two men were brawling. The woman had a crooked walking stick in her hand and was beating at the two men. Several patrons leapt back out of the way of the commotion as glasses and chairs tumbled on to the floor. Others were laughing aloud. "Here, now Megs, dear," said the larger of the two, a burly woodsman named Pete. "I was just teachin' this lout some manners."

He picked up a little man, who had apparently mouthed off at him, and brushed the dirt of the floor off him as one might brush a cloak. Jeffrey was amused at the old lady's name, 'Megs.' *It suits her somehow*, he thought.

"Well I run a civil place," she said. "And none of that rough stuff or you can take it outside with the rest of the trash!"

"Right you are, Megs," the large fellow said soothingly. "And to show you how much I respect your place, I'll buy this leech another round." With that, everyone went back to their business. The room itself served as a tavern and the inn's dining room, where Megs served up her crude menu of local favorites, washed down with large tankards of ale. Tonight's offering was warm gruel and bread, of which Jeffrey quickly had quite enough.

The walls were paneled with dark wood and decorated with all manner of trophies—birds, fish, deer, boar—even a unicorn with a dusty red scarf covering its eyes that gave the place its name. The little fellow gladly accepted his refill and the two went on into conversation as if they had been in good fellowship all evening long.

Jasper Pickworth was still talking to the fellow who had brought the horse and one other man. Jeffrey wondered what they might be talking about when all three looked back at him, and with a little nod of Jasper's head, resumed talking.

"And who might you be?" came a voice, which he recognized as belonging to Megs.

"Oh, hello," said Jeffrey, caught off guard. "I'm Jeffrey Jefford, traveling with Jasper Pickworth to Gillingham."

"Jefford? Jefford? Killian Jefford's boy?" she asked, seating herself.

"Killian was my grandfather," Jeffrey answered.

A smile beamed across Megs's ancient face, revealing numerous gaps between tobacco- stained teeth. She slapped her knee and howled, "Killian Jefford's grandson? Well strike me dead!" She ordered a hot tea brought to the table.

"Did you know my grandfather?" looking around as if someone might be listening but not really knowing why it might matter.

"Know him?" she cackled, "Why, 'twas his road gave life to this town," she said. "Ah, Killian. Handsome figure of a man. I swore to him that as long as I lived no Jefford would ever pay me for my hospitality. You haven't paid yet, have you boy?"

"No, ma'am," Jeffrey said. "But I have plenty of money..."

"Jefford money is no good in my place," she said. "Never will be."

"Thank you, ma'am."

"Then you're Malcolm's son?" she asked, sipping on her tea.

Before he could answer she swung her stick around and rapped someone hard across the knuckles. "You, there! Don't be gettin' up without paying!" The man who'd received the blow cursed the woman and plunked down some copper coins, swearing he'd never come back to THIS hovel. The men around the table laughed.

"How do you do that?" asked Jeffrey. "I mean...you can't see..."

"You don't need eyes as long as you have wits, boy," she said, winking as if she *could* see. "My ears and my nose tell me everything

I need to know t' run this place. Besides—he tries that just about every night. Sort of a little game we play. That your bird?"

Jeffrey had forgotten about Corinth, who was perched above him on the antlers of a large deer. He had been flitting about the room and squawking occasionally and Megs had apparently picked up on it above all the rest of the noise. "Yes," said Jeffrey. "That's Corinth. He's a great friend. How did you know he was up there?"

"Because, boy, I use my ears. Like I told you, eyes are only part of seeing. You gets used to not having them so you make something else work for you."

"Corinth is a bit of a scoundrel at times," Jeffrey said, thinking back to the incident with Mr. Pickworth's watch. "He seems to know when something is valuable to a person and sometimes he goes after it."

"Animals makes the best friends," said Megs, nodding. "So how is your father? And how come you're so far from the Trout and Truffles?"

"Ah, well, we're looking for him," said Jeffrey. "He set off nearly a year ago with a one-eyed fellow and another chap and we haven't seen him since."

"A one-eyed fellow," Megs murmured.

"But I received a note that said…"

"Jeffrey, my boy!" Jasper was standing behind him at the table.

"Come join us now. We have business to discuss and I'm sure this good lady has other affairs to tend to."

"Are you this boy's guardian?" she asked, addressing Jasper.

"I am his agent, madam," said Jasper.

"Even better, then," she said. "Listen to this and start doing your job proper." She motioned with her finger that they should move in closer so she could lower her voice. Jasper was annoyed, but did as she said. "The boy just mentioned a one-eyed fellow," she began. "Does that interest you?"

"Possibly," said Jasper, seating himself and motioning to Jeffrey not to say anything else. "Why do you ask?"

"Well, a few months ago we had trouble with a one-eyed fellow," she began. "M'friend Tom told me he had a shiny eye—you know—a glass eye. Liked to show it off to people for a drink. He was with two other gentlemen and got roaring drunk. Well that's not unusual in this place, mind you. I run a respectable place, but a tavern is, after all, a tavern. So this fellow with the patch starts going off about how he was going to be a very important man one day. Got into a few shouting matches with some of the others.

"Now, people are always spouting off in public places like this and so I pays it no never mind. When he finally left, I heard him holler, 'Come on Malcolm, my boy. Let's get on with it.' The reason I'm telling you this is because I didn't think of it until you told me who you are—Malcolm Jefford's son. Later on, I was told by several people that Jefford was definitely with the man."

Jeffrey looked up excitedly at Jasper.

"Very touching, madam," said Jasper. "But hardly of consequence. We had already deduced that the party had traveled this way."

"Ah but that's not the end of it!" she snapped. "Lawyers think they know everything. Well, listen to this! It's not by accident you're here tonight. Just two nights ago he was here again—the man with the eye. I could tell by that blustery manner of his. Except this time he was alone."

"Jack?" Jeffrey whispered aloud. He looked at Jasper. "I thought Finius killed him in a fight."

She looked in Jeffrey's direction. "Yes—Jack was his name, I believe. But Malcolm Jefford—your father—was not with him. Had on his patch of course, but this time he was missing the eye.

Said he lost it in a fight or some such thing and was working my customers for drinks by offering them a peek under the patch. Besides bein' disgusting, I don't like people botherin' the paying customers."

Jeffrey's jaw dropped as the woman continued, "So I says to him—'Here now! What ever happened to all this talk about you becoming a very important man?' You know—I was giving some of his own back to him. 'And where is Jefford?' I says to him. 'He was the only respectable one in your bunch.' Well, this fellow breathing his liquored breath on me says, 'Blast that name!'

"He threw a pewter tankard across the room. I got on to him about that as you might know. 'Those two planned to move in on my doings,' he starts screaming. 'Take it right out from under me.' Then he smiles. 'But your poor ol' Jefford met with an accident dearie. And I know where he is now. Finius tucked him away in Gillingham. Poor man. Thinks he's safe. He's a goner for sure—both of them are. But I plan on finishing off Jefford myself if he's still alive!' He stayed a bit longer and then left. Bound for Gillingham, I'd wager."

"Anything else you can recall?" asked Pickworth.

Megs tapped her chin.

"Seems he mentioned Rurik."

Jeffrey looked up at Jasper who was shaking his head in disbelief.

"He's going to murder my father!" Jeffrey said. "We have to get to Gillingham!" Jeffrey got up as if to leave, still reeling from the possibility that his father was about to be killed. "Megs, who is Rurik?"

"A shady fellow," offered Jasper. "Thieves and scoundrels from all over Humus meet with him to bargain their ill-gotten goods—jewels, artifacts, rare books—all of dubious but unquestioned sources. Lives in Gillingham. But if anyone can tell us about this business, I'd bet my last eden it would be Rurik"

"Rurik," repeated Jeffrey frantically. "Mr. Pickworth! We have to get to Gillingham immediately! Before Jack does."

"Jeffrey, we have to trust what Finius said in the letter," Jasper responded. "We are to meet him and then let him escort us to your father. As his lawyer, I am obligated to follow the conditions set forth in his communication."

"But you're *my* lawyer, too," said Jeffrey. "Remember? When Finius wrote that letter several weeks ago, he thought Jack was dead. The conditions have changed since that letter was written. Jack's already made his move."

Jasper looked at the young man tenderly. "I suppose as your lawyer I promised to get you to your father, didn't I. The problem is, we're at least three days' hard journey from there. And this blackguard has two days' ride on us."

"We could get fresh horses and ride all night," Jeffrey said. "Start tonight."

"Too dangerous," said Jasper.

"Is there no other way?" asked Jeffrey desperately.

The old woman gave a sly smile. "Depends," she said. "There are ways to Gillingham and then there are ways."

"What do you mean, Megs?" asked Jeffrey.

She motioned the two to follow her to the back room. Leading them through the murky atmosphere of the Unicorn, she brought them to a small office. After they were seated she began to whisper. "I shouldn't be telling you this, but in memory of your grandfather, I'm bound to." She leaned in as did Jasper and Jeffrey. "I know a secret way to Gillingham. A passage that cuts underground through the old mine from when they were taking ore out of these hills. The hills of Aerath are filled with tricky old shafts.

In my younger days, I took the tunnel myself, and I suspect that a young fellow like you could make it in one day."

"Megs! Really?"

Megs reached behind her into a dresser and pulled out a small, brownish paper. It was a map. She laid it out in front of Jeffrey and Jasper. Pointing to the map, she continued. "Right here. This is where the shaft was cut. Problem is, the present owner of that passage is very particular about who travels through—and he demands quite a pretty price up front. Has a keeper at the entrance who takes certain payments."

"I don't care," said Jeffrey. "I'll give him whatever he wants. I have some money coming to me, don't I Mr. Pickworth?"

"True, young Jefford," said Pickworth, looking about and raising a finger to his lips, hushing Jeffrey so as not to raise too many eyebrows with talk of money. "But you don't have it yet. And I'm sure this fellow is not one to take your word for it."

Jeffrey's heart sank.

"I'm afraid he's right, boy," Megs agreed. "The keeper of this passage will not take anyone's word in place of gold. Have you nothing else of value? Did you bring anything else of worth?" Jeffrey thought about it. What did he have...a few coins to get him to Gillingham, a noisy black bird. That was it. Except for...

"I have a family heirloom with me," he finally said, "a very special sword that was taken years ago in battle."

"Ah yes, the sword," said Jasper, looking at Megs. "But what a shame that would be. It's been part of your family history for so many years."

"I would give away anything to get my father back alive," argued Jeffrey. "Megs, would he take my sword?"

Megs leaned back in thought, chewing on a fresh cut of tobacco. She scratched her chin a bit. "Possibly," she said. "You might give it a try. I'd take it with you and see, but he has all sorts of weapons. He prefers items more easily disposed of, like gold, rare old coins, uncut gemstones…"

The three sat in silent thought around the table for a moment. Suddenly, Jasper slapped the table with the palm of his hand so loudly that the tavern outside their closet grew quiet for a split second before resuming its normal din. "The coin!" Jasper suddenly said. "Perhaps the strange coin might attract this blackguard's attention."

"I can't do that," Jeffrey protested. "The coin is the very thing we need to get the reward so we can save my father's life. I'll hang on to that," Jeffrey answered.

"But if you don't get to Gillingham in time, your father's needs will be meaningless. We may need to give up the coin now and plan on using our wits later. How bold are you, Jeffrey?" Jeffrey thought about it for a moment. The letter stipulated he must bring the coin with him to Gillingham. But if he didn't get to Gillingham in time, Jack would murder his father! Perhaps he could bargain with this fellow. Perhaps he was more reasonable than they made out. "We're wasting valuable time," Jasper remarked.

Jeffrey looked at the two faces staring back at him. Megs seemed genuinely concerned for the boy. Jasper was simply waiting for the boy to make what he believed to be the only logical choice afforded him right now.

"When your opponent has the advantage, you settle the first round quickly in anticipation of the second round," Jasper finally said. "First rule of law!"

"Would you talk to him then," Jeffrey asked, almost pleading.

"Of course, my boy," Jasper answered magnanimously. "I'll be right there to negotiate on your behalf."

"Make the deal, Megs," he said. "Tell your friend we want passage and will pay him. But give no details about the payment. Perhaps we can bargain with him, yet."

Megs nodded that she understood. Jeffrey raced out of the little room, knocked over a chair in the common room and dashed up the stairs. Corinth flew up the stairs behind him. The crowd in the tavern barely noticed him.

Jasper and Megs came into the room and Megs sat down at a corner table. While they waited for the boy to come back with his things, Jasper looked down at Megs and smiled.

"Megs, old girl, you're a right proper actress," he said, plopping down several gold coins. "You missed your trade."

"Did I, now?" she cackled, biting on one of the coins to make sure it was genuine. "But you never told me this was Killian's grandson."

"You never asked," Jasper said as he sat down on the chair beside Megs.

"They won't hurt the boy, will they?"

"How should I know?" Jasper snorted. "I'm only his lawyer. In the end he would have been destroyed anyway. We are merely expediting the issue for a price."

"You're sure he has the coin with him? The one that's bewitched?"

"He has it," Jasper answered. "And he shall hold it until the end. Jack and Finius will have no part in even looking at the coin, much less laying their grubby hands on it. Especially while he has the sword. If that fool father of his had brought the coin along in the first place, none of this would be happening. Took us nearly a year to sweat it out of him that he'd left it with his son. Accursed coin."

"They must want those things badly," said Megs. "I wouldn't trust their kind. You could get paid off in something other than gold."

"Don't worry about me, old dear," Jasper said. "If they want the sword and coin, they'll come through, all right. And they want them!"

"And you?" Megs said, spitting accurately over her shoulder. "Will you touch the coin?"

"Lawyers don't handle curses, old girl. We merely expedite them."

They laughed heartily and toasted one another. Megs got up from the table and moved back to her place behind the bar. Before long she was haranguing her customers as usual. But she kept looking upstairs, toward the room where she could now here Jeffrey scurrying about, gathering his things.

"Poor lad," she sniffed. "I only hopes they make quick work of it."

It seemed like forever before their escort returned with Megs's courier and the news that the gatekeeper would receive the young man, but only if he came alone and with stones and the coin. Further, he reserved the right to refuse passage if the stones didn't measure up or if the coin proved unworthy. Jeffrey readily agreed to the terms and set out immediately.

"May fortune smile upon you," Jasper called out. "Farewell, young Jefford!"

Jeffrey wasn't completely sure of the escort who was leading him into the darkness beyond Roxbury. Though the man knew his trails, he certainly knew no manners. He was not at all sociable.

Try as he might to strike up a conversation, all Jeffrey got back was a grunt now and then as they continued along the dark road.

The town was behind them and soon they came to what seemed to be an opening in the road—a large meadow. He was leading them off the road now.

"Is this right?" Jeffrey wondered aloud. The man grunted in affirmation, pointing to a low hill in the distance that could just barely be made out in the scant glow of the moon through the ever-present cloud cover. It made sense, Jeffrey thought. It was, after all, a mountain passage they were heading to. Still, he kept his sword handy as the mountain loomed larger the closer they moved toward it. He could feel Corinth under his cloak, his claws digging in from time to time.

The man himself was not much bigger than Jeffrey, though probably 20 years his senior. He wore a cap pulled tightly over his ears and a long black coat. He had boots with very large buckles upon them and smoked a very smelly chub pipe about the size of his thumb. As to his features, he seemed almost fox-like in appearance with large eyes and a seemingly endless crooked nose—probably from some scuffle in Megs's rowdy dive, Jeffrey surmised. His large, yellow teeth only added to the gruesome picture and Jeffrey consciously avoided speculating on his trustworthiness.

After crossing the meadow and enduring about an hour of ducking low branches while listening to all manner of beasts real and imagined, they came to a halt. The escort pointed to a little ravine that led into complete darkness. "Over there?" Jeffrey asked, squinting in the darkness. Foxface grunted an affirmative.

He wished that he had brought along a torch now. But Megs assured him that a light in this dismal place would only invite the worst sort of trouble. The thought of his father somewhere ahead emboldened him. Jeffrey dismounted and shouldered his knapsack, rousing Corinth who returned to his perch when all was settled for the hike. "Aren't you going to take me there?" Jeffrey asked, as the man turned to leave.

He grunted and pointed once more in the direction of the ravine. Jeffrey was about to protest further when he looked into the darkness and blinked hard. Were his eyes playing tricks on him? No, there was definitely a speck of light that seemed to be moving like a firefly in the distance, beckoning. Jeffrey turned to remark about the signal and found himself quite alone—the man was gone.

"Well Corinth, this is it," said Jeffrey, as he began walking toward the light.

The air had turned much cooler since they had left Roxbury. And in the distance, Jeffrey could hear the sound of a waterfall or a rushing river. Several times he stumbled over pinecones and bits of debris as he continued undeterred toward the light. What was he to say to the gatekeeper? What sort of man was he? Perhaps he would reason with a young man trying to save his father's life. Perhaps the promise of a share in the treasure would compel him to let Jeffrey pass through with the coin.

Jeffrey reached the bottom of the ravine and was now level with the light, which seemed only a few yards ahead of him. He called out to the light but got no answer. He felt Corinth's claws digging into his shoulder as if the black bird was tensing up too. "It's all right, Corinth," said Jeffrey, watching the beacon ahead. "But these people are certainly unsociable." The bird squawked in agreement. They walked another hundred feet or so and Jeffrey called out once more.

"You there, with the light! Are you the gatekeeper?"

"Quiet!" came a harsh response. "Just keep coming along."

Jeffrey finally reached a point in the narrow chasm where he could make out a figure carrying a small oil lamp. He was a rather large man, but before Jeffrey could make out any features, the light was abruptly extinguished. Corinth squawked and flew to a nearby branch. Jeffrey continued making his way toward the man whose presence he could now both sense and, unfortunately, smell.

"Did you bring it?" came a voice out of the darkness. "Do you have the coin?"

"Yes, but can't we have some light?"

"Are you alone?"

"Of course," said Jeffrey. "Except for Corinth."

"Who's he?" came an alarmed response.

"My raven."

"Oh."

"So…can we have some light now?"

"I suppose it will be all right now."

Jeffrey watched as a spark ignited the small lamp, giving scant light to the area—more of a dim, macabre glow, really. The man held the lamp close to Jeffrey's face, so that as he strained to see who was holding the light, he was still unable to make out specific features on the cloaked and hooded figure other than red eyes glaring back from the hood's darkness.

"Is this the boy," inquired the hooded man, in a strange, raspy voice.

"That's him," replied a vaguely familiar voice from behind. Jeffrey was startled and turned to see a little weasel of a man grinning at him with a waxy, gnarled grin. "There, there, smile for uncle, boy," came the voice.

That was the last thing Jeffrey remembered.

Chapter 6

DARK REUNION

A strange echoing sound mixed with murmurings and fuzzy laughter filled Jeffrey's ears as he began to awaken. He wasn't sure where he was, so he lay still for a moment trying to recall what was happening. Perhaps he would soon awaken in his own bed at the Trout and Truffles. One thing was certain—his head was throbbing.

He opened his eyes and saw the blurred figure of a man standing over him. He could make out neither what was being said, nor who was speaking, but it all seemed too noisy and bothersome. Why would all these people be in his bedroom? A constant drip-drip-drip sound of water also assaulted his head. Where was he? He realized he was not in his warm bed at the Trout and Truffles but on the dank floor of some sort of cavern or mine. He was tied up, as well.

"He's moving," said a voice.

"Let's finish this and get on with it," said another. "This place is haunted."

"Nonsense!" came a voice Jeffrey recognized immediately. "You never rush a job like this before all of the pertinent information has been obtained! First rule of law."

"Pickworth?" Jeffrey muttered. "Mr. Pickworth? Is that you? What's happened? Was there an attack or something?"

"There, there," said another voice. "Drink this cool water."

Jeffrey recognized the face with the patch over one eye bending over him with a cup in his hand. "Jack! Where is my father?"

"Drink this first, lad," said Jack soothingly. "Then we'll talk."

Jeffrey's thirst overcame his confusion and he greedily gulped down the best water he had ever tasted. Jack positioned Jeffrey so that he could sit upright. Jeffrey looked around at several faces in the dimly lit room. He indicated the ropes. "What are these for?"

"Ah, Jeffrey," said Jack sighing. "Seems like you have fallen into some rather wicked company."

"Mr. Pickworth?" Jeffrey said, looking at his former guide.

"There are very important events unfolding Jeffrey," Jasper said. "And you have blundered squarely into the middle of them."

"But never you fear, boy," said Jack. "If you cooperate with these fine men I'm sure all will be well."

"Right down until they cut your throat and dump you into one of the shafts," came another voice. Laughter echoed through the large room.

Jeffrey was still recovering his senses. By now he could make out about five figures. The echo and dampness told him they were definitely underground. There were small lanterns here and there, and the smell of ale and tobacco filled the dankness with a staleness that, coupled with his aching head made Jeffrey nauseated.

"Now then Jeffrey," said Jasper. "We have a question for you. And if you cooperate with us, we shall see that you are safely delivered back into you mother's waiting company and the matter shall be considered closed."

"What matter?"

"The matter of the coin…naturally," said Jasper.

The coin! Jeffrey looked at what was left of his things. They had been strewn about the mine floor in frantic disarray. He noticed that the man with the hood was tearing through his bag and that Finius had taken charge of the sword. Even the dagger he'd tucked into his boot was missing.

"The coin?" said Jeffrey. "Is that what this is all about?"

His head still smarted. He squirmed in his bonds and felt for the coin sewn inside his shirt. Yes, it was still there.

"Where is my father?"

"You'll never see that fool again unless you help us," screamed the man in the hood. He spoke with a strange accent. "You hear me boy?!" Jeffrey could see glowing red eyes deep inside the hood. The others edged away from the man as he raged at Jeffrey.

"Just tell us where the coin is, lad," said Jasper. "We've searched your things and your person. Obviously you've concealed it cleverly somewhere. Now, just tell us where and we will unite you with your father."

Finius snickered.

Jeffrey's burning mind was beginning to size things up. He realized that the coin was of greater importance than he'd imagined. Perhaps it did have some strange powers. Whatever secret it held, so long as Jeffrey was in possession of it, these villains would certainly spare him. His father had seen this too. The pain in his head irritated and emboldened him.

"I have secured it," he said, "And will release it upon seeing my father." He glared at the man in the hood. "And if you kill me or have done anything to my father, you shall never have the coin. Ever."

Jasper looked at the hooded man as if wondering what they should do next. Jack began reasoning with Jeffrey, as if the two of them were great friends and he was trying to help him. Meanwhile, Jasper conferred with the hooded man, who Jeffrey learned was named Lorogos. He saw the men nodding in agreement. "Pickworth you rat." said Jeffrey. "How could I have trusted you?"

"Because I am a convincing person," said Jasper. "I have cajoled many a jury into sending an innocent man to the gallows or setting a murderer free. You're a fool, Jeffrey. A decent young man, to be sure, but a fool. Now for the final time—where is the coin?"

"First my father," Jeffrey answered resolutely.

"Very well," said Jasper resignedly. "The pit."

Jeffrey suddenly felt himself being hoisted up by a rope tied to his ankles. As he struggled in protest, Lorogos simply carried him off as if he were a roll of flax. The others followed. The sound of rock sliding hard against rock echoed through the chamber and then Jeffrey found himself hanging upside down, suspended from a crossbeam over a small, black opening to the blackest, most foul-smelling pit he had ever seen.

"Have you ever heard of a shina, Jeffrey?" asked Jasper.

"Never," said Jeffrey, trying to put on a brave front but curious as to what he could hear skittering about in the pit below his head.

"What do they educate young people with these days?" Jasper asked in an exasperated tone. "Well sir, the shina is a very rare beast that dwells in abandoned mine shafts and caves in these parts."

"Interesting" said Jeffrey, attempting a nonplussed attitude.

"Quite," continued Jasper. "These creatures, though only about two feet in length, have an enormous capacity for consuming flesh—live flesh, mind you. They never touch something already dead." Jasper paced back and forth as if giving a lecture. "But—and this is the part I believe you shall find most interesting, Jeffrey—these gruesome creatures can eat the skin off an entire animal while the poor thing is still alive. A matter of seconds! Can you imagine? I suppose it's because they feed in such great numbers."

"I am sorry, young Jefford, about the letter that b-b-b-brought you here," stammered Finius. "But you can see that it turned out that the coin was of greater value than we r-r-r-realized. It was either your life or ours."

"Quiet, Finius," shouted Jack. "You were in this like the rest of us. His blood be on all our heads!"

The foul odor from the pit made Jeffrey choke. He could also hear what sounded like many animals moving about below, claws scratching at the sides of the pit. Lorogos took out a knife and held it against the rope that was all that separated Jeffrey from the hideous flesh-eaters below. He awaited the signal to cut it. "Sounds as if they are hungry tonight," said Pickworth, laughing. The others joined in as well. "So what'll it be?" the lawyer asked.

Jeffrey couldn't believe that they would actually kill him until they obtained the coin. He decided to continue his game. "How do I know that isn't just a bunch of stray cats or something down there?"

"That's easily proven," said Jasper.

He made a quick nod of his head and Lorogos grabbed a man behind Finius—the fox-faced guide who had brought Jeffrey from Megs's place to the ravine. The poor man looked to Pickworth in wide-eyed terror, struggling against the hooded Lorogos before being casually tossed into the pit. Jeffrey had never heard such screams in his life. Every person there, with the exception of Lorogos who seemed to enjoy it, was unnerved by the rending, ripping, grunting, and chewing sounds of the man being flayed alive by the razor-sharp teeth of the shina. Finally the screaming subsided to a low moan, then grew quiet except for some unmistakable, gastric noises and belching.

"Not the most refined diners," said Jasper. "But quite enthusiastic."

"Suppose I tell you where the coin is," Jeffrey said, sweat pouring from his drenched blond hair. "How do I know you will not murder me anyway?"

"You have my word," said Jasper solemnly. "As a lawyer."

Jeffrey managed a laugh—even in his predicament. "Your word? How about Jack's' word? Or Finius's solemn vow? Right."

"Then down you go, boy," Jasper sneered.

"Wait a minute, Pickworth" protested Jack. "If he goes down, then the coin goes down with him. Then the only payment we get is an even worse end. I've a better thought, anyway." Jack walked to the front of the pit where Jeffrey could see his ugly face, even more hideous in the dim light and upside down. He had apparently found his glass eye in Jeffrey's stuff. Now that eye stared vacantly at him. "Suppose we paid a visit to his mother…"

With that Jeffrey shook violently and began struggling wildly against his bonds. He was shrieking they'd better leave his mother out of this. She was sick and couldn't stand this sort of excitement. Besides she had never harmed anyone—least of all this bunch! Jasper Pickworth winked at Jack.

"Hold him steady," shouted Lorogos.

Jack reached over to secure Jeffrey, whose wild swings were nearly pulling the crossbeam out of its setting. He reached around Jeffrey's side and then suddenly froze as if he had discovered something. He patted the boy's neck. "What's this?" he said, feeling through the material of Jeffrey's shirt. Lorogos immediately understood and pulled Jeffrey off the crossbeam and threw him onto the hard mine floor. Jasper and Finius crowded over Jeffrey as Jack ripped most of the shirt off him and came up with a shiny gold coin.

"The coin, the coin, I have it!" Jack shouted victoriously.

Then, as if recalling his fear of the coin's purported powers, he quickly handed it off to Jasper, who immediately set it down on a rock outcrop. He, too, didn't want to touch it. Jeffrey tensed, waiting to be thrown to the Shina. The men in the room crowded around the rock ledge, looking at the coin and congratulating each other. Jasper Pickworth brought a lantern to the ledge to inspect it more closely. His victory smile turned quickly sour and he glared at Jeffrey menacingly.

"What's the matter," asked Jack.

"Look for yourself," he said turning away angrily.

It was an ordinary gold eden!

Jack threw the eden down to the ground. So the coin was still not in their possession after all! Jeffrey suddenly realized what had happened. The night his mother had sewn the coin into his shirt, she had spilled a bag of gold edens on the floor. She must have accidentally sewn this coin into his shirt by mistake—which meant that the sword-struck coin was still at the Trout and Truffles!

"Where is the real coin, boy?" Jasper demanded.

"He tricked us!" whined Finius.

"Where is the coin?" repeated Jasper. "It couldn't possibly have any value to you. You don't understand its importance."

"And you do understand it?" Jeffrey countered. "You would kill a man—or possibly several men—for an oddly-minted coin?"

"There's more to this than you know, boy."

Jack took a short-bladed knife from his boot and held it under Jeffrey's chin. He pressed the cold blade against his throat. "Last chances come only once, young Jefford," he said, his eyes cold with murder. "Where is that coin?"

"I—won't—tell," Jeffrey managed in a show of defiance, sweat pouring down his forehead. "And if you kill me or go near my mother, you'll never know."

"Hold there, Jack," crowed Jasper. "That's it. He left it with his poor, sick mother!"

"Such a nice woman too," said Jack, grimly shaking his head. "Pity."

Lorogos laughed.

"No!" screamed Jeffrey. "She doesn't have the coin!"

"Then for the last time, where is it?" demanded Jasper.

"Right here!" came a new voice from the darkness of the mine.

"Who's there?" Jack yelled, holding a lantern toward a dark shaft.

"Over here!" came the voice again, but from a different direction.

All heads turned toward the opposite side of the shaft.

"I told you this place was bewitched!" said Jack.

"We'll see if it's flesh and blood or spirit that vexes us," said Lorogos.

Lorogos picked up a discarded pick and began swinging it viciously at random, trying to hit the source of the voice. Jasper had to duck to avoid being caught by one of the wild backswings. The voice seemed to move all about the room, adding to the confusion and infuriating Lorogos. Jeffrey was completely confused but could swear that he heard a voice whispering from behind him to close his eyes tight and, "Be prepared."

"Watch it there!" Jasper shouted, narrowly escaping the pick's reach.

Suddenly a brilliant flash of light exploded.

The men screamed in anger and panic and fell to the ground, immobilized by the sound and light. Another sharp explosion and flash. They began swinging at the air, hitting each other and stumbling over the debris on the mine floor. Lorogos threw the pick in a rage, which slammed into a beam causing a cloud of rocks and debris to shower down upon the room. Curses and angry confusion filled the area as the men dodged falling rocks and choked on the dust. Jeffrey, felt the ropes drop off him and then a pair of hands helped him up.

"Who are you?" Jeffrey managed as his invisible rescuer led him into the mine.

"Don't talk now," answered the voice, pulling Jeffrey along.

Jeffrey held on to what was apparently the cloak of the man who was guiding him—but he could see nobody! From behind, he could hear Pickworth ordering that the boy must not be allowed to escape. Jeffrey and the unseen stranger continued down the shaft for a bit and then turned off the trail into a very narrow passage which eventually opened into an enormous room. There were several torches about that cast misshapen images of strange beasts and other conjurings of the imagination onto the damp walls.

They continued like this for what seemed a very long time. The mine had become decidedly cooler, and the mysterious person who had saved his life led him to a dead end—a blank wall that was not exactly encouraging to Jeffrey.

"Here we are," said the voice.

Jeffrey was about to ask just where "here" was, when a stone door swung open, revealing a passageway. "In you go, my boy." Jeffrey peered into the tunnel and could see a dim light some distance ahead. "It's quite safe, I assure you," reassured the voice.

"Thank you," was all that Jeffrey managed as he lowered his head and walked through the passageway. After a few hundred feet or so, the tunnel turned sharply to the right and opened into a large room.

Jeffrey could hardly believe his eyes. Here, deep in the ground was what looked like a large, fully-furnished cottage. He entered the room and felt as if he were stepping into another world. The room had several torches burning brightly, creating a cheery atmosphere that he had long since forgotten. Why, it was a charming room not unlike those he had known back home at the Trout and Truffles! "Sit down, sit down," came the voice in a very cheery tone.

"Thank you, sir," said Jeffrey, plopping down on a very soft chair. "You are a sir, aren't you? I mean you are a man…a human? Or are you?"

Booming laughter filled the room. "Dreadfully sorry, Jeffrey," said the voice. "One moment please!" In an instant a kind-looking older man stood in the room near the entry. He sat down next to Jeffrey. "I'm glad to see you're recovered," he said.

"They'll be recovering by now, too," Jeffrey said, looking back toward the mine.

"Yes but they shan't come this way," said the stranger.

"How do you know?"

"These mines are very tricky," he said. "And they don't know them as I do. Besides, there are certain creatures about who are sympathetic to me."

Jeffrey hoped the shina was one of them! "Thank you for helping me."

"Of course."

"How did you do it?"

"Do what?" said the man.

"Become invisible."

"Oh, that. All in its time, lad," said the old man, who was taking off his boots. "I shall explain all very soon. Here, drink this."

The man poured for both of them from an ancient-looking tea set on the small table beside him. Jeffrey sipped his tea and studied the old man and the room and thought it all very bizarre. But it was very good tea and Jeffrey relaxed for the first time in what seemed like days. In fact, he was getting drowsy. Who was this man? And why had he saved him? He studied the kind face looking back at him. Was this a friend of his father's, or perhaps some distant relative? He started to thank his rescuer once more, but the old man simply hushed him.

"You rest now, Jeffrey. We shall talk soon enough. All will be answered then."

"You know my name?" Jeffrey said sleepily.

"I know all about you, Jeffrey Jefford."

And even though Jeffrey had a million things he wanted to ask the old man, he felt himself more and more relaxed. Within seconds he drifted off to sleep as if he had taken some sort of elixir. He dreamed that the King himself was serving Jeffrey Jefford a plate of trout and truffles at the family inn, his parents looking on dotingly behind him.

Chapter 7

A WARM RECEPTION

WHEN Jeffrey awoke, the smell of sweet bread filled his nostrils. He smiled to himself as the comforting aroma warmed his heart like his grandma's special treats always managed to in the dreariness of winter. "Dreamy, wonderful feeling," he smiled to himself and opened his eyes.

Then he remembered. And he hurt.

Jeffrey found himself in the cozy little room with a little fire burning in the very cozy fireplace. A pot was simmering over the fire. All in all, the place had the feel of a very hospitable inn and was a welcome situation compared to the dank, chilly mine. But whose hospitality was he enjoying?

"Here you go, Jeffrey."

Was this all a silly dream? He reached up and felt his sore head. No, at least, not that part. The bump was certainly real, as were the cuts and scrapes. What was left of his shirt was in tatters. In a few foggy minutes, images began to come back to him: The conversation at Megs's tavern. The deal made to secure quick passage through the supposed secret tunnel to Gillingham. His rough captivity at the hands of those he had formerly trusted. Dangling above the shina's pit. Finally, in all probability, the saving of his life by this kindly old man who was now serving him this wonderful broth.

He looked at the kindly looking gentleman who had rescued him. Perhaps he was an angelic being of some sort…or a disgraced knight trying to make good…or…. He certainly didn't give the impression of being a warrior type. Twice now, the old man had burned himself on the fire fussing with the pot. He looked like he could be anyone's grandfather or uncle. And yet he was different.

"Sir?" Jeffrey ventured.

"At your service, young Jefford," answered the strange man as crisply as one of the royal guards at the castle in Edenshore.

How indeed? Since the man intended him no harm—at least for the moment—it seemed likely he was an ally. But, knowing the sorts of scoundrels that were turning up in this adventure, Jeffrey played it all very cautiously.

"Who are you?"

"Introductions!" the old man exclaimed so exuberantly it made Jeffrey jump. "That's what is wanting here. My name, though of no consequence, is Alexander Thaniel deManques VIII. You may call me Thaniel."

"Thank you," said Jeffrey, whose head buzzed with the name. "Thaniel VIII? The eighth what?"

"Good question," said the old man pensively. "The eighth deManques, I suppose. But I shall answer more fully when you have answered me this even greater question: Who is Jeffrey Jefford?"

Jeffrey thought for a moment in his still cloudy mind.

"Why that is me, sir. I am Jeffrey Jefford."

"But that is no answer," said Thaniel very casually, as he poured himself another tea. He glanced up toward the mantel. "Does your bird partake?"

Corinth was greedily eyeing the bits of pastry. "Yes, of course," answered Jeffrey, looking at the bird. "He partakes of just about anything he can carry away."

"Splendid!"

The old man soothingly coaxed the large, black bird down from the fireplace. Within a few moments Thaniel was acting as if he had made a new friend. Jeffrey smiled at this notion.

"He is only pretending to be your friend," Jeffrey snickered. "That raven is loyal only to my family."

"Perhaps," said Thaniel, as he fed a morsel of meat to the bird. "But sometimes a brief understanding is better than none."

He winked at the bird. Jeffrey could have sworn the bird winked back. He rested a few more minutes, finally beginning to relax. He was sore, but he was also safe. He looked at the old man who'd found a pipe and begun cleaning it.

"Please, sir," Jeffrey finally asked, "What is this all about?" He looked about as if suddenly remembering that someone else should be in the room. He sat up anxiously. "And where is my father?"

Thaniel looked at the boy and then settled back into his chair. He continued gazing at Jeffrey as he stuffed some sweet-smelling tobacco into a very long pipe and lit it up. He created quite a billow of smoke that swirled around his head. Then, taking the pipe from his mouth he leaned in toward Jeffrey.

"Two excellent questions," he said. "And both the same question, really. Because the matter of what this business is all about and where your father is are the same matters. I shall be honest with you in all that I know."

"Thank you, sir."

"Thaniel," corrected the old man. "But allow me to finish my pipe while you finish your broth. Then there is much to do while we talk." Jeffrey nodded. They sat in silence for several minutes, sipping, puffing, and thinking. Then Thaniel stood and slapped his hands together and looked at Jeffrey.

"You must know that your father was duped from the beginning," Thaniel began. "Excuse me if I get some things together while we chat. We'll be leaving shortly. Now, all this matter of treasure and maps and such was partly a device to get your father out into the open with the coin. Deception masked in a bit of truth is quite convincing. That was it. Brilliantly conceived, I must admit."

"Jack and Finius," muttered Jeffrey, angrily.

Thaniel laughed. "Those two? Hardly clever enough to come up with the details of this sort of plan." Thaniel looked about the room as if trying to remember where he had placed something.

"Then it was Pickworth," mused Jeffrey. "I should never have trusted him with all his sentimental talk of helping me."

"True, Jasper Pickworth, your one-time lawyer, probably helped plan the scheme. Clever man. Never trust a lawyer, Jeffrey! First rule of law!" He winked at the boy.

Jeffrey managed a smile at hearing Pickworth's maxim once more. Obviously Thaniel had heard of Jasper Pickworth. "But even Pickworth is not the primary mover in this. Someone else is behind all this, Jeffrey."

"Certainly not that brute called Lorogos," Jeffrey said.

"Lorogos," muttered Thaniel. "I thought I recognized him."

"You know him?"

"Only distantly," said Thaniel. He looked at Jeffrey's bemused stare. "Pickworth, Jack, Lorogos—they are but minor players in this drama. No, Jeffrey, someone else with a vile passion and a dark heart who will do whatever he must to recover that coin is responsible. And that is why we must be off at once!"

"The coin again," Jeffrey sighed.

"The coin," Thaniel said. "Yes."

"So…where is my father?"

"I cannot say, boy," Thaniel said grimly. "But prepare yourself for the worst. I'm sure he met with foul play. Murdered, most likely."

Jeffrey sat back, nodding with an understanding that indicated he wasn't at all surprised at the answer, though he certainly did not want to hear it. He threw his head back and rubbed his eyes with both hands. "Murdered? For that coin?" he asked bitterly.

"Oh, it's not just *this* coin," said Thaniel. He put down the compass he was packing in a small chest. "Look, boy, I don't know if your father is alive or not. But you saw the intent of these villains back in the mine. They will stop at nothing to secure the object of their quest. I saw them throw one of their own to the shina, just for amusement."

"What were you doing in the mine?"

"I live here," Thaniel said, indicating his home.

"But you helped me," Jeffrey continued, "like you were expecting me."

"I was," Thaniel said, winking.

He put his hand on Jeffrey's shoulder.

"As to your father, perhaps he is alive. And if he is, we shall find him yet, but not if we stay here." Thaniel returned to packing a couple of small bags. "You see, Jeffrey, the coins are the whole point of this business. If there is any chance of finding your father alive it shall involve the coins. That is why we must be off at once!"

"Coins!" Jeffrey snapped. "Don't you mean coin? The coin I have?"

"No Jeffrey, I mean coins."

Jeffrey stood up and angrily paced about. He was angry about everything now; angry about his father; angry about his throbbing head; angry that he had trusted Pickworth, angry about not knowing what everyone else seemed to know; angry at the thought of coins and maps; and angry for being mixed up in it all. "What is this about, old man?" he seethed.

"I'll provide some details as we gather things for the journey, but we need to get out of here quickly," Thaniel said calmly.

"Where are we going?"

"To your home, of course," Thaniel replied, as he wrapped a kettle in some cloth, placing it in the seemingly bottomless bag. "Among other places. But first we are going to your family inn." For the first time in several hours, Jeffrey's face lit up. "And by the way, you may call me Thaniel, but not 'old man.'"

Jeffrey managed an apologetic smile. Thaniel smiled back reassuringly, looking at Jeffrey. "And now, as to this business, as you say, about the coins." Thaniel stood up and moved to the other side of the room. Reaching for the intricately inlaid wall, he pulled on a particular portion of the inlay and it opened, revealing a small, square cavity. Reaching inside, Thaniel pulled out a small, leather-bound box. He walked back to Jeffrey and sat down. The old man closed his eyes as if in prayer for a few moments. Then, opening the box, he produced a coin, which he handed to Jeffrey.

"Does this look familiar?" Thaniel asked.

Jeffrey examined the coin. He held it up to the candle on the table. There was no doubt in his mind that this was like his father's coin—the one brought home by Killian Jefford so many years ago. Same strange markings, same inscription, but there was something different. What was it? "There's a pair of sandals on this coin," said Jeffrey, handing it back to Thaniel. "It's the same as father's, but for that."

"As I said, Jeffrey, coins, and not coin. There are more. And what is on your father's coin?"

"Father's is similar but it has a sword on it instead of the shoes."

Thaniel leaned back and closed his eyes.

"*Copis*," he whispered.

"What was that, sir?"

"*Copis*," said Thaniel. "You have *Copis*!"

"And that is good?" Jeffrey asked.

"Very good! Thaniel smiled.

"But what is it?"

"Everything and nothing," the old man said cryptically. "One piece of a puzzle. One-sixth to be exact, but a very significant one, indeed. And a very powerful ally to one who knows how to coax its power." Jeffrey was more confused than ever. "You see?" Thaniel said, holding the coin. "I have the *Juaracas*—the sandals. Your grandfather believed he was bringing home a very interesting relic for your father's collection. Well, indeed he did bring something very interesting. He brought home the *Copis Spiritus*—the Sword of the Spirit!"

"Swords? Sandals? Coins? Puzzles?" Jeffrey whined, holding his head in his hands. He looked at Thaniel grimacing. "And there are four more of these? My head is boiling!"

"Yes, yes," said Thaniel excitedly. "Six coins in all. That is why they went after your father. And that is why they have been after me: the coins."

"Are they really worth killing a man?"

"Jeffrey, in the wrong hands, they are worth killing *all* men."

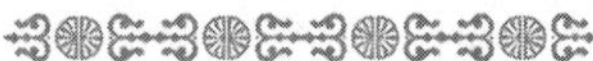

Within a few minutes, Thaniel had packed and tidied up the room. He took one last long look and then turned to his young guest. "And now we must be off, lad! No saying when I'll see this place again. Best leave it in good shape for the next occupant. Come along."

"Why such a hurry?" asked Jeffrey.

"We must get there before they do!"

"Where?"

"I told you, boy," said Thaniel, helping Jeffrey with a cloak, "to your inn."

"They are going to the Trout and Truffles?"

"Listen to me, lad," said Thaniel tenderly. "We are dealing with vicious and cunning brutes who are in the employ of a darkness you could not possibly understand. They will let nobody stand in the way of their mission to find the coins. Not a boy, and certainly not his mother, however innocent. That is why we must be off at once!"

"But the inn? Why would they go there?" His eyes grew wide as he finally realized the situation. "You think they know the coin is at the inn?" Jeffrey swallowed hard. "I mean—I just found out myself when they ripped the mistaken coin out of my shirt. My mother had sewn it there."

"Look, boy," the old man said tenderly, "your mother was mistaken. I'm sure that she probably put it back in that little hiding place you told me of with the ordinary edens."

"When did I tell you that?" Jeffrey asked, confused.

"In your delirium while recovering from that head blow," Thaniel winked at him. "you talk in your sleep! And if the coin is in your mother's possession at the inn, then I suspect they will have figured that a mistake was made. Pickworth is no fool. Even Jack mentioned going back to the inn."

Jeffrey's eyes grew wide. "If that's true..."

"Then your mother is in grave danger," Thaniel said solemnly.

The old man pulled a brick out of the mantel and a door slid open at the rear of the room. It was another entrance into the mine. He handed the boy one of the bags he had packed and bid him follow. "I have much more to tell you but we really have to leave and I can explain it all on the way."

"Let's hurry!" said Jeffrey, stirred into action. He started for the door but stopped. He looked around. "Where is my..." He then remembered that all his things had been wrecked in the mine when Jack and the others were searching for the coin.

"My sword!" he said with great disappointment. "Finius took the Sauren sword!" Corinth flew down and lit on his shoulder.

The old man handed him a small knapsack that was surprisingly heavy for its size. "The sword is lost to those scoundrels," Thaniel said, as he began snuffing out the little candles and lamps. Thaniel guided the boy through the increasingly dark room. "They have a bit of a head start on us. But if I know the type, they will stop at an inn or two along the way for some drink."

"One inn in particular," said Jeffrey, as Megs's face flashed before his eyes.

Chapter 8

THE JOURNEY BEGINS

THE journey back through the tricky mine seemed a lot longer to Jeffrey than when they had first entered. Perhaps it was because the first time through he was dazed from his bruised head; or maybe it was the astonishment of being led to safety by an unseen rescuer; or the shock of finding himself betrayed by men he had trusted. Most likely, it seemed to be taking such a long time because of the danger hanging over his mother.

"A bit farther," was ever the phrase of encouragement Thaniel would speak. He had managed some clothes and a cloak for Jeffrey, something akin to a cowl and very monkish, in Jeffrey's estimation, but quite warm. Thaniel was dressed similarly. Both carried knapsacks for the journey. Corinth took to the safety of Jeffrey's tunic, burrowing inside for warmth.

When they finally reached the surface, Jeffrey was completely lost. This did not look anything like the woods he had traveled with Pickworth. In fact, it looked as if they were in another country altogether. The trees seemed as thick, but somehow different. They were not as tall as the forest he had grown up in. There were less flowers and small shrubs, too. In the distance, he could see a grayness that spanned the horizon. He was probably the first Jefford to travel so close to the mist that was such a mystery to the people of Humus.

Thaniel led them to a small clearing where they seated themselves to rest on a fallen log. Corinth took off into the trees overhead. Jeffrey wished he had his sword with him and began looking about for some sort of weapon. The old man motioned for Jeffrey to be still and then began to murmur to himself, as if in prayer. Jeffrey stood, a bit annoyed. He was ready to get moving again, before those villains arrived at his mother's door. He looked at the woods about him. Yes, they were definitely in a different region. Thaniel had evidently brought them out through a completely different passageway under the mountain. What an amazing man, Jeffrey thought to himself, though still annoyed at the delay.

A strange howl in the distance startled Jeffrey. He looked in the direction of the noise but saw nothing. It sounded far off, but who could tell in these dense woods. Perhaps there were still werewolves about, as old Pickworth had intimated. If only he had that sword! He scowled at Thaniel who was only just now finishing up.

"You're in too much of a hurry," Thaniel remarked.

"Well, yes I am," Jeffrey stammered. "You kept telling me we must be off. Why have we stopped? I thought we were in a race!"

Thaniel took his pipe out and began packing it.

"*They* are in a hurry, Jeffrey," he said. "They are driven by greed and fear. *We* are making haste with purpose. I told you that my pass put us safely ahead of them."

"*They* are with horse," Jeffrey bit back.

Thaniel smiled at Jeffrey's consternation. "Patience, Jeffrey. Our exit on this side of the mountain places us miles ahead of their party. I was praying for the journey and expressing thanks for our mission." He winked and added, "I prayed for horses, too."

"Next time you're praying, you might ask about my father," Jeffrey requested, picking up a stick and swinging it around like a sword. "Ask your god to watch over my mother, too. And see if you can find out how I got caught up in the middle of this business!"

Thaniel only nodded and smiled at the boy. Jeffrey had never seen such piety in action. The only association he had ever had with a holy man was an itinerant monk who had passed through the inn when he was a little boy. Turned out the man was wanted for murder and was eventually caught and condemned. But Thaniel seemed sincere enough. Jeffrey watched as the old man apparently finished his praying.

"Sir?" asked Jeffrey, as he helped Thaniel to his feet. "To whom do you pray?"

Thaniel put away the pipe and stretched his arm, looking at the trees. "Why, to Him who made all this," he said, "the trees, the land, you, me…" He laughed. "Yes, and even you, Corinth!"

The big black bird screeched in delight.

"The one who made us?" Jeffrey asked, puzzled.

"Yes," said Thaniel. "Surely you pray?"

"Well, yes, of course," he mustered. "We have priests in our region, or did. There is an old abandoned abbot near the inn." He looked sheepishly at Thaniel. "They say it's haunted now, but one time it was filled with holy men. Men like yourself who prayed…" Jeffrey's voice trailed off as one who had wandered into unfamiliar territory. He knew of some clerics in the family from a long time ago. But the recent family history had run less to prophets and more to profits.

"Nothing quite as empty as a once holy place that has lost its purpose," mused Thaniel. "Happens to buildings…happens to people too, Jeffrey. But He to whom I pray is no whimsical god of trees or animals."

"But what is his name?" Jeffrey asked.

"Nobody knows, boy," said Thaniel. "We only know that He has always been. That is what matters."

"But if He has no name…"

"Ah, here are the horses I was expecting!" Thaniel interrupted.

As if on cue, a young man emerged from the woods holding the reins of two fine horses. He was blond like Jeffrey, only older. Thaniel approached the young man and had a brief discussion with him. He nodded and, after a quick glance in Jeffrey's direction, bade Thaniel farewell and disappeared into the woods.

"Quick work on that prayer," Jeffrey said, happy to see the horses.

"Yes," said Thaniel. "Prayer is always good. And a little advance planning! You'll find that we have many friends in this endeavor."

The horses were beautiful creatures. Thaniel's mount was a chestnut-colored beauty with a broad chest and gentle demeanor. Jeffrey's horse was as black and glossy as Corinth. Thaniel watched as Jeffrey approached his horse. He couldn't tell whether Jeffrey was sizing up the horse or the horse was sizing up Jeffrey.

"He's a proud one, lad," said Thaniel. "You'll have to work as a team. Learn to trust one another."

"I know horses," said Jeffrey defensively as he moved to the horse to mount him. "A little coaxing, a bit of a treat, and you can get these stupid animals to do anything."

Upon those words the black horse moved the rear of his body to the side, knocking Jeffrey into a small puddle. The boy landed with a splash, looked up at the horse, and imagined an insolent look back. Thaniel laughed heartily at the exchange.

"As I said, he is a proud horse," he said while helping the boy up. "And quite unique, as there's not another horse like him in all Humus. Nova Fannum even, I'd wager."

"How fortunate for me," Jeffrey retorted, brushing mud off his cloak.

"Indeed," said Thaniel, mounting his horse. "His name is Fortis, and you'd best ask permission before you mount. He's quite particular. You must say, 'By your leave.'"

The horse snorted.

"I will not!" Jeffrey responded. He looked at Fortis, who snorted again with determination. Jeffrey looked at his muddy cloak. "But this time I will. If only so we might be off. I'll master this horse, though, before we reach the inn!"

He stepped toward the horse and pitched an overly dramatic bow. "By your leave, Fortis," he said. Fortis simply stared at Jeffrey, as before, but this time he gave the boy no trouble as he mounted him.

"You see?" said Thaniel, smiling. "Teamwork!"

Jeffrey rolled his eyes.

Thaniel looked at the sky. "We'd best continue. These woods are treacherous after dark. There is a good stopping-place we can reach by twilight if we get moving."

The remainder of the day was spent mainly in silence. Thaniel said it was best not to be talking too openly about their mission. All, he promised, would be divulged tonight when they stopped. So Jeffrey contented himself with ambling along on Fortis. They passed through several deeply forested areas where branches and even whole fallen trees blocked the barely perceptible trail.

"Aren't there better roads?" asked Jeffrey scornfully as a branch scratched his cheek once more. "We might as well be cutting a new trail."

"There are better roads," admitted Thaniel, who was himself holding a branch aside so Jeffrey could pass under. "But there are none quicker. These are old smuggler's trails. The elves ran the mines and some dwarves worked them. But the dwarves got it into their heads to begin hoarding the better gems for themselves.

"They would mine the very mountain we just left and take the stolen jewels across this region to the port at Aarpon. The elves, having a bit of the magic, finally caught on and, in their fury, buried some 600 dwarves alive and put a spell upon them. They rest somewhere beneath our feet."

He looked back at Jeffrey's wide-eyed countenance and added, "Or perhaps they do not rest. Some say these woods are haunted by maddened dwarves looking for the gems that cost them their lives."

Jeffrey looked down at the dark trail, imagining hundreds of dwarves' voices screaming for mercy. He shuddered a bit. Silly story. Still, he wished he had that Sauren sword!

"Here we are!" Thaniel announced. "We stop just ahead for the night." Jeffrey craned his neck to see around Thaniel but was able to see nothing in the way of an inn or house or anything that looked inhabited. He was getting cold. He was hungry. He frowned. And he was getting tired.

Corinth suddenly flew from Jeffrey's shoulder and into the top of a tree. He squawked loudly, fussing in and out of the limbs. Jeffrey watched, amused. He had seen Corinth go after other birds before. Scrappy little beggar!

"What is it?" Thaniel called back.

"Oh, nothing. Corinth is protecting us!" Jeffrey smiled as Corinth came gliding back. He was glad they were stopping for the night. His tired eyes were beginning to trick him. He didn't tell Thaniel, because he thought he would laugh at him, but in the branches where Corinth had flown, he was sure he had seen a small, black creature staring at him. He shook it off and followed Thaniel.

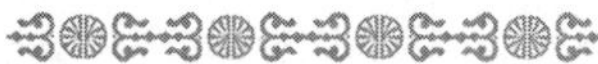

They entered a small, wooded ravine through which a creek flowed. There were trees enough for cover and the water was certainly adequate, but what about a place to sleep? Why had they come here?

"Where are we? I don't see anything here."

"That says quite a lot about a person, Jeffrey," said Thaniel, reining his horse to a stop. "Some can look into emptiness and see everything; others can see everything and still come up empty."

Jeffrey could hardly believe his eyes. Or perhaps the bump on his head had been harder than he thought. For in front of them, as if out of nowhere, was a sparkling waterfall, some 60 feet above them. It was quite beautiful, and in the dusky light of evening, seemed enchanting. Jeffrey rubbed his eyes hard. He would have sworn that it was not there only seconds before.

Thaniel climbed off his horse and moved over the rocks to the edge of the waterfall, which cascaded like a shimmering curtain. He climbed up a bit onto the slippery rocks and disappeared behind the falls, yelling for Jeffrey to tie up the horses and follow him. Jeffrey did as he was told and edged over the wet rocks to the edge of the falls. Corinth dove into his cloak, readying himself for the deluge. "Easy, Corinth," said Jeffrey, adjusting his cloak to make a warm spot for the black bird. He peered in behind the curtain of water and saw no opening.

"Where are you?"

"Through the waters," came a voice from deep within. "Come on."

Jeffrey saw a flicker of a light from within. He stepped very delicately under a large outcrop and, craning his neck around the corner of the rock, saw the rest of the opening. It was a cave under the falls! The old man was certainly agile, Jeffrey thought to himself as he almost slipped twice into the onrushing falls. Finally, he found a firm footing and stepped into the opening.

"You certainly know your way around," Jeffrey said as he warmed himself by the fire that Thaniel had somehow already built. Corinth emerged and, finding no perch, flew to a sharp outcrop about 30 feet up on the wall opposite Jeffrey.

"I've known about this place for some time," Thaniel answered.

"How did you build that fire so quickly?" Jeffrey asked.

"Oh I didn't build it," said Thaniel, warming his hands. "He did."

Jeffrey looked to see a young man, probably in his twenties, bringing a pot to the fire. The young man looked up, wrinkling his nose at Jeffrey. "The world is full of places of refuge," said Thaniel, packing his pipe for a fresh smoke, "If one knows where to find them, Jeffrey. This is Ethan."

Ethan nodded as he set the pot down on the coals. He was in a cloak of the same sort as Thaniel's and looked to be at least as tall as Jeffrey. He could almost be Jeffrey's twin except that he was older and his hair a darker blond.

"I have tea for you, uncle," he said to Thaniel. "And some stew. I'll take care of your horses."

"Excellent! Thank you, Ethan."

"How was Fortis?" Ethan asked Jeffrey.

Jeffrey managed a disagreeable smile at Ethan while looking around for something he could throw at him. Thaniel opened the steaming pot. "No finer fare in these woods!" Jeffrey was still looking about, confused. "Do you not know these caves, Jeffrey?"

Jeffrey looked about the cave—really more of a very large crack that opened at the falls. The light allowed him to make out the strange formations that occur in most caves. And there was evidence of an animal here or there. Otherwise it seemed a very normal cave. Jeffrey shrugged.

"Looks like the regular sort of cave one sees," he said, "except for the waterfall. But I have never been this far from the inn, or so close to the great southern mountains. I see nothing out of the ordinary."

"Ah, but you're only looking and not observing. Just as the Great Mist of the mountains hides something behind its impassable edges, so does this waterfall hide something. Use your mind as well as your eyes. Look to the walls. What do you observe?" Jeffrey was hungry and really not in the mood for anymore of Thaniel's puzzles. He also wondered who this Ethan was, but resigned himself to the situation and began looking intently at the dark, damp cave walls. At first, he could only see moss and other discolorations in the rock.

"Can you give me a hint of what I am supposed to see?"

Thaniel ignored him. Jeffrey was about to give up, but Ethan's snickering at his inability to see whatever it was that Thaniel wanted him to see urged him on. He moved in close and still saw nothing. But then...what was this…?

"Writing!" he exclaimed, his voice throwing an echo. "There is writing of some sort on these walls."

"Not just some sort," said Thaniel, who was seated near the fire and pulling some bread and cheese out of his sack. "It is a very particular sort—a definite language. Now sit! Both of you! Let us enjoy this delicious meal."

Jeffrey began to eat greedily until he noticed that both Thaniel and Ethan were silently praying. He stopped eating until they were finished and began eating. As far as Jeffrey was concerned, they might have been dining in the King's own banquet hall in the palace at Edenshore. The stew—a venison and wild mushroom concoction—was very good. Jeffrey tried to mentally put the recipe together for future use at the Trout and Truffles. They all sat in satisfied silence for a few minutes, enjoying the savory venison stew and the comfort of the fire. As they sipped their tea and relaxed, Thaniel lit his pipe and indicated the walls once more.

"So what do you think, Jeffrey," he said. "What sort of writing is that?"

"Nothing I recognize," said Jeffrey, whose knowledge of other languages was limited to the few words of Jorish he'd picked up at the inn. Ethan smirked and Jeffrey shot him an annoyed look.

"But you've seen that script before," said Thaniel. Jeffrey concentrated. "Think, boy. Where have you seen that writing?"

"Of course—the coin! I recognize some of the lettering from that coin of my father's."

"Splendid. And so it is. It is Fannish, a very ancient and holy language. This is my native tongue as we speak it in Nova Fannum." He looked at the writing. "Or once did and hope to again one day."

"Nova Fannum?" Jeffrey asked, running his hands across the strange inscriptions. They were written in an ochre hue in characters about the size of Jeffrey's thumb.

"Yes, my homeland and a noble, priestly language spoken in a nobler, holier time." He put his hand on Ethan's shoulder. "This writing was once a sacred and beautiful part of Nova Fannum's life. It was the language of holy writ and sacred scrolls. It was the language of Him to whom we pray and whose law we keep. It was the language spoken by prophets and kings…"

"Was?"

He looked at Jeffrey, teary-eyed. "Let's just say it is no longer spoken in Nova Fannum; is it, Ethan?"

"At least not by anyone who values his life," Ethan answered.

Thaniel nodded silently.

"Where is Nova Fannum?" asked Jeffrey. "I have never heard of such a place."

"I suspect not," Thaniel said.

"Is it to the south—beyond the mountains?"

"In a sense," said Thaniel.

"More toward the sea or in the peaks, themselves?"

"Yes," said Thaniel.

"Well, which is it?"

"It is all of those, Jeffrey," Thaniel said, sipping his tea. "Nova Fannum is high in the mountains and down near the sea. It is to the south and in the north. In short, Jeffrey, Nova Fannum is in every man's heart, if he seeks it. But no man from Humus has ever seen Nova Fannum, though one day all men shall see its King."

"Then it is not a real place. It is merely part of the lore of your religion."

Thaniel frowned. "What are they teaching in Humus?" he sputtered. "This language is real enough. And the coins, you've seen them. Nova Fannum is real indeed, boy."

"Then how do you get there from here?" Jeffrey persisted.

"Through the waters, Jeffrey, through the waters."

"The waters? I'm afraid I don't understand," said Jeffrey, looking to Ethan, who merely shrugged at him. "So, who wrote this on the wall?"

Thaniel sat back and puffed on his long pipe. He took a piece of brown bread and gave a portion to Corinth, who devoured it greedily, then flew away. Corinth perched himself near the entrance in the hopes of seizing a mouse or some other cave vermin. Jeffrey could still not believe the old man had actually befriended that fickle bird. Ethan settled in close.

"These words were written a long time ago," answered Thaniel. "Yet not really so long, by myself and my five brothers. Ethan is a son to one of those brothers. He is my nephew and my only surviving relative, to my knowledge."

Jeffrey and Ethan exchanged glances. "You live in these caves?" Jeffrey asked.

"Not so much live in them as wait in them," Ethan said. "I am here because my uncle asked me to be here when you arrived. And I'm here because it is time."

"Time for what?"

"The writing on that wall is a vow, Jeffrey," Thaniel continued. "It is a blood oath sworn between my brothers and myself. Do you know what such an oath means?"

Jeffrey swallowed and shook his head, no.

"It means that I shall die before I fail in my purpose," Thaniel said solemnly, looking at the writing. "I swore this oath with my brothers. That is why I know that Dontel was murdered. He would never have given up the coin to Jack. He would have died first, as have the others. I fear that I represent the last of us." He smiled and mussed Ethan's hair. "Along with Ethan here who will honor his father's name and keep the oath with me." Ethan smiled a sad sort of smile and nodded.

"But what was the oath?" Jeffrey asked.

"Earlier, you asked me what this is all about, Jeffrey, and I promised to tell you. I brought you to this cave for a number of reasons, apart from the fact that this is also on the way to your inn. I must now swear you to secrecy, Jeffrey. From here on out nothing I tell you must ever cross your lips to anyone else."

"I swear it," Jeffrey whispered.

"Then you must trust me, lad. I promise that all will be disclosed, but not here. Not now. Jaarad will explain all."

The old man settled himself in a bit and reached for his bag. Jeffrey watched him pull out the book he had earlier packed. He thumbed through a few opening pages and then with a sigh that seemed both melancholy and nostalgic, looked at Jeffrey.

"This book, written in Fannish, is a chronicle of my land," he said. "The Annals of Nova Fannum was one of the books in the immense temple library of which my brothers and I were stewards. Before the dark times, all the people of Nova Fannum were quite literate. Knowledge is essential to virtue, Jeffrey. But when knowledge is misused or neglected, it becomes an instrument of wickedness and license for the most unholy behaviors."

He leafed through several pages.

"My story is of a great land and a greater king; a glorious place and time; a virtuous people and a royal priesthood. It's a history of purity and piety; and, sad to say, of treachery, evil and corruption. It is full of hopeful prophecy and devastating consequences…"

He stopped and leaned in toward his audience.

"But these are words better kept for Jaarad."

"When will we see him?" asked Jeffrey.

"Soon enough," said Thaniel. "He is expecting us."

He looked at Jeffrey with compassion. "Ah, poor lad," he said. "Caught in a world that is not your own in the middle of a war that is not of your making. And yet our deeds will eventually affect all people everywhere."

Jeffrey looked down at the fire. It popped loudly and startled him.

"Not so long ago," Thaniel continued, "when it became apparent that the star was on the rise foretelling the Great King's return, my brother came to Humus looking for me. He had been in hiding in Nova Fannum—always stalked, ever in danger of a hunter lurking everywhere."

"Spies?"

"Agents," said Thaniel. "They serve a usurper named Hendras, called in unfriendlier circles, "Blackheart." And while it is true his power, for now, is limited in Humus..."

"Blackheart?" Jeffrey repeated.

"...he has spies and villains in his employ that reach even into Humus. Pickworth and Jack, for example. Lorogos, too."

He looked at Jeffrey.

"And one vile and cruel man in particular whose sorcery, I'm sorry to say, also serves him in Humus as well. He is Blackheart's second and probably the one behind your father's disappearance. Phaesus by name, he is bent on returning the coins to Nova Fannum at any cost, and seeing his dark master forever enthroned."

"So what happened to your brother?" Jeffrey asked.

"Murdered, I'm sure. Dontel fell prey to the thieves who took the coin and murdered him in some common act of crime."

"He had the coin my grandfather bought."

"Of course, boy," said Thaniel, stirring the fire. "The vow we took as brothers on that black day was a vow to the death. Blackheart seized the armor, but we had already taken the coins which give it power. Without the coins in place the prophecy will never happen. And without the prophecy, the armor is useless. No, Jeffrey, not one of us would ever give up our coin without first giving up his life."

He looked up from the fire.

"This is why I know that my brother was murdered and the coin stolen."

"So Jack and Finius took the coin those many years ago, never knowing its true value until after they had pawned it to the thieving monks for common currency," surmised Jeffrey. "And then my grandfather bought it from some unscrupulous dealer who had taken it in commerce from the monks!"

He continued, thinking hard. "And then Pickworth and his lot were engaged by this Hendras..."

"By Phaesus, more likely," said Thaniel. "When it became evident that the time was drawing near. To be sure, there are many who know of the coin's existence in Humus, but Phaesus had to follow the coin's trail, person by person. I'm sure he murdered as he went. That monk, Thaddius, was likely a victim of this affair. Not that he didn't deserve it, having fallen in with a band of thieves. Also, the dealer from whom your grandfather bought the coin years ago, all of them murdered. The killers cover their tracks but leave blood in their wake."

"But why does he need the coins?"

"The coins represent the fullest possible power available to him. They each have certain properties which, when in place together, create an irresistible force for good or for evil. It's obvious that Hendras is reaching into Humus for the coins. Ah, Jeffrey, his heart is as black as the darkness of this cave. It is totally devoid of anything pure. The time must be shorter than I thought."

"What is this 'time' you keep speaking of?"

"The time of the King's promised return to Nova Fannum," Thaniel answered. "The one who will make all things right. As I said, the twin stars have begun their ascent. When they reach their zenith in the constellation, the appointed time will have arrived."

"Then it began just in the last year," reasoned Jeffrey, "when they first approached my father."

"Or shortly before that," Thaniel said. "Very recently, to be sure. As I said, the encroaching darkness over Humus speaks of the gathering power of Hendras. For the time it is contained. But, if he succeeds, it shall spill over this land like a great dark flood. Nothing shall suppress his will."

Jeffrey nodded, thinking again of how the darkness had indeed become more pervasive and the days shorter of late.

"Jeffrey, the reach of these events is universal. It is a war that has begun in a different world, yet all worlds shall be affected by the outcome, for good or ill."

"But we see no twin star in our skies,"

"The stars of which I speak don't appear in this sky but in the skies of Nova Fannum, as you shall see. Remember, Jeffrey, Nova Fannum is not simply another land hidden in the mists and mountains of Humus. It is another world, hidden in the hearts and minds of men. It is a place all men dream of, yet it is not a dream. It is a land of great possibility, of fantastic creatures and wonderful people. Or at least it was, in better times." He closed his eyes, as though gazing upon Nova Fannum in his mind.

"Blackheart's ascent has turned all that was pure into that which is dark. Where beautiful unicorns and golden rams once roamed there are now one-eyed sentries and vile flesh-eating beasts, profane reflections of noble beasts gone before. All sorts of hellish creatures thought extinct by your people, or imagined in the most lurid minds, are gathering in Nova Fannum as one wicked army—dedicated to their master's every whim, and serving as Phaesus's network of spies. It is a very different world where evil is on high."

"Hendras, you said?" Jeffrey asked, thinking aloud.

"Hendras was his priestly name," said Thaniel. "But Blackheart is how we know him. For that is what he is." Thaniel sat silent for a few moments.

"Thaniel, I don't understand something. If all of the other brothers are dead, then where are their coins?"

"As far as I know they are secreted in various places and with various people loyal to the cause," he answered. "As I said, there is a resistance, chief among them, a secret army called the Servatrix. They and their families are sworn to find the coins and hold them for the Castus, who is to come and restore the Kingdom. I suspect they have some of the coins. Perhaps the enemy has some, I don't know. But we'll meet the Servatrix soon."

He clasped his hands.

"So there it is. I have one of the coins. Your father was in possession of one. And Ethan here, has one," he said, smiling at Ethan. "The other coins we shall obtain in due course."

"You have one of the coins?" Jeffrey asked, looking at Ethan.

Ethan nodded. "Ethan's father, Corin, took *Cassis*—the helmet," Thaniel said.

Ethan reached inside his cloak and pulled out a coin with a helmet struck into its face. Jeffrey examined it and handed it back to Ethan. "But what does your coin do?" he asked. "Can you become invisible, too?"

Before Jeffrey had finished the question, Ethan's form took on that of a giant cave bear, slathering mouth wide open and teeth bared. Jeffrey screamed and jumped behind Thaniel, who was laughing aloud. Just as quickly, the bear changed back into a smirking Ethan, tucking the coin back into his cloak.

Jeffrey sputtered as Ethan doubled over in laughter.

"*Cassis*," explained Thaniel, "has the ability to influence another's mind. To allow it to see things as *if they are*, though they *are not*; or to see things that are *not* as though they *are*. But it only influences men and women who have no understanding of true belief, Jeffrey. For true belief sees things that are not as if they were, and then watches them become! Understand?"

"Not at all," said Jeffrey, still mad at himself for having been so startled.

"Suffice it to say that Ethan opened the image of the waterfall *that* is to your mind, as well as the image of the bear, that *is not*. His assistance in our effort shall become invaluable as we deal with men whose minds are closed to truth. A darkened mind is always vulnerable, Jeffrey. Now you can see the importance of not allowing the coins to fall into Hendras's hands. The power of the armor with the coins is unstoppable."

"What about this king of yours? Why should he allow all this, if he is as powerful as you say?"

"I know it is difficult to understand, but He allows us to make the choices that create our destinies. He will not interfere with the prophecy or its outcome. It is a test of our hearts, Jeffrey. He will not interfere with our chosen destiny. That is why we must prevail with the coins. Jaarad will explain all."

After a few moments of silence, they began settling in for the night. Jeffrey used his outer cloak for a pillow and the three lay down around the fire.

"Just don't do the bear thing again,"

"Don't worry, I won't. At least not until it's good and dark..."

"Great!" Jeffrey said as he lay down and pulled his cloak up over his eyes.

Chapter 9

HOMEWARD BOUND

THE morning came quickly for Jeffrey. Although he'd finally managed to fall asleep after the eventful night, he only got a couple hours' rest. Thaniel and Ethan were already up and ready when Jeffrey met them outside the cave. Both their horses were saddled and ready to go, with Ethan smiling and holding their reins.

"'Bout time you awoke," scolded Thaniel good-naturedly. "We must make your home before nightfall—before our opponents get there."

Jeffrey was angry with the old man for stopping overnight. "If we had kept going we'd be there now," he said, as he asked permission and mounted. "Why did we stop?"

"For a number of reasons, Jeffrey. For one thing I am not as young as I once was. For another, the forest is far too dangerous to travel through at night. Also, I wanted to pick up Ethan. His skills will be valuable to us as the journey continues. But mainly, boy, you needed to see for yourself that cave. You may return there again one day."

"I might return *here*?"

"As I said, places of refuge are of great value, especially when they are so concealed as this one."

"Concealed?" said Jeffrey. "I bet lots of people around here know about this place."

"What place?" asked Thaniel.

Ethan smiled as he mounted his horse.

"Why the waterfall, of course," fumed Jeffrey, looking back.

"Waterfall?"

Looking back, Jeffrey was astonished to see an ordinary ravine, with ordinary rocks and ordinary trees and shrubs. The brook continued babbling through, but any hint of a cave behind a waterfall was gone. In fact, the waterfall was gone as well!

"Where did it go?" He jumped down and ran to the brook, then looked at Ethan, who was grinning to himself. "Very clever, Ethan. At least it wasn't a bear."

"That wasn't Ethan's doing," said Thaniel. "This place is a holy place of refuge, seen only by those with a pure intent. The priests of Nova Fannum created it centuries ago."

Jeffrey stared blankly at the ravine wall, his head throbbing with the information he had taken in.

"Come on boy," Thaniel said. "We need to be off if we're going to reach your mother by this evening."

Jeffrey shook his head, muttering to himself. He walked over to Fortis and started to climb back into the saddle. Fortis moved quickly to the side, knocking Jeffrey down, giving him a dismissive look. Thaniel and Ethan laughed.

"Very funny," Jeffrey said, dusting himself off.

"Remember, Fortis has his sensibilities," Thaniel smiled.

"I will not ask a horse's permission to mount him!"

Ethan and Thaniel looked at each other.

"Then get used to walking," said Ethan. "For that is a very special horse. Treat him right and he will one day surprise you—even save your life." Jeffrey looked at the horse. Then he looked back where the waterfall and cave had been. He sighed.

"By your leave, Fortis."

"I don't believe he heard you," said Thaniel.

"By your leave!" Jeffrey yelled, and Fortis relaxed and allowed himself to be mounted. "You stupid beast."

"Beast, yes, 'stupid,' no," said Thaniel, as they started down the ravine trail. "After all, he got what he wanted."

"I wish I could get what I wanted," said Jeffrey.

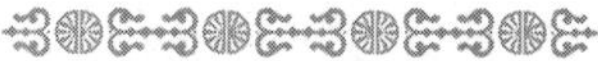

The trip through the ravine was slow going. Passing through unfamiliar territory, Thaniel led the group out of the ravine and across a large meadow. The horses no longer had to travel single file and Jeffrey drew up next to Ethan, who was riding a beautiful gray horse he called Cosmos. Corinth flew from tree to tree along the way, staying in view of the path. Ethan looked over at Jeffrey and nodded. After a few moments of silence, Jeffrey finally spoke.

"What's your country like? I mean Nova Fannum."

"I've never been there, at least, not in my memory. My father fled before I was born. But from the stories I have heard, it was unbelievable. And our family home was very large."

"I have always lived in the inn. This is the farthest I have ever been from my home."

"You're lucky," said Ethan. "I have never known my home. And my parents were killed when I was very young."

"I'm not sure if my father is still alive," Jeffrey responded, plucking a leaf from a low branch. "But my mother will be glad to see me again." Ethan nodded and the two fell silent for a while. About an hour later, Thaniel stopped as the trail topped a hill. He pointed out some low-lying hills to their northwest.

"Those hills should be familiar to you, Jeffrey," he said. "Your inn is on the other side just a bit farther." Jeffrey could hardly believe it. It seemed like years since he had been home. He urged the party onward, galloping down the trail. He could hear Thaniel yelling behind him and Fortis slowed to a measured pace. He grabbed Fortis' dark mane and urged him on. The horse continued walking at the same pace, ignoring him.

"Some horse," said Jeffrey. "I thought he was a champion."

"Only when ridden by a champion," said Thaniel.

Jeffrey could hear Ethan chuckling.

"OK, Fortis, let's see what you are really made of," he whispered. "You are supposed to be this magnificent creature. Let's go!"

Nothing.

"Come on Fortis! I want to get to my home! Go!"

Nothing.

"Stupid horse! If you only knew of the sweet treats I have in the stables…"

Before Jeffrey could even finish his sentence, Fortis reared up as though possessed! He took off down the trail. Jeffrey looked back at Thaniel and Ethan in triumph, barely keeping up with the saddle. "Yeahhhh!" Jeffrey hollered. "Go Fortis!"

"Jeffrey wait!"

But off they went. This must be what the riders in the Aurora Cup feel like, Jeffrey thought. Maybe he should enter Fortis next year. Jeffrey could see the blurred images of trees passing by. A few times he barely managed to escape being knocked off by a low-hanging limb.

"Watch it, Fortis," Jeffrey hollered. "Look out, there!"

Fortis continued galloping at full speed, and Jeffrey was thrilled. He was getting the feel of this horse and liking him more and more. "Blackheart himself couldn't catch me on this horse!" Jeffrey yelled.

Looking back, he could see the figures of Ethan and Thaniel making their way through the dust they had kicked up. Ahead of him was the outcropping of red granite that he had shown to Pickworth. They were only a few miles from the inn! Jeffrey looked back to tell the others that they were nearly there. He pulled on the reins, bringing Fortis to a stop and waited on the trail until they caught up to him.

"There," he said, pointing to the familiar rock. "My father called that Red Point when he was a child playing here. I hurt my arm here. We are almost at the inn! Just a few more miles! See? We're back on the Shadberry Way! There's the hill with the bald spot...and there's the peak of Mount Cornyn...and just over these hills is the inn."

"You're very excited to be home," said Ethan.

"Of course," said Jeffrey. "Don't you enjoy going home?"

"I have no home or family," Ethan said, "except for Thaniel."

"Sorry, I forgot."

"It's all right."

"Hey you can stay with us at the inn! We can run the place together."

For a second Ethan perked up at the prospect of partnering with his new friend and having a nice place to stay. But then he shook his head. "We have to do something else first," or the other things won't matter."

"Well good luck to you, then. I haven't told Thaniel this, but I've decided that when we get back, I'm going to give him the coin and then step out of this whole affair."

"What's that?" came a voice from behind.

Jeffrey looked back embarrassed that he had been heard.

"Sorry, Thaniel, but this is the end for me. You can have the coin when we get there. I'm done with it all. When I get home I'm through."

Ethan looked at Thaniel.

"I'm sorry to hear that, Jeffrey. Ethan and I will, of course, keep the vow we took. You are under no such obligation."

"Right," said Jeffrey, looking at Ethan. "You two may always stay at the inn."

"Very generous," said Thaniel.

"All of you," he continued, "The whole Servatrix!"

"I will inform them," Thaniel said, puffing on his pipe.

"I mean no charge."

"Thank you."

Jeffrey looked at the two men.

"Don't you see that I am all wrong for this?"

"You must follow your heart, Jeffrey," was all Thaniel said.

They continued down the road for a few silent minutes.

"What is that?" asked Ethan.

"Oh that's an abandoned miner's hut," Jeffrey explained. "There was..."

"No, I mean THAT," Ethan said pointing down the road.

They all saw it at the same time. On the road ahead were what appeared to be piles of clothing and different colored rags. Jeffrey and Ethan rode on ahead. It only took a moment to realize that there were several corpses lying in the road. Ethan jumped off his horse first.

"Are they dead?" asked Jeffrey.

"Yes, but not long. I bet they were alive a couple of hours ago."

Jeffrey thought he recognized one of the men from the mine. He wasn't sure about the other two. Thaniel by now had caught up with them. He climbed off Treasure, his horse, and looked over the bodies. When he bent over the last of the dead men, he was taken aback. He stood and shook his head grimly. "Very well, lads, what do you two make of it?"

"I think I know. There must have been an argument," Jeffrey said, looking about. "Perhaps as they got nearer the inn they argued."

"Ethan?" Thaniel asked.

"Looks more like an ambush to me," he said, pointing out the various vantage points that ambushers might employ. "They didn't have a chance."

"Perhaps," said Thaniel. "Except that ambushers usually use weapons. Do you see any marks on the bodies?"

"You're right," said Jeffrey, who had never seen a dead body. "There is no blood. So what killed them?"

Thaniel looked at the young men. He also scanned the woods about them.

"What killed them isn't as important as who," he said. "And if I am right, then we haven't a moment to lose."

He looked at Jeffrey,

"We must get to the inn. How much farther, Jeffrey?"

"Not far," he said, "That way. Maybe an hour. In the direction of...that smoke..." Jeffrey gulped.

"Smoke!" Ethan repeated. They looked in the direction Ethan was pointing. Just at mid-rise of the hills a line of smoke was visible.

"That's where we are going," Jeffrey said, fear seizing him. "In that direction. The inn." Then he shuddered. "My mother!"

He kicked his heels into Fortis' side and the horse took off down the trail. Thaniel and Ethan did their best to stay close, calling for him to hold back in case their enemies somehow beat them to the inn. Jeffrey was stone-faced, his eyes set on the line of smoke that was now billowing darker. They passed the old monastery as if Fortis had wings. Jeffrey looked back to encourage the others to hurry on.

Then everything went black.

Chapter 10

FAMILY BUSINESS

TWO blurry images with muffled voices...blue sky...branches...an acrid smoky odor...and a throbbing head, again. This was getting old. Jeffrey closed his eyes and rested a bit more. He dreamed he was falling off a cliff while riding Fortis. Flashes of faces and objects raced by—Thaniel, Pickworth holding a chess piece, his mother, Ethan grinning, some coins...

"He's coming 'round now."

Jeffrey felt a cool cloth across his forehead.

"I was afraid we had lost him. Jeffrey! Open your eyes, lad."

Jeffrey opened his eyes and saw Ethan and Thaniel kneeling over him, Ethan holding a cup of water, which he put to Jeffrey's lips. He drank it greedily and blinked a few times, sitting up. The wet rag fell from his forehead.

"What happened?" Jeffrey asked groggily.

"When one rides headlong on Fortis, one must never look back," said Thaniel, filling his pipe. "Especially in these woods. We laid you across your saddle and Fortis carried you here."

"You hit a branch," said Ethan. "Or perhaps the branch hit you."

Jeffrey managed a very sore smile. Then he noticed that Ethan was leaning against a lamppost—specifically, the lamppost in front of the Trout and Truffles. They were home! He asked about his mother and the house and...

"Now, boy, I'm afraid it isn't good," was all he heard as he saw what was left of the smoldering inn. "There was a woman..."

Jeffrey ripped the bandage off of his head and screamed.

Silence.

"A woman?"

He turned to look at Thaniel and Ethan who remained silent. Then he saw the still-smoking ruin of the Trout and Truffles. Making his way up the path to what had been the front door, Jeffrey stepped over blackened wreckage. His feet were getting warm as he moved across a fallen timber that he recognized as the old mantel.

Everywhere was smoking wood, broken crockery, and the detritus of what had once been a fine old inn, now a complete ruin. He bent down and picked up a sooty piece of metal—the commemorative plaque. Jeffrey turned back to Thaniel and Ethan, holding the still warm metal.

"We buried her over there," Thaniel said, pointing toward a rose-covered wall. "She was already dead. I'm sorry, lad."

Jeffrey began to cry. He walked over to the fresh grave and stood for a few moments. His father had been pulled into this affair because of his wanderlust. He understood the risks. But Cornelia? She was innocent in all of this. He couldn't help but smile a bit as he knelt down.

"You always said his dealings would be the death of you."

He picked a rose and placed it atop the grave.

"I guess you were right."

He sat there for a few more minutes and then walked back over to where Ethan and Thaniel had tied the horses. He couldn't believe this was happening. Maybe it was all a hideous dream? Thaniel hugged Jeffrey. Then he and Ethan knelt to pray. Jeffrey's tears were already turning angry. He looked at the two.

"Praying? Now? For what?"

"For you," said Thaniel quietly.

"To that god of yours? The one whose name you don't even know?"

Thaniel nodded. "He knows your name, Jeffrey."

"He's a little late. If he is your god why didn't he help us?"

"Sometimes there are no answers, Jeffrey," Thaniel said. "Sometimes what happens is the result of evil men doing evil things. Other times there is no good answer at all."

"Now what do I do?" Jeffrey looked at the grave. "I mean, after I hunt down and kill the animals who did this."

Ethan looked at Thaniel. "Perhaps part of that problem has already been settled for you, Jeffrey," Thaniel said. "The men on the road already paid with their lives. Accounts will be settled one way or another."

"Nothing's settled until Pickworth and the others pay for this as well," Jeffrey said, bitterly. "How could they kill her?"

"Pickworth is a cunning brute," Thaniel began. "And Jack is a scoundrel. But I'm not certain they did this. I don't even know if they have arrived yet. It's strange that there is no sign of their horses or evidence of their having been here."

"Then what about the men on the trail?" asked Jeffrey. "And my mother? Surely it was Jack and Pickworth who killed her. Perhaps they got in a fight over the coin and those men on the road came up short. I bet Pickworth made off with everything!"

"If only it were that simple," said Thaniel, as they sat down to eat some food that Ethan had brought along. "No, lads. It's an altogether different party—led by one whom I mentioned before in the cave. An adversary loyal to Blackheart and far more cunning than Pickworth. One whose power in Humus is increasing." Thaniel began pacing as he pieced the scene together in his mind.

"He first murdered the men on the road who had probably been stationed by Pickworth to ambush us. He then murdered your mother. Perhaps he even took the coin. He is murdering as he goes, you see, following the coin. And if I am wrong, and Pickworth *did* kill your mother, burn the inn and take the coin—then rest assured, Jasper and his thugs are the next to die."

"So it was Blackheart's doing that killed my mother?"

"I believe so."

Jeffrey paused for a moment.

"Thaniel?"

"Yes, Jeffrey?"

"I want to finish this."

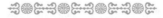

The next morning, Jeffrey rummaged through what was left of the inn. He found a few family trinkets that survived the fire, but nothing of value. Some parts of the wreckage were still smoldering. Corinth watched it all from a makeshift perch on the one wall that hadn't collapsed. After a while, Thaniel asked him what he was looking for.

"The coin, of course. I was thinking, perhaps my mother hid it in the wall. I'm looking for that compartment. Right about here..."

"They have the coin now, Jeffrey. Your mother never knew its true meaning, poor woman. I wonder why Jack hasn't yet arrived."

Corinth squawked loudly as he pulled at something in the rubble. Jeffrey watched as the bird tugged and tugged and then plucked something from the debris. He flew over to a tree and perched with his treasure. Jeffrey wiped his sooty forehead.

"I guess you're right, Thaniel," he said. "If the coin is here it will be impossible to find. If only she..."

The sound of a fast horse galloping at them made them turn. A lone rider came shooting out of the woodland path that continued north from the inn. Jeffrey recognized the baker, Max, who often came to the inn.

"Jeffrey?"

Max dismounted and ran to Jeffrey. His wife was not far behind him, coming up the trail as well. Max surveyed the wreckage, shaking his head in disbelief. The woman, a buxom lady with large teeth, jumped off her horse and gave Jeffrey a crushing hug, weeping as she held him in her massive arms. The baker nodded at Thaniel and Ethan. Jeffrey smiled at them.

"We're so sorry, Jeffrey," Lorina, the wife said. "We only just heard. Where is Cornelia?"

Thaniel, Jeffrey and Ethan exchanged knowing glances.

"Is she...?"

"She died, Max. She's buried over there."

Lorina burst out in fresh tears. Jeffrey backed away just in case she should decide to hug him again. She walked over to the grave, weeping. Max stood with Jeffrey, still in disbelief that the Trout and Truffles was no more.

"Was only last week I spoke with her," she said. "Always spoke of you, Jeffrey. Always knew you'd come back. Many's the night I came out here to light up that old lantern for her."

"Max, did you see anyone else around here?" Jeffrey asked. "I mean, strangers?"

Max thought for a moment.

"Nobody," he said. "You think this was not an accident?"

"Not at all," said Thaniel. "But these days, what with all the brazen thievery about, one never knows."

"Hmm, true," said Max. "No, Jeffrey. She was quite alone. She spoke of no stranger. But she did speak strangely. I mean the last time I saw her."

Thaniel and Jeffrey looked at each other.

"How did she speak strangely?" Jeffrey asked.

"It was like she knew something was going to happen to her," Max said. "You know how your grandmother acted before she died, Jeffrey? Remember how she wanted to get her affairs in order? Well, your mother asked me for a great favor. Asked me to take her several miles down the road, a half-day's ride to your old family home. You know, the house built by one of your uncles?"

"Yes, I know that place."

"Well, of course I took her on a wagon. She had a box with her and she asked me to wait for her. I waited for nearly an hour. Just about the time I was ready to go in after her, she came back on the trail. But," he held up his finger dramatically, "she did not have the box with her. I guess she buried it out in the woods somewhere. We continued on into town and she stayed with my wife and me that night."

Jeffrey swallowed hard, nodding.

"She never told me what she buried out there. But I think she knew something was about to happen—you know—got her affairs in order so to speak."

Jeffrey thanked the baker and his wife and watched them disappear down the pathway. When they were out of hearing, he turned to Thaniel.

"That's it!" he said.

Jeffrey suddenly started digging with renewed vigor. He had gotten used to the hot spots in the debris. Thaniel and Ethan came over to where he was furiously pulling out pieces of wood and stone.

"The key!" Jeffrey said excitedly. "I left the key to the family vault with mama! She always insisted on keeping the coin there! The old ruin is at the point in the trail where we break off for the vault. You see? She took the coin there just a few days ago!"

"Outstanding!" exclaimed Thaniel, "and where did she keep the key?"

Jeffrey stopped digging and looked up. "She wore it around her neck," he said quietly.

"Jeffrey, we didn't see a key on her when we buried her."

"Then it must be here somewhere! Help me!"

The three began digging through the rubble. They worked for an hour before Ethan's foot broke through and the whole floor was in danger of collapsing into the cellar below. Thaniel urged them to move on. "But I must have that key," said Jeffrey. "It's the only way into the vault."

SQUWAK!

"Not now, Corinth," Jeffrey said, brushing away the shiny raven.

Jeffrey saw a wide grin on Ethan and Thaniel's faces.

"What?"

"Your bird," Thaniel said. "Look!"

Jeffrey turned and saw Corinth holding what was left of a leather thong in his mouth. On the end was the key, smudged with soot. "Corinth! Good eye!"

SQUAWK!

"But you might have showed us this earlier and saved us the time we spent digging around," whined Jeffrey. "Idiot bird."

SQUAWK!

Jeffrey took the key and held it up. "This is it! The vault is a day's ride."

"Good work, Corinth," said Thaniel. He tossed the bird a morsel of dried meat. "Once more, the ravens have saved the Jeffords!"

"He might have done it a bit sooner!"

As the three left the ruins of the Trout and Truffles, Jeffrey could hardly believe his eyes. A flood of memories overwhelmed him as they started down the road. He was now wearing the key around his neck once more. As they started, he suddenly stopped and jumped off Fortis.

"Jeffrey! What are you doing?" yelled Thaniel. "We need to be off!"

Jeffrey ran over to the lamppost and very carefully lit the lantern. He looked at his mother's grave and whispered, "For you mama."

"Keep close to them but not too close. When they open the vault we will fall upon them at once."

"But suppose the vault is empty? If we don't have that coin…"

"Then we kill them and take whatever coins they *do* have!"

"But only after we have destroyed any evidence. Let them lead us to the vault and open it for us. Lesson here: always let your opponent do the work. First rule of law!"

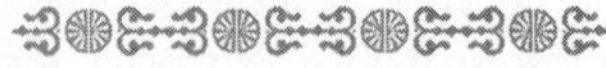

The trip to the Jefford hidden vault was a melancholy and mostly silent journey. Thaniel and Ethan let Jeffrey ride up ahead of them a bit. Alone with his thoughts, Jeffrey regarded the very different course his life had taken. No longer was he Jeffrey Jefford, the innkeeper and son of an innkeeper. He now felt he was a young man in search of meaning in all of this, bent on vengeance, and determined to bring honor to his family name.

As for the business of the armor and coins, all that still didn't seem real to him. He believed the story—but did not yet appreciate its significance as Thaniel and Ethan and this mysterious group called the Servatrix did. He was feeling more and more trapped in a fight that was not his, yet which had devastated him personally. And so, when he asked himself why he was leading these two to the family vault in search of a legendary coin, all he had to do was remind himself of a smoldering inn and a murdered parent.

The next morning, Jeffrey led the group into a narrow cavern, with cascading waterfalls on either side. It was a beautiful spot and Thaniel commented about how much it reminded him of a favorite spot in Nova Fannum. They stopped to water their horses.

"Of course, that was before Blackheart," Thaniel said. "Until then, Nova Fannum was beautiful beyond your imagination. You never saw it, Ethan. But there are, or were—colors there that defy anything your eyes have ever seen."

"And now?" asked Jeffrey, wondering how anywhere else could be as pretty as the spot where they were stopped.

"And now, it is only two colors," sighed Thaniel. "One, really, a dullish gray."

"No color?" asked Jeffrey. "How can that be?"

"Because, lad, when evil is in command or in threat, true colors emerge—dark, lifeless colors. Thus, the land has taken on the appearance of that which controls it, something dark. Everything behind the mist that borders Humus is colorless." He looked at the skies of Humus. "Your own land is increasingly dark, Jeffrey. You have even said so. Humus will one day be colorless as well, if he succeeds."

"Humus? Colorless?"

"As I said, Blackheart's lust for control has no end. Once he has secured Nova Fannum, he intends to conquer all of Humus and spread his dark kingdom. That is why his agents are here already. And that is why we must get the coins before they do."

Another hour brought them past the ruins of the old Jefford house and out of the cavern. They entered a clearing where large boulders were strewn about as if a giant had been throwing them haphazardly. Among the rocks was a reddish point, an outcropping, actually, that resembled an arrowhead. Jeffrey motioned the others to be quiet and looked about to make sure they were quite alone. "This is it," Jeffrey announced, as he tied Fortis to a branch. "This is the vault dug by my great-grandfather."

They followed Jeffrey around the arrowhead rock and up the side of the cliff on the other side. It was steep, but one could just make out steps that had been carved into the rock. About halfway up, Jeffrey took out his key and, looking around once more, pulled a false rock out of the wall. Behind it was a small, metal plate into which he inserted the key. Thaniel was amazed as a portion of the cliff, invisible up until now, swung inward into a dark room.

"Well done, grandfather," said Thaniel. "I would never have found such a place."

"Nor has anyone else," Jeffrey said proudly.

He lit a torch that hung on the inside of the door and beckoned the others follow. They came in with him and Jeffrey lit several lanterns until, at last, the room was quite navigable. Once their eyes grew accustomed to the light, they beheld what was left of the Jefford family heritage.

"I have only been here once," Jeffrey said, peering at the many chests. "As you can see, my family saves everything."

In fact, there were all sorts of things strewn about, as if the last person here was in a hurry. There were many suits of clothes, all black of course, hats, dresses, shoes. There were several chests of jewelry, though Jeffrey explained that most of the really valuable things had been sold off. There were a few pieces of furniture, a chair, desk, candlesticks, but no sign of a coin. Ethan moved to the farthest corner to search the floor there.

"Looks more like a rummage market than family treasures," muttered Ethan.

"I never said we were rich," Jeffrey said, setting down a small figurine that he had picked up. "Not any more."

They combed the room for an hour.

"Does anything look out of place?" Thaniel asked. "What would your mother have done with something she deemed so valuable?"

Jeffrey scratched his head. "I think she would have kept it at her side," he said. Suddenly, his eyes focused on a jacket she had been making for him when he left with Pickworth. Jeffrey grabbed the cloak and began running his hands over it.

"What is it boy, " Thaniel asked.

He and Ethan crowded over Jeffrey.

"This coat," he said. "She was working on this when I left. It was a special coat she was making for my father. It was very special to her and would never be here unless…"

The sound of fabric tearing was followed by a howl of delight. He produced the coin and handed it to Thaniel.

"This what you're after?" he asked triumphantly.

Thaniel took the coin, trembling. He could hardly believe that he was holding the *Copis*—the sword of the Armor of Nova Fannum. His eyes teared as he thought of Dontel carrying that very coin for so many years. Ethan looked at the coin as well and smiled at the old man.

"We're halfway there, lads," he said finally, handing the coin back to Jeffrey. "Three coins out of six! That is a powerful weapon, Jeffrey. Your wise mother did well to conceal it in your coat. She must have sensed that it was of great value to have brought it out here. Bless her."

He looked at Jeffrey, who was feeling the sting of loss once more.

"She loved you very much, Jeffrey," he said. "She knew you would need this, I'm sure."

Jeffrey nodded, wiping his eyes. It was silent for a few minutes. Then Jeffrey exclaimed, "Great stars! Another find!"

"What is it?" asked Thaniel, dropping an old hat. "Not another coin!"

Ethan looked up.

"No," said Jeffrey. "Look at this!"

Jeffrey held up an ancient black cloak, vest, boots, pants, and a black feathered cap. The feather was broken off. Thaniel looked at him curiously. Ethan shook his head and smiled.

"These are the clothes of Sir William Jefford! The Hero of Aurora!"

"Ah, your noble ancestor," said Thaniel, glad for the boy but disappointed that he was holding clothes rather than the coin. "Quite appropriate for the new hero of Humus! Especially since you are newly armed with Copis."

Jeffrey was amazed that the warrior's clothing had held up. In a few minutes he was wearing it, hat and all—minus the feather. He checked himself in an old, floor length mirror. Thaniel laughed. All I need is a weapon," Jeffrey said, thinking about the Sauren sword he had lost. "Then we'll put Copis to work!"

"Well, Sir William, looks like you need assistance from a raven once more," Thaniel said looking at the boy's reflection. "Your feather is frazzled!"

Corinth flew down and lighted on his shoulder. "I know a raven that needs a good plucking," said Jeffrey, smiling.

Corinth squawked loudly.

"And I know someone else who needs a good plucking," came a voice from the entrance. "A good plucking indeed!"

Chapter 11

Reunion in the Vault

JEFFREY found himself looking at the pointed end of his sword—the Sauren sword he had lost in the mine. On the other end of the sword was the hooded Lorogos, threatening, as always. Behind him was Jack, eye patch in place and smelling of drink. He staggered a bit as he assessed their control of the situation. Finius and Pickworth followed, pushing their way into the vault.

"Well Jeffrey, looks as if you're in need of a good lawyer!" Pickworth crowed.

"Know where I can find one?" Jeffrey asked.

Jack and Finius laughed loudly.

"Where is the old man?" asked Lorogos. "We saw him come in here."

"He left just before you arrived."

"Nonsense, boy, we know he is here," said Pickworth, looking around. "Here me, Thaniel! I know you are in here. Give us the coins and we'll leave you."

No answer.

"I told you, he left," said Jeffrey.

"And the other boy? Where is he?"

"They left together," Jeffrey said. "There's a secret exit at the river. And besides, we didn't find the coin."

"Too bad for you," said Lorogos. "We missed our chance at the mine. We won't miss it here."

"You certainly didn't miss your chance with my mother, you animals. Killing a sick woman!"

Pickworth laughed.

"Don't believe your eyes. Believe the evidence! First rule of law!"

"What are you saying?"

"The woman was dead when we got there, lad," said Jack with a tenderness that was almost believable. "Just minutes ahead of you. And the place was already burning. We sent some men to tell you so you might come to terms with us. They haven't returned yet."

"Nor shall they," said Jeffrey. "The same justice that is coming your way found them. They're dead."

Pickworth looked at Lorogos.

"Nevertheless, we didn't kill your mother," the lawyer said.

"Why should I believe you?"

"Because it's true," said Jack.

"Which means you had better hand over the coin," said Pickworth. "If there is a third party brutal enough to kill our men hunting for it, then the sooner you dispose of the coins, the better for you. News travels fast where treasure is concerned. Better to deal with us than those who would kill an innocent woman." He looked about the cave and called out. "Hear that Thaniel? Show yourself now old fellow, or the boy will join his mother on the spot."

Lorogos took his cue and lunged at Jeffrey grabbing him and holding him with the sword at his neck. It all happened so fast that Jeffrey couldn't even think. Thaniel's form immediately became visible, standing near Jeffrey. Finius held the sword out in front of him anticipating a counterattack.

"There he is," said Pickworth. "Come to his senses!"

"Release him," said Thaniel.

"No, Thaniel! said Jeffrey angrily. "I'd as soon die."

"Soon is a good word for it," whispered Lorogos in Jeffrey's ear.

"The coin," said Pickworth.

"Some answers," said Thaniel. "Then the coin."

"I'm a lawyer," said Pickworth. "And I am the one asking the questions here."

"Then surely, as a lawyer, you can appreciate a little quid pro quo?" suggested Thaniel, sitting down. "Questions and answers between adversaries, so to speak."

"Of course," said Pickworth. "Quid pro quo. Very well, ask away. But I reserve the right to answer only questions I deem acceptable."

"Let's get this over with," said Lorogos.

"I agree," said Jack. "Let's sweat the coins out of them and leave."

Jeffrey was forced down at the feet of Lorogos so he could be attended to quickly. "To begin with, we are working toward the same goal," said Thaniel, "to find the coins. What do they mean to you and who is your employer?"

Pickworth laughed. "Two questions, but I'm in a generous mood," Pickworth began. He paced the room as if he were deliberating before the Royal Court in Edenshore, comfortable in his element. "The coins mean nothing to me except the possibility of great monetary gain. Your motivation for finding them and mine are worlds apart. Your problem is politics—mine is poverty. And as to the identity of my employer, I have never met the gentleman, though I soon shall. He always transacts business through Lorogos here—his agent—who also happens to be a prince among his…er…kind."

"I see," said Thaniel, eyeing Lorogos. "And how did you become involved with such esteemed company?"

Pickworth looked at the captive audience. "I don't mind telling you," said the lawyer. "You'll likely not repeat it. But you might appreciate it."

Lorogos grunted impatiently. But Pickworth relished in crowing about how he had come so far. Indeed, to go forward without letting someone know the intricacies was maddening—so he welcomed the opportunity. He seemed very relaxed as he recounted.

"Some time back I was in my offices in Graulet's Harbor working on some dreary case or other. My life had become so dreadfully predictable. Sending men to the gallows or saving their worthless necks for a price. Routine is the death knell for a fertile mind. After all, how many cases can one win before it gets tiresome?"

"Indeed," Thaniel said smirking. "May I have a pipe?"

"Of course," said Pickworth. "What is a smoke between friends?" Pickworth watched as Thaniel packed his pipe and lit it. Everyone was careful for what trick the old man might try. He looked at everyone's intent gaze as he puffed away.

"I'm afraid that's all it does," he said.

Pickworth laughed. "I had a knock on my door late one evening," the lawyer continued. "I was astonished to find a rather seedy-looking character, hat in hand, holding out a communication that was addressed to me in beautiful lettering. I recall thinking to myself, what a contrast between the roughness of the messenger and the elegance of the message. I read the contents of the message, which, to my surprise, instructed me to await a visitor the following evening. It promised a handsome reward and a percentage of whatever was realized in the enterprise. That, naturally, appealed to me."

"Naturally," said Thaniel, puffing away.

"The next evening, as per the letter, I met with the aforementioned individual, who was hooded and cloaked and insisted on meeting in the dark. Being a good attorney and seeing the gold in his hand, I obliged. He then told me that he was acting as agent for a very important family in Humus, an old family that had fallen upon hard times, but which had visions of new glory."

He looked at Thaniel.

"I cannot give you that name and break my trust, but, needless to say, it is in fact one of the greater families in Humus' history and very significantly tied to the Jefford clan, albeit in a humiliating way. That's what makes this all so delicious."

"Relatives of mine?" Jeffrey asked.

"Not at all, dear boy," said Pickworth, laughing. "In fact they are not even human. And so this creature explained to me that he was interested in recovering various artifacts that had once been Sauren treasures but had become dispersed over time. He would be particularly interested in certain objects that had become part of your family's treasure." He looked pointedly at Jeffrey.

"Such as…" asked Jeffrey.

Pickworth pointed at Finius. "This sword, for example," he said. "That is why I insisted you bring it along, Jeffrey. You were so obliging."

"Saurens," muttered Jeffrey. "I thought they were all dead."

"What I had not anticipated was the business of the coins," continued Pickworth. "Here we were, ready to approach your father, Malcolm. Our intention was to recover only the sword. I had already hired Jack and Finius and sent them on their way to the Trout and Truffles when I was told to wait. There was a new development and much more gold to be had. It was then that the matter of the coins was brought to my attention," he snickered.

"By whom?" asked Thaniel.

"By Lorogos, of course," said Pickworth. "When he told us of the coins, we were suspicious. Apparently some person of means had heard of our venture to recover the sword and knew that Jefford also had possession of a coin of great value and worth much gold if it could somehow be recovered."

"You mean stolen," Jeffrey said.

"Very similar words in this business," said Pickworth. "Lorogos insisted that this was a genuine offer. To prove it, he showed a similar coin to us. Jack recalled the coin he had received from your brother. Same markings!"

"Dontel," whispered Thaniel.

"Yes, your brother," he continued. "Jack recalled the coin he had taken off him and sold to the monks in Wikkam. When we told Lorogos this, the Sauren became particularly engaged. There was much gold to be made by all!"

"My father drooled at the prospects of taking both the sword and the coin from the Jefford family," Lorogos said, glaring at Jeffrey. "A double humbling."

"What happened to Dontel?" asked Thaniel.

"Died," said Pickworth matter-of-factly. "Terrible accident. But the poor man was dying anyway, according to Jack."

"It's true," said Jack. "The man was sick—of mind and of heart as I recall. I liberated the coin and map from him after he died."

"So, when the value of the coins became apparent to us," Pickworth continued, "we planned accordingly. Now, instead of simply going after the Sauren artifacts, we were also after the coin.

I'm afraid I concocted that awful story about Jack's troubled past, as bait for your simple father!"

"My father a seaman!" Jack roared. "The only vessel he ever knew was one that held ale! Ah, but it was all business, lad. Nothing personal."

"Your father refused to take the sword along," said Pickworth. "This rather complicated things. Rather than make him more suspicious we contented ourselves with his bringing along the coin. Lorogos felt we could always come back for the sword." Pickworth looked at Jeffrey. "But apparently your father suspected something unusual about the coin, and he left it in your care. Took us completely by surprise. Imagine the embarrassment, after all that planning to acquire sword and coin, only to come up with neither! It was most uncomfortable explaining that to my client."

"What happened to my father?"

"You don't want to know, boy," said Lorogos. "Let's just say that he had a closer call with the shina than you did."

"You murderers!"

"And so, we had to regroup," Pickworth went on, ignoring Jeffrey. "Thus we contrived the letter from Finius which I presented to you. I gallantly accompanied you to Gillingham where we were to collect sword and coin. We were successful in obtaining the sword. Unfortunately, your foolish mother, in her attempt to secure the coin in your shirt lining, sent the wrong coin with you and here we are. But, no matter. In the end we shall be rewarded handsomely for recovering both the sword and the coins."

Thaniel looked at Lorogos. "I thought he was Sauren, his blood red eyes gave him away. I always heard you could tell a Sauren by his bizarre eyes. So, your once-proud family is behind this?"

Lorogos's red eyes seemed to flame with intensity.

"We have waited a long time to settle the score with Humus and the Jefford family," Lorogos said in characteristic Sauren hissing. "My father is collecting all of the great Sauren artifacts. This sword, the crown, the stones—all of them. Then we shall reign again as masters of Humus! All of the immortals are on our side and every human shall die or become enslaved—beginning with the family of William Jefford!"

He sneered at Jeffrey in his Sir William outfit.

"The next blood on those fine clothes will be Jefford blood, not Sauren!" He laughed.

"The Saurens are quite generous in financing vengeance and plans for grandeur," said Pickworth. "That is to say, they pay very well. I simply couldn't refuse their offer for me to help them procure the sought-after items. The coins, it turned out, were an unexpected bonus, you might say."

"Where is my family crown?" Lorogos demanded of Jeffrey.

"I have never seen the crown," said Jeffrey. "We had only the sword, which my ancestor took off the Sauren king's body."

"Liar!" said Jack, throwing down a gold cup he had picked up. "I saw one of the stones myself. In your home."

"That isn't true," said Jeffrey. "This is the only Sauren piece we have. The crown was lost in the Demeroth Marshes after the battle. History says the stones were already stripped off their settings. It's a matter of record in my family."

"And the coins?" asked Thaniel, looking at Lorogos. "You are simply brokering them for someone else?"

"Glory costs much gold," Lorogos said. "We Saurens are known for making gold through trade and transaction. The coins are a valuable commodity to us, and of greater value to the one who desires to have them all."

"But who is paying you to collect these coins?" demanded Thaniel.

"Calm down, old man," said Lorogos. "It's all a matter of business."

"And as I said, I only recently learned of their value," said Pickworth.

"But what was this man's name?" Thaniel asked.

"I don't remember," said Lorogos, looking at Pickworth. "But he was another of those priests from your supposed land. Not unlike that Dontel, according to Jack's description of your brother. But dressed differently—more elegantly."

"Describe him to me," said Thaniel, obviously shaken.

"Very mysterious," admitted Lorogos. "But quite polished. Rich black robe, velvet hood. But most outstanding was his face." Thaniel held his breath as Lorogos continued.

"His face was a silver mask. I never saw what was behind it, only his black eyes. One deals with many strange types under these circumstances. But when he showed us one of the coins…"

"You're certain he had one of the coins?"

"Yes," said Lorogos. "By then I had brought Pickworth in and told him of the new plan to go after both sword and coin. Jack took one look at the coin and confirmed that he had indeed seen one similar years before. He left the coin with my father with the instructions that we were to search for five others."

Thaniel could hardly believe it.

"Phaesus," he said. "His name is Phaesus."

Lorogos nodded. "He was accompanied by two rather drably dressed guards and a strange flying creature that was always nearby but never in sight. He spoke to it constantly.

"That would be Sestrin, a vile creature who serves Phaesus, his eyes and ears, so to speak—his chief spy. Do you recall what markings were on the coin?"

"A shield, I believe," said Lorogos.

"Yes, same as the others," said Pickworth. "But with the depiction of a shield."

"*Fides*, he has *Fides*. The shield." Thaniel looked worriedly at Jeffrey. "If he has one, he may have others, don't you see?"

Thaniel fell to his knees, pleading.

"You must listen to me," he cried. "You have no idea what forces you are dealing with. This isn't about gold. Don't you see that you are being used to collect the coins for someone who pays only in blood? Someone far more powerful than you or your father is plotting a dark crime against all freedom-loving creatures. He is using your love of gold and glory for his own purposes. You saw what he did to your messengers. The same fate, and far worse, awaits you after you have collected the coins!"

"Enough of this," said Lorogos. "We'll have those coins, Thaniel. You're wasting our time with these fables. Those coins shall pave the way for renewed Sauren glory."

"You mean Sauren destruction," said Thaniel, getting to his feet. "If they succeed in their plans there shall be no future Sauren glory, for there shall be no future in Humus." He sighed. "But as for giving up the coins—I have sworn to die first, just as my brother did."

Jeffrey looked at Thaniel. He smiled proudly. "Maybe you took such an oath," said Pickworth, looking at Jeffrey. "But I'm sure young 'Sir William' here did not."

"And so I did!" sneered Jeffrey. "Let me die."

Lorogos glared at Thaniel. "Now, old man. We shall have the coins with or without Jeffrey's blood on this sword. My family has need of them." He smiled at Thaniel. "When an offer has been made, always take the one that leaves you the greatest long-term advantage. First rule of law, right, Pickworth?"

Thaniel thought for a moment. He looked at Jeffrey. "Take the coins," he said, but spare the boy's life."

"No Thaniel!" Jeffrey screamed. "The oath."

"Oaths are for fools, lad," Thaniel said, handing the pouch over to Pickworth, who examined the contents and nodded to Lorogos. "Give him your coin, Jeffrey."

"No, sir."

"Jeffrey, give him the coin." Thaniel looked deeply into Jeffrey's eyes. Jeffrey was shaking his head. He didn't understand. Lorogos growled and grabbed Jeffrey. He roughly went through the pockets of the old clothing. He smiled when he felt it.

"Here it is," he said, producing the coin. He looked at it. "This one is a sword," he said. "How fitting!"

"And this is of sandals," said Pickworth. "Equally fitting, as we must be on our way as quickly as possible."

"And now where is the other lad who came in here?" asked Jack, who had been searching the vault ever since they came in. "I know there were three of you."

"I told you, he escaped," said Jeffrey defiantly. "And I will not tell you how!"

Lorogos turned to Pickworth. "We need that other coin," he demanded. "We know he has one of them. Do something, Pickworth."

Pickworth rose and thought for a moment. He then spoke quietly to his comrades. They nodded in agreement as he turned to Thaniel. "We know that other boy has one of the coins," he said. "We were informed so by Phaesus. Got the information from that vile creature he keeps around. So, until we have that coin in hand we shall take something of value in exchange."

He glanced at Jeffrey. "Bind him," he ordered.

"What do you want?" asked Thaniel as Finius tied Jeffrey's hands behind him. "The other boy left and I have no idea where he is."

"Then find him," said Pickworth menacingly. "Let's get away from this place." The group exited the vault and climbed down to their horses at the foot of the hill. Lorogos was dragging Jeffrey by his bound hands.

"And when you do find him," said Pickworth, as he climbed his horse, "bring him to us in the Sauren lands, at the Mountain of Sabrek. When we have the coin you may have Jeffrey back. That is, if the Sauren king is in the mood to release the one whose family has brought such grief. Hopefully, the Saurens will be in a generous mood."

"Not likely," Lorogos said, tying Jeffrey to a horse. "So you had best hurry."

"If he is harmed, you'll never see the coin," said Thaniel, as they all left the vault. "And without all of the coins, you may as well have none of them. Phaesus, your master, is not one to be disappointed."

"Bold talk, old man" said Lorogos, as he mounted his horse. "But talk is for fools and lawyers."

"Both of which we have here," said Pickworth laughing.

The party disappeared down the trail.

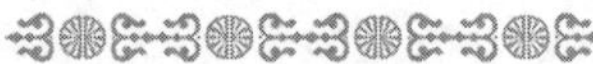

"They've left."

Thaniel watched as what had appeared to be a rocky outcropping in the rear of the vault began to transform itself into the shape of a young man. Ethan emerged from the wall and looked at Thaniel.

"I'm sorry uncle," he said. "But I thought it better to hide than make myself known to them."

"You did right, lad," said Thaniel, hugging his nephew. "We'll need the power of your coin to save Jeffrey and recover the other coins."

"We're going after them?" Ethan said, perking up.

"Of course," said Thaniel. "Sometimes the best move against your opponent is to allow them an advantage—however brief. First rule of law!"

Ethan laughed.

"But we must not underestimate our opponents," Thaniel continued as they moved down to where they had tied their horses. "I had to give them the coins not only to buy Jeffrey some time, but so we might also recover the coin Phaesus left with them. *Fides*! They have *Fides*! After all these years…"

"I'm surprised Phaesus would entrust one of the coins to anyone else," said Ethan, as they made their way down the hill.

"I can assure you he would never part with the coin unless he was certain of its return," said Thaniel. "Sestrin is keeping a watch for him, I'm sure." Thaniel looked up into the trees for any sign of the black creature.

"Of course the other possibility is that he was baiting a trap of his own," Ethan offered. "A trap for us…"

"Possibly," said Thaniel. "He is certainly cunning enough. As commander of Blackheart's murderous private army, he is keenly loyal to his leader and the most feared person in Nova Fannum. Remember, Blackheart's power is limited for now in Nova Fannum. Phaesus does his wicked work for him with sorcery."

"How do you know it's Phaesus?" asked Ethan, as he climbed on Cosmos.

"That mask," said Thaniel. "His face is covered with a mask of silver hiding the hideous evil behind it. Phaesus was a high-ranking priest at one time, but he craved power—dark power. The same sort of power Blackheart draws upon. As payment for his powerful skill in the black arts, his face was permanently disfigured by the evil within him. Thus, the mask. It's Phaesus, to be sure."

They rode along for a few minutes in silence. Ethan was continually checking the trees and dark places in the rocks, certain they were being watched from every angle. "Uncle, what about Jeffrey?"

"The Saurens undoubtedly plan to kill Jeffrey," Thaniel answered. "They have waited a long time to avenge the deeds of William Jefford. But first they need your coin. We'll see that they have the satisfaction of neither!"

"But if we give them the coin we shall have given them all," Ethan said.

"There are coins, and there are coins," Thaniel said, climbing onto Treasure. Ethan tied Fortis to his own horse and signaled he was ready to leave.

"We are facing two enemies, Ethan. Pickworth and the Saurens are concerned with mere gold and glory, so we expect typical crimes of greed from them and pride. But the other enemy. The real enemy. The one who killed those men. The one who murdered Jeffrey's mother. The one who plans to usher in a darkness that will forever enslave the hearts of men. That enemy is playing an entirely different game."

He looked up at the darkening sky.

"And the game is nearly up."

Chapter 12

SAUREN REVENGE

IT was all Jeffrey could do to stay balanced on the horse he was bound to. Blindfolded, he tried to mentally picture where they might be headed. Within minutes, he was completely lost. He could tell they were moving down a slope, and apparently through some very narrow ravines. Other than that, he used his nose and ears to pick out whatever information he could. He knew they were headed to Sabrek, but which side of the mountain? According to family lore, the place was riddled with passes. If only he could get word to Thaniel. He still found it hard to believe the old man had given up his coin and sacred vow so easily.

From time to time, Jeffrey could hear Jack bellowing or Pickworth being his usual persnickety self or Lorogos breathing murderous threats. But he found a perverse sort of compassion in Finius, who rode alongside him and offered a cup of water or a kind word here and there. It was during one of these moments when Jeffrey spoke very quietly to the yellow-toothed man.

"Where are we going, Finius?" Jeffrey asked, speaking very quietly.

"Just a moment," came Finius's voice. "We'll drop back a bit more." After a few moments, Finius spoke up again. "They can't hear me now," he said. "I hope they don't kill you. I wouldn't want that on my c-c-conscience. But if they do, I'll see that it goes quickly."

"Very reassuring," said Jeffrey, swallowing hard. "So where are we going?"

"Sauren mountains," Finius said. "Sabrek. And I don't like it a b-b-bit. Never did trust those creatures. This Lorogos business can drive a man to d-d-drink."

Jeffrey could hear Finius taking a drink from a bottle of some sort. When he spoke again the fresh aroma of cheap wine filled the air. "Saurens! Think they are going to become rulers in Humus again. Mind you, that's their business. Long as I get p-p-paid."

Jeffrey thought for a moment. "Finius, I could pay you. One day, I shall be very rich."

"What's that, boy?" Finius blurted out rather loudly.

"Shhh," cautioned Jeffrey. "If you help me now, I will see that you are rewarded. I have many important friends and one day I will be very rich."

Silence.

"We're near the mountain," said Finius, scanning the horizon. "The Sauren lands are just ahead. Good luck to you, Jeffrey." With that, Finius rejoined the others, bringing Jeffrey's horse along with him. The trail of men on horses was winding down a foothill path toward the base of the mountain. The shrubs were low and sparse, and the trees were mainly evergreens. Lorogos was speaking of how the Saurens had made this fortress mountain their last foothold in a world that had passed their glory by long ago.

"Was a time when Saurens were the most feared and respected race in Humus," Lorogos said. "No human dared look us in the eye."

"Indeed," said Pickworth, holding back a yawn. He was getting tired of hearing this Sauren spout off about how great his people were and how young and insignificant they considered the upstart human race. He had decided that as soon as he closed the deal he would have no further commerce with such a prideful and bitter client. Unless, of course, the price was right.

"It will happen again," Lorogos said, "When the sword is returned to us."

"That sword," said Pickworth. "You put a great deal of stock in that sword. Why is that so special to your…kind? Why not simply make new weapons and begin your campaign afresh?"

Lorogos wasn't sure if Pickworth was being sincere or sarcastic. "Because it was forged in the very heart of this mountain sacred to the Saurens," said Lorogos. "It was created by Sabrek I, the first Sauren king. It is vested with magic powers, and once reunited with the crown and both are reconsecrated, my nation shall become once more unconquerable. One day the sword and crown will lead my nation to greatness."

"Apparently my ancestor didn't find your people so unconquerable," called out Jeffrey from behind. Finius cuffed the boy's ear.

"Mind your t-t-tongue!" he said.

Lorogos laughed. "Let him rant," he said. "It will be the last defiant act he can manage. Yes, your accursed ancestor defeated us. But only because we misused the sword's magic. It turned on us because we were too proud then. But now, with a proper consecration, and the sword reunited with the crown, we shall eradicate the memory of Sir William Jefford!"

They rode on a bit farther until Lorogos stopped. He looked around at the darkening woods. They had come to a little clearing at the foot of the mountains. There was a stream nearby and evidence of an old encampment. He nodded his head. "This is it," he said. "We'll stop here and wait to be met with royal escort."

Pickworth was glad to stop, although he personally didn't enjoy seeing the Sauren take command of the expedition. Still, they were in his country now and since he had not yet been paid by the Sauren king, he went along with it all. Jack was eager to break out the drink and ordered Finius to get a fire started. Within a few minutes, camp was made and the men were sitting about eating and drinking—mainly drinking.

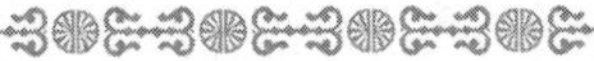

Saurens and humans had always been at odds. Only a common enemy, or in the case of Pickworth, a common lust for gold, brought them together in brief, shaky alliances. Though they had once been numerous, and held great portions of Humus, they had been gradually pushed aside by the emergent humans, who seemed bent on exterminating the wood folk and other eldritch races.

The Black Water Wars was the Sauren's last great effort to throw the humans out of their territory and push them back to the coasts. For a whole year, the uprising was successful. Trolls and other creatures, sharing a common hatred of humans, allied themselves with the Saurens and enjoyed early successes, most notably the massacre of the human settlement at Churchgaard in the Black Water region.

The humans began falling back in disarray, and for a while it appeared the Sauren-inspired war would be a short one. But the Jefford family, led by William Jefford, rallied the human army at Bekworth and stood their ground. The battle was joined in the dark of night (for that is the only time trolls will fight) and by most accounts had come to a bloody draw. But the Saurens and their allies, the trolls, pressed the attack, and William Jefford was separated from his command for several days. It was then when the legend of the ravens was born as he and his men were spared dying of thirst when the birds led them to a source of fresh water.

The last and greatest battle of the wars came about when the Sauren army gave chase to a few scouts that William had sent ahead of his main body of troops. Thinking that a rout was at hand, the Sauren king ordered a full frontal attack. Saurens and trolls poured over the hill—right into William Jefford's trap. The Saurens suddenly found themselves outflanked on both sides, as humans charged out of the misty darkness. The battle only lasted a few minutes and the Sauren army was slaughtered. William Jefford personally ran down the Sauren king and after a few minutes of fierce fighting, killed him with a single axe blow to his head.

After that battle, Sauren dominance of the region was broken and the creatures retreated to their main stronghold at Sabrek, where their hatred festered as they dreamed of future glory. Now, led by Lorogos's father, Sabrek III, they intended, with the return of the Sauren sword and financed by the recovery of the coins, to have vengeance and reclaim their former glory.

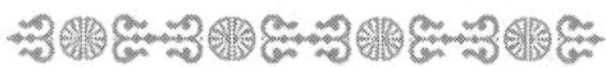

Jeffrey leaned against a fallen log, nibbling on a bit of stale bread Finius had brought him. He was very tired. In such a short time, he had lost his parents, the family inn, the sword, the coins, and...

"Hey, what now?" Jeffrey said, brushing at his neck. He'd felt a tug on his blindfold.

"Finius?"

No. He could hear Finius singing some ridiculous song that came upon him when he'd had too much ale. He listened for the others. Yes, he could account for the entire party. There was Jack, bellowing as usual about how he would spend his share of the gold. Pickworth was lecturing arrogantly on some point of law. Lorogos threw in a comment now and then about his coming glory. And of course Finius, warbling his inane drinking ditty.

"Ouch!" Jeffrey said. Something had pricked his ear. And again.

"Corinth!" Jeffrey whispered.

The bird tugged again at the blindfold. Within minutes he had the cloth down around Jeffrey's neck. For the first time in hours, Jeffrey opened his eyes. In front of him about 20 yards away, the drunken party of kidnappers lounged about the fire. Jack had just thrown a rock into the fire, singeing Finius with sparks. Everyone laughed as Finius danced about screaming that he was burning alive.

"I knew your thieving ways would come in handy," Jeffrey said to the black bird. "If only you could bring me a blade." Corinth flew off, startled by someone approaching. Before Jeffrey could turn to see who it was, a hand came over his mouth to keep him from making any noise. It was Thaniel. He whispered for Jeffrey to stay quiet and be ready for anything.

"But what's going to happen?"

"Just stay alert," said Thaniel. "And don't believe everything you see or hear!"

Jasper Pickworth was getting impatient. He felt that a man of his knowledge and experience was demeaned to be left in the company of such louts. He was disgusted with Jack and Finius. Even the prospect of finally settling with the Saurens and getting paid was becoming secondary to getting away from these seedy scoundrels. He looked at the men, dazed in their ale and talking nonsense. Still, he found their unscrupulous natures quite handy. Noticing Lorogos off by himself brooding, Pickworth wandered over to engage the Sauren prince.

"How long until our escort arrives?" Pickworth asked.

Lorogos looked up at Pickworth, knowing his reddish eyes glinted in the moonlight, evoking a shudder from the human lawyer. Lorogos laughed. "Humans frighten so easily. When Saurens are in full battle regalia, we allow our complete forms to be seen. It strikes fear into the hearts of men. They'll be here soon—at the peak of darkness."

"I've heard that Saurens are rather reptilian in appearance," said Pickworth, obviously peering into the darkness of the hood covering Lorogos's face." Lorogos began to pull the hood back. "But I am not that curious," he exclaimed.

Lorogos laughed. "You see? Humans are weak! Don't worry, my greedy friend. You'll get paid. You held up your end of the deal and brought us the sword and the coins."

Pickworth looked at his drunken partners. The thought of sharing any of the proceeds with those two was becoming more and more irksome. He was seriously thinking of dissolving the partnership. Discreetly, of course.

"Where is the sword?" asked Pickworth.

"Here," said Lorogos, patting his cloak. "Near my hearts. I can't abide Finius clutching it in his grubby hands now that we are in my land."

"Hearts?"

"Saurens have two hearts, lawyer. That is why we are so noble. As for the sword, I will deliver it to my father personally. But don't worry, you and your friends will get all due credit when the escort arrives."

"And here *they* are," said Pickworth, standing up, "I presume."

Lorogos turned to see a group of hooded figures approaching the camp. They carried weapons and moved quite stealthily. One of the men bowed low before Lorogos.

"My Prince!"

Lorogos greeted the escort in Sauren.

"Where is my father?"

"The king awaits your return," the Sauren guard said, looking up at Pickworth. He then added in Pickworth's language. "He also sends for your human servants." The Saurens laughed among themselves.

"Servants indeed," snorted Pickworth.

"You hear that, Jeffrey," said Thaniel, as Jack and Finius were rudely roused from their drunken sleep. "The escort has arrived. Now remember, they have *secutor fides*—the shield. We must recover that coin before it gets back to Phaesus."

"Hmph," said Jeffrey. "I thought you came back for me. Here! Untie my hands."

"We did come back for you, boy. But we'll have to allow you to continue as their prisoner for a bit more.

"But..."

That was all Jeffrey managed to say before Thaniel slipped the blindfold back up over his eyes.

"Don't worry. We'll save both you and the shield. Stay brave, lad, and have faith. We're going into the dragon's bowels."

"We?" Jeffrey whispered.

Jeffrey heard Thaniel's deft steps disappearing somewhere behind him. He hoped that Thaniel knew what he was doing in all of this. In a moment, he felt himself being roughly pulled up.

"Come on boy," said Finius's drunken voice, "Time to meet his majesty."

"You mean his *maker*," Jack snickered. Jack and Finius stood Jeffrey up and tore the cloth off Jeffrey's eyes.

"The Saurens want you to look their king in the eye," Jack said. "Personally, lad, I like you. But business is business. Your father knew that."

Jeffrey remained silent. He wished he could tell them how sorry they soon would be; that any moment now, Thaniel would outwit them and recover the coins. The Jeffords would once more best the Saurens. Just wait until Thaniel comes through. Those were the things Jeffrey was thinking when he suddenly heard Thaniel's voice call out.

"Lorogos!" A voice came from the darkness. "Lorogos! We have the coin!"

Jack turned, his hand gripping a knife. Lorogos ordered his guards to investigate and they rushed to the area where two figures emerged from the darkness. Jeffrey watched in horror as

Thaniel and Ethan walked into the camp. They were giving themselves up!

Chapter 13

SAUREN HOSPITALITY

THE Saurens were in high spirits as Lorogos, like a returning hero, led his captives into the heart of the Sauren mountain. Mt. Sabrek was a veritable fortress, with innumerable crags and clefts topped by an unassailable plateau which comprised the Sauren's principle camp. Sauren troops lined the pathway leading into the royal grounds, jeering at the captives. They were especially venomous in their tirades against Jeffrey, for every Sauren knew that it was his ancestor who had humbled their proud nation years before.

Thaniel and Ethan walked just ahead of Jeffrey. They had been spared the indignity of being bound, in order for Lorogos to demonstrate his complete control of the situation. Lorogos, shining as prince of the Saurens, rode ahead on horseback. Pickworth, Jack and Finius, also being on horse, drew confused stares from the throng. But the Saurens seemed to understand that those three stood with them in this situation. Jack and Finius waved and winked at the Saurens, as if they too were being celebrated. As for Pickworth, he simply wanted to collect his fee and depart as quickly as possible.

Ahead of them stood the rocky castle, really more of a tower, in which the Sauren king held court. The torchlight procession, the hissing crowd, and the thousands of glowing red eyes in the darkness created a chilling effect on all the humans. Jeffrey felt as if they had entered the Lowerlands that the priests had spoken of in his childhood. Perhaps they had.

Suddenly, they were made to stop as a low trumpet sounded a long, drawn-out tone. Another horn answered and then all eyes shifted to the platform atop the stone stair leading up to the tower. There, in regal Sauren splendor, stood Sabrek, King of the Saurens. The Sauren crowd raised a great cheer as Lorogos met his father atop the stairs, bowing low and, per Sauren protocol, kissing the king's feet.

Lorogos spoke with his father, who looked down at the humans as they talked. He seemed particularly interested in Jeffrey. The king made a motion and Lorogos waved the party up the steps. Pickworth ascended the stairs and bowed low as Lorogos had. He even kissed the scaly feet of the king. Jack and Finius did the same. Then Sauren guards took charge of Thaniel, Ethan, and Jeffrey and escorted them roughly up the stairs. The king looked them over, whispered something to Lorogos, and they entered the tower.

It wasn't until they were all standing before the king in his council hall that Jeffrey finally got a good look at the Saurens. They were indeed rather reptilian in appearance, with large scalelike plates covering their bodies. Greenish-blue in color, Saurens had a human-shaped head, although to Jeffrey they seemed more turtle than human. Their most outstanding feature was the glowing, reddish eyes which contributed to an overall malevolent appearance. Jeffrey snickered to himself. He thought they were more frightening in their armor or hooded than uncovered.

For his part, the Sauren king seemed delighted to have a Jefford seated in front of him after so many years of humiliating memories. He was in generous humor, offering his human captives such Sauren delicacies as raw bear with wild mushrooms and oiled boar's snout. The king even opened his own stock of wonderful ales, which, of course, made Jack and Finius more than happy. The humans sat at one large table and were served by Sauren pages dressed in white and red robes. Thaniel thanked the servants as food was placed before them.

"You'd best eat hearty, Jeffrey," Thaniel said quietly. "You'll be needing the nourishment."

"For what?" asked Jeffrey, still annoyed at Thaniel's willing surrender, "We're all as good as dead, now."

"Nonsense," said Thaniel, "You must believe."

Ethan sat quietly next to Thaniel, eating some savory venison.

"Why haven't you given them your coin?" Jeffrey said to Ethan. "That's why you're here, isn't it?"

"They haven't asked for it yet," said Thaniel. "They plan to make a great show of the 'presentation,' most likely. At any rate, Ethan is only doing as I ask."

"Some oath you both took," said Jeffrey, picking at his food.

Lorogos, seated at the royal table with his father, stood and announced that, in honor of this great day, they should drink to Sauren glory—past and future. Everyone stood and faced the king, raising their cups. The king nodded to the crowd, smiling with his jagged teeth and acknowledging their homage.

"And now," Lorogos continued, "we bring tribute to his majesty."

On cue, two Saurens entered the room bearing a large golden tray covered in a velvet material. With great ceremony, they approached the king, their eyes downcast. They stopped in front of the two royals. Lorogos stood and dramatically uncovered the tray, throwing the velvet behind him.

"Father, I return to you the Sauren sword!"

The room exploded in applause as Sabrek reached out and took the sword from his son. He acknowledged his son and raised the sword over his head. Pointing it toward the ceiling, he uttered some words in Sauren that nonc of the humans understood and reverently lay it on the table before him. The king stood to address the multitude.

"For too long, we have borne the indignity of the past. Our nation lost its way and then its place. But the return of this sword is the beginning of a new age for the Saurens—a glorious path of conquest and empire. I thank these, our human allies, for their service to this kingdom."

He indicated Pickworth and the others. Pickworth immediately understood and made a nervous bow to the crowd. The king caught the eye of an aide who began to interpret for the humans.

"It isn't often that Saurens and humans can reach accord, but this time it was meant to be. And soon, with their further help, we shall recover the crown and stones and begin our conquest of Humus in earnest."

Shouts of "*Glory to the king!*" echoed through the chamber.

"Thus we shall allow these humans to go and continue their search for the other relics of our glorious past. But as you know, the sword is only a portion of the good fortune overwhelming this kingdom. For I have an agreement with a great land, whose interest in certain coins will give us the gold we need for conquest!"

Again on cue, a page entered the room. This one bore before him a large, velvet pillow upon which lay three coins: Thaniel's, Jeffrey's, and the one left by Phaesus. The page knelt before the King, presenting the golden coins. Thaniel strained to see them, and then caught Ethan's eye. Ethan discreetly nodded.

"Our great ally from the land called Nova Fannum has assured me that there are six coins in all—three of which we have!"

Applause.

Lorogos whispered something to the king, who looked down at Thaniel. He then motioned Thaniel to stand. "My son tells me that you have brought the fourth coin to us. Very wise of you. I can assure you that, for your diligence in this matter, the Jefford spawn will die much more quickly than he might otherwise have."

"For that, I thank you," Thaniel answered, observing guards beginning to cover the two exits from the room. "Come along, Ethan."

Thaniel and Ethan started toward the king. Lorogos motioned for the Sauren guards to close in around his royal father. When they stood before the Sauren king, Thaniel bowed his head. Ethan, following Thaniel's lead, did the same.

"Watch him," cautioned Pickworth. "He's full of tricks."

"Who has the coin?" asked the king.

"I, sire," answered Ethan. Jeffrey could hardly believe what was happening.

"Give it to him then," ordered Lorogos. "And be quick about it." Ethan looked at Thaniel, sighed, and with a tear in his eyes, opened his hand. There, on his palm, was a coin—the coin with the emblem of the helmet. The king snatched it out of his hands.

"Your majesty," said Pickworth timidly. "May I speak?"

The interpreter whispered into the king's ear. "Of course, of course," said the king, who was thrilled with the coin and placed it beside the others on the pillow. Pickworth approached the king.

"Your majesty, it has been my experience with human nature that when one gives up too easily one either is insincere or a fool. Thaniel is no fool. I would like to examine the coin, if I may. We have been fooled before..." The king agreed and Pickworth took the coin and made a show of examining it carefully. After a moment, he was satisfied and returned the coin to its place with the others.

"It is genuine, your majesty," Pickworth gushed. "My congratulations to you and your noble heir!" The king smiled his reptilian smile. Pickworth, obviously conscious all eyes were on him, began to take on the confidence of a lawyer and begged once more to speak, seeing an opportunity to hasten his lot's departure.

"And now, your majesty, in regard to the reward for these efforts," he began. "My partners and I are anxious to begin our quest for the remaining coins and the Sauren crown and stones. We desire nothing so much as to bring further glory to your name. Sources tell us the Demeroth Marshes are the most likely place to begin our search..."

"Of course, of course," said the King, motioning with his hand. "I have fresh horses for you and safe escort to our borders. Find me the other relics and the two other coins and I shall double your reward! See that they are given their reward."

"Yes, sire," said an aide, who left the room.

"Thank you, majesty," said Pickworth. "Come Jack and Finius, we best be off. The sweetest hospitality is brief. First rule of law!"

After Pickworth was gone, all eyes returned to the king. What would he do with the other humans? Saurens loved to make sport of humans before they killed them. Some hoped for killing games; others for something much more slow. Whatever the king decided, they were sure it would be fitting.

"Majesty, may I say something?" asked Thaniel, after he had taken his seat once more, "Something about the coins?"

The king nodded.

"Majesty, the person you are dealing with, this Phaesus, is a ruthless and cunning man who is not to be trusted. You have two hearts, majesty. This man has none. He serves a powerful sorcerer whose soul is as black as the emptiness inside of him. His master is even now gathering dark forces in preparation for an invasion of Humus. By turning these coins over to him, you will deliver into his hands a most unimaginable power from which no land will be safe, including your own realm."

The king held up his hand for Thaniel to stop speaking. He looked at Lorogos and smiled, then, turning to Thaniel, asked. "Your name is Thaniel, is it not?" the king asked.

"Yes, majesty," Thaniel answered.

"You are a priest from your land."

"Yes, I serve the Great King."

"I was told by Phaesus to expect such talk from you. He also said you would try to convince me not to turn the coins over to him. I see that you are surprised that Phaesus knows of your involvement." He smiled. "You and your friends have been watched since you left the mines in Gillingham. Phaesus knows your every move."

"Sestrin," said Thaniel bitterly. "That wicked creature."

"Just so," said the king. "Sestrin watches and reports—and you have managed not only to lose the coins but deliver them right into Phaesus's hands. He said that, in fact, you are a fugitive from his land. You are a convicted traitor to be either held for him or put to death at my discretion. Then he shall turn the coins over to their rightful owner, for which service my kingdom shall be well paid—in gold as well as in military alliance. Therefore, I'm sure Phaesus would thank you for delivering the coins to him so quickly."

Thaniel looked at Ethan and shook his head. "Very neatly done, I must say. Phaesus is well-suited to his office as master of security for that dark realm." Thaniel fell to his knees. "Nevertheless, majesty, please understand that he will one day turn on you. I beg you to reconsider your relationship with this dark-hearted sorcerer, lest you and your kingdom and all of Humus be destroyed. You don't understand the forces these coins will unleash, and you underestimate the wickedness of Phaesus's master!"

The king lunged to his feet, glaring at Thaniel. "And you underestimate Saurens!" he roared, "Human insolence. Get them out of my sight! You will join Jefford in the manner of death we choose. I promised noble Phaesus that it would be something particularly creative if it was Sauren justice that finished you. And so it shall be. In fact, Phaesus shall be here in person to enjoy the spectacle."

"What? He is returning here?"

"Of course," said the king, sipping at his cup. "He knew you would come for the coin with the shield. That is why he left it. And now he will see you die. He will arrive in time to collect the coins and witness your execution three nights hence. All of you!"

The dreary accommodations in which Jeffrey and the others now found themselves were very different from the Sauren hospitality they enjoyed just a few hours earlier. Though they were free to roam their cell, any thought of escape quickly dispelled. The walls were thick with slime, seeping putrid water that worked its way in around the stones in a bubbly ooze.

The only way in or out was a small door in the ceiling atop a narrow flight of stone steps. Apart from that door, the only opening was a vent about 50 feet above them in the center of the steep ceiling, which added to their misery by letting rain drip in. Theirs was, indeed, as Killian Jefford would have put it, "a most doubtful disposition."

The door flung open and Ethan was kicked into the cell to tumble roughly down the slippery stone steps. The Sauren guards above laughed and slammed the heavy door loudly. They could still be heard laughing after the door was shut. Thaniel and Jeffrey ran to Ethan, who was badly scraped up. Within a few minutes, though, he was his old self.

Thaniel looked at his nephew. "I was wondering if they would put you in here. They only just threw me down an hour ago." He showed Ethan his badly cut elbow.

"They let me walk," Jeffrey said proudly.

"Yes, well I'm afraid it's because, as far as the Saurens are concerned, you're the big catch," said Thaniel. "They'll take no chances with you."

"What do you mean?" asked Jeffrey.

"He means that they plan to kill you in a very special way. The guards know they would, at the least, take your place on the program should you break your neck and not be available." said Ethan. "Hope you enjoyed the walk."

"Hmph," snorted Jeffrey. He still thought they were a bit jealous.

Thaniel watched Jeffrey with amusement. For the fourth time in as many hours, he was investigating every inch, every indention, every hole for a means of escape. Ethan sat next to Thaniel, picking the mold off the cheese which had been tossed down the stairs at them. Jeffrey stopped in the middle of the room and looked up—just in time for a large drop of rain to hit him in the eye. "You know, they could at least have sealed this tomb," Jeffrey said, rubbing the water out of his eyes. "Anyway, tomorrow it will all be over."

Ethan looked at Thaniel. "For whom?" asked Thaniel, "Us, or them?"

"Why for us, of course," said Jeffrey, sitting next to Thaniel. He pulled what was left of a cover over his cold shoulders. "Tomorrow is the third day, and we're to be the main event for your friend Phaesus's gala departure. Remember, right before he slips away with the coins." He hit himself in the forehead. "By the Great Ones, I wish I'd never laid eyes on that coin! I should never have left the inn with that gasbag Pickworth!"

Thaniel looked at Jeffrey. "Ah, Jeffrey," he began. "The die had already been cast. The mere fact of your family's possession of the coin was enough. They had been trying to take it in a more subtle way. But, even if you hadn't gone along with their plan, they would have eventually gotten around to you. Phaesus would have seen to that."

"Perhaps," said Jeffrey. "But at least I would have made a fight of it. And maybe my mother would have survived."

"Doubtful," said Thaniel. "And I'm afraid it would not have been much of a fight. Phaesus would have quickly and most painfully dealt with you and your mother. He would have delighted in watching your slow death even after you had divulged the whereabouts of the coin. He prefers to remain in the shadows. Just the fact that he has crossed over into Humus tells me the time is shorter than we'd thought. Your mother already died at the hand of this monster. Do you wish her death to be pointless? Or shall we do something to avenge it and give it meaning?"

Jeffrey was tearing up. "But how? Look where we are! We die tomorrow. Tomorrow, Thaniel! I see no great meaning in any of this. Tomorrow, they'll have our lives and the coins."

"As I said, Jeffrey," Thaniel said slyly, "there are coins and there are coins."

Rolling his eyes toward the ceiling in mock sarcasm, Jeffrey caught a movement and shouted, pointing to the little opening in the ceiling. "Did you see that—that thing!?"

Thaniel and Ethan looked up at the opening. They could see the gray skies over Mt. Sabrek. Ethan laughed it off, but Thaniel was quite interested. "What did you see, Jeffrey?"

"A black, shadowy creature," he said. "I know you think I'm seeing things that aren't there, but I promise I saw it. It was looking at us. And it had these bluish eyes that seemed to glow. I remember seeing it on the trail, but I didn't say anything because I knew you'd laugh at me."

"He's here," said Thaniel, looking up, "Or nearby."

"Who?" asked Jeffrey, choking down a piece of the cheese off which Ethan had managed to scrape most of the mold.

"Phaesus," said Thaniel. "You just saw his eyes. His spy, Sestrin."

"What kind of creature is it, uncle?" asked Ethan, looking nervously upward.

"Sestrin was one of the priests in Nova Fannum. After Blackheart's rise to power, he offered his services to the new regime. Unfortunately, he was quite greedy, but not very intelligent. He was caught in the temple treasury after hours. Phaesus turned him into this vile creature and uses him to spy on his enemies. It was Sestrin who led Phaesus to your inn, I'm sure."

"You mean the creature can speak?" asked Jeffrey.

"He speaks with his eyes," said Thaniel. "His binding to Phaesus is such that his master sees what Sestrin sees and hears what Sestrin hears—at least when he wants to."

"You sure have a lot of strange people in your land," said Jeffrey.

Thaniel nodded in amused agreement. He looked again at the opening in the ceiling. There was nothing there but the opening to the gray skies. He began thinking aloud. "Phaesus has come to collect the coins from Sabrek. He had obtained *Fides*, the shield, himself and left it here as bait for us. I must admit he succeeded there. We have three coins among us: *Juaracas* the sandals; *Cassis* the helmet; and *Copis*, the sword. That leaves two outstanding coins: *Lorica*, the breastplate that represents the righteousness of the King, and *Balteus*, the belt."

"What is *Balteus*?" asked Jeffrey.

"Truth."

Jeffrey couldn't believe what he was hearing. The situation was quite grim. "Sir, we haven't one coin, much less three," he said.

"Ah, Jeffrey," said Thaniel, shaking his head. "Remember what I said? There are coins and then there are coins!" He looked about carefully and reached into his cloak. He pulled out a coin with the emblem of the helmet upon it. Jeffrey was amazed.

"But I saw..."

"You saw what Ethan wanted you to see, along with everyone else present. Among its other properties, *Cassis* allows one to cloud another's mind. You saw a gold eden. What you—and the others—thought you saw was the genuine coin. And now, with this coin's help, we shall obtain the other coins and be out of here before Phaesus arrives!"

"I should like to see this Phaesus's face when he picks up the fake," admitted Jeffrey.

"As would I, but Phaesus is powerful. He will see through the trick as soon as he touches the coin. By then we must be well on our way."

"Where are we going?" asked Jeffrey.

Thaniel looked at the boy tenderly.

"I would tell you lad, but the less you know right now, the better. You cannot reveal what you don't know. Same as Ethan, here, you both must simply trust me." He motioned for Jeffrey and Ethan to move in closer.

"Now, as to executing our escape from this place..."

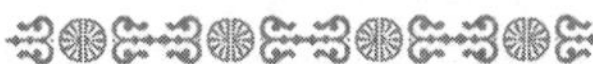

Outside the cell where Thaniel and the young men were being held, two Sauren guards stood, bored and hungry. They were glad these humans would be executed the next day, not only at the prospect of the spectacle, but so they could get back to their normal duties. The two were part of a detachment that preyed upon people who wandered off their farms or got lost in the woods, earning bounties for humans killed. The conflict between the two races had been ongoing for centuries. In fact, human parents often frightened disobedient children with stories of ugly Saurens slithering into the rooms of naughty children at night and kidnapping them. Ironically, Sauren parents did the same with their own kids—except the creatures of the night were human!

"How will they be executed?" one of the guards asked.

"Oil I think," said the other. "I'd just as soon roast them alive and share in the meat. I'm sure they will have something special in mind for the Jefford."

The other guard chuckled in agreement.

"Guard! Guard!"

The Sauren sentries looked at each other.

"Please help us! There is something wrong with Jeffrey!"

The guards heard the sound of someone screaming from the cell below. One of them opened the small wooden door in the floor and looked down into the darkness.

"What is happening down there?" the Sauren hissed. "Get quiet!"

"Help us," came the response. "It's Jeffrey. I think he took poison."

"What?!" said the Sauren, flinging open the door. "If anything happens to Jefford it will mean our own necks! The Saurens raced down the narrow stairs. Reaching the bottom they saw Thaniel bending over the lifeless form of Jeffrey Jefford, who had a trickle of blood coming out of the corner of his mouth.

"What happened?" demanded the Sauren, throwing Thaniel aside. "Where did he get poison? Tell me!"

"I have no idea," said Thaniel, picking himself up. "He was standing there one minute and suddenly started choking and fell where he is."

The other guard looked panicked. He set his weapon down and began shaking Jeffrey trying to revive him. "If he dies we will have to kill ourselves," the Sauren said. "Do something."

"What is happening down there!" came a voice.

Everyone turned to see Lorogos descending the stairs.

The guards fell to their knees immediately. Thaniel looked wide-eyed and backed away from the body of Jeffrey. Lorogos ordered the guards to stand their ground, walked over to the boy and nudged him with his foot. He looked at Thaniel.

"Is he dead?"

"Apparently, and by his own hand rather than entertaining a Sauren mob tomorrow."

Lorogos turned to the trembling guards. "And you allowed this?"

Silence.

"You know what Sauren honor demands of you," he said, looking at the guards.

The guards looked at each other. Each took his sword out and put it to the other's neck. They looked to Lorogos and he nodded quickly. Thaniel averted his eyes. The Saurens, shouting their oath of loyalty to the king, plunged their swords deeply and fell to the floor, dying.

Thaniel watched their few seconds of death throes. "Poor chaps," he said. "Though I must say I appreciate taking advantage of their sense of duty!"

"Can I get up now?" asked Jeffrey.

"Yes, of course," answered Thaniel. "We must hurry," turning to Ethan, "Are you all right, nephew?"

"I've never ordered an execution before—human or otherwise," he said.

Thaniel placed a hand on Ethan's shoulder. "Your transformation into Lorogos was quite convincing. You did what had to be done. Better stay in his form for now. We have to find someone who will tell us where the coins are kept and lead us to them."

Jeffrey was looking at the dead Saurens. He took one of their short swords and pulled a long leather strand from one of their uniforms. He looked at it for a moment and smiled, "I think I have an idea."

"Out of my way," ordered Lorogos. "I have the Jefford spawn with me."

The Sauren guards were surprised. Human prisoners moving through the royal compound at the stronghold in Sabrek was not unusual, but a human of this historic significance being escorted by Lorogos himself made quite an impression. And that is exactly what the Saurens stationed about the tower were seeing: Lorogos, a Sauren guard, and Jeffrey Jefford, his hands bound behind him—walking through the prison.

"Mind you, Lorogos is always a bit on the angry side," whispered Thaniel.

"Don't worry, uncle, I'm working on it!" glaring at the guards as he stalked by. Every one of them lowered their eyes at the approach of their "prince." Ethan continued his disdainful rant, praying they didn't run into the real Lorogos. When they came upon Delkor, a Sauren whom Thaniel recognized as one of

Lorogos's aides from the meeting with the King, they stopped. Delkor looked up, astonished at what he saw.

"My prince, what are you doing here?" the confused aide said. "You've always said the prison was too dreary for a royal."

"Jefford is an important prisoner, to our history as well as our future." He looked at Jeffrey. "He has agreed to tell me where the stones are hidden."

"Splendid!" exclaimed Delkor. "I will fetch a scribe!"

"Why? Are you too good to write for me yourself? This is a sensitive matter. Tell me, where are the coins and the sword kept tonight? All this evening's toasting one thing and another has not served my memory well," he winked, belching loudly.

Delkor chuckled nervously. "In the treasure room, my prince—I'll bring a lamp."

"Ah yes, of course," said Lorogos. "Please accompany us, Delkor. Serve as scribe and help me with questions."

"I would be honored, my prince."

"Very good," said Lorogos. "Walk ahead of us and dismiss the guards as you see them. This information must be kept secret. Saurens tend to stray when there is treasure to be had. We'll be right behind you."

"Yes, my prince," said Delkor, pondering his good fortune at being allowed to sit in on so privy a matter.

"Bring the prisoner!" Lorogos ordered, as they followed Delkor through the corridors.

"Very clever, Ethan," said Thaniel, quietly, "having him lead us to the room."

"Yes," muttered Jeffrey, "As long as we don't run into the real Lorogos. And quit overacting. This isn't the theater in Nistrum."

Ethan smirked, "You take care of your own bit of acting. Anyway, you heard Delkor. He said Lorogos is never in these parts of the tower."

"But what happens if we *do* see the real Lorogos?" asked Jeffrey.

There were a few seconds of silence. "Well then," said Thaniel philosophically, "to borrow from an old Sauren proverb, 'It's every Sauren for himself.'"

"Great," muttered Jeffrey, "at last, a plan."

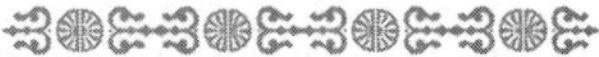

"Er, sire," said Delkor. "I said the treasure room. Over here." He pointed in the opposite corridor.

"Ah yes," said Lorogos, turning around. "It's been a while…this way then, Jefford! You, guards! Leave us!"

The Sauren guards looked at each other in consternation as the strange party made their way down the hall toward the treasure room. Delkor unlocked the massive door with an ornate key from his belt, opening it with a flourish for Lorogos, who strode in, unimpressed. The startled treasure warden looked up from his ledgers, only to have his personal guards ordered out of the vault by the prince, who seemed in a foul temper.

The room was large and neatly organized, earning a gruff compliment from Lorogos. There were several chests against one wall, and links of gold chain piled in that corner. The opposite wall held racks of ceremonial weapons. Shelves and display cases contained quite a bit of gold, both in coin and jewelry. Jeffrey was shoved into a chair and the guard who accompanied him stood at his side.

"If Pickworth saw this room he'd never leave it," Jeffrey whispered to Thaniel.

"Hush, boy," cautioned Thaniel.

"Now, Jefford," said Lorogos, pacing in what he deemed to be interrogation mode. "You told me you were ready to disclose the location of the remainder of the coins and where the stones may be found. Speak truth, or your friends' lives are forfeit."

Jeffrey looked up at Lorogos. "Yes, that's right. But before I betray my family I wish to see the articles I gave up. I want one last look at the Sauren sword and the coins. Then I'll be ready to discuss the fate of your accursed stones."

"Whelp of a human dog!" Lorogos roared, swatting Jeffrey's face. "You are in no position to make demands of me. You're lucky to still be living, for however short and painful a time. In fact, I've changed my mind and you'll see nothing but the end of a hot blade."

The warden snickered.

"Then I won't tell you."

Lorogos looked around, becoming more and more agitated. The warden backed off a few paces. "You what?"

"I won't tell you," Jeffrey said, "blade or not!"

Lorogos nodded his head in understanding. "Delkor, what do you suggest for one who has information but will not talk?" Lorogos said, turning to the aide.

"Highness, we have many convincing tools, just down the hallway."

"Warden, what say you?"

The warden, in the white robes of a Sauren bureaucrat, bowed slightly. "My prince, most of my information comes from books rather than beatings," he said. "But it seems to me that what he asks is of little consequence since he will be put to death on the morrow, anyway."

Lorogos seemed to weigh the answer. He suddenly became serene and amiable, turning back to the warden.

"Who in here holds the coins and sword now?" Lorogos said.

"They are here, sire," said the warden, "in the vault."

"Fetch them then," he said. "We may as well honor this dead man's wish." Delkor looked at Lorogos strangely. "You heard me," Lorogos said. "Bring the coins and the sword. Now!"

The warden nodded and raced away. Delkor didn't like these breaches of protocol. Bargaining with a prisoner simply wasn't done, but he had learned long before not to cross Lorogos. The three waited for what seemed like an hour. From time to time they looked at each other nervously. Finally, he returned with a small box and what was apparently the sword, wrapped in a velvet cloth.

"Here we go," whispered Thaniel. "Get ready."

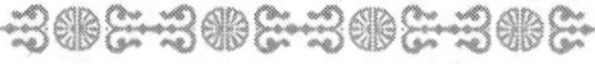

The sight of four of the six coins of the Armor of Nova Fannum almost brought tears to Thaniel's eyes. Not only did he think of what they represented for the future of his land and the rest of the world, but each coin represented the sacrifice of a brother who gave his life rather than surrender one of the coins. And now here they were—displayed in a black velvet-lined case—holy symbols in most unholy hands. Thaniel's eyes glanced at Ethan, who, for a moment, forgot about his Lorogos guise.

"Uncle, look!" Ethan said.

Jeffrey and Thaniel both looked at Ethan with eyes that told him to be careful. The warden apparently didn't hear these words, although Thaniel wondered about Delkor who still seemed uncomfortable with Lorogos's odd, untimely visit.

"They are indeed beautiful," admitted Lorogos. "And the sword! I have waited so long to see its return. Let me hold it once more." The warden began to unwrap the velvety covering. Thaniel and Jeffrey prepared themselves for whatever might happen. The warden started to hand the sword over when Delkor grasped at the weapon's remaining covering.

"Your highness is aware of Sauren protocol. This sword is not to be touched again before its consecration by blood." He looked menacingly at Jeffrey.

"I'm well aware of Sauren custom," snapped Lorogos. "And this sword will indeed be consecrated in blood." Ethan grasped the haft and held the blade to Delkor's throat. Gasping, the Sauren aide fell to his knees. Thaniel and Jeffrey seized the warden, forcing him down, also. Suddenly, Ethan and Thaniel appeared to the Saurens as themselves. Delkor was astonished.

"Sorry uncle, my concentration slipped," he said.

"Never mind," Thaniel said, relieved to see his nephew's form once more. "But we must deal with these two."

Delkor looked first at Ethan, who the moment before appeared as Lorogos, and at Thaniel who no longer resembled a Sauren guard. He sneered at them. "I should have known you were not the true prince," Delkor said. "Lorogos would never have come to this room before the consecration."

"Convincing enough to fool you," said Jeffrey. Ethan handed him the Sauren sword. It felt good in Jeffrey's hands once more.

"For the moment," Delkor admitted. "But you're a long way from leaving this fortress. With or without the coins." Thaniel took the three coins and put them in the little leather pouch around his neck. He handed the gold eden that Ethan had used to fool the Saurens to Delkor.

"Have a souvenir of our little adventure." Delkor picked up the eden.

"And here is another," said Jeffrey. He brought the butt of the sword's hilt down hard upon Delkor's head. The Sauren fell across the table, unconscious. The warden looked at the men with frightened eyes.

"I am a simple warden," he said. "I am no warrior."

"A frightened Sauren?" Thaniel mused. "Remarkable."

Jeffrey placed the tip of the blade under the trembling warden's throat. The Sauren swallowed heavily. "I was remanded here from my position as cupbearer to the King. Like you, I saw through Phaesus's evil plans and said as much—and the king demoted me to treasure steward."

"Very sorry to hear that," Thaniel cut him off. "But we have problems of our own. Now, tell us how to get out of here."

"Please sir," protested the warden. "If I tell you, I shall have to kill myself. It is the way of our people."

"Yes we saw that code played out a few minutes ago," said Thaniel, thinking of the two guards who drove their swords into each other's neck. "But you need not die."

"How?"

"Come with us. Lead us out of here and join us. You know that the Saurens are being used by a far greater enemy than they realize, an enemy bent upon destroying all of Humus. This unholy alliance with Phaesus will end in your kingdom's destruction. Join us, and you may be able to make the difference that preserves your kind."

The warden looked at Thaniel. "It's true," he admitted. "Phaesus captivated the king in a way that no other human has ever done. It's as if he were under a spell."

"And so he is. And we haven't much time, so you must choose now. Take your chances with us, or die by your own hand and accomplish nothing.

"Or at Lorogos's behest," the warden added, "He plans to deal further with me after the matter of the coins is settled. Loss of face and all that. Very Sauren, you know." The Sauren thought about it for a moment. He looked about the treasure room and down at Delkor, who would awaken soon and alert the Tower. Could he trust these men? He looked at Thaniel. What choice did he have?

"Very well, I will go with you. But we must go quickly, while the guards are still scattered. And we must secure Delkor. His head is harder than you'd know."

Ethan and Jeffrey tied up Delkor and hid him in the vault at the back of the room. They dealt him one more blow to the head for good measure before emerging from the room. The warden had gathered a few things for his journey. Looking around one more time, he sighed. "Very well, I'm ready. Understand, it isn't that I enjoy human company, but the greater enemy that threatens us all and has deceived my king compels me."

"Common threats make uncommon friends," said Thaniel. "Ethan?" As if cued, Ethan took up Cassis and suddenly appeared as Delkor. Jeffrey became a Sauren guard. The warden remained himself and Thaniel merely concentrated on Juaracas and vanished. The warden stood, gaping.

"Oh by the way, close your mouth, take a breath and tell us your name."

"Kreelin."

"Kreelin. Welcome to the Servatrix."

Chapter 14

THE SERVATRIX

KREELIN'S nervousness was quite apparent as he led the group in single file down the darkened, narrow corridor. The rarely-used passage he'd brought them to avoided the main guard posts. Jeffrey was glad to have his sword back. Though it felt good in his hands, he'd be the first to admit he hoped he wouldn't have to use it. Not yet, anyway. Thaniel had secured the coins in his little pouch. Ethan, still looking like Delkor to whomever they might run into, was behind them.

"Easy, Kreelin," Thaniel said. "We'll make it yet. You must have faith."

"We have a long way to go, human," the Sauren advised, "and if we are caught, I will be dealt with even more severely than you. You can afford to have faith."

"Then we'd best not get caught."

"Good plan," said Kreelin, pulling his hood more closely around his face.

The stairs of this lofty keep, the main building in the Sabrek complex, seemed to wind endlessly. Jeffrey was surprised at the many twists and turns they had taken. Hopefully, this was a back way out of the place, but Thaniel had told him that the Saurens were by nature stealthy, so, for all he knew, this could be the main route for the dark-sighted Saurens. Fortunately for the group, Kreelin knew the Tower quite well. "This is where they were going to take you," Kreelin said, indicating a doorway on their right. He smiled his crocodile smile at them.

Jeffrey peeked into the room, only to see all manner of horrible-looking torture devices. Some of the contraptions were beyond his imagination, and he didn't really want to take the time to figure out their nefarious purposes. Thaniel and Ethan also took a brief glance inside the room, gulped nervously and picked up the pace. "Nice, Kreelin," said Jeffrey. "Thanks for showing us."

Kreelin smiled.

After a few more minutes they stopped. Kreelin held his hand up and then motioned them forward to a large door at the end of the stone hallway. He slowly opened the door. Outside, about 40 feet away, stood a single guard. Beyond him lay a path to a small building—and beyond that was forest. The guard's back was largely to the door, but he was at an angle where, if he should look to his right, the door would be clearly in view. He leaned against the corner of the Tower, standing his post.

"There will be one more around the other corner," Kreelin muttered, "Over to the right.

The group paused for a moment. Thaniel put his hand to the little leather pouch at his neck, having a particular coin in mind, and vanished. Ethan and Jeffrey smiled. Kreelin was dumbfounded. The coins really were magic! He'd be glad to be getting away from all this nonsense.

"I'll take care of our friend," Thaniel said.

"We need to hurry," Kreelin said. "The Tower will be awakened soon, because executions always take place at first hour."

"How prompt you Saurens are," said Jeffrey.

"Gratification delayed is gratification denied, we always say!"

"Quiet," came Thaniel's voice.

The door slowly opened a bit and Kreelin shut it.

The guard was, like all guards of all armies everywhere, bored. He even stretched once as Thaniel slowly crept up behind him. Thaniel took time to survey their situation. Like Kreelin said, there was a guard to the right, out of sight of the doorway. He stood looking toward the forest. Thaniel looked back along the path of their escape at the Tower. It was enormous. He stepped a few feet toward the path which led into the woods. Yes, this was it! Then he turned back toward the guard nearest the door.

CRACK!

The guard looked up. He didn't see anyone, but he had heard something. He remained quite alert for a few minutes, looking around, sniffing the air about him and even leaving his post and walking toward the woods. The other guard motioned that he hadn't heard anything. Thaniel looked down at the little branch he had accidentally stepped on. He was sweating. How was he going to take care of both guards? The question became moot, as the nighttime silence was shattered by a familiar and terrifying voice.

"You there, guard! Stand your post!"

It was Lorogos.

From inside the doorway, the sound of the real Lorogos almost made Kreelin faint. The group wondered what to do. The door suddenly pushed open and Thaniel reappeared. "Quiet!" He looked at Kreelin. "What is he doing here?"

"I don't know," Kreelin stammered. "Unless…"

"Listen!" said Ethan. "He's speaking."

"The prisoners have escaped," said Lorogos. "I have already personally killed six of your worthless comrades for letting this happen. If they get through that doorway, you'll be joining them. Now, get more guards out here between them and the cover of that forest! Who trained you idiots?"

The Saurens rushed around and within minutes the Tower was coming alive. Kreelin told them that it wouldn't be long before they were caught. "Please kill me," he begged Jeffrey, who was still hanging on to the Sauren sword. "And then kill yourselves, if you have any brains at all—it's the only way."

"Nonsense," said Thaniel.

"But it's true," said Kreelin, falling to his knees and grabbing the end of the blade, pointing it toward his neck. "The only thing worse than a prisoner escaping is being the one who allowed them to escape. Now, kill me!"

Ignoring Kreelin, Thaniel thought for a moment. They could hear footsteps approaching from above. Kreelin continued begging that his life be taken. Thaniel suddenly looked at the others.

"I have a plan. It's desperate, but approaching footsteps inspire many an enterprise."

"We're doomed," Kreelin whined.

"Not now, Kreelin. Quiet yourself..."

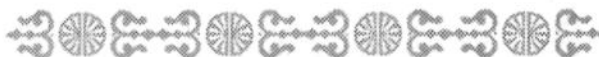

The door to the Tower burst open and Thaniel and Jeffrey emerged in single file, hands above their heads. Behind them, brandishing the Sauren sword to their backs, strode Kreelin. Ethan, his mind on Cassis, looked once more like Lorogos, bringing up the rear. The deception of the coin was so complete that even Ethan's voice was that of Lorogos. Not only that, but the coin made Ethan's words come out in Sauren—very handy, since Ethan knew not a word of the language! The guards outside called to their captain and ran to the group. Some of them looked confused, having just seen Lorogos.

"Spread the word. The prisoners are caught," snapped Ethan. "But find that one other human boy. He is still somewhere in the Tower."

The guards stood about, dazed. How could Lorogos move so quickly from the yard to the Tower?

"Now!" Ethan yelled.

The guards hurried into the Tower door. The captain moved to take custody of the prisoners. Ethan waved him off. "I've already lost them once. You get a party together and find the other human. He could be anywhere by now!"

"Not quite anywhere," came a familiar voice.

Ethan turned to see Delkor and a smiling Lorogos, with a company of guards.

"I admire your courage, but first I'll have the sword and coins—then your heads."

The guards moved in to take custody of the prisoners once more. But Ethan remained in character, glaring at the guards. "What are you doing? Take him. He obviously has the coin and wants to take these prisoners off my hands. He is the missing boy with the bewitched coin! Take him!"

The guards stopped in their tracks and looked back at Lorogos.

"Good thinking, Ethan," whispered Thaniel.

"What are you waiting for?" Lorogos roared. "Take them!"

The guards hesitated. They looked to their captain, who seemed just as confused. One infuriated Lorogos was bad enough, but two raging princes had career-ending potential. Finally, the captain stepped out and called out quietly, "My prince?"

Both Ethan and Lorogos answered him.

"I am the real Lorogos!" they both shouted. Lorogos continued, "They are using the coin against your weak minds! Seize them now."

The guards again started toward Ethan.

"You fools!" Ethan shouted back. "If you don't obey me I will have you and your families boiled in your own stinking fats! I have the sword."

The situation was rapidly deteriorating, as more and more guards arrived, carrying torches and weapons. This was not lost on Thaniel, who determined that if they didn't break out now they would never make it. Lorogos took a sword from one of his captains and started toward them. The guards were thrilled at the prospect of Lorogos fighting Lorogos to the death.

Suddenly, a screeching sound came from overhead and everyone looked up. It was Sestrin, diving from the sky at Ethan. The attack startled him and he immediately lost mind of the coin and his shape shifted back to that of Ethan! The guards were astonished. The evil wight flew away as quickly as it had appeared, shrieking in insane delight.

"Sestrin," Thaniel said bitterly. "Which means Phaesus must be…"

"Here, priest!"

Thaniel and the others watched as the guards parted, revealing a tall man in a black cloak at the end of the Sauren column. He was hooded and, just as Thaniel had said, his face was a silver mask, reflecting grotesquely the light of the torches. He strolled toward Lorogos who, having taken custody of the coins, immediately handed them over to Phaesus.

Thaniel whispered for everyone to be ready.

"Ready for what?" asked Kreelin.

"Just do as he says," said Jeffrey, "if you want to get out of this alive."

"Why didn't you just kill me earlier," Kreelin muttered.

"Is that all you guys think about?"

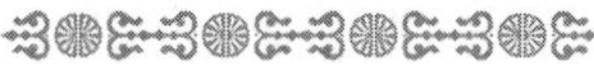

"I would have a few moments alone with the priest," Phaesus said.

Lorogos agreed, ordering the others bound and watched in the courtyard while Thaniel and Phaesus walked to a small garden area. The only person who accompanied them was one of

Phaesus's elite guards from Nova Fannum. Phaesus laughed at the Sauren attempt at landscaping.

"Not like Nova Fannum, eh, priest?" he asked Thaniel.

"No. It has color."

Phaesus ignored the sarcasm. Thaniel looked up. He could hear Sestrin fluttering around somewhere above them. He looked at Phaesus.

"I've had my eye on you from the start, you know," Phaesus said, as they sat at a bronze table. "You never had a chance. And now you have dragged the poor boy into this mess."

"He came of his own free will," said Thaniel, "after you murdered his mother."

"Ah that," Phasesus said. "She was quite strong for one so sick. She died at her own hand. Never told us where the coin was hidden. Had I gotten to her before she killed herself she would have talked, I assure you." Phaesus stood, his flowing robes dripping down his form. He pulled a strange-looking flower from a nearby shrub and sniffed it.

"Now what?" asked Thaniel.

Phaesus produced a small black bag and proceeded to lay the four coins out on the table. Even in the darkness they seemed to shine, dancing in the light of the torches. The fallen priest looked at Thaniel as he played with one of the coins. "Four of six," he said, "After so many years, to have them together once more. It doesn't seem possible that it has been so long."

"How did you come by *Fides*?"

"Actually I came by *Fides* quite early," Phaesus said. "Your brother, Therin, who took this particular coin never even made it out of the Temple before being cut down. Had he used the coin's power, he might have made it. Instead he was killed by one of the guards."

"Therin," whispered Thaniel.

"Yes," Phaesus said, looking at Thaniel, "and Dontel, Corin, Bartemus, and Jarrol. All dead, and their chosen coins now in our care." He looked down at the coins. Thaniel saw the coins reflected off the silver mask, creating a bizarre effect around his eyes. "The others shall soon be in our care as well."

"*Lorica?*"

"The breastplate?" purred Phaesus. "We believe we know where to find that coin, too. The rebels have it. I should have news of its recovery soon enough. My agents are already moving on it."

"You mean Pickworth?"

Phaesus laughed. "It's amazing what humans or Saurens will do for gold or glory. In the end, they will be served by neither. No, I'm afraid Pickworth is going to a very different reward. I'm sure he has been paid in full by now." He sipped from a glass that was at the table.

"And what about Graysil?"

"Ah, yes, Graysil." Phaesus mused. "Of the lot of you, he was my favorite. True, your brother Graysil remains unaccounted for. He made off with *Balteus*, the truth. Fitting, somehow, that the coin representing truth should be the last to be revealed, but it's only a matter of time."

They were silent for a moment.

"Why, Phaesus?"

Phaesus looked at the old priest. "Why?" he said, laughing.

"Why do you serve wickedness?"

"That's easy," Phaesus said, "Because righteousness doesn't pay. I tried to serve with the best of you. In the end, I was ignored and passed over, as others were promoted to higher positions in the priesthood."

"That was because you were perverting the truth," said Thaniel. "Your heart had turned to sorcery rather than faith."

"You and your haughty class rejected me," said Phaesus. "You rejected the superior knowledge I tried to give you. And now you shall be destroyed by that very knowledge! Blackheart's time will soon arrive and the prophecy and your notions of freedom and these criminals calling themselves the Servatrix shall all be crushed."

Just as he finished a howl was heard, and guards began scattering for cover. Arrows were flying to their marks from the woods. Commands were shouted to call out fresh troops as Saurens tried to regroup amid the confusion. A Sauren aide to Lorogos found Phaesus and bowed down.

"Well what is it?" Phaesus demanded.

"We're under attack, sir,"

"Attack? By whom?"

"The Servatrix," the Sauren trooper answered.

Phaesus glared at Thaniel, snatched up the coins and stuffed them into the black bag.

"You were saying about the Servatrix?" Thaniel asked.

Phaesus glared at Thaniel and was about to say something when an arrow skimmed his hand, making him drop the coins. Thaniel quickly snatched the bag and turned to flee. Phaesus's eye turned red with rage. "Kill him!" he ordered.

The Sauren guard raised his sword to kill Thaniel. He suddenly stopped—his hand dropping the sword. He looked at Thaniel and crumpled onto the tabletop with a Servatrix arrow through his neck.

Phaesus looked about, realizing his peril. He saw several Servatrix fighters closing in. "This isn't over, priest!" he said, vanishing.

Everything became a strange, bloody blur. Thaniel heard the sound of arrows flying by, men yelling, orders barked by commanders and the harsh clank of sword against sword. He saw human and Sauren engaged in killing each other in vicious combat, once more. Thaniel's first instinct was to find a weapon. He picked up the dead Sauren's sword as an arrow whizzed by his ear. The Tower was fully engaged by now, and Lorogos was standing in the middle of troops ordering a counterattack. He could not see Jeffrey or Ethan.

"Thaniel, Priest of Nova Fannum!"

Thaniel turned and saw a bowman in a black and red uniform calling to him. Around his neck was a small medallion with a suit of armor insignia—the sign of the Servatrix. His face was covered by a black cloth, except for the eyes. He motioned Thaniel over to him.

"Out of the way!" he screamed at Thaniel, nocking a fresh arrow.

An axe came flying by, just off Thaniel's shoulder. Thaniel watched, horrified, as the axe hurtled toward the bowman. A brilliant flash of light emanated from the man's chest as the axe bounced harmlessly off him. Thaniel ducked just as the archer let fly the arrow, killing the shocked Sauren who had thrown the axe. The bowman approached Thaniel. "We must get you out of here," he said, keeping his eyes on the battlefield.

The garden and courtyard of the Tower complex was becoming a mass of blood and confusion as Sauren fought Servatrix in front of the Tower. Several other uniformed Servatrix fighters ran to Thaniel. The Servatrix raiding party was already falling back.

They hadn't come to besiege the Tower—only to rescue its prisoners.

"Come with me, sir," the bowman said.

"But the others! I can't leave them."

"We took them," said the other fighter, "Or at least one of them. The other slipped away into the woods, but we'll find him."

The bowman who had rescued Thaniel was getting angry. "You heard him," he said. "But you must come with me now! The Saurens are responding in strength." Thaniel took a look back toward the Tower where moments before he had stood with Jeffrey and Ethan. He tried calling out to them, hoping to get the attention of whichever one was not accounted for, but the noise of battle drowned his voice. The Servatrix bowman grabbed his shoulder. "Please sir, we must leave now, or die for nothing!"

Thaniel nodded and followed the archers into the woods disappearing into the darkness. He took one last look behind him at the carnage inflicted upon the Saurens by the Servatrix and disappeared into the blackness.

Chapter 15

FAMILY REUNION

OVER the next several hours, the Servatrix raiding party made their way through the forest on paths known only to them. Thaniel did his best to keep up, impressed with their speed, silence and discipline. He was glad to be away from the Saurens but would much rather have been horsed on Treasure. Along the way, he inquired from this or that fighter about Jeffrey or Ethan, but none seemed to have heard of or seen them. Perhaps they were with one of the other parties. Thaniel could only hope that he would see them at the main gathering…wherever that was.

The main body of Saurens following them had long since given up the chase. Never ones to venture too far out into uncontrolled territory—their drubbing by William Jefford taught them that one—they figured they would meet again on a future battlefield more suited to them. Only Lorogos and his hand-picked warriors continued the hunt, determined not to let the sword slip into the hands of a Jefford yet again.

"We're almost there," came the whispered words Thaniel had been waiting for.

Ahead of him, he could see the silhouettes of figures against small lights—torches and lanterns, it turned out—all heading downhill. Within minutes, Thaniel felt a cool rush of damp air, indicating the entrance to a cave or tunnel of some sort. The men remained quiet. It wasn't until they reached a large opening that he could hear the murmur of conversation.

Thaniel was amazed at the size of the underground chamber. It was obviously a natural formation, and the torches reflected eerie figures like menacing giants on the walls. The returning party was welcomed by other men and women, who saw to wounds, fetched fresh food and water, or greeted loved ones with warm embraces. Thaniel looked for Jeffrey and Ethan but still saw no sign of them. There must have been hundreds of people in the area, counting women, men, fighters, and even a few children.

"Thaniel?"

Thaniel turned to see the warrior who had rescued him from Phaesus hours before. He had lost track of him on the trail. "I never was able to properly thank you for getting me out of that rather dubious position...," Thaniel began.

"My pleasure, Uncle!" Thaniel's jaw dropped. He looked at the fighter, whose face was still hidden behind a black and red cloth mask.

"Who are you?" Thaniel asked, trembling.

The fighter took off "his" mask, revealing the face of a girl about 18, with brown hair and sparkling green eyes. She smiled at her uncle, who could only tear up. He didn't need any further introduction. He could tell by her eyes that this was the youngest daughter of his brother Graysil. Her name was Kierlin.

"Kierlin, Kierlin," was all he could manage. He held her for a few moments. "It's been a lifetime since I beheld any of my brothers' children." His smile faded and he looked into her eyes. "Graysil? My brother?"

"Dead," Kierlin said. "But true to his vow, uncle. He never revealed where he hid the coin, *Balteus*."

Thaniel nodded in understanding as she brushed away a tear. "How did he die?"

"Betrayed," Kierlin said, as they walked through the large cave to a place where they could sit, "Like the rest of them."

She noticed Thaniel's curiosity about their surroundings. "This is a sort of emergency camp, where we hide when we are campaigning. You'll meet our leader soon. He hasn't returned yet."

"What of your cousin, Ethan, and Jeffrey, the young man accompanying us?"

"I believe they are with him," she said, looking toward the entrance to see if there was any sign of the remaining war party. "I know they brought your horses along. We have a hidden stable above."

He looked at Kierlin once more—this time like a doting uncle rather than a fugitive priest. "My goodness," he said, "Kierlin, daughter of my brother Graysil, a freedom fighter? I would never have imagined it!"

She smiled. "Father had taken me to a safe place in Nova Fannum," she said. "But with Phaesus's men closing in, he handed me off to Aarlon. He's like my guardian. You'll meet him soon. He's also the armorer for the Servatrix. Anyway, we were on the run for a while, but when Nova Fannum was finally overcome by the darkness, we crossed the mountains into Humus. By then, the Servatrix was already established."

"Yes," said Thaniel. "You are truly Graysil's daughter. I'm very proud of you, and your father would be proud as well."

"About the coins...," she began.

Thaniel put his finger to her lips and glanced around cautiously, looking for a more private spot, away from the common area of the cavern. When they had settled on a rough blanket, Kierlin reached into a small bag, from which she produced a coin. He took it and smiled.

"*Lorica*, the breast plate," he said. "That explains your protection from the axe back there at the Sauren keep." He placed it in the pouch with the other coins. "How did you come by it?"

"My father gave it to me with the box," she said. "He'd retrieved it from one of my aunts, my uncle Jarrol's wife. I've held it since, awaiting the arrival of the other coins. I now turn it over to you with the prayer that all of them shall soon be reunited."

Thaniel nodded, his voice quivering, "Five of the six. It has been a long time coming." He wiped his eyes. "You mentioned a box?"

Kierlin nodded and pulled a small lacquered box with an embossed image of two swans. Thaniel smiled at the sight of it, recognizing it from his childhood—it had been his mother's. "My father also gave me this, or rather, left it for me. It belonged to my grandmother."

"Yes," said Thaniel, taking the box. He held it up and looked it over as if examining a precious artifact, then looked over it at Kierlin. "I remember mother treasured this. It came to her from one of the greatest collections in Nova Fannum. Quite unique."

He laughed and looked at his niece. "I'll tell you a story about your father. One time, when we were all young, Graysil actually took this box from mother's room without her permission, and he lost it. For three days, we looked and looked for the box. Our mother was broken-hearted—or so we thought. She moaned and fussed and cried. She was very emotional—not to mention a very good actress. It turned out that she had it all the time!"

Kierlin snickered at the thought of her father and uncles scurrying about their house looking for this very box.

"As it turned out, Graysil had left it on the mantel. She'd found it and taken it back to her room to see how long it would take for someone to confess."

They both laughed.

"Well when your father finally did confess, she made quite a sport of it. And she said this to all of us boys: 'Lesson here young gentlemen. That which is sacred to the heart never really leaves it.' I never forgot that."

"Nor did father," Kierlin said, opening the box.

Thaniel looked at her with curiosity. She pulled out a folded piece of paper with writing on it. Thaniel watched as she very carefully unfolded the letter. He reached out to take the letter.

"I'll read it, Uncle," she said, "although I know it by heart. Before my father died, he assured those in whom he had the greatest confidence that he had not divulged the place where the coin was hidden. But he said that I was to receive this box, and that the contents of this box would reveal all. I'm afraid I was never any good at riddles."

"Let's hear it, niece," said Thaniel, closing his eyes so he could take in the communication from a long dead brother.

Kierlin looked about to make sure they were quite alone. Though they were probably out of earshot of the other Servatrix, she spoke very quietly:

Dearest Kierlin,

You know the fate which has overtaken me. You also know the grave responsibility entailed in the return of Baleteus to the rightful one. Therefore I give you these words that my mother gave to me years ago and will help you find the coin: ***That which is sacred to the***

heart never really leaves it. *Good-bye my little love. May the Great King return to reclaim his place in Nova Fannum.*

Thaniel read the note several times. As he did he took out the little pouch of coins that he wore around his neck. He shivered to think that only a short time before Phaesus actually had his hands on all four of these! And now they had a clue in this cryptic note which might lead them to *Balteus*, the belt of truth! If only they could get things in place before the prophesied time!

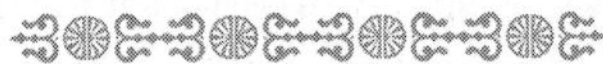

"Thaniel!"

Thaniel turned to see someone rushing toward him. It was Jeffrey! The old priest stood and hugged the boy. Thaniel looked up, teary-eyed, and saw Ethan approaching off Jeffrey's shoulder. Thaniel embraced his nephew. The two young men were dirty, a bit bloodied, but very much alive! Thaniel looked up and said a brief prayer of thanks.

"Uncle, the coins?" asked Ethan.

"Here, with me," he said, patting the pouch under his cloak. "Thanks to your cousin here."

Ethan looked around to see Kierlin, still seated and smiling at the impromptu family reunion. Ethan walked over to her.

"My cousin?" he asked.

"By your uncle Graysil," said Thaniel. "This is Kierlin. And she saved both my life and the coins."

"Hello cousin," Kierlin said, standing.

"Hello," said a bemused Ethan. "And thank you for rescuing my uncle."

"You mean *my* uncle," she said, smiling.

They laughed.

"Oh, this is Jeffrey," said Ethan, indicating Jeffrey.

Kierlin and Ethan laughed at Jeffrey, who seemed enthralled with Kierlin. He was looking at her in her warrior outfit, long brown hair and sharp eyes. He had never seen such a strange mix of fighter and female.

"Jeffrey!" said Thaniel. "This is my niece and Ethan's cousin, Kierlin."

"Hello," he stammered.

"So you are the descendant of the famous William Jefford," she said. "I hope some of his fight was passed down to you."

"I can hold my own," he said. "Like any Jefford."

"I'm sure," she said smiling.

"Hmph," Jeffrey muttered and walked away.

Jeffrey left the little family and walked to another part of the huge cave. From time to time he looked back at them. He would show her, he thought to himself. He patted the Sauren sword that he was once more carrying. She probably thought she was important in her fighting gear. But one thing was sure, he thought, as he looked at Kierlin's face in the torchlight. She was the most beautiful girl he had ever seen.

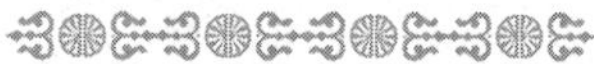

"Priest of Nova Fannum!"

Thaniel turned to see an older man, dressed in the Servatrix fashion, but with much more bloodied clothing. He was bearded and balding and had a great, toothy grin on his face. Behind him Thaniel could see another group of returning fighters. Some were being tended to because of their wounds. Most quietly blended into the waiting arms of family. Kierlin bowed her head slightly and whispered to Thaniel that this was Cren-Jaez, the leader of the Servatrix.

Thaniel stood to his feet. Cren-Jaez waved him back.

"Sit, sit," he said. "Bring food here. And drink!"

Jeffrey joined the group as they enjoyed some tasty venison with brown bread and ale. The chief talked loudly and colorfully of life as fugitive freedom fighters. No matter where the conversation drifted, it always centered itself back in restoring Nova Fannum to rightful authority. Cren-Jaez leaned back, pulling his cloak closer around his neck. He looked at Jeffrey.

"To think you had one of the coins all those years and were unaware of it," he said. "Amazing! And now we have four of them together again. And with the Great King's blessing we shall have them all!"

"My grandfather bought the coin," Jeffrey said. "But he had no idea it would lead to a cave eating venison with a secret fighting group!"

They laughed.

"I'm sure he didn't" said Cren-Jaez.

"Or to my mother's death because of it."

The group silently ate their meal for the next few minutes. Kierlin looked at Jeffrey. She felt sorry for him. Here he was in a strange world, fighting a strange war, caught up in something that had seen his mother killed, his father disappear and his home and his family inn destroyed. She smiled at the far-off look in his gray eyes.

"May I have a word with you, Cren-Jaez?" asked Thaniel.

"Of course, priest," the warrior chief said.

He stood up and the two of them walked over to Cren-Jaez's private area. It was a natural indention in the cave wall which was about the size of Thaniel's little home in the mines under Gillingham. The room was alight with the glow of many ornate lamps and the cave floor was carpeted with rich, luxurious rugs. Even the walls demonstrated Cren-Jaez's apparent love for things beautiful as they were covered with thick tapestries. All in all, the place had the feel of a palace chamber, albeit a damp one.

Cren-Jaez offered Thaniel some hot spiced cider. Thaniel took the steaming cup from the warrior's battle-scarred hands and smiled at the man's gesture. It seemed quaintly out of place—this hulking fighter offering something as civil as hot cider in the midst of so great a conflict. Thaniel sat down on a very comfortable chair. Cren-Jaez poured himself some cider and plopped down on the floor next to him. For a few minutes they spoke of Nova Fannum, common friends and such.

"When last I saw our beloved Nova Fannum, the place had become bleak and desolate," Cren-Jaez said, sipping from his cup. "The colors which so made Nova Fannum remarkable had become gray. Have you seen it?"

"I have heard that when Blackheart seized power all things turned," Thaniel said. "Such is the result of evil's influence on innocence."

Cren-Jaez nodded.

"And so for me it was a matter of either joining up with Phaesus as his second, in charge of all the intelligence and security details, or joining what was in my heart. He would have me arresting the leading citizens of Nova Fannum under the most obscure of suspicions. Whole families were being executed. I could not stomach such evil."

He smiled.

"So, I followed my heart, which was following my King. And so Phaesus has a particular interest in me. Quite a price on my head, I understand."

"And on mine," said Thaniel. "He has managed to kill most of my family in the name of Blackheart. And he knows that as long as I am alive and am in possession of the coins he has much to fear."

"I am honored to turn over custody of *Lorica* into your hands," Cren-Jaez said. "I noticed that Kierlin already did so."

Thaniel nodded.

Cren-Jaez looked about the room.

"Not bad for a band of rebels," he said. "This is only one of our sanctuaries. We have several. The opening in the ceiling allows us to have fires inside. I have some ingenious designers who created a chimney for the smoke. Looks like a natural formation on the outside. Allows us great comfort. Of course we never have fires except at night."

"Wonderful!" said Thaniel.

They sat in silence for a few minutes.

"What next,?" asked Thaniel. "What is your plan?"

"You're the priest of Nova Fannum," said Cren-Jaez. "We were hoping you would be able to tell us. What does the prophecy indicate?"

"The time is near, my friend," said Thaniel, looking up as if imagining the star rising in the sky. "I can feel it. And remember, Blackheart has a great advantage. If he has the coins before the time, he will forever reign in darkness and all is lost. We, however, must have the Armor in place and in the proper hands."

"The Castus?"

"Exactly," said Thaniel. "And that is why I wanted to speak with you."

Cren-Jaez looked intently at the old priest. He saw tears in his eyes, reflecting off the dim light in the room.

"I believe I know who the Castus is," Thaniel said.

Cren-Jaez stood, nearly upsetting the little table that was between them.

"Where is he?" he asked, reaching instinctively for his sword. "We must secure him immediately."

"Never fear, my friend," said Thaniel, grasping the warrior's arm. "He is in the best of hands."

"Where is he?" asked Cren-Jaez, a bemused expression on his bearded face.

"Here," said Thaniel. "He is among us now!"

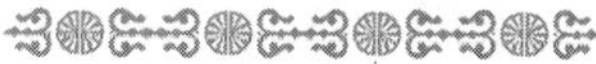

"How long have you been a fighter?" Kierlin asked.

Jeffrey looked at her across the little oven.

"He isn't exactly a fighter," said Ethan. "But he's willing."

Jeffrey gave Ethan a harsh "thanks a lot" glance.

"My family has an inn," he began. "Or rather they had one. But this sword that caused such a fuss shall one day be my avenger."

Ethan winked at his cousin.

"If he doesn't kill himself by charging under a low hanging limb!"

Jeffrey gave Ethan yet another harsh glance.

"Must be nice to have such a dream," Kierlin said, ignoring Ethan's comment. "And such a family. I never really got to grow up with a family. Though I have a wonderful cousin—although he talks a bit too much!"

Ethan smiled at her.

Jeffrey looked at Ethan and Kierlin, two cousins whose fathers had been murdered by the same enemy that had killed his own mother. He could see the resemblance around the eyes. He was glad they had found each other. He thought for a moment of his own family. His mother dead. As far as he knew, his father was dead as well. All of them had suffered tremendous loss because of this struggle. Jeffrey knew why he was committed to seeing this through—he wanted to avenge his parents. But these two—there was more in their hearts than revenge.

"Why are you here, Kierlin?" Jeffrey asked.

Kierlin laughed.

"That should be evident," she said. "Blackheart must be stopped."

"But is that the only reason?"

"Is there another?" she asked.

"To kill those who killed your father."

"Jeffrey, we are here because we believe in what we are doing," said Ethan.

"In many ways we are like you. Our families were devastated by this hideous evil. But beyond that we are loyal to One whose return is foretold, and whose prophecy must be fulfilled. We are dedicated to the Armor's return both to honor our King and to honor the memory of our fathers—not merely avenge their deaths."

Kierlin gave Ethan a hug and a "well said" look.

"Not to mention your mother," she added. "Welcome to the fight!"

Jeffrey turned his head and brushed away a tear.

"This never was my fight," he said, his voice beginning to tremble. "She never asked for this."

"But it was to be," Kierlin said. "And now you are involved in a noble cause."

"Noble cause?" Jeffrey said, smirking. "I'm tired of noble causes. My family is ruined for this noble cause."

He stood and began pacing angrily. He was mad but he didn't know why. Just a moment ago he was in good spirits, enjoying the company of Ethan and his cousin—this strange fighting girl who talked of great causes like some hero from Humus mythology. Maybe he didn't like the fact that she was so sure of what she was doing here and he was not? Or maybe it was just that she was so much better at this than he was? Whatever it was, he was becoming angrier by the minute.

"What am I doing getting mixed up in a foreign civil war anyway? This is your problem, not mine. I'm going to let Thaniel have the coin. From now on my only cause is finding my father and avenging my mother!"

"Revenge is best left to those who can handle a weapon," Kierlin said. "You'll be killed in a moment."

Ethan cautioned his cousin to stop.

"Maybe that would be best!" Jeffrey shouted.

His words were so loud they could hear a faint echo in the cave.

"Anyway leave me alone," he said, sitting down again. "You fight your wars and I'll fight mine!"

Chapter 16

Talking Coins

"JEFFREY, Ethan, Kierlin—a word please."

Thaniel stood over the trio, hands on his hips. They all turned to the old priest, who motioned them to follow him. They walked up the incline that led outside. Once out in the open they continued a bit to a clearing, about a quarter mile from the cave's opening. A very still pond was nearby, so clear that the reflection upon it was like a mirror. Jeffrey breathed the clean early morning air in deeply. It felt good after the confinement in the safe but smoky hideout. He was still seething from the conversation with Kierlin and Ethan.

"We need to talk," said Thaniel, sitting on a fallen tree,

The others made themselves comfortable on the ground.

SQUAWK!

"Corinth?", shouted Jeffrey. "Where are you, boy?"

The others looked in amusement as the black bird glided down from a very tall tree and right into Jeffrey's open cloak. Kierlin laughed out loud at such a pet.

"I was wondering if you had managed to follow us," Jeffrey said, momentarily forgetting his anger. He fed the bird a morsel of food he had brought up from the cave. "Here you go."

Corinth took the food and flew back to his perch.

"That greedy animal," said Jeffrey. "Always thinking of himself!"

SQUAWK!

They all laughed and enjoyed the comedy of the moment. Jeffrey related several stories of Corinth's bad habit of snatching things from people and hiding them away. His favorite story was of finding a gold button emblazoned with the Shadberry royal insignia following the visit to the inn of a rather persnickety royal who had been very particular about his new coat.

"Wonderful story," said Thaniel. "But now I need to talk with all of you."

The young trio looked up at Thaniel, who stood as if making a speech in Edenshore's parliament. His countenance was the most serious that Jeffrey had ever seen. They looked at each other in bewildered silence.

"What is it, Uncle?" Kierlin finally said.

Thaniel looked around and made sure they were quite alone. He began pacing as he spoke.

"My dears," he began. "As you know, we are now on the verge of recovering all of the coins. It is becoming critical that we remain alert and vigilant. Our enemy has tried on numerous occasions to take the coins and thwart the prophecy. He knows that his time is soon up and that the King's return is imminent. He also knows that these coins mean the difference between victory or destruction. Very soon we must go after the remaining coin."

"My father's?"

"Yes, Kierlin," said Thaniel. "*Balteus*—your father's coin."

"But we don't know where it is," Kierlin protested.

"Ah, but he told us all we need to know," said Thaniel. "In a way that only myself or one of his brothers would understand. In that letter he wrote you. It contains a clue as to where he hid that last coin."

Kierlin was puzzled. For years, she had never been able to figure out the cryptic message. Yet Thaniel had only just read the note and understood all? Still it made sense in this business that her father would have spoken from the grave—as it were.

"We'll find that coin when we speak with Jaarad—the Divinitus," said Thaniel. "He'll be able to tell us where to look."

"Jaarad?" asked Ethan.

"Last of the seers," said Thaniel wistfully. "Or at least the last of the true seers of Nova Fannum. He'll help us out immeasurably. And I'm sure he will want to speak with you, Jeffrey."

"Why me?" Jeffrey said.

"Why to help you vanquish our enemy, of course."

"*Our* enemy?" Jeffrey snapped, glaring at Kierlin.

His head was swimming and he found himself getting angry once again. He was no fighter! He had just been told as much by this silly girl dressed in warrior's garb. And now he was to join the fight with new vigor?

"You mean *your* enemy! I was facing a crooked lawyer, a one-eyed scoundrel, and his very human friends. And I think I can manage them eventually. But *your* enemy? Coins of power—great darkness. I have no argument with the power you are contesting. And now my mother is dead because of this mess. I just want to find my father alive!"

His words echoed angrily in the meadow. Jeffrey blushed with embarrassment. He calmed himself down and continued speaking.

"I mean all due respect and best of luck to Nova Fannum and all but..."

"Jeffrey, haven't you yet realized that your enemies and mine are the same?" Thaniel said, sitting down. "I speak of an enemy of all that is decent. True, the humans you encountered thus far are evil men—but they are unwitting pawns in the hands of a far greater threat."

Thaniel stood and looked at his reflection in the pond.

"Yes, you can defeat your human foes. But you won't avenge your mother. And your personal revenge won't stop the enemy of which I speak. Blackheart's name speaks well of him. His heart is black with sorcery and dark powers. And he will stop at nothing to destroy you and recover the coins."

"Destroy me?" yelped Jeffrey. "I am not at war with this Blackheart!"

"I'm afraid, Jeffrey, that the war is with all men," said Thaniel. "And you are quite in line for destruction. Even if they recover all of the coins you must die. Don't you see that Blackheart's appetite for conquest is unchecked? After Nova Fannum is secured, he will be unstoppable and Humus too will fall...and all lands."

"But why?" asked Jeffrey. "I don't know these people. I only came to help my father. I ended up losing my mother and the inn. If there is a chance I can walk away from this and find my father then maybe I had better do just that. I'm not here to get mixed up in some religious war from your world."

Thaniel sighed and reached into his cloak, pulling out the familiar pouch of coins. He held the pouch for Jeffrey to see.

"I know that they seem like a trifle," Thaniel said. "To you this must all seem a terrible nightmare. But to we who understand, these coins represent the destiny of everyone who loves decency and all that is good."

Jeffrey snatched the pouch from Thaniel. Ethan stood up, ready to grab the coins and fight Jeffrey if need be. Jeffrey shook the coins so that the jingling could be heard by everyone.

"These coins, including the one my grandfather bought," he said, emptying the pouch into his hands. "I wash my hands of them!"

Jeffrey held the coins out for everyone to see. Ethan looked at Thaniel and shook his head. Kierlin kept her eyes on the coins. Satisfied that he had made his point, Jeffrey began to pour them back into the pouch; but he noticed a strange look on all of their faces—Ethan, Kierlin, even Thaniel—were all staring wide-eyed at his hand. He really had made his point, he thought.

Then he looked down at the coins—they were glowing in a curious, purplish haze!

Jeffrey's jaw dropped as he dropped the coins thinking they might burn him. The coins scattered on the ground and immediately stopped glowing.

Thaniel and Ethan couldn't believe their eyes. They looked at the coins and then each other.

"Uncle, he couldn't possibly be…," began Ethan.

"Of course he could," said Thaniel, tearing up in his eyes. "And is!"

Jeffrey's eyes were fixed on the scattered coins. Thaniel came to him and placed a hand on his shoulder.

"Jeffrey, do you see now that there is more to this than a mere religious war?" Thaniel asked. "This is a battle for the souls of men. It is a war that will determine destinies for many millennia.

And like it or not you are already mixed up in this. The question is whether or not you will fight."

"I told you, Thaniel," said Jeffrey. "This is your war."

"Pick up the coins, lad."

"Are you kidding? They'll burn me or something."

"Quite the contrary," said Thaniel. "Now pick them up."

Jeffrey looked at Thaniel.

"You must trust me, lad."

Jeffrey sighed and reluctantly did as he was told and the coins once more began to glow. Jeffrey's eyes never left the eerily glowing coins in his sweaty palm.

"Why do they glow?" he asked.

"Because they are speaking, Jeffrey," said Thaniel. "They speak when empowered."

"By what?"

"Not by what," said Thaniel. "By whom."

"By whom?" Jeffrey repeated.

"By the one who was foretold," said Thaniel.

Kierlin started to say something but Ethan stopped her.

"But you empowered them also," Jeffrey said. "In the mine you became invisible. And Ethan's coin allowed him to play on the minds of men..."

"Yes, they will respond to whoever holds them, to a degree," Thaniel explained. "They respond to one's belief in their power—or rather belief in the One through whom their power is derived. But they only speak when you hold them. Did you notice that? You see, I understand the coin's power and can use it as needed. As can Ethan. As unfortunately can Blackheart or Phaesus. That is why they fear the coins. Remember Jack's reluctance to hold the coins? Even Pickworth was intimidated by them. But the coins have never before spoken to anyone as they are now speaking to you."

Jeffrey's face wrinkled in confusion. He held the glowing coins up to his ears as if trying to hear something.

"Speak? I don't hear anything."

"The light, Jeffrey," said Thaniel. "They are speaking through the light. Just as our Great King is of the light. I'll show you."

He took the coins from Jeffrey and they stopped glowing. He showed Ethan and Kierlin. Ethan took the coins and held them. Nothing. Jeffrey couldn't help but smirk at Ethan's attempt. Kierlin declined a turn. Then Jeffrey took the coins back and they immediately lit up again.

"See? The coins speak to only you."

"I don't understand," said Jeffrey, growing weary of where Thaniel was taking this conversation. All the while he kept his eyes on the coins. "I held these before and they didn't do this. Why should they start talking now?"

"Because it is time," said Thaniel. "That is why they have started talking. It is the time being fulfilled—called the prekaros."

He looked at Ethan and Kierlin.

"The time is much closer than I realized."

Thaniel motioned Jeffrey closer to the pond. They stood and looked at each other in the reflection of the water.

"Do you remember what I said about these coins?" asked Thaniel. "Life and death are in their destiny. There is a prophecy, Jeffrey. We were appointed to find the coins and place them in the proper hands—the one called the Castus—who will precede the Great King's return by putting on the armor and..."

He sensed the boy's confusion.

"Anyway boy, all this must be done before Blackheart gets his hands on them."

"Yes, and?" asked Jeffrey, very suspiciously.

Thaniel took Jeffrey's hands in his and knelt before him.

"In the *proper* hands," he whispered, his teary eyes were closed as if in prayer." And in the proper place the coins would tell us who the Castus is..."

After a few seconds Jeffrey pulled his hands back in revulsion. He looked at Thaniel who was now staring at him with a strange, albeit pleasant expression.

"What?" asked Jeffrey. "What are you looking at? Is something wrong with me? Why are you acting so strangely?"

Thaniel pointed to the pool. Jeffrey looked at his image—he saw a somewhat gaunt, bruised, young man with a bruise on his forehead. Thaniel looked in the water as well and saw something quite different. Jeffrey's eyes met Thaniel's in the reflection.

"What do you see, Jeffrey?" Thaniel asked.

"I see myself," he answered. "And I see you."

"I see something quite different," said Thaniel, staring at the boy's reflection. "Quite another person."

"Don't tell me," said Jeffrey nervously.

Thaniel indicated the boy's image which had a strange, purple hue from the coins' light and bowed to one knee, as did Ethan.

"Behold the Castus!"

It took about as much time as it took for you to read this for Jeffrey to shudder.

"What?! Wait a minute," he said, shaking his head. He handed the coins back to Thaniel and threw up his hands, pacing the ground excitedly.

"Me? The what? The Castus? Look, Thaniel, I know I got a bump on my head a couple of times back there. But I'm not crazy. Quests. Coins. Maps. Armor. Look old man…er…Thaniel. I originally came looking for my father. I now have a murdered mother and no home and still don't know where my father is or if he is even alive."

He pointed to Kierlin.

"Even she recognizes I'm not much of a fighter. And I am certainly not this "pure" one. I don't even pray to my own gods much less yours!"

Thaniel ignored Jeffrey and asked him to hold the coins again. Jeffrey declined. Thaniel took out one coin. Jeffrey sighed and took it from him, beginning in his mind to plot an escape from the meadow should it become necessary. He wondered if he could find his way back to the inn. Perhaps he could apprentice with the baker?

"Now Jeffrey," said Thaniel calmly. "I want you to look at the coin and think about the possibility that everything I have said is true. Everything. The coin. Blackheart. My brother's plea. Everything."

Jeffrey scowled in frustration.

"Consider it a kindly gesture to an eccentric old man."

Jeffrey sighed and looked at the coin again. Everything that was in him told him to drop the coin and run, yet there was something that held him. He realized it was his growing love for the old man—despite everything.

"Relax, Jeffrey," Thaniel said. "Think about it and believe."

"Believe what?"

"Consider the larger possibility," said Thaniel. "Open your mind to a much larger world than the Trout and Truffles."

Jeffrey smirked.

"Do you really believe that all of the extraordinary events that brought you here were mere coincidence?" Thaniel continued. "Do you not see a larger possibility in these things? Could not what I have said at least be partially true?"

Jeffrey stared blankly at the glowing coin.

"Is there nothing deep inside of you that yearns for the bottom of all this? Something about your real purpose?"

Jeffrey glanced at Ethan, who gave him an encouraging look, and then back at the coin.

"Could it be, Jeffrey, that you were meant to be something more than the host of an inn called the Trout and Truffles?"

Jeffrey swallowed hard, staring at the coin. His hand was trembling. "*Owner* and host," he said quietly.

"Are you the Castus?" Thaniel whispered.

Upon that question the coin's glow turned from the purple glow to a brilliant gold light, filling the meadow with a blinding display. The water reflected the light more brightly than the rising sun, and everyone shielded their eyes. Jeffrey screamed and dropped the coin. Even Corinth screeched and flew down, burying himself in Jeffrey's cloak. Upon dropping the coin, the meadow immediately returned to its tranquil dawn state. Jeffrey checked his hands, thinking they were probably burned. He then looked fearfully and angrily at Thaniel. Ethan picked up the coin.

Thaniel only smiled, nodding his head and looking upward. He then collapsed to his knees as if his heart was failing him. Jeffrey rushed to the old man's aide but to his surprise he was singing in some language he didn't recognize. Jeffrey didn't know what the words were, but he could tell from Thaniel's expression that these were words of exuberance—of joy. He then began saying "thank you," over and over again.

Jeffrey looked about for Thaniel's cup. The old man probably needed some water. Ethan searched his kit and found Thaniel's cup and dipped it into the cool clear pool of water into which they had just been staring. He offered it to Thaniel. The old man's eyes sparkled as he ignored the cup and looked at Jeffrey.

"What is this sorcery?" Jeffrey demanded.

"Nothing as cheap as sorcery," Thaniel answered excitedly. "The prophecy. As I said, the coins yield themselves to the proper hands. Your hands, it seems—even as I thought! And that is why Blackheart must see you destroyed. He is a great sorcerer. But even his black arts cannot possibly stand up to this power. As long as you hold the coins and believe in their power he cannot possibly defeat you. But if he can get his hands on the coins…or if your faith is not strong…he can still win. That is why we must recover that final coin as soon as possible."

Thaniel held the other coins out to Jeffrey before the boy could protest further.

"Don't be afraid of them, lad," Ethan said. "Take them. They shan't hurt you."

He timidly held the coins in his hand as before. The coins began shining—not the gold hue but the usual purplish color. Though fiery in color—the coins were cool to the touch. He held on to them.

"You are the chosen one," proclaimed Thaniel boldly. "You are the Castus."

Jeffrey looked at his reflection. He could see the others standing behind him. Corinth's black beak stuck out from behind his cloak. He looked at them in the water.

"But I don't feel like a Castus," he muttered.

"Now, let's move back to the reflecting pool, boy," Thaniel said. "I want to try something. Time for your first lesson."

He looked back at the others.

"This should prove interesting."

"Lessons too?" Jeffrey fumed.

They walked over to the pool. Jeffrey sighed as they turned to see the coin glowing in the water as before, radiating the now familiar purple tints. He also could make out the grinning face of Thaniel. From a distance Jeffrey looked as if he was holding some strange sort of candle—but many times brighter. Thaniel indicated that he wanted the coins. Jeffrey handed the coins back and the light vanished. Thaniel held up the coin with the sandals on it.

"Now watch!" he said.

Once more the old man disappeared! Jeffrey could clearly hear the old man speaking. Ethan and Kierlin sat down to watch. Jeffrey felt for Thaniel, who had apparently moved behind him. Suddenly Jeffrey was pushed from behind and found himself soaking in the pond. Ethan and Kierlin burst out laughing. Corinth shrieked and flew to the nearest tree limb. Thaniel reappeared, smiling at the very wet Jefford.

"Very funny," said Jeffrey, climbing out of the water.

"I only wanted to demonstrate how one might surprise one's enemy when in possession of the coins," Thaniel explained.

"Can you teach me that trick?" Jeffrey said excitedly, taking Thaniel's hand as he climbed the low bank.

"First of all Jeffrey, it is not a trick," corrected Thaniel. "Second, it cannot be taught. It is something you must compel from within."

"From within?"

"You must believe in the coin—or rather Who the coin represents—if you are to realize its potential. You must compel all the power of the coins if you are to stand against the sorcery of Phaesus and Blackheart."

He smiled at the dripping boy.

"Now, hold up the coin," Thaniel said gently, "and concentrate—but not too much. Just think about the possibility of becoming invisible."

Jeffrey took the coin and it immediately glowed. But when it became apparent that he was not becoming invisible, he became frustrated and berated the whole idea. *This old man is driving me crazy*, he thought to himself.

"Jeffrey, please! You will need the power of these coins to have any chance of surviving; to have any chance of thwarting the greatest evil ever."

Jeffrey looked at Thaniel with a bitter look. Why must he always bring this great cause into it? Still, he held up the coin as instructed.

"Doesn't matter how you hold it really," said Thaniel. "As long as it is in your possession—on your person—you can command its power. Now, think about becoming invisible."

"Rather a strange thought," said Jeffrey. "I have never before been invisible."

"Think about it and believe."

"OK, I'm thinking and believing and nothing is happening."

"Jeffrey, belief must be sincere," Thaniel said. "Your attitude cannot possibly allow you to truly believe. You must lose yourself in this. You must believe that this coin represents something awesome—something holy—and that this power is available to you by that sacred authority."

Jeffrey held the coin for another couple of minutes.

Nothing.

He sat down with the coin.

Nothing.

He spoke to it.

Nothing.

"Don't try so hard, Jeffrey," said Thaniel after a while. "Let's put the coin away. It will come to you when the time is right. Then it's a matter of heart."

"When the time is right?" Jeffrey whined. "Great. The enemy will be closing in and I'll be standing around with a coin in my hand trying to become invisible."

"Very unlikely," said Thaniel. "You will draw from the coin's power when your focus is on others and not yourself. You see, Jeffrey, you want to become invisible so you might take revenge. Restore your father's good name. Your motivation, while understandable, is selfish and impure. The coin will never respond to such an attitude."

"Well it certainly responded to the whole me-being-the-Castus thing," Jeffrey sniffed. "So it makes a target of me but won't protect me?"

"Give me the coin, Jeffrey," said Thaniel. "We'll practice later. And perhaps when I have laid out the remainder of the story you will be encouraged with a different attitude to which the coin will respond. Jaarad will instruct you. He is a master at coaxing the coin's power."

"Jaarad again?"

"Jaarad," said Thaniel. "He intimately knows the power behind the coins and how to coax them. He will teach you to handle the coins as a great weapon for good, until we obtain the final coin and hold the armor intact. He will also teach you how to wield that Sauren sword of yours in the tradition of your great ancestor. Jaarad lives in the Crassus mountains in the Divinitus Shrine."

"The Crassus?" asked Jeffrey. "Those can't be crossed."

"Who said anything about crossing them," Thaniel said. "Jaarad lives in a castle carved out of the solid face of a mountain. He is the last of a noble line of great seers—the Divinitus—and created this refuge in the Crassus as a place of meditative refuge. Now it serves as a refuge until Blackheart can be overthrown."

"They built a castle out of rock?" asked Jeffrey doubtfully. "How could he…"

"Jeffrey, there are great powers and great things that you know very little of," Thaniel said. "Such as the coin you held in your hand. It has enormous potential. But it yields its power only to the deserving or the knowledgeable."

Jeffrey looked down at the coin that Thaniel had returned to the pouch.

"Invisible," Jeffrey muttered to himself. "You can do it? Why not I?"

"You hold it in ignorance," Thaniel said, as they began walking back to the Servatrix hideout. "But be encouraged. Every day you are increasing in knowledge. That is why it speaks to you. Until you had knowledge of the coin's true nature, it could not respond to you. That's why it never spoke when you held it at your inn."

"But…"

"And once you have knowledge, you are lacking only one other thing—the power of sincere belief. There is nothing more powerful. Especially in the hands of the Castus. And once you have all of the coins, your power will far surpass my own.

Knowledge is powerful. But belief is unstoppable. But now we must go to Jaarad."

As they walked back to the cave an overwhelming sense of fear gripped Jeffrey. What was he doing in this mess with a crazy old man, and magic coins, and such? It was time to bring this sickening episode to an end. Perhaps his father was back at the inn now awaiting his own return. And this Castus business?

"Please sir, let me go home," Jeffrey said, sitting up. "I am the son of an innkeeper. I cannot be this Castus. I will not be! I am neither warrior nor hero."

"I must tell you, Jeffrey," said Thaniel. "You have heard only a portion of the story. But this I am sure of with all that is in me."

He stared into Jeffrey's gray eyes.

"The coin spoke, lad. It is destiny. Why you? Who can say? But without a doubt you are the one to reassemble the six coins before the Great Time—and to reclaim in the name of the great King the Armor of Nova Fannum. We have five of them—and we're soon in possession of the sixth."

"And suppose I do not?" Jeffrey snorted. "Suppose I leave this nonsense to another Castus and return to await my father and rebuild the inn and forget about it all."

Thaniel sighed.

"There is but one Castus—and you are he."

"And suppose I refuse?"

Thaniel stopped walking. Ethan and Kierlin watched as their uncle closed his eyes and was silent for a moment or two. Then, as if prophesying he began speaking.

"If you fail to live up to your destiny, then, Jeffrey, a great evil will befall us from which all that is pure will never recover. Blackheart's appetite for power grows daily. He beckons a darkness that he wishes to unleash on all of creation. A darkness—the likes of which has never before been unleashed—will emerge with great power and permanence and pervasiveness.

"A perverse alliance grows as well. Vile creatures are gathering in support of Blackheart as Phaesus creates an army of horrible creatures that have not been seen in eons. Wicked monsters. Nightmarish creatures. Unimaginable beasts. And as to your little world and your little inn—even unto all of Humus—they too will be swept up in its horrible grasp. All that you hold dear will be swallowed in darkness and occupied by creatures who have not seen the light of day in many years."

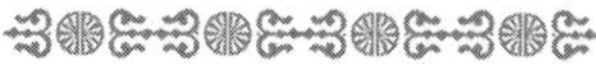

High above them, shielded by the thick leaves, if one was looking very sharply, one might have seen a small, dark form seated on a branch. Sestrin watched the group as it made its way back toward the Servatrix underground sanctuary. He smiled, sensing his master's reading of the situation through his hidden perspective. Phaesus must be pleased. Having heard and seen all through Sestrin's discreet spying, Phaesus had discovered not only where the Servatrix were hiding, but he now knew the one person who could prove catastrophic to all their plans. He would report to Blackheart that he knew the identity of the Castus—and that he would destroy both he and the Servatrix at first opportunity. He would also see to Jaarad…

"Thaniel!"

"Kreelin! We wondered what became of you!"

The old Sauren, former archivist for the Sauren king and now a fugitive with a price on his head, greeted Thaniel warmly. Ethan and Jeffrey were glad to see the former enemy who had helped them escape the Sauren tower at Mt. Sabrek. Kierlin was taken aback to see a sworn enemy in fellowship with some of her own.

"I arrived earlier and came to find you," said Kreelin. "Though the Servatrix posts were most unbelieving of my story, as you can imagine. I was finally recognized by one of their officers as having been with you in the escape. Humans!"

"We're glad to see you, dear friend," Thaniel said, hugging the cloaked and hooded creature. "I can see by your red eyes that you are glad to see us as well."

"I'm glad to see anyone," Kreelin said. "Lorogos has a price on my head and Sauren bounty hunters are quite relentless."

"Never you worry," Thaniel said. "We shan't be in Sauren territory much longer."

"I don't know if that's a good thing or a bad thing," said Kreelin, as they entered the Servatrix cave and began the long, slow descent.

"Nor do I," muttered Jeffrey, who was bringing up the rear.

PART II

NOVA FANNUM

Chapter 17

THE DIVINITUS

THE next few days seemed a blur as the Servatrix worked hard to bring together the supplies needed for the journey to Jaarad's stronghold in the Crassus Mountains. Thaniel was to lead the expedition which would take Jeffrey, Ethan, Kierlin, and Kreelin, as he so dramatically put it, to speak with "the heart of wisdom before confronting the heart of the beast."

Cren-Jaez offered a troop of his finest warriors to see the group to the frontiers of Humus, all the way to the edge where the misty mountains began. He warned of Sauren scouting parties in the area. Thaniel declined graciously, believing the more light of foot the better. With Lorogos still stinging from the recent defeat dealt him in the loss of both the coins and the Sauren sword, the subtler a party, the better. And once they began crossing the mountains, the narrow passes would be better served by stealth than security.

Jeffrey still had it in his mind that he could always quit this venture. Yet, the prospect of actually traversing the mountains which had been the stuff of legends—a feat never before done by any known citizen of Humus—he couldn't help but be enticed. He sat next to Ethan that last night before they departed. They were both thinking about what lay ahead, and the prospects of what was at stake.

"You still wondering what happened to your world?" Ethan said, eating a piece of dried venison.

"What world?" Jeffrey answered smiling. "My world is gone. But I find myself wanting to go back to nothing, rather than continue in this quest that has taken control of my life. One day I'm Jeffrey Jefford, son of an innkeeper. The next day I'm Jeffrey Jefford, the Castus and forerunner to the Great King of Nova Fannum."

He shook his head.

"I don't know if I can do this, Ethan," he said, looking up from the cup he was drinking out of. "I don't know how to be this Castus. I don't know what to do."

He teared up. Ethan pretended not to notice.

"Jaarad will help you," said Ethan. "When we get to his place in the mountains he'll reveal much more. He is very wise."

"Right," said Jeffrey with a sigh. "The Divinitus. More words he'll give me. Ethan, what good is a weapon to fight a war that my heart isn't in?"

Ethan looked at his friend. He placed his hands on his shoulders.

"Jeffrey I don't understand all of this myself. But this much I know. I believe you are the Castus—someone my father would have died for. And I also know this, Jeffrey. I would die for you too; because somehow it's right. And because you are my very best friend."

Ethan got up and walked away. Jeffrey watched as the young man disappeared into the darkness of the cave. He wiped away the tears in his eyes as the weight of the burden seemed to crush him. He stood up and looked around.

Here and there were different fighters, busying themselves for the struggle, checking their weapons and supplies. To his left was Thaniel, speaking with Cren-Jaez. Standing alone with his thoughts was Ethan, whom he was beginning to love like a brother. All of these people were engaged in one way or another in one thought—the great quest of Nova Fannum. And Jeffrey realized that they were depending upon him.

He looked up.

"I've never prayed to you before," he whispered. "I hardly pray at all. But Thaniel says that you are a real King who hears and responds to prayer. So if somehow this is all real…if I am this Castus…then please show me that it will be all right and that I will know what to do. Because right now I'm lost in this."

He glanced at Thaniel, across the area, his face lit by the many lanterns.

"And I don't want to let my friends down who are willing to die for me and this cause they see as so worthy. Please, king of Nova Fannum, see me through this. And help me to be worthy of all these things and show myself strong. Let me be worthy…"

"Jeffrey?"

Ethan was standing next to him. Jeffrey stopped praying and acted as if he were stretching and yawning.

"Were you praying?"

Jeffrey turned to Ethan.

"No I was just…"

He smiled.

"Yes. I figured it couldn't hurt."

Ethan nodded.

"I was praying as well."

He held his hand out to Jeffrey, who took it in his own. They clasped hands for a moment. Ethan looked at him sharply.

"We are brothers now, Jeffrey," said Ethan. "And you are the Castus. And I pledge to the Great King never to leave your side in this struggle."

Jeffrey thanked Ethan.

"One more thing," Ethan added. "As I was praying the King spoke something in my heart that I believe is for you."

Jeffrey raised an eyebrow.

"You will never be worthy enough," Ethan said. "But He will always be worthy. And that is why you can conquer the enemy."

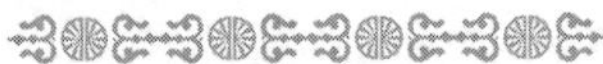

Early the next morning the group began the journey south toward the mountains that divided Humus from the legendary land of Nova Fannum. The first couple of hours were spent maneuvering the trails Kierlin knew that were used by the Servatrix. They had organized in this part of Humus after Blackheart's takeover. Their goal was to stay out of the path of Sauren sentries and bounty hunters in the pay of Lorogos.

Thaniel consulted a map that had been created by Cren-Jaez's scouts, and which should get the group safely to Jaarad, the Divinitus. From there, Jaarad would instruct them as to the proper passes through the shroud of mist that covered the mountains. There was, supposedly, a tunnel pass under the mountains that would help them cross into Nova Fannum secretly—but this was all unconfirmed.

For Jeffrey, in spite of everything, this was something of a dream. Every boy growing up in Humus spoke of one day penetrating the great mountains. There had always been talk of lands on the other side, but nobody had ever successfully made it through to the other side. Ships had never been able to round the southern most points of Humus either, because of the strange current that always flowed north and never allowed for even the most daring sailors to break through the invisible wall of physical boundaries and superstitious lore.

As the party set out, Jeffrey noticed sentries along the way. These guardian angels, as Thaniel called them, were some of Cren-Jaez's finest archers, and kept watch on the group as they continued through Sauren territory. Before long they were out of the hills which surrounded Mt. Sabrek and into more familiar territory. Jeffrey recognized certain features and knew he was not very far from the ruins of his home. A quick stop at the Jefford family vault proved worthless. Thieves had apparently broken in after word got out where the vault was. Jeffrey figured someone had watched them all along.

It was good to be riding Fortis again. Stubborn as he was, he was by far the fastest and most clever of the horses they had with them. Along with Corinth, who flew ahead from tree to tree, Jeffrey felt in good company—at least good non-human company. Jeffrey looked back at Kreelin, who had never before ridden a horse.

"How are you doing, Kreelin?" Jeffrey asked.

"Managing," Kreelin answered unconvincingly. "But this horse doesn't seem to want me on him."

"He doesn't know you," said Ethan, who was in the lead atop Cosmo. "And he isn't used to Saurens riding him."

"Well pardon me that," Kreelin snorted.

Everyone laughed.

That evening they camped near the foothills of the mountains, just shy of the mist that would soon encompass them. Though legend had it that the mist was poisonous, Thaniel explained that it was actually simply a thick, ever-present fog which separated Humus from north and south.

"There has always been mist in these mountains," Thaniel said, as they sat comfortably around the evening fire. He smoked his pipe and spoke of earlier times.

"But the idea of a poisonous border has been around since humans could imagine such things. Dangerous. Mysterious. They were not to be penetrated."

He knocked his pipe against the log he was leaning on.

"We had borders of a sort in Nova Fannum. But not because of monsters or poisonous clouds. We believed that Nova Fannum was a world to itself, and nobody ever thought of leaving the boundaries afforded by the Great King's grace."

He stopped to light his pipe.

"But when Hendras—that is Blackheart—took over, the grace lifted and, like these clouds of Humus myth, so our boundaries took on a poisonous aspect. The color lifted and the darkness descended. That bleak, colorless world now represents the threat that hangs over all of us, and the hideous crimes that they hide in my beloved land."

He sighed.

"It's a very different Nova Fannum to which I return."

"Sir?" came a voice.

It was Kreelin, who in typical Sauren fashion preferred the darkness as a sanctuary to the campfire.

"Yes, Kreelin."

"How much farther to the one whom we are seeking?"

"In three days we should arrive at the Shrine of the Divinitus," said Thaniel.

"I've never heard of that place, uncle," said Kierlin.

"Built many, many years ago," said Thaniel. "The Pallasites were an order of wise men who dedicated themselves to a monastic life and built this shrine to wisdom on the outer edge of Nova Fannum. They were the only people who lived outside of our world. Added to their mystery, I suppose. They heralded the great events and it was from this order that the King's prophet was chosen for the annual message to the nation. Jaarad is the last of these. Very wise; blind and yet seeing. A great, holy man."

Thaniel looked grimly at the others.

"And unless Blackheart is stopped he shall be the last."

"He is blind, Uncle?" asked Ethan.

"The order requires it," said Thaniel. "They give up their sight in order to see more clearly."

"A blind man will teach me how to use my sword," Jeffrey said, smirking at Ethan. "That should be interesting! So just what does he see?"

"That which is worth seeing, I suppose," said Thaniel, who turned from the fire and wished everyone a good night's rest. "And Jeffrey? The more shallow something is, the easier to see through it. I imagine he'll see through you right away."

Ethan snickered as he said good night.

That morning Jeffrey awoke with a sharp pain in his back. He rolled over and looked at Ethan, who was already awake.

Reaching behind him he felt a large pinecone that had fallen into his bedding. He threw it into the fire and he and Ethan watched in amusement as it exploded in little pops that awakened the rest of the camp.

"I wondered what was getting me," Jeffrey said. "I dreamed I was being attacked by rats or something."

"You lads go and fetch fresh water," said Thaniel, who was warming his hands by the fire. "Thank you, Ethan, for getting the fire started."

"We didn't build that," Ethan and Jeffrey said in unison.

"Kreelin built that," said Kierlin, who was packing her things. "He was up early and said he would be back in a few moments."

"Where did he go?" asked Thaniel, looking about the forest. "He doesn't know these parts."

"Foraging I believe," said Kierlin. "Anyway he took Jeffrey's sword with him for protection."

Jeffrey jumped up and looked at the place where he had left his sword. He looked angrily at Kierlin.

"You stupid…"

"Jeffrey!" That will be quite enough of that," Thaniel said.

"She gave him my sword! He just walked off with it!"

He paced around a bit.

"You better check the coins and see if they are missing too!"

"Really Jeffrey," said Kierlin. "He needed some sort of weapon. I'm sure he'll be back with it."

"Never give away my things again," Jeffrey said, glaring at her.

They sat about the camp for a minute or two saying nothing. Ethan worked to get the horses packed and ready. The sun was finally beginning to shed some light in the area. Off to the south was a grayish horizon, just at the tree tops.

"That is our destination," said Thaniel, lighting his pipe. "Those are the Crassus mountains we must enter. The Pallasites are located there."

Jeffrey said nothing, still angry. Ethan felt bad for his friend and for his cousin. But he thought Jeffrey was being a bit dramatic about it all.

"Will Jaarad be expecting us, uncle?" asked Ethan, hoping to change the mood.

"I'm sure he is expecting some communication as the time approaches," said Thaniel. "After all, he is a mystic of sorts. It will be good to see him again."

"Perhaps he can tell me where my sword is," said Jeffrey, still brooding.

"You mean this sword?"

Everyone turned to see Kreelin emerging from the woods holding a bag in one hand and the Sauren sword in the other. Jeffrey smiled immediately and then became embarrassed for his behavior. He didn't dare look at Kierlin. Ethan smiled at Jeffrey.

"Well, well, the thief returns to the scene of the crime," Ethan said.

"Quiet, Ethan," Jeffrey whispered loudly.

"Were you concerned about the sword?" Kreelin asked. "I surely didn't mean any harm."

"No harm done at all, Kreelin," said Thaniel. "What have you there?"

"Mushrooms! These make an excellent steak and will provide just what we need to make the trip today. We Saurens are excellent foragers."

Jeffrey sheepishly took the sword from Kreelin's hand and nodded a thank you for returning it. Within minutes the Sauren prepared a wonderful meal of grilled mushrooms, brown bread, and hot tea. Everyone was quite content. They enjoyed the peace of the forest, a warm fire and a full belly for several minutes. Then Thaniel announced it was time they started off. Jeffrey felt like he could have stayed there all day long. Within minutes Kreelin managed to remove every trace of a camp ever having been there—another skill of the stealthy Sauren types.

For the remainder of the day they continued their southern trek, getting closer and closer to the mountains that both compelled and cajoled them. The mist was beginning to show itself now, lapping at the legs of the horses. Jeffrey had seen such mists on lakes before, but never had he ridden into one that was becoming increasingly dense. At one point in the long ride Kreelin and Jeffrey rode close to each other.

"Kreelin tell me something," Jeffrey said.

"Yes, what is it?" the Sauren answered.

"Why do the Saurens want this sword so badly?"

Kreelin was silent for a moment.

"You see, Jeffrey, that sword is a part of Sauren history—Sauren pride," Kreelin began. "It is as important to us as…well as the armor is to Nova Fannum. And there was great magic invested in that sword by the first Sabrek."

He laughed.

"Or so they say. The legend says that when the sword and crown are once more united, the Saurens will subdue all of their enemies. Anyway, Lorogos will never feel like a true Sauren with a mandate to conquer until he can take that sword into battle. He has sworn to rise up against the humans and destroy them—drive them into the sea or mountain caves. But until he has that sword which your ancestor took from the Sauren king, he will never feel that he has the legitimacy to strike out."

For the next hour Kreelin spoke of Sauren history and various cultural and artistic interests he held. Jeffrey was astonished that a creature from so brutal a people was in many ways well-read and even refined. He remarked on this very thing and Kreelin laughed and nodded in hearty agreement.

"That's why I was made archivist," Kreelin said. "Not much of a warrior in me but something of a thinker. It is the Sauren way to devote one's talents to the nation—whatever it may be. Saurens such as I are relegated to books and keepsakes, catalogs and accounting. Thus I became Royal Archivist and Keeper of Sauren Treasures. Not a bad title. Plus it allowed me to study the historic relics I had always read about."

He looked about as if being watched.

"But now I am making history. I am a fugitive with bounty hunters after me and Lorogos after this sword and crossing these mountains into who knows what."

Kreelin scanned every tree, every bush, and every rock, seeing shadowy phantoms behind them all—and all of which looked like Lorogos. Jeffrey laughed aloud at Kreelin's fussy attitude.

"Don't worry about Lorogos," he said reassuringly. "He would never venture this far from Mt. Sabrek. And anyway we'll soon be completely covered by this mist."

"Except for one thing, young Jefford," said Kreelin, taking little comfort in the mist which now rose up to their saddles. "Sauren eyes can see in mist—it's bright lights that we cannot tolerate. The mist will not hide us."

Jeffrey nodded his head in understanding.

"In that case we'll just have to take care of Lorogos the old Humus way—with cold hearts and cold steel," he said, patting the sword that was on his saddle.

"And foolish human pride," Kreelin said under his breath nervously. He sighed and added, "I shall never return to Sauren lands again."

Over the next two days the group began a slow, steady ascent. The landscape transformed from woods, streams, and ancient trees to smaller bushes, wildflowers, and rocky ground. They had entered the foothills of the great Crassus peaks. Thanks to the supplies brought by Kierlin, and Kreelin's knack for disappearing into the forest from time to time and coming back with some delicacy, they never went hungry. And water, though becoming increasing scarce, was still in ample supply.

But the most notable feature was the fog, which was increasingly difficult to see through. Jeffrey looked back over the miles they had traveled. It might be the last semi-clear view of his land he would ever see again. He had now gone farther south than any other Jefford in history, so far as he knew. His father would be proud if he was here. He looked over the rich, forested land of Humus and dreamed of going back one day in triumph. He also thought of the threat which Thaniel insisted imperiled it all. It was this threat that kept him moving.

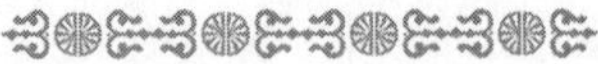

"This is it," came Thaniel's voice in the mist which now completely engulfed them. "This is it. The trail in three directions. From here I'm afraid we'll have to lead the horses. The trail is very tricky."

The others dismounted, each holding his own horse by its rein. Within the mist that covered them Jeffrey could just manage figures but was unable to discern detailed features. It puzzled him that Thaniel could see anything.

"How can you tell this is the right trail?" asked Jeffrey, whose face and arms were scratched up by low-hanging limbs and branches. "I can't see a thing. What do you see, Kreelin?"

"Believe it or not there are three old trails leading upward," he said. "Steep but manageable."

"Kreelin has Sauren eyes that are suited for this sort of thing," said Jeffrey. "How is it that you can see in this soup?"

"You forget, Jeffrey," said Thaniel. "I have these coins. And one of them—formerly Ethan's coin, the helmet—leads me. It will guide one if one lets it. Jaarad would never leave instruction. He knew that whoever sought him out would have the coin to guide him and was therefore genuinely loyal to the Great King."

"The coins guided you?" Jeffrey asked with a bit of apprehension as Thaniel reached into his breast cloak and pulled out the coin pouch.

"Of course," he said. "Much more reliable than mere eyes. As I said, they speak to the one who holds them. They have been directing me all along."

He handed the coins to Jeffrey.

"And now they say that it is time for you to lead us."

"Me?"

"You are the Castus," said Thaniel. "You need to lead us by the coin's prompting. If you listen with your heart they will guide you."

Jeffrey held the coins in his trembling hand. The others watched as this exchange of authority took place. Ever since Thaniel had pronounced him the Castus he had said that this day was coming—when he should take the coins into Nova Fannum. Jeffrey swallowed hard and thanked Thaniel.

The old priest placed his hands on Jeffrey's shoulders and prayed a silent prayer. Everyone remained quiet as he spoke this blessing over the young man's life. But what difference did it make? He didn't know what to do with them!

"Some Castus," he said to himself.

He looked at Thaniel with an expression that begged instruction. The priest merely told him to stop looking outward and start looking inward—to the voice being spoken to him in his heart. Jeffrey nodded and took the pouch in his hand and began pacing about in front of the three trails which lay before them.

Jeffrey concentrated and conjured and otherwise tried to divine some sort of indication from the coin as to which direction to take. He spoke to it; nothing. He held them over his head; nothing. He even put one in his mouth; nothing. The only response he got was that of Kreelin laughing—the only creature who could clearly see what was happening in the mist.

Thaniel took Jeffrey aside while the others waited. He led him to a small opening in the woods. They sat down.

"I can't do this," Jeffrey said.

He could feel Corinth wiggling inside his cloak.

"Of course you can," said Thaniel. "It is all new to you. But you are chosen. And the Great King chooses nobody without also empowering them for the task to which he has called them. The coins speak to you for a reason—and you must learn to listen to them. Now—return to the path and make your choice. Believe in what you are doing and let the coins speak to your heart."

"But..."

"Have confidence, Jeffrey," said Thaniel, as they walked back to the trailhead. "We will follow your leading. Have faith in the coins, lad."

"The coins I have faith in," said Jeffrey. "It's me that I'm having trouble believing!"

"Jeffrey is going to take us up the appropriate pathway," Thaniel announced loudly. "Listen to him."

Jeffrey swallowed hard and turned away from the group. After a moment with his head bowed he made his decision.

"That one!" he declared, pointing to the path on the left.

"That one it is," said Thaniel.

"Wait a minute," said Kierlin, stopping the group just as they started up the path. "I know he's the Castus and all—but just a minute ago he could get nothing. Now he's suddenly making a choice? How do we know this is the right path?"

"I told you," said Jeffrey. "The coins chose this path!"

"That will be quite enough, Kierlin," said Thaniel. "Now up we go!"

And so single file, leading their horses, they went up the trail chosen by Jeffrey: Thaniel in the lead, followed in turn by Kreelin, Kierlin, Jeffrey, and Ethan. After the first couple of miles, Ethan got closer to Jeffrey and tapped him on the shoulder. He whispered to him so Kierlin wouldn't hear.

"So tell me the truth," he said. "How did you do it?"

"Easy," said Jeffrey, motioning with his hands. "I flipped a coin and the decision was made!"

Ethan laughed so loud everyone turned and wondered what was so funny.

The Crassus Mountains had always been an enigma to the people of the north. Even the bravest mapmakers of Humus could only shrug as to what lay deep within, or how far south they stretched, or what lay on the other side. Speculations were that all sorts of wild creatures, monsters, and other hideous races that had been driven out by humans long ago lived in these mist-covered peaks. These tales alone kept most of Humus at bay and added to the mystery surrounding these cloudy towers of rock.

The mountains themselves were void of animal life, though there were a few large birds—eagles mainly. Thaniel assured everyone, with little comfort, that there were indeed other living creatures in these mountains—just not the type they wanted to run into. The trees, which had been taller and straighter below, had become more piney and scrubby, with low-hanging branches that Jeffrey and the others were constantly pushing out of their faces. The land ever-changing, within a few hours even these trees became more and more sparse. And the ever-present mist was giving way to the grayish, rocky landscape that surrounded them.

By the time they had reached a high meadow, the sky was much brighter, though still draped in clouds. The trail the party followed dipped into a small ravine. The sides closed in on them as they continued on. To Jeffrey it seemed they were in a giant trenchwork, so smooth the sides of the rock on either side of them appeared. In an hour they came to a cliff that shot straight up like a granite fortress. Everyone stopped.

"Now what?" asked Ethan, looking at the imposing obstacle. "We'll never be able to climb that."

"And what about our horses and provisions?" observed Kierlin.

Thaniel looked at the rock wall.

"What about it Jeffrey?" he asked.

"I wish you'd stop saying that," said Jeffrey. "How should I know?"

Silence.

Jeffrey walked to the edge of the cliff and looked up. It must have been 200 feet or more, almost straight up. There was no way around it and the only way that seemed open was to turn back. He looked at Ethan and swallowed hard. Ethan gave him an encouraging smile—albeit a weak one.

"Now what, Castus," Kierlin asked doubtfully.

Ethan stared at her harshly.

"I have to confess something about my decision back there," Jeffrey began.

"Look!" cried Kreelin. "A tunnel in the rock!"

Ethan ran to the cliff and he and Jeffrey inspected the rocky facing. They came up short and turned, shrugging their shoulders.

"Let me help you," said Kreelin. "Remember I can see these things."

Kreelin walked to the rocky wall. Everyone thought that perhaps the altitude was getting to Kreelin as he stood with a triumphant stance. He realized they were not following him.

"Don't you see it?"

Kreelin walked toward the rocks and disappeared! An opening appeared where he had vanished, as if it had been carved in the rock for centuries. It had been so dug out that one could only see it from the perfect angle. A brilliant work of concealing something that was completely unconcealed!

"How like the Pallasite monks!" Thaniel said in delight. "One cannot see what is completely visible—just like these blind prophets who see everything! Wonderful!"

"Let's hope they build as well as they don't see," said Jeffrey, looking dubiously at the ancient tunnel.

The old shaft seemed to go on for miles. Thaniel smiled and told everyone to enter. One by one the group entered.

"There's room for all," Thaniel said. "Even the horses! But they'll have to be blinded. Put some cloth around their eyes."

"How did they do this," asked Ethan, as he entered the tunnel.

"Are they sorcerers?" Jeffrey asked.

Great laughter filled the tunnel. Everyone was startled. Jeffrey reached for his sword. Kierlin for her bow. Thaniel, however, grinned and told everyone to calm down.

"I am Jaarad, young Jefford!" boomed a voice that echoed through the tunnel.

"Jaarad?" Jeffrey managed.

"And it is not sorcery at work here, I assure you. Come, all of you, and be welcome and we shall talk!"

Thaniel laughed at Jaarad's words.

"You see?" the old priest said. "He knows we are here and is expecting us!"

Jeffrey turned to Ethan and whispered. "Pretty creepy, that voice everywhere and nowhere."

Ethan nodded.

"Well, anyway the last time I was welcomed into a tunnel I ended up with a lump on my head. This time I am taking no chances!"

Jeffrey reached into the coin pouch and pulled out a coin. He smiled and showed it to Ethan—it was Cassis, the helmet.

"At least I can get some comfort from these things," he said triumphantly, looking back at Ethan. "No lumps this time!"

That was the last thing he remembered.

"He's awake now."

Jeffrey opened his eyes and blinked a couple of times.

"I thought these coins were supposed to protect me," he moaned as Kierlin treated the cut on his head. He had been unconscious for several minutes.

"They will protect you," said Thaniel. "They protect, guide and keep. But only from external enemies. I'm afraid personal foolishness and free will cannot be overcome by any force."

"Hmph!", Jeffrey grunted. "All I know is my head is getting the worst of this adventure."

"Try using it for something more than low branches and unseen rocks," came a vaguely familiar voice, followed by general laughter.

The voice in the tunnel!

"Jeffrey, I am honored to present to you Jaarad, Divinitus of the Great King of Nova Fannum!"

Jeffrey looked to his side. There, seated on a wooden chair was a gentle-looking man in a dark blue cloak. His eyes were closed and his expression quite joyous. He was smiling at Jeffrey. He opened his eyes, and though sparkling with wisdom, they were obviously vacant—the man could not see. He held his hand out to Jeffrey and Jeffrey took it.

"This is my greatest honor," Jaarad said. "After service to the Great King, of course. We have all been waiting for this, Jeffrey."

Jeffrey nodded his head and muttered a thank you.

"I know you all must have questions, but first we must eat!"

With that he guided the group into a dining hall, fully furnished and set for a simple, but most satisfying dinner. The group was astonished that the old prophet lived so well so far from his homeland and so deep in the mountains. He explained that the princes of Nova Fannum had built and added to these quarters for centuries—ever since the office of prophet was established in Nova Fannum.

"Of course supplies don't come as regularly as they once did," Jaarad said, as they devoured the meal of mutton and potatoes. "But there are some young loyalists of the priestly lines who risk running Nova Fannum's sealed border to bring me news and supplies. I don't require much. Eat up, rest, and then we shall talk!"

And they did.

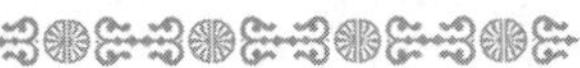

After the meal and a few hours' rest, the group assembled in a large meeting chamber next to the dining room. Jaarad was almost embarrassed at the accommodations. He took them on a tour of the palatial quarters built into the side of the cliff.

"The engineers of Nova Fannum were so clever that the sides of the structure and the exterior of the cliffs are indistinguishable," Jaarad explained. "This permits the resident prophet to be very discreet as to who enters and who does not. Makes it quite difficult to find. Even for a Sauren!"

Kreelin laughed and nodded.

"Discretion is a particularly useful thing in these foreboding times."

"Excuse me, sir," Jeffrey interrupted.

"Yes, Jeffrey," Jaarad replied, stopping the tour.

"But how do you know who you are letting in? I mean your eyes…"

"You mean because I cannot see?" Jaarad asked.

Kierlin and Ethan gave Jeffrey surprised looks.

"Well…yes sir."

"Ah, but what good is a prophet who cannot see?" he replied, smiling. "I cannot see as you see. But see I do!"

Ethan gave Jeffrey a shove for his question and the tour continued.

The tour ended in a very comfortable room that Jaarad called his Receiving Hall. The room was adorned with beautiful tapestries depicting some of Nova Fannum's great cities, as woven by some of the finest artisans in the nation. Jeffrey thought it a shame that Jaarad could not really enjoy all of the splendor that surrounded him. But somehow the blind seer was unaffected by it all. It just didn't seem to matter to him. But it bothered Jeffrey that it would matter to him were their places reversed.

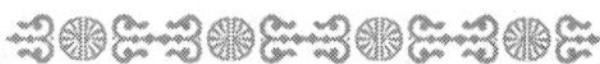

"So tell me, Jeffrey, what do you think about all of these things hurling at you at one time?" Jaarad asked.

Jeffrey nearly missed the question. He was enjoying the warmth of the cheery room in which they were now seated. The glow of the enormous fireplace reminded him of the great room in the Trout and Truffles and he drifted in and out of a dreamy state.

"Jeffrey! Jaarad asked you a question," Thaniel said.

Ethan and Kierlin snickered.

"I'm sorry," Jeffrey said. "Just thinking."

"About your home," said Jaarad. "You were thinking about your home and how much you miss the love of your family and the warmth of the fireplace you shared with them."

"That's exactly right," said Jeffrey, astonished at the accuracy of Jaarad's assessment. "How did you..."

Everyone laughed.

"Oh yes, you're a seer," Jeffrey said. "I forgot."

Laughter again.

"Ah, Jeffrey, have no shame," Jaarad said. "They laugh at you now but they love you as well. You are like a young lion—awkward at first but in the end graceful, powerful, and dangerous."

"Dangerous," Jeffrey repeated, thinking of the jibes he had taken for the bumps on the head and the awkwardness with the coins and the William Jefford outfit he was sporting. "Dangerous to myself mostly."

"Let me tell you something in all seriousness," Jaarad said, leaning forward. "You have not even begun to explore what it means to be the Castus. It's completely bizarre to you and therefore you feel unsuited for the role. And dangerous is a good word for what you are feeling. Like a child handling a sword. But hear me, lad. When the time comes you will begin to be that young lion and will stand proud, capable, and purposed."

Jeffrey glanced at the others who were silent. Ethan gave him a friendly wink and Thaniel was tearing up.

"It will not be easy," Jaarad continued. "But it will be glorious."

He leaned in and smiled.

"But anything glorious is never easy—not if it is truly glorious."

Jaarad looked at the others.

"And now, my friends, I must meet with Jeffrey and Thaniel. For the things I shall share with him are for their ears alone."

Thaniel looked at the others, who excused themselves.

"If you don't mind I'll bed down in the rocks outside," said Kreelin, looking around the room. "It's quite beautiful in here. But—pardon the indiscretion—Saurens prefer something a bit darker and a bit colder. I saw a nice little opening in the rocks which will suit me just fine."

"Very well, Kreelin," said Thaniel. "Don't stray too far. We have precious little time to hunt for wayward Saurens."

Kreelin laughed and left the room. Ethan and Kierlin followed, choosing to wait in the Great Room where a fire awaited them. Rewen, the servant who lived in the enormous place with Jaarad, provided them with fresh drink and biscuits.

While Jaarad poked at the fire, Thaniel whispered to Jeffrey.

"Jeffrey, you must listen to all that Jaarad has to say to you. His words just might save your life one day."

"Yes, and yours," Jeffrey said, smiling.

Jaarad offered a hot drink to Jeffrey and Thaniel. It was a creamy white drink he had never tasted before. Thaniel seemed quite excited. Jaarad smiled.

"You like it,?" he asked.

"It's wonderful," Jeffrey said, downing the last bit in his glass. "What is it?"

"Ah, that is Dju-mar," said Jaarad. "It is a favorite in Nova Fannum."

He settled back in his chair.

"My mother used to give me that on special days."

"We had this only on holy occasions as well," said Thaniel. "My brothers and I would sit and drink and enjoy. Wonderful times."

"Ah, Jeffrey," Jaarad continued. "Nova Fannum was such a beautiful and glorious land then. Full of grace and love and the majesty of the Great King and people who loved his law. And the colors? You think the flowers of Humus are beautiful? I have heard that the Pomley Fields near Edenshore are marvelous in the spring. But by comparison the colors in Nova Fannum are…were incredible!"

"But you're blind."

"I wasn't always blind, Jeffrey" said Jaarad. "As Thaniel told you. That small sacrifice came with the glorious call to be a seer."

"That seems unfair," said Jeffrey, looking at the tapestries. "You gave up your sight for what? To be a holy man in a mountain?"

"To see," said Jaarad. "I gave up my sight for insight. And believe me, Jeffrey, I received the better end of the bargain."

"But…"

"But we have a very short time," Jaarad continued. "And you must be off to Nova Fannum before long."

"Nova Fannum?"

"Of course," said Jaarad. "The final coin is in Nova Fannum. At least that is what the clue tells me from Kierlin's letter."

Thaniel pulled the letter from his cloak.

"Thaniel read it to me earlier," Jaarad said. "And I agree with him. I also believe that Graysil conveyed the place where he secreted the final coin before he was murdered. What is that line again?"

Thaniel read from the letter.

That which is sacred to the heart never really leaves it.

The room was silent for a moment.

"What do those words mean to you, Jeffrey?" asked Jaarad.

Jeffrey looked at Thaniel but saw no comfort or help in his eyes. He wanted to sound as if he was insightful—Castus-like, as it were. But he came up empty.

"Well they are certainly poetic words..."

"Indeed," said Jaarad. "Graysil was very poetic. But there is something more here. This is poetry with purpose."

Jeffrey sighed.

"Well if it's a location we're looking for then maybe a map would help," he said. "I bet that the hiding place is on the map that Jack showed my father at the inn."

"Possibly," said Jaarad, his eyes closed.

"Remember, Jeffrey," said Thaniel. "The map Jack took from my brother was a map of Humus and not of Nova Fannum. We believe this coin to be in Nova Fannum."

"Then how am I to know?" Jeffrey said, frustrated. "I have never seen a map of Nova Fannum much less been there in person! I have no idea where the coin would be. How can I find a place without a map?"

Jaarad looked at Thaniel.

"He gives up easily," he said.

Thaniel remained silent.

"Hold on!", Jeffrey protested. "I'm not giving up. It's just..."

"The words, boy," Jaarad said. "What do the words say?"

Thaniel read the line again.

That which is sacred to the heart never really leaves it.

Jeffrey cleared his throat as if preparing to speak before the royal court.

"OK, well. Obviously if someone holds something dear they hold it close to their heart," Jeffrey began. "So in a sense it never leaves your memory. It stays sacred…"

"Yes that's true," said Jaarad, who reached for a pipe in front of him and deftly loaded and lit it in a matter of seconds. "So where would the coin be hidden?"

"In his heart?"

"Exactly!" said Jaarad. "Or at least some sort of heart."

Jeffrey looked at Thaniel and indicated that maybe the old seer had lost his mind.

"Thaniel, you'll find an old map or two in the chest. Bring them in and study them. They have markings on them. Places that no other maps indicate. And very likely places that a holy priest would hide so holy an artifact."

He smiled and turned toward Jeffrey.

"After all, as Jeffrey so wisely said, how can one expect to find a location without a map?"

"That's not exactly what I meant," Jeffrey muttered.

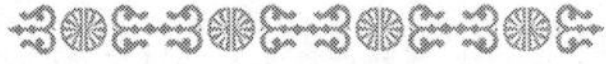

Thaniel found several old maps in a leather chest near the door. He brought them out and examined them. In a moment he buried himself in studying the leather and paper scrolls which were evidently quite old. He smiled and unrolled a scroll that revealed a map written in the Fannish script of which Jeffrey was seeing more and more.

"It's good to see Fannish again," Thaniel said, pouring over the map on a small table. "Especially in so hospitable a place."

"Thank you, priest," said Jaarad. "And now, Jeffrey, as Thaniel studies we shall talk. I know that you have been curious in this rather murky business that you find yourself caught up in. I don't blame you. But in a way I envy you. Yours is a great possibility for a great cause—something greater than yourself."

"I hope I'm up to it," was all Jeffrey could manage to say.

"Don't worry, lad," said Jaarad. "Nobody is 'up to it.' That is why it is such a great cause. If you were 'up to it' as you put it, the cause would be less than great."

"I see," said Jeffrey, settling in the chair and not really seeing at all.

"What Jaarad is saying Jeffrey," Thaniel said, looking up from the map, "is that the greatest cause—the greatest purpose in one's life—shall always be beyond his capability to achieve. That is where faith comes in. And that is what makes the cause great."

"Well done, Thaniel," said Jaarad. "He's quite right."

Jeffrey stood up and began to pace a bit. He looked around the room they were in and was still clutching to the hope that maybe he was dreaming all of this and would soon wake up.

"I don't know causes," Jeffrey said. "And I don't want to disappoint you. But I am not a hero. I'm not Castus. I can't fight well. And I'm no good at puzzles. I only found this place by luck!"

He picked a medal off a display table and held it as if holding a coin in his hand.

"The only reason we found you, Jaarad, is because I flipped a coin and made my decision! You call that being a Castus?"

"Did you find me?" asked Jaarad, his eyes closed and hands folded.

"Well yes, but…"

"And were you looking for me?"

"Yes. Thaniel told me…"

"Then the coins guided you."

"But I was not even thinking about the coins," Jeffrey protested. "I simply wanted to make a decision because people were mad at me."

"Jeffrey, the coin guided you precisely because you weren't thinking about them," said Thaniel. "You simply wanted an answer and needed one. What you don't realize is that you provided exactly what the coins require to respond."

"Desperation?" Jeffrey asked, smiling.

"Faith," Thaniel said.

Jeffrey was about to respond when Jaarad spoke up.

"And now to this business," he said. "And a black business it is, Jeffrey. I shall tell you what you need to know about Nova Fannum and the coins and the prophecy…"

"And the Castus," Jeffrey said.

Jaarad smiled.

"Yes, and the Castus."

Jaarad arose from his chair and walked to a large, luxurious looking book case with gold fittings and leaded glass. It was still curious to Jeffrey that such beautiful things were housed in a place dedicated to blind holy men. Jaarad opened the cabinet and reached in, very far, to the back of the shelf. His hand came out holding a green, leather-bound book. Thaniel smiled as if he recognized it.

"That looks like your book," Jeffrey said, thinking about the book that Thaniel had taken along from the mine in Gillingham.

"Very much like it," said Thaniel in a whisper. "But this one is more complete."

Jaarad brought the book to the table that sat between him and Jeffrey. Jeffrey wondered how the old man would read to them since he couldn't see. Jaarad placed the book down on the table.

Taking a key from around his neck he laid it on the book and pursed his lips for Jeffrey not to make a sound.

"I shall now read to you of things that happened many years ago, Jeffrey, realizing that it is all a part of the future. This final chapter of these chronicles was written hastily by Graysil, brother to Thaniel. It was written in his own hand. He left this with me in his flight from Blackheart in hopes that one day the restoration would come."

Thaniel took the book and ran his fingers over the writing, as if taking his brother by the hand. His eyes teared up at the hastily written text. It was definitely Graysil's writing—even the flourishes in some of the lettering remained despite the obvious hurry he was in when he wrote. Phaesus must have been hot on his heels when he wrote these words. Thaniel wiped away the dampness in his eyes and handed the book back to Jaarad.

"Did he have the coin with him?" asked Jeffrey. "When he gave you this?"

"No he had already secreted it in Nova Fannum," said Jaarad. "He gave me this book and the letter to his daughter Kierlin, which I later sent to Cren-Jaez. She was to have it when she was older. He had held out in Nova Fannum for many years before being discovered. He only just escaped with Kierlin before they closed in and destroyed the others in his house. Ethan's father was among them."

Jeffrey couldn't help but think of how this wickedness had made orphans of the people he had now grown close to. He especially thought of Ethan, his best friend now, with his melancholy but determined attitude.

"Now listen," said Jaarad, "I will tell you of the sacred oath taken by Thaniel's brothers, and of the mission which has befallen you; and the power and promise it holds either for a coming age of glory—or an abysmal darkness."

"Excuse me sir," said Jeffrey, "but are you going to read these words?"

"Still concerned about my sight?" Jaarad said, smiling. "This is a Pallasite Key, Jeffrey. The last one known to exist from the days of Nova Fannum's glory. It unlocks all books, all languages."

He placed the key that he had taken from his neck again and placed it on the book. This time the key glowed! Jeffrey sat back, astonished at the sight. Thaniel hushed him and before he could ask what was going on, a voice started to speak, reading the text. They all sat back and listened to Graysil's final testament.

Chapter 18

GRAYSIL'S PLEA

FROM the chronicles of Nova Fannum as recorded by the priests of the Holy One to be kept until the day of restoration upon the Great King's return:

And now this book shall sealed up be, for you, dear friend,
to hold and see
And know that long is dust, the one whose writing you
behold.
My prayer is that whoever reads shall one day help restore
with deeds
The glory of the days renowned, and righteousness of old.
A holy place, a blessed race once we were and proud;
But now a dark and loathsome land, of death, and pain
and shroud.
'Twasn't quake nor flood nor fire, that took my happy land;
But treachery and wicked counsel, craft of a wicked hand.
Now, know that darkness had not always ruled us in this
place,

For Nova Fannum, beloved land, was filled with joy and grace.
Mere words will not suffice for me to tell you of its beauty;
Of noble citizens ever holding honor as their duty.
Words I'm sure that seize your mind, of paradise I bring,
Yet, understand that none would be—apart from the Great King.
Creator, Builder, Holy One—sovereign to wise and simple,
He ruled in glorious majesty enthroned in our Great Temple.
Doubtless, you who read this now, have gods you call your own,
Of wood and mud, of tree and sky, of gold and jewel and stone.
But know this now, however bold this statement may appear:
There is but One Great King; it is He whom we hold dear.
We know not what to call him, nor have we seen His face,
He brooks no graven image and desires to rule by grace.
And yet he bids us know Him, and gives us life and land
It is by His strength we live and breathe, and by His mighty hand.
It is by His word we celebrate with sacrifice and feast,
And through His law established He His prophets and His priests.
Thus Nova Fannum gloried in the greatness of its King,
And all the peace and fortune that such holiness can bring.
For a thousand years or more in holy covenant we flourished,
Thriving in his Presence while upon His Truth we nourished.

Then one day appeared a sign both close to us and far,
Our wise men sought the meaning of a bright and morning star.
For in the skies of Nova Fannum twin lights shone, and bold;
But we who knew the prophecy, knew what must now unfold.
For it was written long ago the King would one day leave,
That we the people, by our own choice, should continue to believe.
As long as we kept holiness and covenant and love,
Our fortune would continue from a Guardian above.
And then as if assurance was the thing we needed best,
He fashioned a great armor that would keep the land at rest.
The Armor of Nova Fannum—as this holy suit was called—
The symbol of our land, our faith, in the Temple was installed.
Six pieces there were forged in prayer to make the suit complete;
Helmet, sword, breastplate, shield, belt and sandaled feet.
So long as Nova Fannum served their sovereign, it was said,
This armor would protect the land and keep it from all dread.
But how, you ask, could empty armor keep our good land free?
Because this was not mere earthly armor, though not all could see.
Each separate piece, He imbued with powers to command,

But when assembled whole, the armor meant salvation for
the land.
Perhaps the greatest prophecy of hope we were to learn,
Was the promise that our King to Nova Fannum would
return!
And so the priests kept vigil o'er the Armor day and night,
And worshiped its Creator and held him in delight.
But woe to men whose faith is weak and falters over time
For good intent has paved the way for many a craven crime.
So it was when the King's return seemed only to delay.
Our people lost their heat for Him—and lost hearts often
stray.
And to our shame and utter grief a pretender then arose,
One whose heart deceived all men—mostly his own, I
suppose.
He held the throngs with clever speech and wooed them to
his sway
Until, at last, were but a few who truly held the Way.
Starting with the temples, he tore the altars down
And replaced them with his graven image, his own
foreboding frown.
Feasts and song and sacrifice continued as before—
But now the people understood 'twas HE they should adore.
His name, though foul to speak it, was even more a shame,
He called himself the Great White Heart, though Blackheart
be his name.
But blasphemy of blasphemies upon a midnight fey
He declared himself the King returned, demanding we obey!
And with his hand-picked council—all wicked to be sure
He took the reins of power like disease that has no cure.
In reverence or fear the people worshiped this foul beast

Who demanded adoration—be they commoner or priest.
But there remained a core of people loyal to the Lord,
Who met in secret hope of holy government restored.
To Blackheart's priestly orders we feigned obeisance from the start;
We bowed to him in body as we scorned him in our heart
Yet symbol of the hope of our dear King's return remained
For the Armor of Nova Fannum stood before us, unprofaned.
And so we in quiet vigil by the Armor took our stand,
Believing by the prophecy that it would save our land.
But Blackheart through his prophets knew the Armor posed a threat
And ordered its destruction—Then paused and said, "And yet…
"Let us ascertain for our self what this Armor does foretell,
And learn a thing or two about the returning King as well."
And so his wise men searched the texts and to their utter fear
Discovered that indeed the King's return was drawing very near.
And of the Armor found they that its power was quite true;
And told all this to Blackheart to see what he might do.
He took it to the Council, their wisdom to engage,
And questioned every prophet, every priest, and every sage.
And to a man they realized that the Armor was the key;
But if Blackheart wear the Armor, perhaps they would stay free.
"If what is written of this Armor and its power all be true,
What better way to rule this land—and other nations too?

Have the Armor now brought in—its power we might discern."
He laughed in scorn and added, "We'll see about this King's return!"
And so he gave the order and his captain called his men
And they went to seize the Armor heaping sin upon more sin.
But 'ere they lay their wicked hands upon the holy prize
Six priests, all brothers, took a vow they would not compromise.
And stole away each one a coin, a symbol of the Armor's might
Six coins for six brothers—and took them in their flight.
And with each coin they took with them the Armor piece by piece,
So Blackheart's men were bested by this band of loyal priests.
And so we six were scattered—a priestly class no more
Each with sacred coin to long await the King's reward:
For a second star shall rise one day when His return is near.
Signaling an age with no more pain and no more tear.
Addendum
Lo, the stars are on the rise
Seen above with faithful eyes
And shorter grows the Blackheart's reign.
For he knows as we, that the coins must all be found,
To return the peace to all of us and restore the rightful crown.
Come then Castus, take your place, fully armored and full of grace,
Come usher in our Sovereign King and you make your Temple stand

For lo, the Castus must come first, before the starry peak
And then The King comes forth in glory, evermore to speak.
And so I write these feeble words in hopes that there is time,
And pray that it is not too late to stop this evil crime.
Whoever reads must find the coins and keep them for the King,
For His return will crush the dark and cause our world to sing.
So as my final testament, I leave this in your hand,
In hopes that you will join the quest and free our heart-sick land.
For should you fail or falter or ignore this woeful plea,
Then every land shall suffer—and no man shall be free.

Thaniel settled back, his eyes shut as if he were reliving the days of which he just heard. He thought of Graysil, his determined brother who died fighting the good fight. Jeffrey sat spellbound, hiding a tear from the others. Jaarad took the key and placed it around his neck once more.

"Nova Fannum was a wonderful place, Jeffrey," he began. "Filled with promise and prosperity and ruled by a holy King. Nobody saw him, not even the High Priest of Nova Fannum. But every year a great feast was celebrated in His name, and the Prophet, guided by the heart of the King, would speak forth the pronouncements for the upcoming year. Ah, it was glorious! Such wisdom, such purity…"

"What would he say?" asked Jeffrey.

"Blessings, Jeffrey. He spoke blessings over the land and people of Nova Fannum. He decreed a holy order and established ordinances to be kept. He conferred knighthoods and granted titles. He gave us law, Jeffrey. He gave us freedom to enjoy lives of virtue and honesty. Most of all, He taught us the law of love. As long as we kept the laws and taught them to our people, Nova Fannum flourished."

"And you were one of His priests?"

"AM one of His priests," Thaniel corrected. "And always shall be. Yes, He established the priesthood to teach the people His ways and to comfort those who were in need. My family was ordained a part of the priesthood many hundreds of years ago. I represent the last of that prophetic line, so far as we know. The rest have been hunted down and butchered or are in hiding. But there is, as you know, a resistance..."

Jeffrey smiled at Thaniel. "Yes, the Servatrix."

"They hope to be a part of the restoration for which Graysil and many others gave their lives," Jaarad said. "And they are willing to die for it as well. They would also die for you, Jeffrey. As would I and Thaniel and Ethan, I dare say."

"Die for...me?"

"Well, for the cause you represent," answered Jaarad.

"Sir, where is this land of yours?"

"As I told you, Nova Fannum is written in the heart of one who seeks after it. And to those who seek with all of their hearts, there is a way."

"But what is the way?"

"I told you, lad," Thaniel said. "Through the waters."

"But..."

Jaarad laughed aloud. "Don't worry Jeffrey. The way will be opened to you when it is time."

"Do you know the way?" Jeffrey asked Thaniel sheepishly.

Thaniel nodded his head.

"You see, Jeffrey, there were four Ways," Jaarad began. "The Way of Air, the Way of Fire, the Way of Earth, and the Way of Water. These were gateways into Nova Fannum that were created by the priesthood in anticipation of the day when the greatness of our King's love would invade Humus. He has a heart for all of His creatures."

"So you know where these places—these ways—are?"

"Of course," said Thaniel. "But Blackheart saw fit to seal the Ways in an attempt to prevent any possibility of the Castus emerging. Legend says the Castus will come from the other side. So Phaesus found the location of the Way of Fire in Mount Caerendor and the Way of the Air near your town of Dalidor. The Way of Earth was discovered early on. But there is still one way open—the Way of Water. That information was held by only my brothers and myself. I am sure none of us ever succumbed to talk or torture."

"So the Way of Water is still open?" asked Jeffrey.

"As of this moment it is," said Jaarad. "But Phaesus's agents are everywhere looking for it. And that is where you will be headed tomorrow."

"It is at the Pool of Socaren, near Brestley," whispered Thaniel, as if there might be unfriendly ears about. "About a day's ride."

"To continue," said Jaarad, "there is in Nova Fannum a great temple which housed the priests and was the home of our Great King. He was…"

"Excuse me sir, you say that you never saw Him?"

"Quite right," said Jaarad.

"Then how do you know He was there?"

Jaarad glanced at Thaniel, who had returned to his maps. "The same way we know He hears our prayers and answers them, Jeffrey, Thaniel said. "The same way that the waterfall was in the ravine, even though you didn't see it at first. The same way the writing was on the wall, though you didn't notice it."

"But you can't see Him! What good is a god you cannot see?"

"Let me ask you something, Jeffrey," Thaniel responded. "What good is a god that you *can* see?"

"Well, if you can see him at least you know that he is there."

"I see," Thaniel replied, setting the map down. "Have you ever seen a god, Jeffrey?"

"I have seen many such statues and paintings of..."

"That isn't what I asked. Those are only idols. Images. Artifacts. They are not the real god."

"But they depict the real god!"

"So someone must have seen these gods at one time or another to be able to depict them, correct?"

"I suppose so. Otherwise they would not create an image."

"Really? I would much prefer to believe in a God I cannot see, than devise one that I can scc or, worse still, have some other fellow design it for me and then call upon it. Seems much too easy that way, if you ask me."

Jeffrey wrinkled his nose.

"Now, to get on with it," Jaarad said gruffly. "There came a time when the Great King announced through the Prophet that He must leave Nova Fannum for a season. It was to be a great test for His people. He would leave behind the priests to carry on the teaching of the law and the Prophet would continue to speak for Him in His absence. The King promised one day to return upon the rising of twin stars to the north. Naturally, we were perplexed at such a notion, but our new chief priest, a great man named Hendras, assured us that our faith was being purified and that we should be better for it upon the Great King's return.

"In lieu of His Presence among His people, the King created the glorious Armor of Nova Fannum, a wonderful suit of six pieces, suspended over a golden table at the temple's center, above the Altar of Fatuma. The Armor was to be in place until just prior to the King's return, at which time the Castus should put on the Armor, ushering in The Great Age of Purity."

He looked at Thaniel who nodded enthusiastically. "The sacred stone of Fatuma rests at the center of the Temple," Jaarad continued. "And above it—suspended in the air as if held by an invisible hand—stands the full Armor. You see?"

Jeffrey nodded.

"And so a priestly order was established and set apart for the sole purpose of the Armor's keeping. The first high priest of the Order of the Armor—that sacred and ancient fellowship—had each of the coins crafted to be an insignia of sorts. They fit in special slots on Balteus—the Belt of Truth. Of course, it was not until much later—some 600 years as you measure time in Humus—that we learned the coins themselves had been vested with power to house the spirit of the armor and perform certain tasks."

He laughed a grim sort of laugh. "Now, of course, the coins convey the hope of a kingdom. That is why we are in this great contest to find that remaining coin before our enemy does."

Thaniel nodded and spoke. "Truth, Jeffrey. The belt binds the suit of armor. Just as truth is the binding force of the universe. As Jaarad said, the Armor was bound together by a belt in which the six sacred coins fit—each coin depicting a piece of the Armor—and each invested with power commensurate with the piece of armor it represented. Thus, the work of the Order began, maintaining the Armor against *that day*, the return of the King."

Jaarad turned toward Jeffrey.

"May I have the coins?" he asked.

Jeffrey took the pouch from around his neck and handed it to Jaarad. The old man almost cried as he felt the coins. He held them cupped in his hands, relishing the moment he had waited so long to enjoy. Then he took them one by one, examining them, as he held them in his bony fingers. When he was finished he handed them back to Jeffrey, saying, "Jeffrey, you must wear the Armor at the Fatuma Altar one day."

Jeffrey nodded as if he understood though he really did not. "But a caution," Jaarad continued, "The prophecy indicates that the Castus must present the Armor at the time of the return *complete*—meaning with all six coins in place on the belt." He leaned in and continued, whispering, "But if the Armor is profaned before the King's return, or if it should not be in possession of the true Castus before the appointed time, a great darkness will befall the land and all that is sacred will be lost."

He leaned back. "'Whoever rules the Armor rules the rest,' we used to say. Whoever is king in Nova Fannum when the stars peak shall reign forever."

"But what was the Armor made of?" asked Jeffrey. "Why is it so special?"

"Doesn't really matter," said Thaniel. "It is only special because the King pronounced it so. It might just as well have been made of stone. It would still be sacred because the King said so. You see, the Armor represents the King's presence—His pledge, as it were—while He is away. Through its remembrance Nova Fannum continued to prosper—or falter. But without the coins, the Armor is compromised."

"So it is magic armor!" Jeffrey said excitedly.

"Not magic," corrected Jaarad. "This is not sorcery. Blackheart's men are well versed in those forbidden crafts. This is not magic. This is something pure—something unsullied by compromise with dark powers. Understand, Jeffrey, we do not *worship* the Armor. We merely kept it as our King's guarantee and a reminder of His law and love. And so long as the law was maintained in the hearts of the priests and people, Nova Fannum did well. It was a thing of blessing that protected us, kept us…so long as it was in pure hands."

Thaniel gazed down into the fire.

"But men tend to stray, given enough time," Jaarad continued. "Hendras arose to lead us. Within time his holy mask was stripped away and his true nature emerged. While the rest of the priesthood studied their sacred texts, Hendras bargained his soul and mastered sorcery. His black arts captivated the priesthood and within time he surrounded himself with willing accomplices and claimed to be the new King. The once beautiful land became as colorless and morose as its pretender king—there is no color there now."

"Only a bleak, dull grayness," Thaniel interrupted. "The sky. The fields. The food. The people. Even the flowers are gray. Like these ashes." He stirred the fire and a cloud of ash billowed.

"The people were enchanted by his speech and taken captive by his magic," Jaarad continued. "Through Phaesus they established the holy covenant—a dark covenant more like—and forced the people to drink of an unholy communion which keeps them servile. Some sorcerer's brew and probably the same stuff he used on the Sauren king. Those who refused to partake were killed immediately.

"We saw through him right away. But the people were taken in. In time, he installed his own prophet so that even that sacred voice became his own. Apart from a few loyal holy men, the Armor lost its significance and the prophecy was lost to memory. He called himself the Great White Heart."

Thaniel scoffed, "Though Blackheart be his name!" they intoned in unison, smiling at Graysil's words.

"You see, Jeffrey, he is after the coins and will stop at nothing to obtain them. Nor to murder whoever is in his way, including you."

"But why? I have never even heard of this Hendras fellow."

"Ah, but he has heard of you," said Thaniel. "Or at least he has traced the coin to your family. He murdered your mother, and, should he discover you are the Castus, he will unleash Phaesus and his army of unholy agents in full fury. He must act quickly. He must possess these coins to accomplish his dark purpose."

"So why hasn't he simply come and taken them?" Jeffrey asked. "If he is such a powerful sorcerer."

"Blackheart is powerful indeed," said Jaarad. "But his power is limited—for the present. Without the coins, he cannot bring to bear the full measure of the Armor's power. But his strength is gathering. You've said yourself you noticed that it was getting darker in Humus? It is because the time is near. And if he isn't stopped, Jeffrey, the darkness will overwhelm all lands. Including yours."

Thaniel stood and looked toward the entrance of the room. Slowly, as if browsing some of the many books in the room, he made his way toward the door. Suddenly he rushed to a window which was open and looked outside. He thought he had seen a shadowy figure just outside the opening. After a few seconds he relaxed.

"What is it, Thaniel?" Jeffrey asked.

"Nothing, nothing," Thaniel answered. "Just checking…"

Thaniel walked back to the others, still glancing at the window from time to time, then sat down with them.

"So why can't we simply hide them until the King returns?" Jeffrey continued.

"Because, lad, it isn't enough to simply hide the Armor," Jaarad said. "It must be worn by the Castus on the Fatuma at the King's return. And what a glorious return it shall be! For when the King arrives, the color shall return to Nova Fannum and all men will finally see the Great King for who He is—and He shall become their King as well." He teared up. "And all men shall be free!" he finished, looking tenderly at Jeffrey.

"But the armor must be in place and in the proper hands," Thaniel reminded Jeffrey.

"These hands?" Jeffrey asked. "Are you sure?"

Thaniel glanced at Jaarad and continued. "The Prophet foretold that prior to the Great King's return, twin stars would rise in the northern skies. Afterward the Castus—the Pure One—would be revealed and would present the Armor to the King and then the King would return to rule forever from His temple in Nova Fannum. The Castus is the forerunner of the King, you see."

"But Blackheart wears the Armor now?" asked Jeffrey.

"No, no," Jaarad said. "Even he understands that the game must be played by the rules set forth. Only the Castus will wear the Armor in advance of the Great King. But, blasphemy upon blasphemy, Blackheart intends for Phaesus to bring the coins back and to wear the Armor, as Castus, and affirm Blackheart as king forever. After that, the real conquest begins."

Thaniel's eyes teared.

"The twin stars have begun their ascent in the north, Jeffrey," Jaarad said quietly. "And when they reach the center of the Craxuz Triangle all will be lost if the Armor is not presented to the Great King by the Castus—the Pure One. That is why we must get to that last coin before Blackheart's agents do. You see, all they need is one coin to profane the prophecy. But they need all six in order to complete their conquest. We, the priests, must present all six *with the Castus* or darkness will conquer all—first Nova Fannum, then all Humus."

Thaniel continued studying the map. Occasionally he looked up, or rubbed his aching eyes, and looked at Jeffrey and Jaarad. The three of them sat silently, only the crackling of the fire breaking the silence of the room. Suddenly Thaniel pounded the table and laughed aloud. "Of course! This must be it," seizing the map and bringing it to Jaarad as if the old man could see it.

"What is it?" Jaarad asked.

"Graysil's clue to us," Thaniel said. "'That which is sacred to the heart never leaves it,' right? It has to be the ruins of the temple on Kalul. The Sacred Heart! Remember, Jaarad?"

"Of course, the Temple of the Sacred Heart! It was built centuries ago, and abandoned later. Graysil said he loved going there to meditate and visit the island in the middle of Lake Chenior. He must have hidden it there!"

"Then to Chenior we must go!" Thaniel concluded.

"It's on an island?" asked Jeffrey.

"Actually the temple is the island," said Thaniel. "Or most of it. It's in the middle of the lake. We played there as boys."

"Brilliant conclusion, indeed," said Jaarad. "Glad all my efforts toward your instruction didn't go entirely to waste."

Jaarad walked to the cabinet and produced yet another book, this time a red leather-bound tome. He placed the book down and turned to Jeffrey.

"And now to more unpleasant matters. I must speak to you of Blackheart's intentions and the despicable methods he is using to accomplish his crime."

Jaarad took up another key that he had taken from the cabinet. This time he unlocked the clasp that held the book firmly closed. The lock clicked and the clasp was open. Jaarad opened the book. Jeffrey could see it was filled with words and pictures of strange creatures and bizarre people he had never seen before.

"Blackheart has through his dark powers and with the willing assistance of Phaesus, conjured and summoned all the creatures of darkness who have been in exile since the Great King's first arrival," Jaarad said. "Every manner of evil beast that once populated these lands and has since become a thing of myth and legend, has now become part of the gathering army of darkness."

"What sorts of creatures?" asked Jeffrey. "Surely you don't mean dragons and such things as in this book?"

"I do indeed," said Jaarad. "And far worse. It's all in this manuscript I am sending with you. This book, *The Codex Prodigium*—the book of unnatural creatures, is forbidden knowledge, Jeffrey. It will be quite an education for you—and perhaps will save your life. Knowledge can do that, you know. That is why it is essential that you learn the strengths and weaknesses of these creatures as pertains to the Armor's abilities as exhibited through the coins if you are to succeed."

Jeffrey was still having trouble with the idea of facing a three-headed cyclops, two-headed dogs, and giant spiders. It was almost laughable.

"Monsters?" was all he could stammer.

"Oh yes," Jaarad said. "Of every description—living, dead, undead—horrible beings which existed at one time or another, before being vanquished by strength or arms or banished from our world by unbelief. Many of the monsters familiar to your childhood lore are rooted in reality. It is these legendary folk that Blackheart is drawing to himself with promise of dominance once more."

"Dragons in Humus?" scoffed Jeffrey. "That will be the day!"

"A very black day, and one that will overcome a skeptical mind very quickly. And not just dragons, mind you. Even now, within the once-sacred land of Nova Fannum there are cadres of these creatures loyal to Phaesus and Blackheart: trolls and ogres, cyclops and broges. Nature itself has been poisoned, taking on a propensity for wickedness. Ants, scorpions, spiders, rats, and other mundane creatures have gained monstrous proportions and evil appetites—all in response to Blackheart's perverse powers. Nova Fannum has become Nova Profannum. These eagerly await your arrival with orders to kill you all."

He paused. "And once in place, and once the armor is compromised, they will be released over into Humus to continue their conquest in earnest. Dragons in Humus? Oh yes, lad. Dragons and more. Phaesus has engaged the Sauren king as well. They've been promised that they too will be in on the conquest—though Blackheart will, no doubt, dispose of them once the conquest is complete. The evil within him is not disposed to sharing power."

"You see, Jeffrey," said Thaniel. "The only thing restraining Blackheart is the possibility of the Castus completing the mission as the Great King's herald. If you succeed, all that is dark will be forever vanquished."

He placed a hand on Jeffrey's shoulder. "But should you fail, all that is evil will forever enshroud Nova Fannum and, in turn, all Humus. In dismal and hopeless darkness, an eternal midnight shall be established, the depths from which nothing pure shall ever rise again."

Chapter 19

PRACTICE

"JEFFREY!"

No response.

"Jeffrey, wake up!"

"He still asleep, Ethan?"

"Yes, Uncle, but not for long." Ethan looked around the room and found a quill from an ink well. He put a finger to his lips to shush Thaniel and began tickling Jeffrey's nose. Thaniel choked back the laughter as Jeffrey began rubbing at his nose, moving his hand as if a fly were bothering him. Ethan could barely contain himself. Finally Jeffrey hit himself so hard he woke up.

"What!? Get away from me!"

"Time to get up," said Thaniel, passing him a cup of very strong hot tea and herbs. "We have much to do and then we must be off."

Jeffrey sat up on the bed and stretched. He looked at Ethan's belongings—already packed for the trip. He frowned at his friend.

"Can't you just be normal?" he asked. "No matter where you are, you're always ready to leave."

"My father trained me that way I guess," said Ethan, lacing up his boots. "And my uncle. Being prepared is half the battle."

"Yeah, well a good night's sleep is the other half," Jeffrey said, laying back down. He set his tea on the table beside him. You go out and train and tell me all about it when you get back."

"Sorry lad but no time for that," said Thaniel. "Ethan?"

"Right!" The next thing Jeffrey knew, he was being dragged across the floor by his leg. He and Ethan began wrestling and started to laugh. Thaniel was enjoying the spectacle until they turned the table over, spilling the tea and breaking a glass pitcher.

"The Divinitus will see you in the courtyard," came a voice from the door. It was Rewen.

"Thank you Rewen," said Thaniel, a bit embarrassed. "We'll clean this up."

"No need," said Rewen. "It's refreshing to have youth in the house. But the seer is waiting for all of you. I have a small breakfast waiting you there as well."

Thaniel thanked Rewen again and told the boys to hurry and get ready. Within minutes Ethan and Jeffrey joined Thaniel, Kierlin, and Kreelin in the courtyard of the rocky home of Jaarad the Divinitus of Nova Fannum. After a quick meal, they joined Jaarad, who was seated near a strange-looking disc perched on top of a pedestal. It almost looked like a sundial, except that the markings were not set for keeping time.

"The courtyard," as Rewen called it, seemed more like an alleyway to Jeffrey. It was apparently in the center of the complex, but had been constructed in such a way that it only received light from the sun for about three hours of a day. It was otherwise like a prison compound, with stone walls high on four sides.

The crystal blue sky seemed like it was at the end of a long tunnel, high above them.

"Come, come," said Jaarad in a cheery manner. "Today we learn about the coins and how they will serve you!"

Jeffrey made an uncomfortable smile. He felt silly in this position of expectation and pressure to perform: like an unprepared actor setting foot on the stage. He imagined that Kierlin was halfway wanting him to fail just to teach him a lesson; that Ethan wanted him to do well but probably didn't expect him to; and that Thaniel was probably having second thoughts about it all. And what with the William Jefford outfit and holding the Sauren sword, he stood out even more—or so he felt. Some Castus!

"Over here, Jeffrey," Jaarad said, waving with his hand. "Did you bring your sword?"

"I brought it," said Jeffrey, walking over to where Jaarad was seated. "But I have never used it."

He looked back at Kierlin and Ethan.

"No matter," said Jaarad. "Give me the coins for now."

Jeffrey took the coins and gave them to Jaarad. The blind man turned his head toward Ethan and Thaniel, and gave them encouraging smiles.

"Now Jeffrey, as to the coins," Jaarad began. "These five coins, and eventually the sixth, comprise the Armor of Nova Fannum, or in lieu of, certain properties associated with the particular piece. Your coin, for example, Copis Spiritus, is associated with the sword. It will allow you to fight like a practiced warrior when called upon. It will vanquish the most vile evil when used with pure motive."

Jeffrey took his sword and swung it around a few times in mock combat.

"You mean without taking a lesson I'll be able to fight?" he asked.

"But you are having lessons right now, lad," said Jaarad. "And don't ever think you are somehow fighting. It is by the Great King's authority and by His power that you shall accomplish anything at all."

"I just meant…"

"*Copis* will create in you the ability to strike a deadly blow against evil," Jaarad said. "If you trust it you will not miss your mark."

Jeffrey smiled at the prospect of being the greatest swordsman in Humus.

"The other coins you are somewhat familiar with," Jaarad continued. "*Juaracas* the sandals, *Cassis* the helmet, *Lorica* the breastplate, and *Fides* the shield. *Balteus*, the belt of truth is as far as we know undiscovered—but we know where to look for it—thanks to Graysil's cryptic message in his letter. Now let's see how the coins respond."

Jeffrey took his stand, not really knowing what he should be doing.

"Excuse me sir?"

"Yes?"

"But what do they do? I mean—how do they work?"

Jaarad turned his head toward the others who were standing and watching from the side of the courtyard.

"Thaniel! What has this boy learned?"

"Only that the coins are available to him for the King's glory," said Thaniel. "He hasn't really explored them. Tried the *Juaracas* but didn't quite master it."

"We could see him like we see him now," Kierlin chimed in.

"Thank you, Kierlin," Jeffrey muttered.

"Well Jeffrey," said Jaarad. "Let's begin your education."

Jaarad reached into the pouch. He then selected one coin and held it up.

"*Cassis*—the helmet," he began. "This extraordinary coin represents the salvation that only our King can bring. It protects your mind and helps you to cloud the minds of others—as you saw in the Sauren tower. But," he held up a finger, "in the hands of the Castus it can also discern the minds of men and allow you to know what they are thinking. Very handy as you can imagine."

He handed the coin to Jeffrey.

"Now—what am I thinking of?"

Jeffrey's eyes got wide.

"You mean what are you thinking?"

"I just said that," said Jaarad.

Laughter from the others.

"I'll make it easy for you," Jaarad said. "I am thinking of someone in this very courtyard. I have the person's name in mind."

"Didn't I see this act in Oxbury?" Jeffrey asked, trying to ease the tension.

"You focus," said Jaarad, handing the crown back to Jeffrey. "But relaxed focus. You must allow the coin to respond to your trust in its ability."

A few moments which seemed like hours passed. The others looking on remained quiet, wondering how Jeffrey would fare. Ethan silently hoped for his friend. Kierlin was proud that he was trying so hard. And Thaniel? He just prayed. Even Corinth was quiet, perched high up on a windowsill above. After a few minutes of this, Jeffrey decided that a bad guess was better than no guess at all.

"Kierlin!" he announced.

"Wrong."

"Ethan!"

"Wrong."

"Kreelin!"

"Right."

"Hey it works," Jeffrey said, smirking.

"Not exactly," said Jaarad.

Thaniel came over to them.

"Remember what I said, Jeffrey, you must rely on the coin to do the work, but it is your faith which will inspire its action."

Jeffrey gave him one of his now familiar looks of disbelief.

"Meaning?"

"Meaning," said Thaniel, "you are trying too hard."

Jeffrey turned around in anger and kicked the dirt.

"Too hard, not hard enough. Stay focused, stay relaxed. Which is it?"

"As usual, Jeffrey, the truth lies somewhere in between," said Jaarad. "This is not something natural you are attempting. It is something from outside of you. This not your own power, but power that is available when your heart is purely motivated and when your attitude is humble."

Jeffrey looked at the blind seer.

"I was *not* spoiled by my parents!" he said.

Jaarad laughed aloud and looked toward Thaniel.

"That is exactly what I was thinking!"

"But you're wrong," said Jeffrey. "I am not spoiled."

"Who cares?" said Thaniel. "You discerned his thoughts! You see? You weren't thinking about how to make it happen—you simply believed and were open to the coin's ability."

"I'll never figure this out," Jeffrey muttered to himself. "Whatever happened was an accident. What good is some power I can't even control?"

"Control will follow," Thaniel said. "You need to get a feel for it is all."

"But..."

"Well done, Jeffrey," said Jaarad. "And my apologies for wondering about your upbringing. You are obviously not spoiled."

"Hmph!" Jeffrey said.

Kierlin was snickering somewhere from behind. He turned to see her looking at him and whispering to Ethan.

"And I am *not* spoiled!" he said, staring at her.

She laughed some more.

"And no, I do not have a girlfriend!"

Kierlin blushed.

"Probably never will, either," she said, leaving the courtyard.

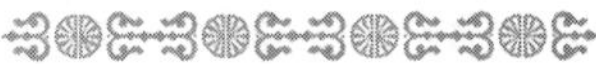

One by one Jeffrey attempted to conquer the coins and coax their power. Jaarad did his best to explain the significance of the coins and their resident powers. But the coins seemed determined to frustrate Jeffrey's efforts—however noble. Ethan stayed in the courtyard to cheer on his friend. Kreelin set out into the woods to hunt for fresh meat. Thaniel was dozing off to the side. And Jaarad continued with great patience to teach Jeffrey how the coins might be used.

Was he just stupid? Had the coins made a mistake in calling him the Castus? He wanted so badly to succeed—not so much for the cause of Nova Fannum but because so many people were now depending on him. Maybe he really wasn't trusting, as they kept saying. It seemed to come so easily for Thaniel and Ethan. Why did he have trouble believing in the coins and this holy returning King they represented?

The following day was spent on, "*Fides*, the shield, will provide protection from all external weapons and projectiles," Jaarad said. "It allows you to block or move or otherwise protect yourself from threats. You will master it in time."

Jeffrey's splotched outfit testified to his inability to stop the projectiles—in this case some very ripe fruit—from hitting him. Ethan's aim was dead-on. The object was for the coin to protect Jeffrey from being hit by anything. It wasn't working. And much to Jeffrey's frustration, Ethan enjoyed pelting Jeffrey with fruit a bit too much.

"I feel like a salad," Jeffrey said, shaking the juice from his hand.

"Yes, well if the fruit were real weapons you'd be dead," Jaarad said. "So better to take friendly fruit from Ethan than from Phaesus's deadly missiles. You'll get it eventually."

"You keep saying I'll get it eventually," said Jeffrey. "I don't have time to get it eventually. I need to know how to use the coins now."

"You will, Jeffrey," said Jaarad. "You see, these coins respond to a person who believes in their Maker and in His ability to produce through them. Faith is something that must be practiced; but when practiced becomes stronger. One day the coins will work without your giving them a notice."

"How could that be?" asked Jeffrey.

"Because faith that is practiced becomes a living thing—a river of sorts connecting you with the source of that faith. It will become second nature to you. But it takes time. And it must be practiced. Faith that is declared but not deployed is useless. So work we must!"

SPLAT!

"Stop it Ethan, I wasn't ready!" Jeffrey yelled, wiping the red fruit from the back of his head.

"Sorry!" Ethan said, laughing.

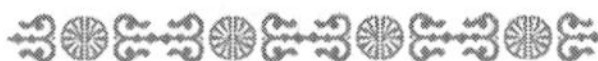

And this was how the rest of the day went. Apart from Jeffrey's brief success with Cassis, which was admittedly accidental, he was unable to attract any of the coins' powers. If indeed he was this Castus, then why weren't the coins simply falling into place? Why must he work at it if they were supposed to be at his disposal? Coin after coin saw the same frustrated and increasingly embarrassing results.

Lorica, the breastplate, was a weapon of righteousness that allowed the wearer to discern evil or danger. In Jeffrey's case, rocks were used to represent threats to his life. Jaarad's instructions were that, should the shield fail him, the breastplate would alert him to attack. The bruises on Jeffrey's chest and mid-section thrown at him by Rewen, however, said otherwise.

"Does he have to throw so hard?" Jeffrey whined, rubbing his sore chest.

"If he doesn't throw them hard you won't be motivated to employ the shield and breastplate," Jaarad instructed. "Pain motivates."

"It also hurts," Jeffrey whined.

Jaarad waved Jeffrey over.

"Let me have the coins," he said.

Jaarad took the coins and stood up.

"Thaniel, will you come over here, please?" he asked. "And Ethan, please bring Kierlin back to the courtyard."

He turned to Jeffrey.

"Now Jeffrey, I will show you the full complement of power these coins bring," he said. "And once the sixth coin is in place you will have the completed representation of the Armor of Nova Fannum. Of course the true Armor will not manifest until the day you are in the Temple."

"But sir, when does this happen?" Jeffrey asked. "I mean, if we get to Nova Fannum too early we shall have to hide out until the time. And if we are there too late it won't matter."

Jaarad smiled.

"You will be there on time," he said reassuringly. "Because you are a part of the prophecy."

"But if it's all a prophecy then it's set right?" asked Jeffrey hopefully. "I mean, I can't mess it up, right?"

"The prophecy is set," said Jaarad. "But it can still be 'messed up' as you put it."

"What good is a prophecy that can be changed?"

"A just one," Jaarad said. "It is a promise made and which will be kept, but it is a conditional promise. Surely your Mr. Pickworth talked to you about such things."

"What good is a prophecy that might not come true?" Jeffrey asked.

Thaniel placed his hand on Jeffrey's shoulder.

"And what good is a prophecy that comes too easily," the old priest said. "Remember what I told you, Jeffrey. Our King wants us to want this. He has created a possibility for you to believe in

Him and watch this unfold. If we believe and trust and do, we win. If we do not, darkness overcomes. In any case the Great King will not interfere with the outcome except in response to our actions."

"But," Jeffrey began.

"And there is Kierlin," Thaniel said, motioning her and Ethan over.

Rewen came with them, holding a cloth-bound sword. He stood silently as if awaiting further instruction. Jaarad moved to the center of the courtyard and, holding the coins, nodded toward Rewen. Without a word, the servant unwrapped the sword he was carrying and approached Jaarad. He moved behind Jaarad and raised his sword, as if to strike down upon the blind man's head.

"What are you doing?" Jeffrey demanded, raising his own Sauren sword.

The others gasped aloud as the sword came swooshing down. Jeffrey watched in terror, mouth open. Kierlin shut her eyes. Ethan turned his head away. All awaited the horrible sound of steel meeting skull. Instead they heard a clinking sound—as of steel meeting steel. The sword failed to hit Jaarad!

Again and again Rewen hacked away at Jaarad, who stood peacefully. Finally Jaarad asked Rewen to stop—not because he was in danger but because Rewen's panting was getting so heavy it was obvious he was out of breath.

"Kierlin, please fire an arrow at me, will you?" Jaarad asked.

"What?" Kierlin answered. "Shoot an arrow at you?"

She looked at the others.

"I assure you I'm quite safe," Jaarad said.

"Still, I won't," she stammered.

"Very well," Jaarad sighed. "Jeffrey, why don't we test that infamous sword of yours out. Surely the renowned Sauren sword could harm me."

Jeffrey looked at Thaniel.

"You want me to hit you with my sword?" Jeffrey asked.

"Of course," said Jaarad. "And no Jeffrey, I am not senile."

"Sorry," Jeffrey said, blushing at Jaarad's quick read of his thoughts.

"OK lad, you're wasting precious time," Jaarad said.

Jeffrey walked over to Jaarad with the sword drawn. He stood silent for a few seconds. He looked at Ethan who merely shrugged. Finally he turned to the old man and raised his sword.

"I can't," he said, lowering the sword.

"Rewen, take his sword and see what happens," Jaarad said.

Rewen did exactly that and, as before, hacked away at the old man at a number of angles. Jaarad was untouched and quite relaxed. At one point he vanished, only to reappear a few seconds later about 30 feet away. Rewen walked to Jaarad and raised the Sauren sword one more time with the same result. Then he lowered the weapon.

"You see, Jeffrey," the old man said. "I'm quite protected. As shall you be. But only when you begin trusting the One behind these coins and not who holds them."

Jeffrey nodded, still amazed at the coolness Jaarad displayed as Rewen hacked away. Finally, as before, Rewen stopped and lowered the sword. Jaarad thanked Rewen, who wrapped up the sword and disappeared inside. The others crowded around Jaarad and Jeffrey, relieved that the lesson was over. They stayed a full two days until Jeffrey displayed an aptitude for the coins—however weak.

That final evening at the meal, the conversation was scarce. Everyone was in a mixed somber and excited mood at the prospect of leaving the hospitality of Jaarad for the Way of the Water, the Pool of Socaren, near Brestley. Their journey was about to take a very different turn. Up until now everything had been a sort of preparation. But very soon they would cross from the familiar world of Humus to the mysterious land of Nova Fannum. Rewen excused himself after the dinner was served and Jaarad turned to the group. The table at which they all sat was set with simple but satisfying game meat and bread. Kreelin had managed to bring back a large stag and Rewen saw to it that the venison was well cooked.

"You will of course be leaving tomorrow," he began. "Yours is a perilous task, but a magnificent one. Fraught with threat but protected by One greater than all of us. I suspect that even in Nova Fannum where you will be in the wolf's jaws, you will also find friends and refuge. In a way, I envy you."

He turned to Jeffrey.

"And you, my lad," he said, his sightless eyes tearing up. "You will serve the Great King well. Everything you need, you possess. You must simply trust in your heart."

Jeffrey agreed with an unconvincing but sincere smile.

"You believe there are people in Nova Fannum who will help us?" Jeffrey asked.

"Undoubtedly," said Jaarad. "And that is where *Lorica* will help you. It will discern between evil and good. It will warn you of a malevolent presence. Remember, Jeffrey, you cannot trust anyone. The people there are crushed by the burden of a tyrant who has robbed them of their spirit and placed them in a colorless land. Many have drunk of the dark communion which they call the Cup of Bliss. The fight has been taken out of them. But others do not fight because of fear. And fear keeps many a good man from taking a stand."

He smiled.

"But I suspect that they will rise to the occasion when they see you revealed as Castus," he continued. "Even the downtrodden have their limits. And hope can overcome all fear."

"Jaarad, how can we defeat Blackheart?" Ethan asked. "And Phaesus? I mean, they are killers and sorcerers and..."

"They will be defeated by something greater than mere sorcery," Jaarad said. "Don't you worry, Ethan. Or any of you. Evil stands no chance against the Armor and the one who wears it. When that day comes, the Armor shall help you overcome."

"I just hope I am the one wearing it," Jeffrey mumbled.

"I just hope I'm standing behind you," Ethan said.

Jaarad roared with laughter and everyone joined in.

Chapter 20

THE WAY OF THE WATER

THE trip down the mountain went much more quickly than Jeffrey had imagined. He was glad to be back in the open air, even though he enjoyed Jaarad's conversation and hospitality. Even Fortis seemed glad to be leaving. Perhaps the rather dank stables Jaarad provided was too much for him. He didn't even buck when Jeffrey forgot the customary salutation before mounting him.

Jeffrey looked back at the mountains that towered before him. Buried in the mist of ages, the Cassis mountains would have to be conquered another day. He and Ethan decided that after the business of the Armor was settled, they should cross the mountains and go down in history. But for now, the way home led through Brestley, where the Way of the Water would allow them entrance into Nova Fannum.

Corinth was particularly chatty this morning, flying from tree to tree and alerting the group of every threat—consisting mainly of squirrels, rabbits, deer, and other woodland creatures. Kierlin laughed at the noisy bird.

"Is he always this loud?" she asked.

"I'm afraid he wouldn't do if we were sneaking up on someone," admitted Jeffrey. "But he is part of my family history and never deserts me."

"Ah, yes," she said, holding the reins of her spotted horse. "The ravens of Sir William. Charming story. It's amazing to me how family legends and myth can become almost believable."

Ethan snickered as Jeffrey shot Kierlin an angry glance.

"It's a true story," said Jeffrey. "It's recorded."

"By some family member looking to make a name, no doubt," Kierlin said, pressing Jeffrey. "Probably some distant relative looking to make a few coins for drink."

"You for one should not be talking about strange family legends," Jeffrey said. "I'm riding a horse that hates me to a land I never heard of because some king you can't see says I am a Castus with some bizarre coins—*all* because of your family's weird heritage. Talk about charming!"

"Hmph!" Kierlin snorted.

Jeffrey winked at Ethan.

"I know, right?" he said.

Ethan laughed.

Along the way, unknown to the others, Jeffrey continued trying to get the coins to respond to him. A couple of times he thought he could feel something happening and would look at Ethan or Kierlin to see if they noticed anything. Once he actually managed to disappear—from the neck up. Kierlin almost shot at him with an arrow thinking it was some kind of headless specter, but Ethan stopped her at the last second.

Kreelin seemed most nervous, convinced that at any moment they would be fallen upon by Lorogos and his party who were thirsty for revenge. He looked about, using his sharp Sauren eyesight, and noticed everything that moved through the woods. Thaniel tried to reassure him that they were quite safe, at least until they moved off the mountains, but Kreelin would have none of it.

"I know Lorogos," he said. "He will not rest until the sword is in his hands and all of our blood is dripping from it."

"But surely he has given up by now," said Jeffrey, ducking a low-hanging branch on the trail. "He can't possibly know where we are headed."

"Doesn't matter," Kreelin said. "We shall be dead soon."

Ethan laughed.

"Your confidence is very reassuring, Kreelin," he said.

Kreelin pulled his hood down over his face a bit more.

"He'll never give up the sword until he has done everything he can to get it back," he continued. "There is magic in the sword that he must have if the Saurens are to be great once more."

Thaniel, who had been listening to all of this from the front, decided it was time to rest the horses and stop for the night. They had arrived at the bottom of the mountain trail and the flat, forested beauty of Humus spread out before them like a green carpet. Darkness was approaching fast. Ethan tied up the horses while the others began the routine of making a camp. It wasn't long before they were enjoying the warmth of a fire and the satisfaction of a hot meal.

Jeffrey kept his sword by him constantly. The tale earlier of Lorogos's thirst for blood and honor made him weary of relaxing too much. If Lorogos did appear, Jeffrey was going to fight him. When he said as much, his boldness was met with laughter.

"I'm sure Lorogos is quite intimidated," Kreelin said, as he tossed a piece of wood on the fire. "But he will overcome his fear and fight you."

Everyone laughed.

"I'm not saying he is afraid of me," Jeffrey said, holding the sword across his crossed legs. "Just that I am not going to run this time."

"Excellent," said Kreelin. "That way it will be much easier for you when he cuts your throat."

Thaniel shook his head.

"Nothing will happen to you, Jeffrey," Thaniel said. "Remember, you have the coins as well as a brave heart. You will do well."

Jeffrey smiled at the old man.

"Yes," said Kreelin. "You will do well to give him the sword so he will leave us alone."

"Nonsense, Kreelin," said Thaniel. "One cannot give in to one's enemies. If it comes to a fight, we shall prevail. You'll see. Besides, I am not concerned with Lorogos. There is a much larger enemy we will soon face."

The camp was quiet for a moment.

"Will we see Blackheart at the Way of the Water?" Kierlin asked.

"No, my dear," said Thaniel, as he lit his pipe. "Blackheart will never set foot in Humus until he comes with his army. But they must expect us. They will be alert to us in Nova Fannum. His sentries shall be looking for us."

He looked at Jeffrey.

"That is why you must master the coins, Jeffrey."

Jeffrey looked at the faces around the fire.

"What do you mean?"

"I mean, lad, that we can only do so much in Nova Fannum," Thaniel continued. "We shall be limited and in great peril. But you, as Castus, must do many things alone."

Jeffrey swallowed hard.

"Maybe we shouldn't go in tomorrow," Jeffrey offered.

Thaniel smiled.

"Tomorrow we enter Nova Fannum," he said. "And don't you worry. When the time comes for the coins to respond, you will do well."

"But…"

"You will find your faith," said Thaniel.

"When?" asked Jeffrey. "When will I find this faith?"

Thaniel looked at Jeffrey, his eyes glimmering in the fire.

"When you lose your self, Jeffrey."

Very early the next morning the camp was quickly broken up and the party set out toward the little town of Brestley. Situated on the edge of the Caernor Glen, Brestley was famous for the waters of the nearby Pool of Socaren. Supposedly, these waters had a healing power and the town made its living by selling the water to the sick and the simple. It was also, according to Thaniel, the place of the Way of the Water, the last entrance into Nova Fannum from Humus.

As they passed through the town and ambled through the city square, people stopped in their busyness to get a look at this strange crew. They nodded courteously at Thaniel, Ethan, and Jeffrey, and wondered at Kierlin's warrior appearance. But by far, of particular interest was Kreelin, whose hooded garment covered his Sauren features. Whispers in the crowd finally concluded that he was a royal traveling incognito. The mayor even rushed to bring him a bottle of the famous water. Jeffrey laughed long and loud at this.

The road leading to the Pool of Socaren was something of a pilgrim's trail. The faithful, the sick, the hopeful, and the frightened traveled up and down this lane, some having come from the opposite side of Humus, in hope of restored health.

Thaniel shook his head pitifully. "These poor misguided creatures," he said, as they moved off the trail and down a gently sloping hill leading to the pool's edge. "They hope for something that cannot be found in mere water."

Jeffrey was puzzled.

"But surely some have been healed," he said, glancing back at an old man who walked with a noticeable limp. "Or else they wouldn't keep coming back."

"Hope keeps people coming back," Thaniel said. "And that is a good thing. But misplaced hope deceives. Always hope in that which is true. Truth binds everything together and makes hope meaningful."

Jeffrey thought about *Balteus*, the belt of truth.

"Just as Balteus binds the Armor together," he said. "That is why the coins fit inside the belt! Truth gives meaning to the whole."

"Well done, Jeffrey!" Thaniel said, smiling at him. "And you shall see this for yourself. Once the coin of *Balteus* is in your hands, I suspect things will become much more clear to you. As

Jaarad said, truth has a way of opening one's eyes. Truth is the key to the Armor's potential."

"Uncle! The waters!" shouted Ethan as they reached the pool's edge.

The Pool of Socaren was one of the clearest bodies of water Jeffrey had ever seen. Here and there along the bank were the remains of various altars, holy sites, places of prayer, and mountains of wax from the candles of the faithful who sat at the water's edge waiting for their healing. There were even some graves nearby, stark reminders that hope is not always simply deferred—sometimes it is dashed.

"We shall await the darkness," Thaniel said, climbing off his horse, "Just a couple more hours. Ethan, you and Jeffrey tie up the horses. Kierlin, build a fire. And Kreelin?"

"I saw plenty of game in these woods," Kreelin said. "I'll take care to find something special in as much as it will likely be our last meal together."

Thaniel could only shake his head and smile.

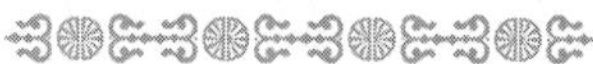

Good as his word, Kreelin found and prepared some outstanding meat, including several ducks which he very cleverly caught with a call he made from a reed. And so, despite Corinth's obvious protest at seeing one of his own eaten, the group enjoyed the game birds very much. The combination of a beautiful sunrise over the water, full bellies and the sweet smell of Thaniel's tobacco made for a very pleasant evening. If it was to be their last meal, it was indeed an outstanding one.

For some reason Jeffrey found himself thinking a lot about the Trout and Truffles. Perhaps it was the feeling of community that the evening had engendered. Or maybe it was the realization that he was about to leave Humus for the first time in his life. But he suddenly felt quite close to his mother, as if she were watching over him.

They sat quietly for a few moments, enjoying the twilight's peace.

He looked over at Ethan and Kierlin and thought about these two cousins who had lost their families to the same enemy. The fire danced on their faces as they sat silently finishing their meal. What must be going on in their minds as they prepared to enter the nation that bore them. Thoughts of revenge? Hope for an end to this lifelong pursuit? He thought about how ridiculous they must appear to Blackheart—an old man, a nervous Sauren, three young fighters, and a noisy raven—aided by a blind seer and a pouch filled with coins. And of course they were, as Thaniel constantly said, armed with hope. Always hope.

"Thaniel, what now?" Jeffrey asked, stroking Corinth behind his neck.

"You'll see," Thaniel said, loading his pipe. "Shortly."

He smiled.

"Listen all of you," he said. "We'll face our enemies soon enough. So sharpen your minds as well as your weapons. For in the end your minds are the greatest weapon you have."

He looked up.

"And now it is time."

Kierlin grabbed her bow and pulled her headgear over her face. Ethan placed a hand on Jeffrey's shoulder and smiled at him reassuringly. Thaniel led everyone to the edge of the dark water. He stood at the edge of the water and spread his hands out and prayed. Jeffrey was amazed that even in the darkness he could make out reflections. More praying! Jeffrey sometimes wondered if Thaniel's religion was really all that different from the other religions in Humus.

For a few minutes all was quiet. Ethan and Jeffrey watched for signs of...what? They really didn't know what they were looking for. Jeffrey was about to make a joke about the meal they had just had when Ethan shoved him hard and pointed at the water. There in the water's mirror-like reflection was Thaniel, hands outstretched. Next to him was Ethan, Jeffrey, and Kierlin. And behind them was Kreelin's tall figure. It looked as if they might step out of the water at any moment, so clear was the image.

It was then when Jeffrey noticed another figure standing next to him in the water's reflection. No, it was a face! He could see a face in the water glowing eerily. The glow grew larger and larger and the water began to swirl. Before he could ask Thaniel about it, the water gave way, as if someone had broken a hole in the bottom of the lake.

The water gave way and disappeared, creating a strange tunnel that went down into the pool. A stairway appeared, the steps and sides made of the water itself. It was lit up in a strange greenish glow and seemed to go on forever. And in the center of the stairs stood a tall figure with the face Jeffrey had seen just a moment before.

The figure walked up out of the watery stairs and approached Thaniel. Jeffrey reached for his sword, but Kreelin cautioned him to watch and wait. Thaniel bowed his head to the man—who appeared to be made of water just like the stairs and tunnel. The watery man bowed his head as well.

"I bid you welcome to the Way of the Water, priest of Nova Fannum," he said. "I am Haustus. May all who accompany you be blessed by the Great King."

"We thank you," said Thaniel. "And we come in the King's name and for His glory. We ask entrance to Nova Fannum on the King's business."

"Then I bid you enter," the Haustus said. "And what do you bring with you to enter this realm?"

"I bring with me Jeffrey, the Castus, and coins of the sacred Armor of Nova Fannum."

Haustus looked at Jeffrey.

"Welcome, Pure One who was foretold," he said. "And where are the holy coins of the Armor?"

Jeffrey took the coin pouch from around his neck and held them.

"Very good," said Haustus. "But first I must hold the coins of the one who is deemed worthy to cross over."

Thaniel looked at the others.

Jeffrey looked at the strange figure in the water and thought about the increasingly bizarre turn of events. He looked back at Ethan and shrugged. Suddenly he felt a burning sensation in his chest. He thought that perhaps Corinth had scratched him earlier in the day. But the feeling was not so much on the chest—but *in* it. He turned to Thaniel.

"All of you get your horses," Thaniel said. "Jeffrey, hand him the coin pouch. This way will remain open for only a short time. He is the water guardian and will let us pass—but we must go quickly."

"Thaniel?" Jeffrey asked.

"He'll give them back when we are safely on the other side," Thaniel said. "It's part of the blessing."

Kreelin looked down the watery steps. He could see the eerie form of fish swimming under the surface. The light coming from the bottom—which could have been one mile away or a hundred—beckoned the party onward. Kreelin gulped loudly.

"We're going down there?" he asked.

"Yes," said Thaniel. "Hurry please."

"Thaniel," Jeffrey said again, feeling his chest with both hand.

"Jeffrey, the coins!"

Jeffrey sighed and took the coins from around his neck. He handed the pouch over to the watery figure. Jeffrey nodded graciously.

"Something you should know about Saurens," Kreelin said, swallowing hard.

"Well?" asked Thaniel impatiently.

"Saurens can't swim," Kreelin said, looking down the watery tunnel.

"You won't be swimming," Thaniel said. "You'll be walking."

"We are magnificent on the ground but helpless as a baby on the water," Kreelin continued. "We have never been a water people."

"Kreelin, trust me," said Thaniel. "The Way of Water is very safe. Besides, you won't be swimming. You'll be walking."

"No," came a voice from behind. "He'll be drowning."

It was Lorogos.

Before Jeffrey could fully comprehend what had happened, Lorogos's Sauren posse had fallen on the group. Ethan and Kierlin were on the ground, Sauren blades at their backs. Jeffrey, sword drawn, looked around in a panicked hope for some sort of help. Maybe the Servatrix were around? Thaniel merely sighed and sat down on a log. Kreelin was shaking violently and fell to his knees, hoping for a merciful jab through the neck. He actually preferred this to drowning and took some comfort in it all.

Lorogos walked over to Jeffrey and stood in front of him. Jeffrey made a stand as if to fight, holding his sword the way Jaarad had taught him. Lorogos laughed and all of the other Saurens laughed as well. Lorogos mocked Jeffrey, imitating his stance.

"You may as well give me the sword, boy," he said calmly. "You don't have the coins. And even if you did I'm sure I would easily kill you."

The coins! Jeffrey looked at Haustus, hoping that the keeper of this final way into Nova Fannum might give the coins back to him. He looked at Haustus hopefully, but only received a rather neutral expression in return. Perhaps it was against protocol for him to take sides in such bloody politics. At any rate no help was forthcoming.

"Well, well," came another voice—as unwelcome as it was familiar.

"Pickworth!" Jeffrey said. "I might have known you would turn up."

"Jeffrey my boy," Pickworth said, as he stepped out of the darkness. "Seems that you are always in need of a lawyer."

"Pickworth," Jeffrey said with disgust. "Why am I not surprised that you would turn up with this Sauren rat?"

"Very good, Jeffrey," came yet another voice, as Jack and Finius emerged, carrying a lantern. "Though as for rats, you are the one caught in the trap."

Even in the darkness Jeffrey could make out the yellowish tint of Finius' snaggly teeth. He grinned with his usual vacant expression. The smell of alcohol also filled the air.

Jeffrey looked at Thaniel.

"Thaniel, I sensed his presence," Jeffrey whispered. "The coin—*Lorica*—was telling me that something was wrong."

"Good lad," Thaniel said. "And now you must sense a way out of this. We must cross into Nova Fannum while the way remains open."

"No whispering lad," said Pickworth. "Didn't your mother teach you that whispering was bad manners?"

"B-b-bad," Finius said.

"What would you know about manners?" Jeffrey asked.

Lorogos walked over to Jeffrey and slapped him hard across the face. He hit him so hard that Jeffrey fell down. Jack winced at the blow. The Saurens snickered among themselves. Kreelin was mumbling a Sauren prayer.

"And now the sword and coins," Lorogos said, holding out his hand.

"The coins are in the custody of Haustus, who guards the Way of the Water," Thaniel said. "You'll have to take that up with him."

"Will I," said Lorogos, looking at Haustus.

Thaniel had a sick feeling in his stomach. He looked up to see the watery figure begin to transform. Within seconds the elegant Haustus morphed into the grinning image of Phaesus! He was laughing and holding the coins in his hand. Sestrin as always was nearby, flitting about in some trees. Lorogos moved over and stood next to Phaesus. The Sauren troops remained alert.

"I'm disappointed, Thaniel," Phaesus continued. "I never believed you would fall for that old trick. Once more the coins belong to me."

He looked at Jeffrey.

"Young Jefford tried to warn you, old man. The coins were responding to him."

He turned to Jeffrey.

"The coins respect your faith," he said. "However weak."

Thaniel could only hang his head. Lorogos laughed.

"Very good, Phaesus," he said. "And now the sword."

"Don't worry about it, Thaniel," Jeffrey said.

"I'm an old fool, Jeffrey," was all he could say.

Kierlin screamed as a Sauren kicked her in the ribs.

"That's for killing my brother at the Tower," he said, and then cursed her in the Sauren language. "You will die slowly."

"Steady," said Phaesus. "These may be useful to me alive for the time being."

The Sauren growled under his breath.

"And now we must trouble you for another item," Phaesus said. "Sestrin informed me about a letter written to this girl from Graysil. It apparently has a cryptic word about the coin *Balteus*."

"Forget it!" Kierlin screamed.

The Sauren guard shoved her face into the sand.

"Quiet, you!" he growled.

"We all know that Graysil hid the coin in Nova Fannum," Phaesus continued. "I don't expect that you will tell us where the coin is. I respect that. But we will take the letter and decipher it ourselves."

Silence.

Phaesus sighed.

The silver mask that covered his face was reflecting the light of the torches and lanterns. He looked around and made an indication to Kierlin's guard to bring her to him. Kierlin's hands were bound behind her. The Sauren picked her up roughly and tossed her at Phaesus's feet.

"Now, my dear" he said. "I'll trouble you for that letter."

Silence.

"Or she will be the first to die right here and now."

"No, Uncle!" she said. "I'll die like my father."

"That coward?" Phaesus said, as Sestrin lighted on his shoulder. "Although I must admit for a priest he was quite sentimental. His last thoughts were of his little girl and of a free Nova Fannum."

Phaesus looked at Thaniel.

"Both are in peril, I'm afraid."

Sestrin hissed in delight.

Thaniel swallowed hard and turned his face. Phaesus nodded to the guard, who put his foot on the back of her head, forcing her face under the water. In a few seconds Kierlin began to thrash about, struggling for air. Thaniel kept his face turned away. Jeffrey looked in turn at Thaniel and at Kierlin.

"Poor girl," Pickworth said. "Caught up in a vow made by her father. And now she must pay its price."

Another minute went by.

"The worst part is that dead or alive we shall have the letter in the end," Pickworth continued. "Such a waste…"

Thaniel looked at Kierlin, and then shook his head apologetically at Ethan and Jeffrey.

"Very well, Phaesus," Thaniel said. "Release her."

Phaesus gave the order. Thaniel reached inside his bag and pulled out Kierlin's letter. He gave Kierlin an apologetic look and handed it over to Pickworth. The lawyer examined it and nodded in approval.

"It's genuine," he said. "I'd stake my life on it."

"Very prophetic," Phaesus said. "Get on with it. You have all the maps and escort you need on the other side. Find that coin!"

"Of course, my lord," said Pickworth, motioning for Jack and Finius to follow him. "The next time you see us will be at your stronghold at Caernclaw."

"With the coin," said Phaesus. "Or don't show your faces."

"With the coin," agreed Pickworth.

"And remember we are dealing with a time element here."

"Never disappoint a client," Pickworth said reassuringly. "First rule of law. Especially one who can turn you into something horrible. Right, Sestrin?"

Sestrin screeched.

"Good-bye, Jeffrey my boy," Jack roared.

And with that, they disappeared down the Way of the Water's stairway.

"The sword," Lorogos said. "I'll have the sword now."

Jeffrey was furious at Kierlin's treatment. He glared at Lorogos.

"There's your sword! he screamed, flinging the treasured Sauren sword into the pool. "Now go and get it yourself."

Lorogos screamed a litany of Sauren oaths.

"This water will be red with your blood before this is over," said Lorogos.

His eyes glowed a reddish, murderous hue from within his hood. He ordered a guard into the water. The Sauren hesitated and several of the others watched him look at Lorogos with pleading eyes. Then he looked at his fellow guards.

"I said fetch it!" Lorogos roared.

"My lord, I..."

Lorogos was furious. He walked to the frightened guard and killed him with a single blow using the guard's own axe. He looked at Jeffrey.

"So Saurens really *are* afraid of the water," Jeffrey said. "Amusing."

Phaesus laughed at Jeffrey's brashness.

"After it, boy," Lorogos said. "And maybe I'll have mercy on you and kill you quickly. Maybe."

Jeffrey laughed.

"You're wasting time," said Phaesus. "Sestrin!"

Sestrin spread his black, bat-like wings and flew out over the water and began circling just above the spot where the sword lay.

"Now, get that sword," Lorogos ordered.

Jeffrey refused.

Phaesus sighed and looked at Kierlin. She began to float, frightening the Sauren who stood guard over her. She hung upside down, helpless. Phaesus looked at Jeffrey.

"Now where should I deposit her?" he asked, as if talking to himself. "Perhaps we should build a fire..."

"Why do they keep picking on me?" she managed to blurt out.

Thaniel shook his head in disgust.

"OK, stop," said Jeffrey. "I'll get the sword."

Jeffrey waded into the water and within a few seconds disappeared under the dark surface. Sestrin continued to circle just above the water. In a moment Jeffrey emerged, dripping and holding the sword. Lorogos stepped out to meet him. Jeffrey held the sword out as if to hand it over but instead brought the blade down hard, slashing through Phaesus's arm.

Phaesus cursed in pain as the hand that held the coins dropped into the water. The sorcerer glared at Jeffrey and reached for the coins with his other hand, but Jeffrey quickly snatched them out of the severed hand. Phaesus made a motion with his hand and caused a lightning streak to shoot out. The light missed Jeffrey and cut in half the Sauren guarding Ethan. Phaesus cursed and disappeared down the watery stairs. The watery stairway began to collapse.

"I have the coins!" Jeffrey yelled triumphantly, holding them over his head.

But before the words were even out of his mouth, Sestrin swooped down with shriek and grabbed the pouch out of his hands. The creature laughed in squealish delight as he disappeared into the watery tunnel just before it completely disappeared. Jeffrey stood in dumbstruck disappointment. For a moment everyone watched as the pool returned to its glasslike stillness.

"You *had* the coins," Lorogos said, snapping Jeffrey out of his daze. "But I have the sword!"

He looked to his guards.

"Kill them all!"

He grinned at Jeffrey.

"I'll personally take care of this one."

The guard watching Kierlin had been distracted by Phaesus's injury, giving her time to spring free and lay hold of her bow. She quickly drew back an arrow. The Sauren laughed as she pointed the weapon at him. He was dead before he hit the ground.

Another Sauren charged Ethan, who had managed to find his knife.

"You mean to kill me with that?" he said, cursing Ethan.

Ethan backed away, tripping over a branch. He dropped his knife and his legs were tangled in the dead wood. He prepared himself for the Sauren's deadly thrust and shut his eyes—but the attack never came. Instead he heard the thud of someone falling. He looked up and saw Thaniel standing behind the Sauren, holding the metal-bound book Jaarad had given them on monsters. He had whacked the Sauren in the back of the head.

"You see, Ethan," he managed. "It pays to read!"

Ethan smiled.

"Need any help Kierlin," he called out.

Kierlin pointed to the remaining Sauren figure running away and disappearing into the woods. She shook her head no as she drew an arrow on him and killed him.

Lorogos had no intention of running. He glared at Jeffrey and approached him menacingly, holding the Sauren sword. His blood lust was so hot that he no longer cared that the other Saurens were dead or dying.

"This sword has waited too long for Jefford blood," Lorogos said. "It shall finally taste it. Even if I should die today!"

Lorogos raised the sword over his head. Jeffrey looked desperately for some sort of weapon, but came up empty. Lorogos brought the sword down hard. Jeffrey waited for the fatal blow. And waited. And waited. But the sword could not touch him! Lorogos swung wildly at Jeffrey, hacking away. But the sword would not touch him at all. The coins were protecting him!

Lorogos cursed and turned toward Thaniel.

"At least you will die, old man!"

"Lorogos!" said Jeffrey.

Lorogos turned to confront Jeffrey—but he wasn't there!

"Here I am, you Sauren fool," came the voice, this time from another direction.

Thaniel laughed.

"Well done, Jeffrey!"

Lorogos cursed Jeffrey even louder, swinging the sword madly in every direction. Mad with rage, he followed the taunting voice. Jeffrey led him down the beach away from the others. They were climbing a small hill, with Lorogos shouting at Jeffrey to show himself, and Jeffrey teasing Lorogos, throwing rocks at him and making him angrier and angrier.

"Appear to me you cowardly Jefford," Lorogos demanded. "You are not worthy of your ancestor Sir William."

Nothing.

Lorogos took another step or two. He looked over the edge of the cliff where Jeffrey had led him. The pool was quiet below—a rocky part of the beach about 100 feet below. In the darkness it looked much farther.

"Where are you, Jefford?"

"Here!" Jeffrey said, appearing from behind.

Lorogos turned, swinging his sword in a final, desperate attack. He turned with such violent force that he lost his footing. The Sauren screamed in terror as he toppled over the side of the cliff. Lorogos had never noticed that he was getting closer and closer to the edge of the waters of Socaren. Not until it was too late. Now he was hanging onto the side for his life. Jeffrey picked up the Sauren sword and stood over Lorogos. The Sauren looked up.

"You shall never have the satisfaction of killing me," he said. "And I shall go to my death knowing about your father."

Jeffrey knelt down.

"My father? What about him?"

Lorogos laughed.

"You shall never know Jefford," Lorogos said bitterly. "And you shall never be able to save him. Not where he is."

"Wait! Don't..."

Then Lorogos let go and dropped into the water. The sickening sound of Lorogos's large body colliding with the jagged rocks was quite final. Within a few minutes the water was as still as before—as if they had never been disturbed. Thaniel walked up behind Jeffrey and gazed into the dark pool. He placed a hand on his shoulder. Ethan and Kierlin approached them from behind. Kreelin had disappeared as usual.

"The coins, Jeffrey," Thaniel said. "Your faith is growing."

"He mentioned my father," Jeffrey said. "He said he is alive."

Thaniel said nothing.

"He was probably lying," Ethan said. "His final offense."

"No, he meant it," Jeffrey said.

"Well anyway you managed the coins," Ethan said, helping his friend up.

"I didn't even know it," Jeffrey said. "It just happened."

"Best kind of faith," Thaniel said.

They all stood in silence for a moment, looking down into the dark water below. The stars reflected on the quiet surface.

"There ends a dark chapter in Sauren history," Thaniel said. "The sad fact of the matter is that Phaesus was merely using the Saurens to get the coins. And now they have lost their prince and the coins."

Jeffrey looked at the sword, still bloody from Phaesus's arm.

"Yes, but I think a new chapter has just begun," Jeffrey said.

"The water," said Kierlin, looking over the pool. "And now the Way of Water is gone. How will we get into Nova Fannum now? There are no other ways."

Thaniel smiled.

"Leave that to me," he said quietly.

"What do you mean, Uncle?" asked Kierlin.

"I mean," he said playfully, "there are ways, and then there are ways."

Chapter 21

ANOTHER WAY

THE loss of the coins to Phaesus was quite a setback to Jeffrey and the others. They moved silently through the woods, not so much to be stealthy as much as melancholy. Nobody felt like talking. Except, of course, Thaniel. As always, he pushed on and talked hopefully and spoke of other greater possibilities, the inevitability of good winning out, and all the other words of encouragement one would expect from such a priest at such a time.

On top of everything else, Jeffrey was thinking about his father. If Lorogos was telling the truth—and a person who is about to die has no reason to lie, be they human or Sauren—then Malcolm might be alive somewhere. If only they could discover where he was being held or what the circumstances were of his disappearance. The more he thought about it, the angrier he got. All he could see in his mind's eye was the smug look of Pickworth, Jack's toothy grin, and the vacant stare of Finius. He vowed their deaths.

"Now what, Uncle," Ethan said, breaking the silence.

"What do you mean, Ethan," Thaniel called back from his lead position on the road. "We have a mission to accomplish as always."

"We have been on this road once before," Ethan noted, as he stroked his horse's neck. "I recognize that abandoned mill."

"Just so, Ethan," said Thaniel, looking at the broken wheel that leaned against the house. "Very observant."

"But Uncle," called Kierlin, "Ethan's right. Even if we do manage to enter Nova Fannum we don't have the coins anymore."

"Phaesus's cunning has indeed cost us dearly," Thaniel said. "But we managed to keep the sword, eh Jeffrey?"

No response.

"Jeffrey is lost in that book Jaarad gave him," said Kreelin. "*The Codex Prodigium*. Although I must say I'm somewhat offended that Saurens are listed in the book as some sort of vile creature. Astonishing!"

They laughed.

"Well you must remember that the book was written by humans," said Thaniel. "And to some humans, Saurens are in fact monstrous."

"Indeed that cuts both ways," Kreelin said in a miffed tone.

"Speaking of cutting, Jeffrey certainly got the better of Phaesus," Ethan said.

"I only wish it had been his head instead of his hand."

"Quite a day," Thaniel said. "But curse that Sestrin! That's twice now he has undone us. The devil! But cheer up, all. Until we hear otherwise we must assume that Phaesus does not yet have *Balteus*. And without *Balteus* I'm afraid he will be greatly disappointed. As I said, truth is what gives meaning to the whole. Without *Balteus* he'll never realize the Armor's significance."

"Incredible!" Jeffrey shouted.

"Well, well, the scholar lives," Thaniel said. "Let's stop here and rest the horses. We'll be at our destination by nightfall."

They tied up the horses near a brook and enjoyed the break in the monotonous travel. Thaniel sat down on a large rock and lit a pipe. Kierlin decided to forage for some berries she had seen a ways back on the road. Ethan sat and closed his eyes. Corinth happily flew from branch to branch, always on the alert for Sestrin. And Jeffrey? His nose was buried in the book—the *Prodigium*—that told of all sorts of creatures, some of which they were likely to encounter in Blackheart's Nova Fannum.

"What have you learned, Jeffrey?" Thaniel asked. "Will you be able to protect us from hideous monsters and undead pursuers?"

"Did you know that skeletons can be brought to life and used as assassins?" Jeffrey said to nobody in particular.

"Only when sufficiently motivated," said Thaniel, winking at Kreelin.

"And Ghoms are all but extinct," Jeffrey continued. "Apart from a few sightings in the northern coastland."

"Ghoms?"

"Little beggars who come into your room at night and suck your blood with such skill that you never wake up!"

"Really? Then how do you know they are so skillful?"

Jeffrey looked up.

"Laugh if you want," he said. "But I for one intend to be prepared should any of these creatures be part of this wicked army Blackheart is assembling."

Jeffrey started looking for various types of moss and herbs and other such items as one might need to ward off, frighten, disable, or otherwise fight some of the creatures mentioned in the book. Thaniel shook his head. Ethan snatched the book from Jeffrey and began thumbing through it. He began calling out names of some of the featured beasts and brutes.

"This sounds like a child's story book," he said. "Trolls and ogres, minotaurs and centaurs, firebirds and harpies, cyclops and dragons—not to mention assorted giant ants, bees, scorpions, centipedes..."

He handed the heavy book back to Jeffrey.

"Uncle, do you really believe in such nonsense?"

"Ethan, in a battle that will be decided by faith, a closed mind makes a poor weapon," Thaniel said. "Whether or not we actually see these creatures is not the point. The fact is that Blackheart is capable of creating such an army.

"And according to Jaarad that is exactly what he is doing," said Jeffrey.

"True Jeffrey," Thaniel said. "But listen. It isn't garlic or tree moss or some herbal potion that will defeat such evil. It is the One greater than all of those things that shall defeat them. It is faith that overcomes evil."

Jeffrey nodded his head.

"I understand, Thaniel," he said, secretly noting a large mossy branch on a cypress tree just off the road. Ethan saw him looking at the limb and laughed.

"Just in case," Jeffrey said defensively.

By that evening the tired group reached a ravine that wound through densely wooded lowlands. Jeffrey knew exactly where they were now and had a pretty good idea where they were headed. When they came to a rocky outcropping Jeffrey looked back at Ethan and they exchanged knowing glances. They were at the waterfall cave where Jeffrey had first met Ethan weeks before.

"We're stopping here for the night?" asked Jeffrey.

"In a manner of speaking," said Thaniel, as he climbed off his horse. "We're passing through."

The party dismounted and Thaniel led them up the little trail to the cave behind the waterfall. The water cascaded as before, frothy and beautiful, concealing the cave behind its flowing curtain. Thaniel motioned for everyone to wait for him and entered the cave. A moment later he returned with a small box.

"It's getting dark now," he said, looking at the sky. "And tomorrow we shall enter Nova Fannum proper. I suggest a good night's rest for all. The cave will do nicely for the night. Ethan, tie up the horses, please."

"I'll help you, Ethan," Jeffrey said, leading Fortis to a clearing. "Why did he bring us back here?"

Ethan looked up at the waterfall.

"The vow," was all he said.

That night as they sat near the very comforting fire that Ethan had built, Jeffrey stroked Corinth and relaxed for the first time in many nights. Here they were, in the cave they had shared weeks before, only this time they were heading into what was likely to be their final journey. His eyes drifted to the writing on the wall, scratched their years before by six brothers who swore to die before they failed in their purpose.

He looked at Ethan and Kierlin huddled in close to the only other living member of their family—their uncle Thaniel. Here, in this very cave, their own fathers, now dead, had written that vow to the death. Thaniel, their uncle, was the last of these brothers. Now he was leading them back into the land that had driven their fathers away to face the villain who had murdered them. It was a bittersweet moment. Jeffrey discreetly moved away to give them some privacy.

He found Kreelin toward the back of the cave. The Sauren was resting, his hood pushed back—a rare sight. Jeffrey sat down next to Kreelin. He looked up. Jeffrey could make out the reddish tint of his snakelike eyes reflecting the fire.

"Ah, Jeffrey," he said, in his hissing Sauren voice. "Do you find the darkness comforting as I do?"

Jeffrey laughed and sat down next to Kreelin.

"I was just giving them some privacy," Jeffrey said, looking back toward the others. "This is a very special place for them."

"So Thaniel told me," Kreelin answered, nibbling on a piece of dark bread. "In a way it is special to all of us."

"How so?" asked Jeffrey. "Have you been here before?"

"They are fugitives, Jeffrey," Kreelin said, looking at the others. "They are from a land that was stolen from them. They return with hopes of restoring their nation. I, too, am a fugitive now. I shall never return to Sauren lands. And you Jeffrey have lost all. You, too, are a fugitive of your past."

Jeffrey nodded in quiet agreement.

"I guess," he said.

"They have lost their family and so have you," Kreelin continued. "And like them, you hope to restore your family fortunes."

"I just want to get through this alive," Jeffrey said. "As to my family, Lorogos spoke as if my father was still alive. I hope things work out for Thaniel and the Nova Fannum. But I just want to find my father—dead or alive."

"Then what?"

"Then me and Ethan will rebuild the Trout and Truffles and become wealthy inn owners and marry beautiful wives and raise our families."

"Ah, human dreams," Kreelin muttered. "Such vanity."

"Is it vain to want to be happy, Kreelin?"

"No, but it is vain to expect it."

Jeffrey smiled.

"Thaniel would say we live in expectation," he said. "This is what he calls faith."

"It is what I call dreaming," Kreelin said.

Jeffrey laughed.

"Don't you believe in anything, Kreelin?" Jeffrey asked.

"Right now I believe in the security of this cave," he answered. "I believe in the moment. The present breath, nothing else is assured."

He looked at Jeffrey.

"The greater question, Jeffrey, is what do *you* believe?"

"Me? What difference does *that* make?"

"What you believe makes all the difference, Jeffrey," Thaniel called out.

"You've been listening," Jeffrey said, annoyed.

"For if Blackheart wins," Thaniel continued, "there will be no Humus in which to rebuild your inn. So much depends on what we believe, Jeffrey. Especially you. For wherever your heart is directed, that is the path you shall take. And all of our destinies are tied in with yours."

Jeffrey gulped uncomfortably.

"Come join us by the fire. We need to talk…and then pray."

"Especially pray," Jeffrey muttered.

Thaniel looked at the faces staring back at him around the fire. He smiled at them all and wiped away a tear from his eyes. He felt more sentimental now than he ever had since leaving Nova Fannum so long ago. He lit his pipe, the smell of which was so ingrained in Jeffrey's mind that he would never forget it.

"This place," he began, "this sacred place is strong in meaning and memory for me. Not just because of those words that your fathers and I inscribed so long ago. We stand on the eve of a great mission. A noble purpose. A great calling. Tomorrow we shall enter a land that is very different from the one I left. A land once filled with joy and promise. Now the joy is gone and the promise long broken."

"Thaniel, how will we get there?" asked Jeffrey. "I mean, where is this other way in?"

Thaniel smiled.

"We are in the way right now," Thaniel said. "This cave is more than a crack in the side of a ravine in Humus. Just as your grandfather so cleverly concealed the Jefford family vault, so did we brothers create a secret way to Nova Fannum—a way that not even Phaesus knows about."

"So he won't be expecting us," said Ethan. "He thinks he destroyed all the other ways in."

"Exactly," said Thaniel. "Apparently he killed the true Haustus, the guardian of the Way of the Water. He then very cleverly assumed his identity and much to my shame tricked me into giving him the coins."

Silence.

"But, since he believes we are in Humus with no ability to cross Nova Fannum's frontiers, he might not be expecting us," said Kreelin hopefully. "A relaxed mind is always more vulnerable."

"Phaesus is never relaxed in mind," said Thaniel. "We must assume that because of Sestrin's spying, he knows everything."

He looked at Jeffrey.

"Especially about Jeffrey being the Castus. He'll never rest until Jeffrey is dead. And he will have sentries all over the frontier."

"Thaniel, now that he has the coins, how can we stop him?" asked Jeffrey.

"Our only hope is in finding *Balteus* before they do," Thaniel said. "Phaesus is no fool. He will search out the clue in Graysil's letter very quickly."

"Then there is no hope," said Ethan glumly.

"True, Ethan," said Thaniel, reaching into his bag. "Except for one thing."

He pulled out a folded piece of paper.

"They will need this to find the coin."

"Father's letter!", Kierlin said excitedly.

Everyone was astonished.

"But we saw you…" began Jeffrey.

"You saw me give Pickworth a letter," said Thaniel, smiling a slyly. "And it was indeed a letter from Graysil. As Pickworth boasted, you cannot fool a good lawyer in such matters! I had seen Sestrin hanging outside of a window while these things were being discussed…"

"*That* is why you were so interested in the window!" Jeffrey said.

"Just so," said Thaniel. "Afterward, Jaarad and I decided that Sestrin's curiosity need not be in vain. We knew that at some point Phaesus would make a move to obtain the letter. So we created the misleading letter—with a false clue for Phaesus should he come for the bait.

Thaniel grinned.

"If my guess is right, Pickworth is poking around the western marshes in an old fortress convinced that he is about to find the final coin!"

The cave was filled with laughter for a few moments.

"So you see, we still have an opportunity to find *Balteus* before our opponents," Thaniel continued. "But it will still be dangerous. As I said, Phaesus's spies are everywhere and the frontiers will be heavily guarded. But since they have no idea about this other way in, they will not expect us!"

"Clever, Thaniel, clever," said Jeffrey.

"Very good, Uncle," added Ethan.

"And now I believe prayer is in order," Thaniel said. "One should never endeavor a great mission without obtaining favor from the Great Commissioner!"

As Thaniel bowed his head in prayer, Kierlin took the letter and opened it. Her eyes welled up with tears. She carefully folded it and placed it among her things. Then she quoted from the letter, looking at the wall where Graysil had signed his name years ago: *That which is sacred to the heart never really leaves it.*

"Thank you, daddy," she whispered.

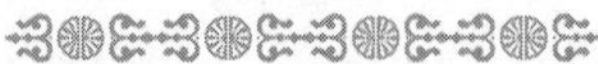

The rest of the evening, Thaniel briefed everyone on Nova Fannum's country and customs. It was a land unlike any other, he said. Nova Fannum, since Blackheart's coup, had become an armed camp—a police state fueled by suspicion and accusation—

in which informants and collaborators abounded and in which decent people lived in fear of being turned in for the price of a drink or some other favor.

"It's amazing how people will turn on their friends and family when times become difficult," Thaniel said. "Therefore we can trust nobody."

He winked at Jeffrey.

"Well, almost nobody."

"So how do we get in," Kierlin asked. "Where is the entry?"

"As I said, this cave is more than just a crack in Humus' quaint countryside," Thaniel said. "It is, as the other Ways were, a portal; a door."

He looked at Jeffrey.

"I told you that one day this place would be important to you."

Jeffrey remembered.

"And so we shall go through this cave and emerge through a waterfall on the other side," he continued. "And enter Nova Fannum!"

"Another Way of the Water," Ethan mused.

"More a way of earth," Thaniel said smiling. "My brothers and I created this portal before we fled. It was the last thing we did. It was the last time we were all together—when we wrote those words in the stone. Your father, Ethan, and yours, Kierlin, and your other uncles. We made sure of our families' safety as best we could and then returned to Nova Fannum and took the coins out of *Balteus*."

"Why didn't you tell me?" asked Jeffrey. "Or Ethan? Didn't you trust us?"

"Because, Jeffrey, disclosure comes in bits and pieces as the situation arises," Thaniel explained. "It wasn't a matter of trust, but timing."

"Uncle, why didn't you take the whole armor?" asked Ethan.

"Too cumbersome," said Thaniel matter-of-factly. "We would have been cut down where we stood. As it was, one of your uncles never even made it out of the Temple. No, the entire Armor was out of the question. But the coins, you see? They represented the Person—the majesty behind the Armor. Just as our faith merely represents the One through whom that faith can operate."

"So they *are* magical," Jeffrey concluded.

"No, no," said Thaniel. "Not magic! I told you. Magic manipulates and uses elements that already exist. But faith—faith is born in the heart of the One who created everything; the One through and by whom all is or becomes. Faith is what gives one hope, Jeffrey, to see those things which are unseen become reality. It is pure and focused on the Holy One who drives it. Magic is born in the hearts of men seeking their own will and dedicated to selfish purposes."

"But what about Cysus, the great wizard who used his power to turn back a storm? Or the Witch of Leedrin who helped people by giving them healing potions?"

"Magic. Witchcraft. Sorcery. They are all the same, Jeffrey," Thaniel continued. "Just because one uses their skills in these arts to do good works does not mean that at the heart of those skills is something self-seeking. True power, legitimate authority comes from the One who made everything. All else is sham and prideful. That is why these arts are alluring, Jeffrey. They appeal to self. Personal power. Control."

He looked at everyone.

"And that is enough on this subject."

"What did Blackheart do," Ethan asked, "when he discovered that the coins had been taken?"

"He was furious, of course," Thaniel said. "Phsesus ordered us found and our homes destroyed. He had Nova Fannum turned upside down. He arrested whatever family members he could and began hunting us down. One by one he caught up to us. All except me. I managed to go underground—literally—near Gillingham here in Humus. I was fortunate to have the *Juaracas coin*—the sandals—which allowed me to become invisible as needed. Saved my neck many times, I tell you."

He looked up at the writing on the wall.

"It was not until the coin of my brother Dontel emerged that I knew Blackheart was on the move. That the time was nearer than I imagined."

"And now you're on the move again," Kreelin said.

Thaniel turned to the Sauren.

"And may it be for the last time."

"Mind your head there, Jeffrey!"

"Very funny, Ethan," Jeffrey said, as he ducked a jagged rock hanging low.

The group was slowly making its way through the tunnel that Thaniel and his brothers had created many years earlier. It was obviously a hastily done job—but under the circumstances these six brothers achieved quite a feat. Just how this tunnel allowed one to travel from one world to another still escaped Jeffrey. He intended to ask Thaniel about it some day.

"What about the horses?" Jeffrey asked.

"They'll be tended to," said Thaniel from the front of the line. "Fact is they are already waiting for us."

"But..."

"Never you mind," said Thaniel. "Animals are easy to move from place to place. They don't resist or ask questions. They simply do as they are told."

Silence.

"Got that, Jeffrey?" Ethan asked laughing.

"All of it," said Jeffrey. "And from here on I will ask no more questions! Here that Corinth?"

A loud but muffled SQUWAK sounded from Jeffrey's cloak.

Everyone laughed.

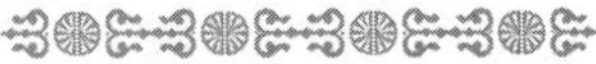

In a few minutes everyone stopped.

"What happened," Kierlin whispered.

"I don't know," Ethan said. "Be quiet."

The party stood still for a moment.

"Do you hear that sound?" Thaniel said, breaking the silence.

At first Jeffrey heard nothing except the breathing of his comrades. But then, almost imperceptible he could hear a sound...a quiet but distinct sound. It was the sound of rushing water...like a waterfall! They continued moving and the sound became louder and clearer. It was definitely a waterfall.

Ahead of them they began to get glimpse of light and soon the cave felt moist. Within minutes the ceiling and floor was wet. It wasn't long before they stood before a waterfall—like the one at the opposite end of the cave—except that this one had a much narrower opening. Thaniel stopped everyone.

"In a few moments we shall enter my once holy land," Thaniel said with great emotion. "The land I left has been transformed by something hideous. Our enemy is relentless and on the alert. We must be careful. I only hope we will be a small part in its restoration."

"A small part?" Jeffrey thought to himself.

"But we have friends here as well. We shall meet one tonight who will give us shelter and provide us with disguise and news."

He looked at Kreelin.

"And now my friend, I must send you back."

Everyone looked at Kreelin.

"What?" said Jeffrey.

"I can fight, sir," said Kreelin. "And you know what a forager I am. I would just as soon die with you here on a noble cause than be hunted down and killed by my own kind should I return."

"You may have my home," said Thaniel. "Keep it until I return. And if I do not return, you may have it. You'll be able to find it. In the mines of Gillingham."

"But sir…" Kreelin protested.

"I'm sorry, Kreelin," said Thaniel. "But a Sauren in Nova Fannum is too dangerous. You will give us away."

"Then why did you let him come all this way with us," Jeffrey said angrily.

Kreelin smiled.

"Because he is wise," he said. "He kept me with you to make sure that I would not turn you in; or to determine that I was not secretly working with Lorogos. In short, he needed me here because he could not completely be sure of my loyalty."

Kreelin looked at Thaniel.

"I must admit I would have done the same."

"No hard feelings, then?" asked Thaniel.

"None," said Kreelin. "You would have made a great Sauren prince, Thaniel. Always suspect. That is one of our creeds. Kept us alive."

Kreelin looked at the others.

"Then off with you," he said. "And if I may extend a Sauren blessing to your efforts: 'May your enemy be at your feet with every step.'"

With that he vanished into the darkness of the cave. Everyone remained silent as the sound of his footsteps disappeared. Soon, only the waterfall could be heard.

"Good-bye my friend," Thaniel said.

"And may your enemy be at your feet with every step!" Jeffrey yelled into the blackness after him. They turned back to Thaniel.

"Well my friends," he said. "We are about to enter a once holy land that has become profaned by darkness. But remember: He who sends us is greater than he who opposes us."

Jeffrey nodded with the others. "I just wish He who sent us was right here with us!" he said.

Silence.

"He is Jeffrey," Thaniel said. "He is."

The others watched as Thaniel approached the watery curtain and, for the first time in many years, glimpsed the land from which he had been a fugitive for so long. He stood silently for a moment. Then he turned back to the others. He had tears in his eyes. He suddenly seemed much older; much more fragile. He even trembled.

He sat down as the others crowded around the entrance. Jeffrey peeked around the side of the watery wall and his eyes beheld for the first time another land.

As Thaniel had said, it was indeed a land unlike any other. Jeffrey had expected something like Humus—a sort of mirror image of what was on the other end of the tunnel. Instead he was shocked to find a land of rolling hills, low shrubs, and trees. He could see what appeared to be a large mountain range on the horizon. The waterfall emptied into a stream which flowed down a hill and emptied into a small lake. It was a beautiful landscape except for one obvious difference: *there was no color!*

"It's worse than I imagined," was all that Thaniel could say.

And indeed it was.

For Nova Fannum, a land once known to its people as luxurious in its rich colors which defied description, had become an ashen tone of black and gray and white. There was no color at all! The trees, the sky, the water—even the flowers—everything was some form of a dull, ashen gray. Jeffrey rubbed his eyes to make sure the darkness of the cave had not affected them in some way. But it was very real…and very gray.

"Jaarad certainly knew what he was talking about," said Jeffrey, looking at the countryside. "He said it was colorless. I thought he meant that in some poetic way."

"It's horrible," said Kierlin.

"Ugly," said Ethan.

Thaniel stood and joined them. Together they stepped out from behind the falls and on to Nova Fannum itself. Corinth excitedly flew into the sky, his black form making it difficult to see against the colorless features of the land. In fact, the country lay before them like a great, gray carpet.

"Corinth!" Jeffrey shouted. "Come back here!"

But the bird was nowhere to be seen, his black feathers blending in with his surroundings. Jeffrey squinted but could not see him anywhere.

"This is what happens when evil is on high," Thaniel said, looking around. "This is the price of evil in ascendancy. Look around. All that has meaning; all that is beautiful or once carried beauty; all that was pure and carried within itself the mark of its Creator becomes distorted and diminished."

He looked at Ethan.

"Or, as you put it, my boy—ugly."

They stood for a moment and allowed their eyes and mind and senses to adjust to this strange world. Then Jeffrey pointed at the others and began laughing.

"Hey you are all colorless!" he said.

"Yeah? Well takc a look at yourself," said Kierlin.

Jeffrey looked at his hands and rushed down to the pool of water where the waterfall emptied. He looked at his reflection and saw the same dull grayness of the world and people around him. The others joined him, looking at their own reflections.

"At least we blend in," Jeffrey surmised, trying to shed some hopeful light on the situation.

"Quite right," said Thaniel, who began looking around. "However, we must be careful. We don't blend in when there is an enemy alerted to our likely incursion. In short, we must remain very cautious."

"Who is this friend of yours?" asked Jeffrey.

"Later," said Thaniel. "For the remainder of the day we must stay in the cave. He will meet us here tonight and escort us to a safe place. Our horses are already there."

They climbed the hill that took them back into the cave behind the waterfall. One by one they entered—except for Jeffrey.

He was waiting for Corinth to return. Thaniel gave him a few minutes and then yelled down to him.

"Jeffrey, please!" he said. "Corinth will be all right. They are looking for people, not ravens."

Jeffrey scanned the trees and skies and still saw no sign of Corinth. Then he knelt down to drink the water.

"What are you doing,?" Thaniel demanded.

"I just wanted to see if the water was as bad as it looked," said Jeffrey, wiping his mouth.

"Well?" asked Thaniel.

"Tastes like water," said Jeffrey.

"What were you expecting?" asked Thaniel, motioning for Jeffrey to hurry.

Jeffrey climbed the hill and stood next to Thaniel. They took one last look around. Still no sign of Corinth.

"Don't worry about that bird," Thaniel said. "Corinth is a smart one. He'll remember how to find us."

Jeffrey sighed.

"I hope so," he said, and disappeared into the cave.

As the grayness of the day gave way to evening, a somber spirit prevailed over the group. The fact that one of their number, Kreelin, had returned to Humus, created an uncharacteristically melancholy atmosphere. Thaniel did what he could to keep things cheery, but without Kreelin's typically humorous, albeit morose comments, the evening wore on slowly. For Jeffrey, the added sting of Corinth's disappearance increased the feeling of despair. He found himself wanting to go home.

Kierlin walked over to Jeffrey and sat next to him. He had the Sauren sword out and was polishing the blade. She smiled at him.

"Some weapon there," she said.

Jeffrey nodded.

"Hope you won't have to use it again," she said. "I'd just as soon get this over with without seeing anymore killing."

Jeffrey looked up.

"Me too," he admitted. "I'm no hero. I got lucky with Phaesus is all. I'll probably end up with my head on his wall for a trophy or something."

Kierlin laughed.

"You sound like Kreelin," she said. "I miss that Sauren."

"Me too," said Jeffrey. "I hope he makes it out there."

"Corinth too," she said. "That little bird always makes me laugh."

Jeffrey smiled.

"Anyway I just wanted you to know that I'm sorry that he flew away," she said. "I know we got off to a bad start. I'm sorry."

Kierlin got back up and moved to her spot on the other side of the opening. Jeffrey watched her and wondered why she had bothered to come over to him like that. He couldn't help but admire her courage and ability as a fighter; she had the confidence that he wished he had. And he found her very attractive—not just physically—but in her dedication to this cause that had thrown them all together. He watched as she sat down and gave her uncle a hug.

"I'm sorry, too," Jeffrey whispered.

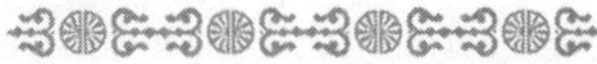

"Thaniel?"

"Thaniel?"

Thaniel sat up and cocked his ear toward the waterfall. He motioned for everyone to be quiet and stood up to see who was calling his name. He was expecting his friend, but in Blackheart's Nova Fannum one could not be too careful. Kierlin made ready her bow and Jeffrey stood with his sword. He also made sure that the way back to Humus was clear—just in case.

Thaniel peeked around the watery curtain and saw a face reflecting the fire inside the cave. Thaniel's cautious countenance became a grin as he welcomed the stranger inside the cave.

"Come in, come in," Thaniel boomed. "My dear friend!"

Jeffrey watched as a man in a hooded robe entered the cave. He relaxed when Thaniel began introducing the man as his friend and their contact.

"Everyone! This is our friend, Colyer," Thaniel said, ushering the man in. "He will guide us to our first stopover."

"Hello," said the man, lowering his hood.

Jeffrey looked at the man. He was about Ethan's height and build, but looked to be about 60 years old. Even so he seemed very fit and Jeffrey was glad to have him on their side. He had a gray beard that was neatly trimmed and a gold earring that gave him a look of a pirate or some sort of scoundrel. Jeffrey shuddered as he thought of Jack for a moment—though this man was definitely Jack's opposite.

"I brought Sedgwin with me," Colyer said. "He has your horses and some clothing to conceal you. I'm afraid the word is already out that there are criminals from a foreign land in Nova Fannum." He smiled.

"Phaesus," he continued, "put quite a price on your heads. Several bounty hunters are on the prowl already."

"Great," said Jeffrey. "Then we're as good as dead."

Colyer shot a glance at Jeffrey and then looked at Thaniel.

"Is he the one?" Colyer asked.

"Yes," said Thaniel. "He's learning. But he is the one."

"I hope your faith increases, lad," Colyer said. "Or your words will become your prophecy. You will all indeed be as good as dead."

Jeffrey discreetly stepped back into the darkness.

"So what is the plan?" asked Thaniel. "Where do we go from here?"

"First thing we must do is get you to a safe place," Colyer said. "Gather your things. Sedgwin will meet us at the trail with the horses that you sent ahead. It's only a couple of hours from here. Then we can talk about plans."

"Is this your house, Colyer?" asked Ethan.

"No lad," he said, looking at Ethan. "You're Corin's boy?"

Ethan nodded.

"Yes, sir," he said. "And this is my cousin, Kierlin. She is the daughter of my uncle Graysil."

"Ah, Graysil," Colyer repeated. "Brave man. Confounded Phaesus to the end."

"Graysil and Colyer were my youngest brothers," said Thaniel. "Twins born late to my parents. They were really novices in the temple when the trouble began."

"Thus these younger children," Colyer said, looking at Ethan and Kierlin. "Well let's not let their deaths have been for nothing, eh?"

Ethan and Kierlin nodded in agreement.

"As for you, young man, I hope you are discovering that the circumstances that brought you into this battle are more than coincidental," Colyer said, looking at Jeffrey. "Quite providential. And now we best be going. Sedgwin will be getting nervous if we don't return soon. You won't need lanterns. Strangely, one development that has occurred since the color has left is that at night the darkness is quite manageable."

"As if darkness be the light," mumbled Thaniel.

Colyer looked up.

"Yes, you remember the prophecy too?"

Thaniel stood for a moment as if trying to recall something. He looked at Colyer and after a few seconds began speaking:

"When color fades this holy land,
When right turns wrong and wrong turns right;
Beware the king who falsely reigns,
As if the darkness be the light."

"Quite right," said Colyer. "And it is so. The land is turned upside down and what was right is now undone. As if darkness be the light."

They all stood in quiet thought.

"You said we best be off," said Thaniel, breaking the silence. "Your man is waiting for you."

"Ah yes," said Colyer. "He will see us safely to the sanctuary."

"The sanctuary," repeated Thaniel. "What is that?"

"A place that we have prepared for the day the Castus should come among us," said Colyer. "We do not all bend the knee to Blackheart or drink his dark communion."

"The communion?" asked Thaniel. "Jaarad mentioned something about that."

Colyer smiled grimly.

"The Modestia," said Colyer. "The purifying cup. The people are required to drink this as part of the worship of the Great King. Its purpose is to cleanse one's heart and mind. It's merely a drug Phaesus created that restrains the mind; keeps it in servile bondage. Brilliant, really."

"You have taken this cup?" asked Thaniel.

"Never," said Colyer. "It is done by family lot. Those who drink it become pacified and open to Blackheart's suggestion. And those who refuse are taken away and never seen again. Rumor has it they are being held in Lygor, on the island of Weest."

He looked at Thaniel.

"When our family was called up, I saw my brother take the drug," he continued. "He has never been the same since. Nor can I trust him. I fled the ceremony and went underground. There are quite a few of us. But we need help...we need the Castus."

Everyone looked at Jeffrey, who shifted uncomfortably.

"Well, right now we need to be going," said Thaniel, coming to Jeffrey's rescue. "Mind what Colyer says. And stay quiet."

Everyone followed Colyer down the slope. Ethan waited on Jeffrey, who was lingering in the cave. Jeffrey turned to his friend and Ethan smiled at him and, sensing that Jeffrey needed to be alone for a moment, left him.

"I'll be out here," Ethan said, and joined the others.

Jeffrey took one last look back into the darkness which led to Humus—to home. How easy it would be to head back. Surely the others would understand. He could go home to his land. To rebuild his life. Perhaps to find his father...

"Coming, Jeffrey?" Thaniel called out.

He hesitated. But he could not leave. Much as he wanted to go home; much as he felt overwhelmed and totally incapable of this whole Castus business, he could not abandon his new friends. He desperately wanted to...and yet...something inside was driving him. Something was compelling him. It was as if knowing all these things about himself—his inadequacies and flaws, his lack of confidence and clumsiness—somehow provided a mysterious assurance. As if things would turn out all right in the end. He couldn't explain it, nor could he logically prove it. But it was very real—and very strong. Was this the faith Thaniel spoke of?

He looked at the waterfall that separated him from uncertainty. Yet, he now knew that his destiny lay in Nova Fannum. If he was somehow part of some great event; some universal and titanic struggle, then he would be the best Castus he could be. He had decided that it was better to die for something that shall always be remembered, than to live for something soon forgotten.

"Coming!" he answered.

He turned back one last time.

"Good-bye, Humus," he said, as he exited the cave.

The trip to the sanctuary, as Colyer called it, was uneventful. Sedgwin, a large man in a coat and hat with the brim pulled down over his brow, met the group just as Colyer had promised. He had all of the horses tied up to several trees. Jeffrey was glad to see Fortis again, and he imagined that Fortis was also glad to see him. In a few minutes the party was horsed and on their way.

The landscape of Nova Fannum at night took on an eerie quality—very different from the day, as in the daylight everything was draped in darkness and shades of gray. But at night the reflection of Nova Fannum's large moon gave everything a surreal, nightmarish quality. Colyer explained that only recently had the clouds begun to lift at night, allowing Lura, the moon, to shine unimpeded.

"I thought the clouds meant Blackheart's power was increasing," said Thaniel, as they made their way down a dark path. "Why should they be giving way."

"Blackheart is giving every indication that he is to be the new and Great King returned," said Colyer. "The clouds were merely a bit of sorcery so that as the day of his appearance approaches, he can even boast that the skies themselves gave way to his magnificence. Creation bowing to creator sort of thing."

"Abominable," was all Thaniel could say.

Colyer added that this retreat of the clouds also coincided very neatly with the recent appearance of the twin stars that would soon reach their zenith. The prophecy indicated that all would see these stars and Blackheart was making certain that the clouds would be unveiled in advance of this great day. Nothing would stand in the way of his being recognized as the Great King.

"He has quite a flair for the dramatic," said Colyer. "Part of what makes him so dangerous—and unpredictable."

"And what about Sedgwin?" asked Thaniel. "Where did you come by him?"

Colyer smiled.

"Poor Sedgwin. His family was either slaughtered or drank the cup a few years back. Ever since he has not spoken a word. I found him wandering in the forest."

He laughed.

"At first I mistook his size for one of Blackheart's creatures," Colyer said. "But he is gentle and a great servant. He is completely devoted to me. He would kill for me or lay his life down for me without thinking twice about it."

"Makes for a good friend," said Thaniel.

"Yes," said Colyer. "And a great enemy to Blackheart."

The horses stopped. Sedgwin, who was in the lead pointed down a hill. In the moonlight, where horse blended with man, he did indeed look like some mythical, hulking creature with four hooved legs—like a giant centaur of old. Colyer raised up on his horse and looked toward the front of the party.

"Ah, this is it," he said. "The next few minutes are tricky so hold on."

"Tricky?" Jeffrey said to Ethan. "What's that mean?"

Ethan shrugged.

In a moment he found out exactly what Colyer meant. The horses were moving slowly down a steep grade. Jeffrey could just make out the trail, which had narrowed considerably. Kierlin dropped an arrow from her kit. Colyer laughed.

"Better you do this at night," he said. "If you could see the drop off just to the side of us none of you would have come!"

"Great," Jeffrey said, just managing to hold on as Fortis brushed a large shrub on Jeffrey's right. "Watch it, Fortis!"

A moment later the horses fanned out as they came to an opening that was pitch black. The horses stopped once more and Colyer gave instructions for everyone to remain where they were. Sedgwin got off his horse and the sound of his footsteps crunching through the grass could be heard disappearing into the blackness. Suddenly off to their right a light appeared as a door opened in the side of a hill.

"Come in, come in," came a very cheery female voice. "Get off those horses. Sedgwin, tie up the horses, lad. Get them in here, Colyer!"

"We're coming, wife!" Colyer answered.

He turned to the others.

"She's very hospitable," he said, and added whispering, "but a bit bossy."

"I heard that!" came the voice.

"Has good hearing, too," Thaniel added.

Within a blink of an eye they found themselves in the "sanctuary" eating hot biscuits and meat and drinking some of the most delicious tea that Jeffrey had ever had. He felt the same warm feelings he experienced when Thaniel had taken him in at the mine. For the first time in a long time he could relax. He hoped.

Chapter 22

In the Sanctuary

COLYER'S wife, Brenetta, was a fantastic hostess and a very good cook. She fussed and dithered and otherwise made herself available to Thaniel and the others. Colyer smiled at his wife, knowing that she was in her element when she was serving others. The Colyer "sanctuary" was a large chamber carved out of the side of a hill. It was complete with a spring running through the center of the floor in an ingeniously engineered duct. The water was clear, cold, and quite satisfying.

"More tea," Brenetta asked in her lyrical voice.

Eager hands went up all over the room. Thaniel lit his pipe and thanked Brenetta.

"My lady this has been a most satisfying meal," he said. "We are all in your debt. And those tarts? Never have I had such a delicacy."

Brenetta blushed.

"Oh please," she said, setting the tea down. "Just a few things I popped in the oven. Practically make themselves."

"They're very good, ma'am," Jeffrey agreed.

Colyer looked at Brenetta as she cleared the table with quiet grace. She excused herself and took the dishes into another room.

"I have been quite blessed," said Colyer. "Brenetta has been my strength."

"She is remarkable," said Thaniel, nibbling on the final tart.

Colyer disappeared from the room for a moment and returned with a large map, rolled up and tied with a black ribbon. He unrolled the paper, and there on the table was a map of Nova Fannum. He began to point out critical areas. The map was written in Fannish, but Colyer explained quite clearly the lay of the land. Jeffrey decided that he may not read Fannish, but he certainly could read the land.

"Here is where we met you," Colyer said. "At the Fresan Spring. You see? Here's the trail we took. This is the trail along here that hugs the cliff. Thousand foot drop. That's why I told you it was just as well that you couldn't see it. Now this is the sanctuary—where we are sitting at this very moment. You spoke of the scared lake, Chenoir? It's here to the west."

"Yes, I have been there," said Thaniel. "The Kalul ruins are where we believe the last coin is hidden—*Balteus*. The Sacred Heart temple."

"Makes sense," Colyer said, reading the letter that Kierlin handed him. "But are you sure Phaesus isn't there yet?"

"I'm sure of nothing," said Thaniel. "But we bought ourselves some time with a false lead that I hope is engaging them. Barring that, Phaesus will eventually figure this out. We'll have to start after it tomorrow."

Colyer nodded.

"Wish I could go with you," he said.

"Not on your life," Brenetta yelled from the other room.

Colyer pointed to his ears and then toward the kitchen.

"Someone needs to stay and keep hope for the others who have not bent the knee to Blackheart," Thaniel said.

"If only there were more of us," said Colyer, dipping his tea. "And it's hard to trust anyone."

"So how can we communicate with people?" asked Jeffrey, looking up from the map. "How can we tell who is a friend and who is not?"

"It's difficult," said Colyer. "Phaesus's spies are everywhere. Not to mention the bounty on your head which has brought out a number of paid killers."

He sighed.

"Worst of all are those who have taken the Modestia—the cup," he continued. "They respond different ways to Phaesus's venom. Some die on the spot. Others become quite vacant of mind. Others turn into servile, thoughtless brutes. But, there is one indicator that always tells on them."

He waited as if for a dramatic pause.

"Their eyes," he said. "Their eyes become black and lifeless. Like button's on a doll. Problem is that by the time you figure this out you are already uncomfortably close to them. But they will largely leave you alone. Most of them are simply resigned to a lethargic, drone-like existence."

"Happy land," Thaniel muttered.

"Indeed," Colyer said grimly. "But you bring hope. And there are a number of us awaiting the moment to break this dark yoke that has gripped our land. We are prepared to fight when the day arrives."

"Servatrix?" Jeffrey asked.

Colyer looked at him.

"Yes," said Colyer. "The Servatrix. We organized years ago, though many of us were slaughtered in a treacherous betrayal. Some have even gone into hiding in other lands, other worlds even."

"We know," said Jeffrey. "We met Cren-Jaez. And Kierlin is a Servatrix warrior."

Colyer looked at Kierlin.

"Cren-Jaez is a great fighter," he said. "One day he shall avenge your father's murder and see Blackheart driven out of Nova Fannum."

"Yes he will," said Kierlin. "And he *is* a great fighter."

"Now," Colyer continued, "you will be supplied with clothing and supplies to get you to Cheno. That is the easy part. The question is: how will you get the coins back from Phaesus? I'm sure he is keeping them in his stronghold Caernclaw."

He pointed to the map.

"Here," he said, "to the southeast of Chenoir. If you are going to get the coins back in time, you'll have to defeat Phaesus here."

"Can it be stormed?" asked Thaniel.

"Not without a gigantic force," said Colyer. "The place is well protected by all manner of unholy beasts and sorcery. It will take something more than force of arms to defeat Phaesus at Caernclaw."

"Like faith?" Jeffrey said quietly.

Everyone looked at him. Thaniel teared up.

"Like faith," Colyer said smiling. "Once Phaesus is defeated and you have all of the coins, you must present yourself, Jeffrey, at the Temple atop the altar. Then the Great King shall appear as promised and Blackheart will forever be vanquished."

There was a moment of silence.

"Sounds easy," said Ethan. "When do we start?"

Everyone laughed.

"Nice, Ethan," said Jeffrey smiling. "But he's right. How are we going to get into Phaesus's stronghold?"

"Jeffrey, tell me something," said Thaniel. "Did you ever have rats in your inn?"

"Yes, sometimes."

"What did you do to get rid of them?"

"Well, when the lazy cat wasn't doing her job, we'd use traps."

Ah," said Thaniel. "And how did you get the rats in the traps?"

Jeffrey smiled.

"We baited them!"

"Exactly," said Thaniel. "And what did you use for bait?"

Jeffrey looked at everyone.

"Well, we used a lot of things. Finally settled on old bread soaked in broth. That's what they seemed to want the most."

"And that is what we shall do," said Thaniel. "We'll bait a trap for the rat!"

"But what will we use for bait?" asked Ethan.

"Jeffrey just told us," Thaniel said. "What the rat wants most."

"*Balteus*?" asked Jeffrey.

"*Balteus*," said Thaniel, looking at Jeffrey.

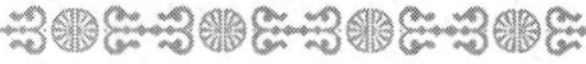

Jeffrey's horrified look told it all. The silence was broken by Ethan.

"Give him the last coin?" said Ethan.

"Are you sure?" said Jeffrey.

All eyes were on Thaniel.

"Are you suggesting that we use Balteus as bait?" asked Kierlin. "If we lose that coin, we lose everything."

Jeffrey nodded vigorously.

"But without the coins we have already lost," said Thaniel. "Hear me now."

Thaniel settled back in his chair.

"We have come a long way," he began. "We have met and made both friends and enemies. We have gained and lost the coins several times. We have established that Jeffrey—for good or for bad or for whatever reason—is the Pure One—the Castus."

"For bad?" Jeffrey muttered.

"We are now in Nova Fannum," Thaniel continued, "ruled by a monster and his wicked servant. Everyone here has lost someone because of this dark ruler. Some of us have lost everyone. We now stand at a point of decision. The one chance we have to overcome the evil and fulfill the prophecy is for the Castus to have the coins and mount the Fatuma Altar and usher in a new and holy age."

"But without the coins—all six of them—we cannot prevail. And darkness, which even now is gathering its strength, will ascend and conquer. Humus will fall as will other worlds. And there will be no hope except we die fighting or take the Modestia and drink from Blackheart's dark communion. The only chance we have is to get the coins. And the only chance we have for getting the coins is to appeal to the one weakness over which Phaesus has little control."

"What's that, Uncle?" asked Ethan.

"The same weakness that plagues us all," said Thaniel. "Pride. Phaesus is so consumed with this conflict that he could never turn down the possibility of having the prize of *Balteus* in hand. That will give us our one opportunity to get all of the coins back."

"But how?" asked Jeffrey.

"We will have one instant, supreme moment when we can strike," said Thaniel. "At the exchange, Phaesus will be distracted with the coin and then he must be killed."

"By whom?" asked Ethan.

"By the Castus," said Thaniel. "Phaesus will never turn down the opportunity of seeing the Castus humbled, with *Balteus* in hand, having given up the chase. You'll have but a second to kill him, Jeffrey. But you must do it."

"It will never work," said Colyer. "Phaesus will never fall for such a trick."

"Pride is a deceiver," said Thaniel. "And it is our only chance. We cannot storm Caernclaw. We must get close to Phaesus."

Silence for several minutes.

"I'll do it, Thaniel," said Jeffrey. "But how will he believe that I have become tired of the chase?"

"Sestrin will help us in that regard," said Thaniel. "By the time we have secured the coin, Sestrin will have found us. Then you will conveniently bemoan this whole Nova Fannum affair and plant a seed in Phaesus's mind that you are looking to get out. You know—whine as usual."

Jeffrey smirked at him.

"Not a great plan," Thaniel continued. "But it's all I can come up with right now."

"It's a horrible plan," said Kierlin.

Ethan nodded in agreement.

"But it's the only one we have," said Jeffrey.

He smiled.

"And if there is one thing I can do well and very convincingly, it's whine!"

"Here, here," said Thaniel, as they all laughed.

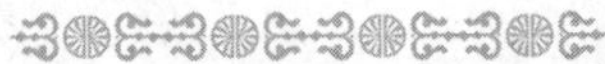

The next morning Sedgwin had their horses ready. Thaniel never explained how he had gotten the horses out of Humus and into Nova Fannum in the first place, but that's for another story. Brenetta made sure that they were sufficiently fed and well supplied with a couple of days meals as they said their good-byes. Colyer walked to Thaniel and spoke with him privately for a few minutes. Thaniel nodded his head and shook his hand.

"Farewell friends," Colyer said. "We'll see you in the great city on a happier day! Stick to the roads. And trust nobody."

Colyer and Brenetta stood together as they disappeared down the road. They said a quiet prayer for them. Afterward they destroyed any evidence of their visitors having stayed with them. Brenetta took one last look down the road and went inside the sanctuary. She was crying.

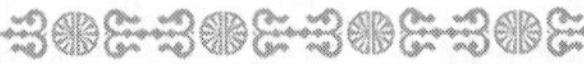

The first couple of hours were uneventful. Apart from the fact that everything was gray, it was a normal forest path in a normal countryside. Jeffrey continually scanned the sky and trees, hoping for signs of Corinth. But he never heard or saw his little friend. What would have made him disappear like that? Maybe the strange bleak colors had driven him mad?

An hour or so later they passed a farmhouse. A man stood outside, near the road. He watched silently, never moving, never waving, never acknowledging Thaniel's greeting as they ambled by. He just stood and watched. It was not until he rode near him that Jeffrey noticed his eyes—just as Colyer described them—black like a doll's eyes. A creepy feeling overtook Jeffrey and he hurried to catch up with the others.

"He drank the stuff," Jeffrey whispered to Ethan as he rode alongside him.

"Hush," said Ethan. "Want these things to go berserk or something?"

"What, you mean they aren't already berserk?" Jeffrey said, laughing. "If this is what Blackheart has to fight with we're in good shape."

"I'm sure Blackheart's regulars are not like that," Kierlin chided.

"Indeed we are not," came a loud voice.

"Stand still. All of you!"

From the side of the road came a strange-looking man in armor. He had a boar-like face, complete with little tusks, and was shouting orders. In seconds, several others came out from the brush and surrounded the group. They were armed with axes and swords, and they pointed and waved them menacingly.

The man who was apparently the captain of this troop walked over to Thaniel. He ordered the old man down. When Thaniel dismounted, the officer walked over to him and stood looking at him for a moment. Then he slapped Thaniel hard.

"You are a spy," he said in Fannish. "You are one of the criminals."

"Me?" said Thaniel. "We are pilgrims. We are simple holy people loyal to our Great King."

"Which king," said the officer suspiciously.

"The *only* King," Thaniel said.

"What are they saying?" Jeffrey whispered.

"How would I know," said Ethan.

"You're the Nova Fannum person," said Jeffrey.

"I was a baby!" Ethan said.

"Both of you be quiet," said Kierlin, who felt for her bow under her cloak.

"You'll have to come with us," said the officer. "Tell them to get off their horses."

Thaniel instructed everyone to dismount. Jeffrey wondered what he was up to but they did as they were told. The officer was laughing with his troops, and Jeffrey could tell they were talking about the horses. They seemed particularly interested in Fortis. They argued for a minute and then the captain screamed loudly and spoke with Thaniel.

"They are taking the horses," Thaniel said. "Or rather the captain is. We will walk alongside them."

Jeffrey looked at Thaniel.

"You mean he is going to ride Fortis?" he said.

"Exactly," said Thaniel, in his be-ready-for-anything voice.

The captain walked to Fortis and mounted the horse. Fortis looked back at his rider with a look that Jeffrey knew very well. He felt for the sword in his belt. The officer spoke softly to the horse in Fannish, but Fortis just stood and refused to move. Within moments he went from cooing to yelling—still Fortis would not budge. Jeffrey looked at Fortis' nostrils, which were beginning to flare, and smiled.

"Get ready," he whispered to everyone.

His guard grunted at him.

The captain cursed Fortis and kicked him hard with his heals. Fortis neighed loudly and reared back. He moved violently to the side, knocking one of the soldiers off the road and into some brush. The captain tried to gain control but Fortis would have none of it. The horse took off wildly with the captain screaming in fear for his life. Everyone watched as Fortis ran very fast under a tree with a low branch that caught the captain by the neck, breaking it and killing him instantly.

The other guards raised their weapons but Kierlin and Ethan were too quick for them. Jeffrey tied to pull his sword out but got it tangled in the clothing Colyer provided. The pig-faced guard grunted in delight as he raised his ax.

SMACK!

Fortis' hooves moved so fast that Jeffrey hardly saw them—but the guard certainly felt them as he was hurled backward unconscious. Jeffrey finally freed his sword and struck another guard in the neck, blood going everywhere. He got sick at the sight of this. The guard who had been knocked down by Fortis was cut down by a well-placed arrow from Kierlin. She turned to see Ethan retrieving an ax from the skull of another guard. The remaining soldier took off into the woods, squealing loudly. Ethan started after him.

"Don't let him escape!" Thaniel called out.

"He won't," said Kierlin as her arrow went through his neck in a streak.

Ethan walked to the guard and made sure he was dead. Then he gathered the horses together. Fortis came strolling up on his own, leaving the dead captain dangling from the tree, his head twisted in a strange angle.

"They know we're here," Thaniel said, looking about. "We best be off as quickly as possible. This was an advance squad. The larger force is not far away."

Kierlin walked over to Jeffrey.

"You OK?" she asked.

Jeffrey looked up. He had been physically ill.

"I never saw someone die that close to me," he said. "Just took me by surprise."

"I know," she said. "But remember. These creatures are evil. And if you don't kill them, they will kill you."

Jeffrey nodded and stood up.

"They didn't fight well," said Ethan.

"Or with much heart," said Kierlin.

"Those were some of Blackheart's scouts," said Thaniel. "They forage and harass in advance of regular troops. They're called the Aperis. Keen sense of smell. Nasty bunch. Rogue, but fearful of their commanders. The better troops are elsewhere. But Blackheart's best troops—his Procudium, are another matter. We won't face them until we get in the city."

"Well at least these Aperisians weren't too much of a problem!" Kierlin remarked, climbing on her horse. "They dealt with the wrong people this time."

"And the wrong horse!" Jeffrey said, grinning.

Chapter 23

CHENOIR ENCOUNTER

"BLAST this marsh!" said Jack, who was stuck again. "I told you horses would do us no good in this gray mud! Are you sure you are right?"

"Hold your tongue," said Pickworth, his own horse having trouble with the muddy ground. "I told you I am an expert at these things. This is a genuine letter. I compared it with other of Graysil's writings. And Phaesus has given me full authority on this expedition—so be careful!"

"Bah!" said Jack. "I still think we should have gone north."

"P-p-perhaps we should turn back," said Finius.

"Quiet," said Jack. "We'll follow the lawyer's instructions—for now."

The party continued on in the muddy bog, moving very slowly. The grayness of the land made things all the more miserable. But still no sign of the ruined fortress that the letter indicated. Jack looked around.

"Nova Fannum is an ugly land," he said. "I should have stayed in Humus!"

"When we find the coin, my friend, things will look much prettier," Pickworth said. "Great reward has a way of overcoming hardship. And *there* it is!"

Pickworth pointed ahead. On the horizon, just over a small hill, the top of a tower could be seen. Pickworth smiled at Jack, whose muddy face grinned back. He clapped his hands together.

"Ale tonight!" Jack said. "Eh, Finius?"

Finius smiled vacantly.

"Let's find the coin first," said Pickworth. "Then we celebrate. Hurry on now, you stupid animal!"

He dug his heels in the horse's sides and with one great lunge; the horse was finally on some dryer land. Pickworth raced toward the tower—all that was left of a once great fortress that guarded the western approach to Nova Fannum's greatest city. Jack and Finius followed, mud flying everywhere.

"We'll live like great princes in this land," said Jack, as he climbed off his horse.

Jack and Finius were covered with mud, but they didn't care. They raced ahead toward the ruined tower that stood about 80 feet tall. They began poking around the yard and looked for something to break down the tower door. Pickworth carefully read the letter to see what their next course must be.

"Well?" said Jack. "Where is it? Where do we look now?"

"Lake Chenoir!" came an icy voice.

It was Phaesus.

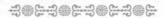

Pickworth swallowed hard and turned to see Phaesus standing over him. Sestrin was nearby, climbing a broken wall. Jack and Finius took off their hats and smiled at Phaesus, indicating that they were very busy looking for the coin.

"You said something about Chenoir?" asked Pickworth, regaining himself.

"You're in the wrong place," said Phaesus. We have been fooled!"

Phaesus glared at Pickworth.

"Impossible," said the lawyer. "This letter is Graysil's."

"Hand me the letter," Phaesus said.

Pickworth took the letter and held it out to Phaesus. A silver, metallic hand, in place of the hand Jeffrey had taken off, grabbed the note. Pickworth stared at the hand.

Phaesus saw him and smiled.

"I shall personally strangle Jeffrey with this hand," he said. "Or worse!"

With that, the letter suddenly burst into flames in Phaesus metal hand. He held it until it became ash. Then he threw it down.

"This letter was a trick," said Phaesus. "They are at Chenoir even now."

"Then we'll be off," said Pickworth. "Come along, men."

"Hold on," said Phaesus. "I have someone on the way to meet them. You fools return to Caernclaw."

Sestrin laughed his hissing laugh. And then Phaesus vanished with Sestrin in a brilliant flash that singed Pickworth's clothes. He brushed himself off, looking at himself in panic as Jack and Finius snickered.

"Quite a dramatic fellow," Pickworth said. "Well, we best be off to Caernclaw."

"I don't like that place," Finius said. "Those bizarre creatures that guard it and skulk around the grounds…"

"No more bizarre than you," said Pickworth. "Let's get moving."

"I h-h-hope that *one* creature isn't there," Finius said.

"He'll be there," said Jack whispering. "But we won't!"

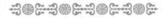

Lake Chenoir had been built as a monastic retreat—where Fannish priests took leaves for times of refreshing and meditation. It also housed one of the four great temples, though it had been destroyed by a fire a few years earlier and abandoned. The temple itself was called Kalul—the Sacred Heart, and sat on a rocky island in the center of the lake. It was a beautiful and serene setting, although it was much more picturesque before the darkness had set in and turned everything the now familiar gray.

"There was once a bridge leading to the gate of the temple," Thaniel said, pointing to the ruined temple. "But what a holy place! My brothers and I enjoyed coming here and having quiet and reflective days of worship and joyous fellowship with the Great King. Sometimes, the Prophet would come himself!"

He sighed.

"But look at it now. Just like the land—drab, dreary, and despairing."

"But housing hope, Uncle," said Kierlin.

Thaniel smiled.

"That's right, Kierlin," he said. "Good girl! Even the most despairing situation houses hope. And somewhere in that ruined temple is *Balteus*!"

"They are crossing the lake now, excellency."

"Wait until they are inside and then give orders to surround the lake. I want them alive. Especially Jefford."

"It will be done as you order, excellency.

"Discreetly, you hear?"

"Yes, excellency."

"I can't believe this bridge still holds up," said Thaniel as a plank groaned loudly. "We used to run across it. Solid as the Greenwoll Rock!"

"I think maybe the Greenwoll Rock smashed into it," Jeffrey said, as his foot crashed through a rotten span, wetting his leg.

Ethan and Kierlin laughed.

"Careful there, Jeffrey," said Thaniel.

"I'm all right," he said red-faced. "I never figured on getting across here completely dry."

"Ethan where did you tie up the horses?" asked Thaniel, as he stepped off the bridge and onto the island.

He scanned the lake's coast. Ethan pointed to a grove of tall trees.

"Over there, Uncle," he said. "Out of sight."

"Good lad," Thaniel said.

One by one the group stepped off the unsteady bridge and onto the rocky island of Kalul in Lake Chenoir. The temple complex took up most of the island, and in some places the water came right up to the stone walls. The building was constructed of immense gray stones, and several towers reached to the sky. It didn't look so bad—until one went inside.

"When you said 'destroyed' you certainly meant it," Ethan said, as he walked into an immense foyer. "Look at this."

Large, charred timbers lay scattered about on the center of the floor, along with a few misplaces bricks and other debris. The light of day could be seen above, where the ceiling had given way. There was also evidence of animals—or worse—that had been running through the halls. Jeffrey and Ethan climbed over the fallen beams until they found themselves in the center of the room.

"Careful there," said Thaniel, looking around the sad state of the room. "This place could collapse at any moment."

"Look here," said Ethan excitedly.

Everyone gathered around the center. Ethan pointed to the floor where he stood on a dusty, but perceptible mosaic of a heart with writing inscribed on it. In fact, as some of the clutter was moved, the stone floor revealed a beautifully inlaid picture of a sword, shield, helmet, sandals, belt, and breastplate in a circle. At the center was the heart on which Ethan stood.

"I forgot about that," said Thaniel, looking at the mosaic. "The Sacred Heart of Kalul. Some of the greatest artisans in Nova Fannum created this, one colorful piece of stone at a time."

"Sacred heart?" said Jeffrey. "Surely it can't be that easy."

"What, the coin?" said Thaniel. "I hardly think so. Graysil would not have made it that easy. But this must be the place. Scatter about, but be mindful."

And so they did. For the better part of the day they explored hallways, rooms, stairs, towers, the grounds—anywhere that might be a likely hiding place for the coin. By mid-afternoon, the searchers were growing weary. One by one they returned to the entryway, Thaniel last of all.

"So this is where you are," he said. "We must keep searching!"

"But we've looked everywhere, Uncle," said Kierlin. "Maybe we got it wrong."

"Nonsense," said Thaniel. "Your father obviously hid this in a spot that is not obvious and yet can be discovered—or he would have never left a clue for us."

"That which is sacred to the heart never really leaves it," said Ethan. "Well I give up. I've thought about those words all day long and still am coming up empty."

Suddenly Kierlin grew wide-eyed.

"No, no," she said to herself. "It can't be!"

She started rummaging through the sack. Everyone looked at her like she was crazy. Kierlin reached in and fished around for a moment.

"What are you looking for?" asked Jeffrey. "The coin?"

"This!" she said, pulling out a pendant in the shape of a heart. "Remember this, Uncle? My father sent this along with the letter and a few other items. I never wear it because I don't want to lose it. But I always keep it near."

"Your heart?" mused Jeffrey.

"Let me see it," said Thaniel excitedly.

The pendant was a miniature—a replica of the stylized heart on the floor. Everyone noted the similarity. Thaniel tried to open it but there didn't appear to be a hinge or any indication that it opened. After a few minutes he gave it back to Kierlin.

"Let me see it," Ethan and Jeffrey said at the same time.

Both tried to grab the pendant and in the confusion, the pendant dropped to the floor and the glass broke off the front, shattering into tiny red fragments.

"Look what you did!" Kierlin screamed, bending down.

Ethan looked at Jeffrey.

"We're sorry, Kierlin," he said.

"No, I mean look what you did!

Kierlin picked up the broken pendant and behind where the glass face had been there was a slip of paper with writing on it. Ethan and Jeffrey looked at each other, both excited and relieved. Thaniel took the little paper and tried to read it.

"The lettering is small," he said, moving to some better light. "But I think I can make it out."

After a few minutes he read aloud:

"Five pieces minus one

And the Armor is undone.

Truth is best that makes one free

And freedom's best when all can see."

Thaniel repeated the cryptic note several times. They sat about thinking and thinking but nobody had any answers. Thaniel paced as he reasoned it out.

"*'Five pieces minus one'* obviously refers to the Armor minus its central piece—the belt of truth," Thaniel said. "Remember. Truth is what binds everything together."

"Right," said Jeffrey. "Jaarad said the Armor is undone when truth is missing."

"*Freedom's best when all can see,*" said Thaniel.

"Maybe he means that he destroyed the coin," offered Jeffrey. "In order to free up the..."

He looked at everyone's doubtful looks. "Maybe not."

They stood around for a few more minutes.

"I know what he means," said Kierlin. "He means that the coin is hidden, but in a free place—a place where anyone can see it if they are really looking for it!"

"Very good Kierlin!" said Thaniel. "You *are* Graysil's child!"

She smiled.

"What do you think, Ethan?" she said. "Ethan?"

Ethan was transfixed on a spot on the floor. They looked at his face and tried to determine what he was staring at. He suddenly bent down and began looking at the mosaic of the heart at different angles. Then he grinned widely.

"Here!" he said. "On the belt! See? Uncle Graysil was telling us that the coin is hidden where we can all see it—but that it is hidden with the piece of the Armor which is most important—*Balteus*, the belt! Without it the rest of the Armor is undone!"

And before the others could even answer he bent down and felt the mosaic tiles on the picture of the belt. His fingers pried up a loose piece of the mosaic, a red stone, and underneath in plain sight was a coin! He lifted it up and handed it to Thaniel. The old man looked at it and his eyes teared up.

"*Balteus*," he said in a hushed voice.

Jeffrey patted his friend on the back.

"Excellent work, Ethan," he said. "You'll make quite a partner with me when we build the inn after this is all over!"

"What a thing to look forward to," Kierlin said smiling.

Thaniel knelt down and prayed. The others stood silently while he did. When he stood, he turned to everyone.

"And now comes the most difficult part of all," he said, handing the coin to Jeffrey. "The last chapter."

Jeffrey took the coin and tucked it into a pocket of the cloak Colyer had provided for him. He breathed a loud sigh and nodded.

"The last chapter then," he said.

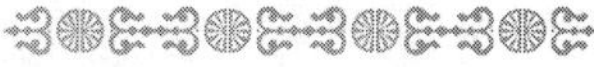

The mood while walking across the lake's bridge was more somber than when they first crossed it. They had accomplished their goal—and yet there was so much uncertainty. They had the one coin that was the key to everything—but now they had to face the brutal enemy whose darkness was so vile and power so sweeping that the land itself had taken on deathly shades of gray.

They walked over to their horses and climbed on them. Thaniel took one last look at the Sacred Heart complex where he had spent many happy times in better days. They waited for him to catch up and take the lead.

"This road will take us to another sanctuary," he said. "We'll meet Colyer there."

Thaniel started down the road.

"By your leave, Fortis," Jeffrey said, and off they went.

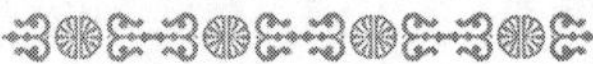

"Shall we take them, excellency?"

"Not yet. Why take only them if they are going to lead us to a whole nest of rebel vermin. We'll follow them to this 'sanctuary' and deal with them all at once. Pull your forces back for now. Give them room. And I want them all alive."

"As you command."

Chapter 24

CAERNCLAW

THEY spent the evening in an abandoned farmhouse, still about a half day from their next haven. The food that Brenetta had sent along was gone, and Jeffrey found himself missing Kreelin and his knack for always finding something for them to eat. All that was left was some bread and a few bits of cheese. Still, the fire in the hearth created a homey feeling and sleep would come easily.

"What a marvelous day," said Thaniel, warming his hands near the fire. "We actually found the coin! Thanks to Ethan's ingenuity and my brother Graysil's crafty mind, we now have the most important piece of all."

"But what does the coin do?" asked Ethan.

"So far nothing," said Jeffrey, who had been trying to determine the same thing. "I have been tying all day to coax its power—but nothing happens!"

Thaniel shook his head.

"I told you truth is the binding tie," he said. "Truth stands alone. It divides the false from the real. You'll know its power at the proper time."

"Uncle, where are we going next?" Kierlin asked, resting her head on Thaniel's shoulder and yawning.

"To the next sanctuary," said Thaniel. "Colyer has set up a station just inside Caernclaw's town. There are quite a few Servatrix there."

"What?" asked Ethan, who was stirring the fire. "That's Phaesus's stronghold!"

"What better place to hide from one's enemy than right under his nose?"

"How about behind his back?" Jeffrey said.

"Unfortunately we don't have time to play a cat and mouse game," said Thaniel. "We have to go to the enemy—into the jaws of the wolves."

"Yeah," said Jeffrey gloomily. "And I'm the first one in!"

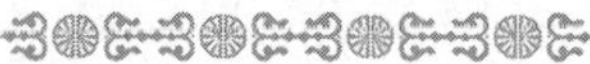

The next morning saw the group up early and on their way. Ethan took the lead, keeping a sharp lookout for any strangers, Fannish troops, or other characters. Though they blended in with their customary garb, they were still wanted fugitives with a price on their heads. They tried to navigate apart from the main road by following a map Colyer had provided. By mid-morning, they could see the wisps of smoke on the horizon from a little village. Ethan pointed it out to everyone.

"That's it," said Thaniel. "That is the town of Caernclaw—Phaesus's fortress. He

is governor over this region among his other duties."

"Uncle, I see people coming this way," said Ethan.

"Undoubtedly," said Thaniel. "Remain alert and calm. The closer we get, the more people we will see. According to the map, the sanctuary is to the south. We'll have to cut through the town itself—right past the main square."

"Great planning," said Jeffrey.

"It's either that or trudge through the poison marshes that Phaesus has created around this town," Thaniel said, "filled with venomous creatures. Colyer said we'd never have a chance there."

"Nice place," said Ethan, nodding at a passerby headed out of town.

No response.

As they topped a low hill, the town of Caernclaw came into view. To Jeffrey it seemed almost like his father's description of Edenshore in Aurora—a walled town with cobblestone roads, chimneys slanted this way and that, roofs of all shapes and sizes, the smell of breads and meats. The only difference, of course, was that this beautiful little town was draped, like everything else, in grey.

They stopped and Thaniel pointed out something else. To the south, a great fortress—the stronghold of Caernclaw from which Phaesus ruled on high. The walls went straight up some 70 feet. It looked like there was a trench or moat around the base of the fortress. And in the center was a large tower that dominated the horizon. If Phaesus was going to have a stronghold, this was just what Jeffrey would have imagined.

"Look at that tower," said Ethan.

"Look at that bread," said Jeffrey, passing by a vendor.

"Look how sad everyone is," said Kierlin.

And indeed, even with the scant commerce of the city that was going on, the people had vacant, forlorn countenances. They were as dreary as the grayness that cloaked them. And one thing else: there were no children around. Not one. It was as if they had walked into a prison built to resemble a town, and these townspeople were the convicted souls serving their sentence.

"Quit staring," cautioned Thaniel quietly. "And look alive. Remember this is Phaesus's domain. No sense in attracting any more attention than needed."

"I don't think they really care," said Jeffrey. "Most of these people don't even seem to see us."

As they turned into a narrow street to the right, a loud bell sounded seven times. It sounded like the noise came from Phaesus's tower. But the bell was not as startling as the result of the tolling: people stopped whatever they were doing and began flocking toward the main square. No smiles, no conversation; just a steady stream of vacant faces headed to the same place. Thaniel continued and the others continued on and soon they found themselves swept up in the crowd and moving inexorably toward the square.

The square itself was surrounded by attractively built shops, all in the typical Fannish style. And in the center was a large platform on which were several men garbed in priestly robes. Several others attended them. There was also a large, brass container, out of which the attendants were dipping a reddish liquid into goblets. The goblets were then being handed to people in line who drank and received a blessing from the priest.

"Phaesus's Modestia," Thaniel said to the others who could hear him. "Notice how they come for it."

"Not him," said Jeffrey, pointing to a man being roughly handled by three large men. "He isn't going quietly."

The men continued to beat him savagely, and finally, when the man was unconscious, they dragged him to a large wagon with bars around it resembling a cage and tossed him in. Several others were in there as well, some awake, some tending to the wounds of others. The crowd became suddenly quiet as the lead priest raised his hands to speak. He pointed to the people who had resisted.

"Woe to those who will not drink the Modestia," he said. "May the fate they bring upon themselves serve as our example that loyalty is both given and demanded."

The people began cursing and cajoling those in the wagon. Some even threw bits of trash and small rocks at them. The wagon moved out of the square slowly, letting most people get a look and a word in. One man in the wagon stood and hung onto the bars. He began screaming as the wagon moved on.

"Don't drink of that sorcerer's brew," he yelled. "It is a cup of death! Don't drink of that devilish cup!"

A rap on his face by a guard with a large wooden stick put an end to his protest. The crowd screamed in delight as the man fell to the floor of the wagon, holding his bleeding face in his hand. As the final people were served, the bell sounded again, seven times, and just as before, the people turned and began streaming away—back to their homes or shops. Within minutes the place was as empty as before. The priests were talking and laughing as they climbed in their wagon and headed toward Phaesus's tower.

"So that is how they do it," said Jeffrey.

"I would imagine that this is being repeated in every town in Nova Fannum," said Thaniel. "This is why Colyer and the others in the Servatrix are in hiding."

"You mean in waiting," said Ethan.

"Yes, of course," said Thaniel. "Looks like we crossed the square with no incident. That communion gave us cover. Now for the sanctuary. Should be just a couple of streets up."

In a few minutes a large figure began approaching them from the opposite end of the alley they had entered. Thaniel cautioned everyone to be alert. But as the figure closed in Thaniel smiled and announced that it was Sedgwin! The mute giant of a man nodded his head in greeting and, after looking around carefully, led them down the alley. Everyone dismounted and led their horse in single file. They stopped. One more look around and Sedgwin pushed a spot on the wall of a building and a door opened—big enough for horse and rider to enter. The door shut and one could not even tell that there was a door unless they had seen them enter.

"Clever," Thaniel said, as the door closed behind them.

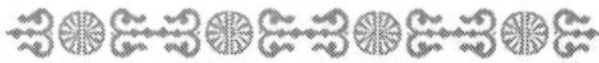

"Send word," came a voice. "Tell his excellency that we have discovered where they are hiding. They are all together in one place."

"Yes my lord."

"And have your forces close in."

"As you command."

"Welcome to Caernclaw," boomed Colyer's familiar voice.

Thaniel and Colyer greeted each other warmly. Jeffrey looked around the large room which served as a meeting/hiding place for the Servatrix rebels. Several men and women looked at him, whispering to each other. Some pointed. A young girl walked over and handed him a rose—a gray rose. Jeffrey smiled at the little girl who ran back to her mother, who nodded her head in greeting.

Colyer led them through the room into an annex that had a large table set with food. They all sat down and enjoyed a very good—and warm—meal. Colyer sat with them, drinking from a large tankard. The walls were decorated with animal heads—stags, boars, etc. Colyer informed them that this had been a hunting club in better days. Now the hunters had become the hunted.

"Who are all those people?" asked Jeffrey.

"Fighters, mainly," Colyer said, wiping ale off his mouth with his sleeve. "Some family members. Some of them have lost their homes to fire or favorites of the regime."

He spat.

"Collaborators!"

"We saw the Modestia," said Thaniel. "Horrible."

"You arrived on an opportune day," said Colyer. "Every seven days at noon the local priest arrives with his swill and the people come—mindless drones. You saw what happens when one resists."

"Colyer, how long do we have?"

"Not long," said Colyer. "An edict has come out of the city that in one week there shall be a prophetic event of some sort. These things were tacked up all over Nova Fannum. Here, read it yourself. You still have your Fannish?"

"My Fannish I have," said Thaniel. "But not my eyes. You better read. It's very small writing."

Colyer smiled and read:

"Be it known that Hendras, the Great White Heart and the Prophet have ascertained through much wrestling in prayer and piety, that the One on whom we have waited shall return seven days hence; when the twin stars have reached the Craxuz Triangle, the Castus—the Pure One—shall usher in a great and glorious age and reveal the True and Great King returned. The King shall arrive with his Holy Army and begin the reconquest of all worlds, so that Nova Fannum will forever be the seat of holy power and authority."

Colyer spat again.

"Sorry but that leaves a horrible taste in my mouth," he said.

"Hendras is mad," said Thaniel. "He is really going through with this prideful madness! And when was that posted?"

"Several days ago," said Colyer. "The stars will reach the center of the Craxuz Triangle in three or four days. And that holy army he speaks of? That's his monstrous collection of humans and beasts that he plans to use to conquer the other worlds—beginning with Humus."

Jeffrey looked up.

"But if we succeed," he continued, "if we can get the other coins from Phaesus and Jeffrey can stand on Fatuma at the zenith, then an entirely different age will dawn. One of true hope and glory."

"But how are we going to get him an audience with Phaesus?" asked Colyer. "That's the trick. Caernclaw is impenetrable. Somehow we'll have to get him close enough to Phaesus to kill him."

"Our only hope is *Balteus*," said Thaniel. "While Jeffrey holds that final coin Phaesus cannot risk losing him."

"Ah, yes," said Colyer. "Baiting the rat."

"So we just need to decide how to get me in to see Phaesus?" said Jeffrey.

CRASH!

A sudden deafening noise jolted the room followed by voices of men screaming, dust flying, children crying, and steel clashing with steel. They were under attack! Jeffrey and Thaniel found each other on the end of the room. Kierlin reached for her bow but the door she was standing in front of burst open, knocking her down. Phaesus's troops poured into the room, taking people captive at sword point. In just a few minutes the battle was over. Every Servatrix member was either killed or captured. The women and children were already being escorted out of the room.

A captain of Phaesus's guard strolled in. The troops stood at attention. They were strange looking, almost wolf-like in appearance, though not as hairy. They had dog-like snouts and canine teeth, but they had the form and ability of men. Strong men. The captain walked over to Jeffrey.

"I am Ladok, captain of the guard of Caernclaw for his excellency Phaesus, governor of this province," he said very calmly in Jeffrey's language. "And you are all under arrest for spying and insurrection."

"Captain, these are innocent friends of mine," Colyer said, indicating Thaniel and the others. "They have nothing to do with this group."

The captain signaled a guard who clubbed Colyer hard on the head.

"Anyone else?" he asked. "No? Good. Get them into the wagon. Phaesus wants to see you—one of you in particular."

They wasted no time tying everyone up and leading them out. Jeffrey stumbled over the body of a man he had just seen sharpening his weapon minutes before. Colyer recovered from the blow and stumbled along with help from Ethan. They were all led upstairs and into a large wagon—a jail wagon—and thrown in. The little bit of hay on the floorboards did little to cushion the rough contact. All their weapons, including Jeffrey's sword had been confiscated. He still had the coin, however, concealed in his clothing. As they got underway the wagon turned south toward the looming fortress Caernclaw—like a menacing giant awaiting his next victim.

"Well at least we got one question answered," said Jeffrey, smiling weakly.

Everyone looked at him incredulously.

"We don't have to worry about how to get an audience with Phaesus."

The crowds jeered the wagonload of prisoners as vehemently as they had those who had resisted the Modestia a few hours earlier. It seemed strange to Jeffrey that they could be so easily stirred from lethargy to violence so easily. Such was the nature of the dark communion, he supposed. The tilt up the hill began as the wagon climbed the road to Phaesus's castle stronghold, Caernclaw.

Built as a southern barrier to the Fannish Plain that opened the way to the city of Nova Fannum proper, Caernclaw was a foreboding stone structure that looked as impregnable as its reputation. What with Phaesus's conjurings and the authority given him by Blackheart, this had become a gathering place of wicked motive and unholy knowledge.

Caernclaw had once been a seminary for the priesthood. Now it was a school of sorcery, and all of the promising practitioners of forbidden arts came here to learn and become disciples of Phaesus. It was all very dark—and very neatly done.

They passed by a large walled-in area where wild screams could be heard. Sometimes one could not tell if they were human or otherwise. There were also strange flashes of light and flames that would sometimes spill over the top of the stone wall. In a few minutes all of the screaming stopped. Jeffrey looked at Colyer, who was sitting up now. Thaniel was seated next to him. Sedgwin was silent in the corner.

"What was going on in that compound?" Jeffrey asked.

Colyer looked at Jeffrey.

"Not sure," he said. "Usually happens on the Modestia days. I'm afraid we may all find out what was happening there. Personally."

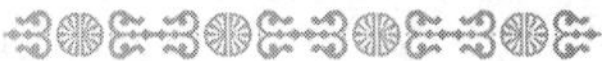

The wagon was pulled by two strange-looking beasts that Jeffrey had never before encountered. They looked like goats but walked on two legs, with massive chests and hair all over their bodies. They even had little horns. Grunting and straining under their load, the goatmen pulled the wagon into the shadow of Caernclaw's tower. The complex was built around the one great building, the tower. Several small buildings were built into the outer walls—soldiers' quarters most likely.

But the most bizarre and unnerving sight were the creatures that wandered about the yard. It was as if nature had gone berserk—they resembled humans but had the grotesque characteristics of animals and other fantastic beings that appeared only in books or nightmares. Some of these Jeffrey recalled from the *Codex Prodigium*, which had been taken with his other possessions. But some of the creatures were altogether unique. Three-eyed, horned beasts, cyclops, lion-men, goat-men, snake-like creatures that were climbing the walls, flying bat-like animals with horrible human-like faces. It was as if hell itself was on parade in Phaesus's compound. Perhaps it was. Jeffrey noticed that the human guards stayed clear of the yard, and remained stationed on the walls. He didn't blame them.

The wagon stopped in front of the main entry into the tower. A foreboding feeling overcame the wagon as a man came down the stone steps to meet them. This was it, Jeffrey thought to himself. From here on, it was all about seizing an opportunity to kill Phaesus and retrieve the coins. Jeffrey was about to say something to Ethan when the man began speaking. Jeffrey could hardly believe it—Pickworth!

"Welcome to Caernclaw," he boomed, as if he were a country squire welcoming his visitors for a weekend hunt. "We have been expecting you. In fact we have been tracking you ever since you entered Nova Fannum."

Pickworth walked around the wagon, peering inside. He was dressed in a cloak similar to that worn by Phaesus, although he didn't have the hood up. He stopped in front of Colyer and smiled.

"Well, old man they finally caught up to you," he said. "I'd say you need a good lawyer except that you have already been tried and condemned."

He stepped back.

"The rest of you shall be guests," he said. "At least for a bit longer."

He walked to where Jeffrey sat.

"My goodness, Jeffrey," he said. "Such a look! If your mother could see such manners. You are the esteemed guest at Caernclaw. You and Thaniel will be the guests of Phaesus in his private chamber. The rest of you have other quarters. Nothing fancy, but then you won't need them for very long. Bring them in. And watch them."

About a dozen human guards in black uniforms rushed out, and a captain began ordering the prisoners out of the wagon. One by one the prisoners were bound with their hands behind them until they stood in a group. Jeffrey and Thaniel were separated out and the others were taken away by some of the lion-men. Ethan and Kierlin looked back and Jeffrey told them good-bye, "for now."

"And now my friends, let us go and meet with Phaesus," Pickworth said, gracious as ever. "But you may freshen up a bit first. Impressions do matter. First rule of law!"

The long walk to Phaesus reminded Jeffrey of the time he and his father had visited a traveling circus that had set up near the inn. People came from all over to see the strange sights as promised by a slick promoter named Marco. This had been one of the few times in Jeffrey's life that the Trout and Truffles was booked solid. One night he and Malcolm stole away to see the circus for themselves.

Marco was all energy and much talk. The circus—just several wagons and a few tents really—was nothing like the yearly carnival in Edenshore with its festive foods, contests, acts, and games. But this was not Edenshore—and this was just fine. What Marco had that, as he so colorfully put it, "no other circus in Humus, and that means the universe" had, was his freaks. Jeffrey remembered being frightened of the poor misshapen people who had no other way of making a living apart from displaying their woeful state. And now, walking through Phaesus's Caernclaw, those same feelings were overcoming him—except that these hideous creatures were of Phaesus's devising and not a natural event.

"Steady lad," said Thaniel. "All we can do is play this out."

Jeffrey nodded silently.

"No whispering, please," Pickworth said. "These guards are a bit zealous some times."

The cyclops looked down with his ugly single eye and scowled at Jeffrey.

"See what I mean?" Pickworth said.

"Where are your partners in this crime?" asked Thaniel.

"Ah, you mean Jack and Finius," said Pickworth. "I'm afraid the partnership was liquidated."

"They were killed?" Jeffrey asked hopefully.

"They ran off," said Pickworth. "Bolted at the prospect of returning to Caernclaw having failed at obtaining the coin now in your possession. Neat trick by the way, planting that letter with its miscues."

Thaniel said nothing.

"I'm afraid there will be no more miscues," Pickworth said. "Ah, here we are."

In front of them were two massive doors, black and daunting. Pickworth fussed with his appearance a bit, and then, knocking timidly, announced that he had arrived with "Jeffrey Jefford of the Trout and Truffles, and Thaniel, priest of Nova Fannum."

The doors swung open and a voice ordered them to enter.

"One freak show to another," Jeffrey thought to himself.

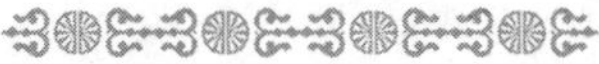

"Come in, come in," said Phaesus, who stood near a large window. "No introductions needed here. We're all old friends. Something hot for our guests!"

The cyclops grunted and bowed his head and left. It was all somehow fitting. The room was quite luxurious, albeit in a macabre sort of way. Blackness pervaded everything, as always in Nova Fannum. But in this setting the blackness was quite at home. The fire in the immense fireplace made the room quite comfortable. The furniture seemed plush and exotic. But the most striking feature of the room was a large crypt that dominated one whole side.

"We'll sit over here," Phaesus said, indicating a corner of the room with some chairs and a large table. He held up a silver metallic hand. "Oh yes. After your rather rude behavior I created an entirely new hand. Quite adequate."

He picked up a metal rod from the fire place and bent it in his hand as one would bend a blade of grass. He smiled at Jeffrey and then turned his head as a fluttering sound was heard from outside. He walked over and unlocked a single panel of the ceiling high window. In crawled Sestrin, who immediately disappeared in the dark rafters.

"Loyalty is hard to come by in Nova Fannum these days," Phaesus said, as they all sat down. "Sestrin was searching for the two traitors who were with Pickworth. He'll find them yet. Ah, our libations."

The cyclops set a tray down in front of everyone. He was attempting elegance and poise, but looked ridiculously out of place—a brute serving a delicate tea set. It was almost comical, except that it was real.

"Drink up," said Phaesus, the red dot of his eyes boring through the darkness of his silver mask. "I haven't forgotten how we served tea in the old days. Eh, Thaniel?"

"Some of your communion tea, perhaps"? Thaniel asked.

Phaesus laughed.

"Of course not," he said. "That is only for special times. Besides, if you are reasonable you won't *ever* drink of that particular brew."

Phaesus poured for the others, sipped his tea and sat back.

"Brilliant idea, however," he admitted. "As I said, loyalty is hard to come by in Nova Fannum these days. Sometimes loyalty must be encouraged."

"But that isn't loyalty," said Thaniel. "That is sorcery. These people aren't loyal. They are merely servile."

"True loyalty is always servile," sneered Phaesus.

"Something your own master taught you?" asked Thaniel.

Phaesus laughed.

"Don't try to provoke me, priest," he said. "I serve a greater cause than the Great White Heart. I am loyal to Hendras but never servile. He needs me far too much."

"The power behind the power," Thaniel said, sipping the tea after thoroughly sniffing it. "Pride behind pride."

"Perhaps," said Phaesus. "But power nevertheless. And that was what was missing here. Something was needed to make us a truly great nation. The prophecy became the catalyst. And the Armor and coins the key. You remember the saying, 'Whoever rules the Armor rules the rest.' We rule the Armor. And now we shall rule the rest."

"What is it you want, Phaesus?" Thaniel said. "You were privileged. You had access to the Great Temple. You served with all of us a Great King. You governed from Caernclaw. Yet you needed more. And so you fell in with Hendras and together your appetites grew for…for what? What is it you need? What is the 'rest' that you need?"

Phaesus scoffed.

"We served a Great King? We bowed to an invisible god, you mean. We all did, Thaniel. I simply decided that rather than serve a god I could not see, I would create a god that all could see."

He smiled.

"Gods that one can see are for more convincing to the masses. Especially when one has other conquests in mind as well."

"Humus," whispered Jeffrey to Thaniel.

"Yes, Jeffrey," said Phaesus, setting his cup down. "I'm afraid your poor nation will be the first to succumb. Then all the other worlds."

"What other worlds?" Jeffrey asked.

Phaesus looked at Jeffrey pitifully.

"I thought you were educating this boy," he said to Thaniel.

No response.

"And now to the matter of the coin in your possession," Phaesus said. "Delicate matter. But quite needful. I must have that coin to accomplish the final piece of this grand design. Surely you can appreciate that, Jeffrey, having had a father who was always in search of something great."

"Unfortunately all he found was you," Jeffrey said.

"Well said," Phaesus remarked. "But now the coin. You must willingly give it over to me."

Thaniel and Jeffrey looked at each other puzzled.

"Part of the game you never knew about, Thaniel. You see, the other coins could be taken. But *Balteus*, once in the hand of the Castus, can only be surrendered willingly. You see, truth, real truth, cannot be taken. It is given. You are the Castus, Jeffrey. No point denying it. But I need the coin."

Silence.

"Not being a fool, I am willing to bargain for it."

He stood up and indicated for Jeffrey to follow him. He walked him to the window and the two of them stood, peering into the darkness.

"You have a quality that the Great King deemed worthy," Phaesus said, his metal hand on Jeffrey's shoulder. "I honor that. In fact it's the only reason you're still living. But I appreciate your position, being a man of position myself. I will give you a fair price for the coin: the lives of you and your friends and safe escort back to Humus."

"Right," Jeffrey said, pulling away. "You'll escort us back to Humus to be conquered anyway. That is, if we get there without a sword in our backs."

"Did I forget mention that once Humus is conquered, we shall need a governor? A prince to rule over Humus from the royal palace at Edenshore? Just think of it, Jeffrey. A Jefford on the royal throne of Humus…"

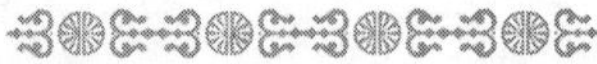

"Any ideas yet?" asked Kierlin.

Ethan looked at her.

"Not yet," he said. "But if we don't do something, we'll end up on that thing's plate for dinner."

Colyer was sitting up. They were in a large, square room. It was stony cold and dark. There were some other prisoners in the room as well, but they couldn't see them well enough to determine who they were. They were all chained together by their wrists.

"That is Phaesus's pride," he said. "A hideous monster called the Manticore. Uses it occasionally to frighten the populace into the Modestia. Comes in handy to take care of prisoners as well. Leaves no trace."

As if on cue, several of the dungeon keepers came in from a side door. They were laughing and talking in some gibberish that Ethan and Kierlin didn't understand. Colyer said they were speaking Gorbish—an ancient dialect known only to their kind: red gorbs. They were hulking, stupid brutal beasts perfectly suited as jail keepers.

They walked to the other end of the room and unlocked one of the shackles. One Gorb held a torch and the other an ax, just in case someone had an idea to resist. They grabbed the first unlucky creature—a dwarf—and brought the remaining man over to Ethan's group. The Gorb threw the man down and secured his chain to Ethan's wrist.

The dwarf was dragged to the large door, begging for his life. The Manticore could be heard scurrying back and forth inside.

The Gorbs opened a wooden panel that revealed a window into the room. One Gorb watched and waited at the window and in a few minutes signaled the other to open the door. The large doors swung open and the hapless dwarf was tossed in. The Gorbs shut the door quickly as the sound of the creature could be heard scuffling across the stone floor toward his victim.

Ethan and the others listened with horror as the dwarf screamed and pounded on the door. Then the pounding stopped and his face appeared in the window, where the Gorbs stood watching and laughing. A final ear-shattering, agonizing shriek came from the room, followed by silence and the sound of the Manticore tearing the dwarf apart. Ethan shook his head. Kierlin stared blankly ahead, her knees drawn up.

"Like I said, no trace," Colyer said grimly.

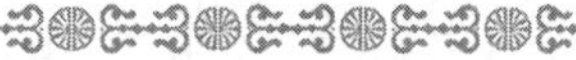

Jeffrey couldn't believe what he was hearing. This man—this monster—was offering him a place of power in the dark world he was creating? The very man who most likely ordered the murder of his mother, not to mention thousands of others? It was laughable. In fact, Jeffrey started to laugh.

"You find it amusing?" Phaesus said.

"More than amusing," he answered.

"In short, we will not turn over the coin," said Thaniel. "Since you cannot obtain it legitimately without Jeffrey's permission, it seems we are at an impasse. And should we have to die, we will do so without reservation."

"Don't worry, priest," said Phaesus. "I'll take care of the reservation. You have a few moments to think it over."

Phaesus left the room.

Ethan looked at the man who was joined to them now. He recognized him as the same person they had seen arrested earlier for refusing to take the Modestia.

"You're the man in the crowd," Ethan said. "The man who fought the cup."

The man looked at Ethan. He was about 30 years old. He had been beaten severely, as his bruised and swollen face told.

"I'm Brandsen," he said. "And who are you? Servatrix?"

"Not all of us," Ethan said cautiously.

"Don't worry about the Gorbs," Brandsen said. "They don't understand us. Nor do they care. They just throw us to the beast when the mood fancies them."

"What is that thing in there," Ethan asked.

"The Manticore? It's something akin to a scorpion, only much bigger. Loves live flesh and eats everything—clothing, boots, bones. Long as it is alive before it eats."

"Nice," said Ethan.

"The people here refuse to fight," Brandsen continued. "They are afraid. If only they showed a will to resist, they could overcome the Modestia. But you saw the level of resistance. Fear is a great killer of resolve."

"Well, we're resolved to get out of here," Colyer said.

"You're Servatrix?" Brandsen said.

"Yes," Colyer said. "And Phaesus has the Castus in his quarters. That's why we have to break out of here."

"The Castus? Here?" asked Brandsen angrily. "Why did you bring him here?"

"To get the coins from Phaesus," said Colyer. "The plan was to get in close and kill him. So far it hasn't gone according to plan."

"As far as we know," said Kierlin. "Jeffrey and Thaniel might be doing better than we think."

"We're not doing so good," Jeffrey whispered.

"Keep it up," said Thaniel quietly. "Apparently your having the coin presents Phaesus with a dilemma. He can't take it from you or the coins won't respond to him. Stay strong, Jeffrey."

"I'm trying," he said. "But I have nothing to kill him with."

They looked around the room for a weapon, but saw nothing they could use. Jeffrey quickly sat back down as Phaesus came back into the room. He sat down across from the two and stared at them for a few minutes.

"My time and patience are running out," he finally said. "I have offered you an exalted place in the future of this nation. Yet you refuse. But now I see why."

He looked at Thaniel.

"This priest is encouraging you in a wrong direction," he continued. "You forget that I hear everything Sestrin hears. So I have decided to separate you from this horrible influence."

Phaesus raised his hand and said something in a strange language. Thaniel froze as if paralyzed and began to levitate. Suddenly the crypt opened of its own accord and Thaniel floated just above it. Then with a smile on Phaesus's face Thaniel was lowered into the crypt and the lid closed with a definite lock.

"What is happening to him?" Jeffrey asked.

"Right now, nothing," Phaesus said. "But for the next hour, your friend shall experience new sensations of increasing pain at five minute intervals. If he lasts the hour, he'll have wished himself dead thirty minutes earlier. Spikes are driving upward, Jeffrey. At the same time, Thaniel is being forced downward. I guess you can imagine the outcome. Soon the spikes will begin to split his flesh, then bore through his muscle. Eventually the spike will come through with convincing force. I've even seen them split bone. A bit old school, but effective."

"Release him!" Jeffrey yelled. "Now!"

"Now I am the one laughing," said Phaesus.

He slapped Jeffrey hard.

"You have one hour before he is dead. Then it will be your friends' turn. But you, I will allow to live in one of my lower cells with some very interesting creatures. Memory is often much worse than death. And the memory of seeing your friends die will be much worse than the comfort death will bring them. Bind him!"

Phaesus left Jeffrey alone as the guards tied Jeffrey to a column in the room.

"They'll be coming for me next," whispered Brandsen. "That will be the last opportunity we have to escape."

"What is your plan?" asked Colyer.

"We have one brief instant when they unlock these, the chain that is on all of our shackles is free," Brandsen said, holding up his wrist. "When they come for me be ready for anything."

"That's your plan?" asked Ethan. "Be ready for anything?"

"You have a better one?"

"No."

"Then be ready for anything."

Chapter 25

Tower Encounter

JEFFREY was completely helpless. Every five minutes one of the guards came to the crypt and turned a wheel on the side causing the spikes to push up more and more. For all he knew, Thaniel was already dead. Jeffrey struggled with the ropes but there was no escaping. The cyclops guard certainly knew his job. The more he struggled with the rope, the tighter the knot was getting.

A chime sounded in the room again—another five minutes! How many more of these could Thaniel survive? The cyclops entered the room and moved the wheel another click. This time Jeffrey clearly heard a groan from the crypt. Maybe he could give the coin to Phaesus and develop a strategy to get it back later on? The cyclops stood by the crypt and awaited the next signal. Jeffrey could only wait as well.

The door opened again and the Gorbs, looking bored, started talking. They walked to their prisoners and stopped. One of them said something and the other nodded and pointed to Brandsen, who appeared to be asleep. The Gorb pulled an L-shaped instrument out and began turning the lock. The other Gorbs stood ready with weapons in hand. Brandsen appeared to be weak, as if he had given up. The lock opened.

At once they all sprung up. Colyer, who was on the end of the chain, pulled hard and took off running like a fish on a line. The chain pulled free from everyone and Colyer grabbed the chain in the middle and whipped a Gorb in the face. The Gorb dropped to his knees in pain, covering his face with his hands.

Brandsen grabbed an ax that the wounded Gorb had dropped and started swinging. A Gorb growled furiously and ran for help. Brandsen threw his ax at the fleeing guard but missed. One Gorb was wrestling with Ethan, his teeth bared. Suddenly he lurched back, grabbing for his throat. Colyer had wrapped his chain around his neck, and together he and Kierlin choked the Gorb to death. They heard the sound of many Gorbs rushing the room. Sedgwin grabbed two Gorbs and crushed their heads together like eggshells.

"Over here!" shouted Brandsen.

They moved over where he was standing, by the big doors that housed the Manticore. Ethan could hardly believe what they were about to do, but it was the best option—as Brandsen said, be ready for anything! The Gorbs poured into the dark room, like hornets whose nest had been disturbed. A shrill Gorb scream filled the room as they found themselves not confronting the human prisoners, but the Manticore!

The beast's tail went into action, stinging Gorbs at random. As more Gorbs came into the room they found themselves pushing against the panicked Gorbs trying to escape. The result was a chaotic death trap in which as many Gorbs were dying by their own hand in the melee as by the Manticore's giant stinger. The escaping humans added to the carnage by throwing random weapons into the crowd.

"This way," Colyer said, leading the others into the Manticore's pen. "There's a door in here!"

They crossed the stone floor and opened the door on the opposite wall. Several injured Gorbs had followed them in to escape the murderous confusion. They shut the huge doors to the Manticore cell. They saw Ethan and the others across the room but didn't seem to care if the humans escaped—they were just glad to have escaped themselves. The door was locked.

"Get those axes over here," Colyer screamed.

Ethan and Brandsen began hacking away at the door, but it seemed to be made of metal rather than wood. Suddenly Sedgwin moved in and with great effort pulled the door off its hinge. Ethan and Brandsen looked at each other and smiled.

"Comes in handy for escapes," Colyer said, as they moved through the open doorway.

"But must be murder on the decorator!" Ethan said.

Kierlin was the last one to move through the opening. She could hear the Gorbs on the outside pounding on the doors and screaming horribly. The Manticore would eat well.

"Where do these stairs lead to?" asked Ethan as they climbed the steps.

"I don't know," Colyer said. "We're making this up. But somehow we have to get to Phaesus's quarters."

At the top of the stairs, they saw someone carrying a torch in the distance to the right. Colyer decided to go left. They followed quietly through a maze of corridors, finally reaching what appeared to be a main hallway. A guard approached and Brandsen indicated that they step back. When the guard—a human—walked by, Sedgwin grabbed him and held a Gorban knife to his throat. Colyer spoke to him in Fannish.

"Where is Phaesus?"

The man was terrified.

"That way," he sputtered as the knife bit into his neck.

"And where are the weapons stored?"

"Over there," the guard said. "In that room."

"Show us," said Brandsen. "But quietly."

The guard led them to a room down the hall where they found all sorts of weaponry, armor, and most importantly, uniforms. They also found their own weapons which had been taken from them when they were captured. Kierlin was glad to get her bow back. And Ethan found the Sauren sword for Jeffrey. He only hoped he was still alive to receive it. In a few minutes they were fully armed and in Caernclaw uniforms.

"What do we do with *him*?" Colyer asked, pointing to the guard.

"This," said Brandsen, crashing the hilt of his sword on the man's head. He fell to the floor. "And now the Castus."

"Must be getting rather difficult in there," Pickworth said. "Too bad. Especially when relief is only a coin away."

Jeffrey didn't look at Pickworth. The lawyer had been with Jeffrey for the last few minutes, chatting as if everything that was happening was Jeffrey's fault. In truth, Jeffrey didn't know if Thaniel was still alive or not. But when the cyclops turned the wheel again and a muffled but distinct scream sounded from the crypt, Jeffrey winced.

"May I advise you?" Pickworth said. "As a lawyer, I mean."

"You mean as a scoundrel," said Jeffrey.

The door opened and Phaesus entered. He looked straight at Pickworth, who shrugged and shook his head. Phaesus cursed loudly.

"Enough of these games," Phaesus snapped. "Open the crypt."

The cyclops hurriedly turned the wheel back in the other direction and Phaesus motioned with his hand. The crypt lid lifted off.

"Untie him," Phaesus ordered. "Let him look at his friend."

Pickworth cut the ropes that held Jeffrey and the cyclops shoved him toward the crypt on the other side of the dark room. Jeffrey didn't want to see what remained of the man who brought him so far. Phaesus ordered him to the crypt. Jeffrey swallowed hard and walked over to the crypt and looked inside.

It was empty!

Jeffrey turned toward Phaesus.

"You fool," Phaesus said. "I did everything I could to get that coin from you, short of killing you. I sent Jack and Finius after your stupid father. I had Pickworth to bring you along. I involved Lorogos and the Saurens. But for the interference of Thaniel, I would have all of the coins by now. Out of respect for the ancient way I have allowed Thaniel to live."

He motioned toward the cyclops who left the room.

"I would have included Thaniel as a part of the new order of things," Phaesus continued. "He would have represented a comforting bridge to the past."

The door opened and Thaniel came in with the cyclops. Thaniel looked at Jeffrey and smiled weakly.

"Thaniel!" Jeffrey yelled. "What happened?"

"A cheap trick but a convincing one," Phaesus said. "The crypt has a false bottom. It serves as an escape tunnel. Although I never anticipate using it."

Phaesus acknowledged Thaniel.

"Jefford stayed pure, Thaniel. He didn't turn the coin over."

"Well done, Jeffrey," he said.

"Not so well for you," said Phaesus, who was increasingly angry. "Jeffrey, you have one opportunity to save Thaniel here and now."

The cyclops walked over with a very large knife.

"I will ask you once for the coin," Phaesus said. "If you refuse I will ask the cyclops to cut Thaniel's throat."

Jeffrey looked at Thaniel, as the blade stroked his throat. The cyclops towered over him in gleeful anticipation of killing him. His hot and hideous breath rolled down the back of Thaniel's neck.

"Do you mind?" he said. "Your breath is horrendous."

The cyclops actually pulled back a bit, as if intimidated by the old priest's gruff warning. Jeffrey couldn't help but smile. Tense as the room was, it was good to see Thaniel being his old cranky self. He looked at Thaniel, who gave a familiar wink.

"Well, Jeffrey which will it be," Phaesus said menacingly. "The coin or Thaniel's life."

Jeffrey looked at Thaniel, whose face was at complete peace.

"Jeffrey knows what to do, Phaesus," he said. "The coin must be surrendered willingly in order for you to invoke its power."

"Power or not I will obtain the coin, priest," Phaesus said. "There will be a Castus with every coin in place. That is all that matters. Sometimes the appearance of legitimacy is all one needs. After Hendras begins ruling, it won't matter anyway."

He looked down at Jeffrey once more.

"Well Jeffrey, which will it be? The coin that is really of no concern to you, or Thaniel's life, which is?"

Jeffrey thought about this position before. He had run such a possibility through his mind and in conversation with Thaniel. The two of them agreed that at all cost—even at the cost of one or both of their lives—the vow that Thaniel had taken to die before giving up the coins must be honored.

And yet a strange feeling overwhelmed Jeffrey: Thoughts of Thaniel stepping in and saving his life; of teaching him about faith and honor; of concern for a young man whose mother was murdered and whose father was missing; of a friend. He looked at Thaniel and suddenly thought of a different possibility. That perhaps Phaesus was right and this was not his concern, not his fight. Why should Thaniel die if Phaesus will get the coins anyway?

It was as if something was compelling him, speaking into his mind. He could hear Thaniel speaking in a muffled garbled sound. But he couldn't understand him. Instead he found himself reaching into his cloak and feeling for the coin. Was this real? Was that what Thaniel was saying? He pulled the coin out and could see Phaesus's silver visage grinning and nodding in approval. Over to the side, Thaniel seemed to be struggling with the cyclops but everything seemed unreal and dreamlike.

Jeffrey held up the coin and could see Phaesus's silver metal hand reaching out for it. He felt strange as he held the coin out, like the time he and a cousin had sneaked some of the inn's ale during a celebration. He looked over at Thaniel and smiled. Thaniel was screaming his name, but it all seemed slow. He read

Thaniel's lips—"I'm sorry Jeffrey." Jeffrey smiled at him like a drunk man.

SMACK!

Thaniel hit Jeffrey hard and knocked him down. The coin flew out of Jeffrey's hands, and Sestrin flew down after it. Phaesus ordered the cyclops to kill Thaniel.

"Look out, Thaniel!" came a voice in the room.

An arrow struck the surprised cyclops in his eye, and he dropped to the floor in agonizing writhing. Thaniel bolted to his left and saw Kierlin and Ethan entering the room. Behind them came Colyer, Brandsen, and Sedgwin.

"Call the guard!" Phaesus said. "I can handle these fools!"

He calmly threw his hand out and stopped an arrow that Kierlin had intended for his heart in mid-flight—it fell to the floor harmlessly. Then he created a ball of light in his hand and threw it at Kierlin, knocking her unconscious. Colyer heard guards approaching from the hallway.

"Sedgwin block this door," he ordered.

The mute giant of a man closed the door and braced himself against it to bar anyone from coming in. Jeffrey recovered his senses and saw Thaniel kneeling over him, smiling.

"I'm sorry lad," he said. "But Phaesus had taken over your mind with his sorcery. You were about to hand him the coin."

"I think I did," he said. "Sestrin!"

They watched as Sestrin picked up the coin and flew toward the window. The panicked creature found the window locked and screeched loudly. Phaesus turned from his fight with Brandsen and focused on the window, which immediately opened. Ethan tossed the Sauren sword to Jeffrey who took a swing at Sestrin but missed. Sestrin held on to the coin and broke for the window laughing.

WOOSH!

The arrow pinned him to the wall so fast he never knew what hit him. He struggled for a few seconds and then dropped the coin. Everyone turned to see Kierlin lowering her bow. Pickworth ran for the coin and grabbed it. But in the face of Kierlin's arrow staring him down, he dropped it. Phaesus was furious and stared at Pickworth.

"Coward!" he said.

Pickworth screamed as Phaesus raised his hand and, with a quick incantation, turned the lawyer into a rat. Jeffrey grabbed the coin, still wet with Sestrin's blood. Phaesus laughed and right in front of their eyes transformed himself into a giant snake. The serpent lunged at Sedgwin, killing him with a single vicious bite to the neck. He then grabbed Jeffrey in his coils before Jeffrey could get his sword in play.

"You fools," the snake hissed. "Nothing can stop this! Open that door now!"

"Phaesus!" Thaniel screamed. "You're forgetting something!"

The snake turned to Thaniel who held a torch. He rammed Phaesus's face with it. The snake shrieked and struck at Thaniel, just missing him. Ethan and the others surrounded Phaesus with their weapons and began attacking him. The snake's grip on Jeffrey loosened and he dropped him and slithered to the other side of the room.

The door burst in and about a dozen fortress troops rushed into the room. Ethan and the others turned their attention to this new threat.

"Jeffrey, go after the coin!" Thaniel yelled. "Find Phaesus!"

Jeffrey was now armed with the Sauren sword and rushed into the darkness after Phaesus. It was so dark he could not see much of anything. But he could feel the slimy floor where Phaesus was bleeding. He soon came to a stairway leading up—as did the trail of blood. He climbed the stairs and emerged on the top of the main tower. There across the roof stood Phaesus.

"Very good try, Jeffrey," Phaesus said, holding the coin. "But as I said, this is one prophecy you won't be able to prevent."

He looked at the sky and indicated the twin stars.

"They are almost set," he said. "Two days and a new era begins. And there will be no meddlesome priests to interfere this time!"

Suddenly a black streak rushed in and snatched the coin from Phaesus's hand and disappeared into the night.

"Corinth!" shouted Jeffrey.

SQUAWK!

Enraged, Phaesus transformed himself into a large black panther and charged Jeffrey, roaring furiously. The cat lunged through the air, teeth and claws bared. Jeffrey pulled out the sword and held it up clumsily. The panther shrieked as the sword tore through his body, knocking Jeffrey down.

Jeffrey was dazed for a moment, as the cat lay on top of him.

"Jeffrey! Are you alright lad?" said Thaniel as he emerged on the tower.

The others followed and looked at the dying panther. Jeffrey and the others stood over the beast and watched as it changed back to Phaesus. Jeffrey pulled out his sword and Phaesus, clearly near death, opened his eyes. The silver mask had now become a grim death mask. He suddenly shot up as if lifted by an unseen hand and stood as if to say something. He leaned against the wall of the tower.

"You're all in for a great surprise," he said, breathing very heavily. "This isn't over. Not at all."

"I'm afraid it is over for you, Phaesus," Thaniel said.

"Is it?" he answered.

And without another word, he leaned out and fell over the side. They heard the sickening sound of the metal and flesh crashing on the rocks below. For a moment everyone stood as if not knowing what to do next. Jeffrey sat down, shaken from the ordeal. The others did likewise. He looked up as Corinth glided in, coin in his beak.

"Corinth!" said Kierlin.

"Saved the coin," said Jeffrey proudly. "His thieving ways always did come in handy. Where did you come from?"

SQUAWK!

They sat for a few more minutes drinking in all that they had been through over the last few days. Down below someone had apparently discovered Phaesus's body. A large crowd soon gathered.

"We're in for it now," said Ethan looking at the gathering of soldiers, creatures and citizens. "Better get ready."

"Wait," said Kierlin. "Listen."

Instead of a raging mob there were cheers and laughter—hesitant at first, but then more and more pronounced. Within a few minutes the cheers gave way to celebration! It was as if a liberation had occurred! The fortress began to empty itself of its troops and the town became alive as former loyalists now took the opportunity to flee Caernclaw forever. Only those who had taken the cup remained impassive and spellbound.

"At least we still have the coin," Ethan said, sitting back down.

"Yes, but unfortunately Blackheart has the others," Thaniel said. "We hadn't counted on that. I'm afraid Phaesus was right. This is far from over."

"Perhaps, but one powerful enemy is dead," said Colyer, who was thinking of Sedgwin who had been killed in the battle.

The sound of squeals and scratching came from the stairs as a rat scurried onto the tower roof. Jeffrey smiled.

"And another has been reduced to a more appropriate state," Thaniel said. "Poor Pickworth. Lawyer to rat in one day."

"I'd call that a promotion," said Colyer.

"That's really not fair to the rest of the rats," Brandsen said.

The rat climbed on Jeffrey's feet as if begging for something.

"Poor Pickworth," Jeffrey said looking down at the pitiful rodent. He should have followed his own advice. Never bet on the wrong side."

He looked at Thaniel and winked.

"First rule of law!"

Jeffrey wondered what the reception would be like below. While everyone appeared happy with the demise of Phaesus, there were still all sorts of misshapen creatures and possibly loyalists around. They didn't have to wait long for an answer. A man appeared in the doorway of the tower and asked to speak with the one who had killed Phaesus.

"My name is Aldron," he said. "Phaesus's soldiers have fled. There are not many of us but we wish to join you. Not all of us have taken the unholy cup.

"Aldron?"

Aldron looked past Thaniel and Jeffrey and grinned broadly.

"Brandsen!"

He ran and embraced the man.

"I guess you are acquaintances?" Thaniel asked smiling.

"Brothers!" said Brandsen.

"I can tell," said Thaniel.

In fact, the men were twins and looked very much alike, although Brandsen was a bit taller than Aldron. The men looked at each other as a large rocket exploded in celebration overhead.

"I thought you were dead by now," Aldron said, looking at the brother he thought was lost to him. "We all thought so."

"Not yet," Brandsen said. "But it's still far from over."

Aldron thanked everyone for helping his brother. He turned to Thaniel.

"You are the priest?" asked Aldron. "What can we do to help you? We are not many but we will fight."

"Hold this place," said Thaniel. "Hold Caernclaw and pray. As word of Phaesus's death spreads, I'm sure others will join you here. But Blackheart won't allow this setback for long. For now, we must depart for the city."

He looked at the twin stars which were about center of the Craxuz Triangle. "Though I don't know what we will do when we get there."

"Phaesus said it himself," Colyer said. "They are still one coin short—the most important coin, thanks to this black bird here."

"Raven," corrected Jeffrey, who was stroking Corinth.

"Sorry," said Colyer. "Anyway, Blackheart will never have a legitimate claim unless he has *Balteus*. Shaky thrones are unhappy thrones."

"And apparently, *Balteus* must be delivered willingly into their hands by Jeffrey," Thaniel added. "Truth given and not taken."

"Meaning?" asked Jeffrey.

"Remember?" Thaniel continued. "Bait the trap, catch the rat. I expect an emissary from Blackheart himself in the next few hours offering you some sort of truce or deal. He must bargain now."

"In which case…?" asked Jeffrey.

Thaniel smiled.

"In which case, we have an opportunity to catch the biggest rat of all!"

Jeffrey was surprised that the people had turned on their ruler so easily. But Thaniel cautioned that theirs had been an easy victory. The test would be their willingness to hold onto this island of freedom in so dark a land. Nevertheless, they left Caernclaw as heroes, escorted out by 40 or 50 people who had never taken the cup or who had been in hiding like Colyer. Jeffrey felt sorry for those whose minds were stilled by the Modestia. Perhaps in time they would recover their wits.

Brandsen and Colyer stayed behind to organize the defenses against Blackheart's expected counterattack. It was sure to come, and they thought it better to stay with their own people and encourage them rather than join Jeffrey in the showdown with Blackheart. And so it was that Thaniel, Jeffrey, Ethan, and Kierlin parted with Colyer and Brandsen, left Caernclaw, and headed south to the great city of Nova Fannum.

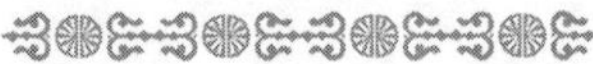

"How long until we get to the city?" asked Jeffrey, as they rode on a pleasant country road.

"Soon," said Thaniel. "By this evening we shall have reached the outskirts of Nova Fannum."

"Then what?" asked Kierlin.

"Then we decide on the final plan," Thaniel said.

Jeffrey didn't like the vagueness of it all. And yet this entire adventure had been one vague direction after another. Here they were having successfully killed Blackheart's second man—and arguably the most dangerous—and on their way to confront the wicked would-be ruler himself.

"You lived in Nova Fannum?" Jeffrey asked, as Fortis ambled along.

"Yes, Jeffrey," Thaniel said. "All of us did. My brothers and our families lived in the Great Temple complex. Nova Fannum was bursting with hope and joy and energy then. It was my hope that, had I a son, he might follow in my footsteps and become a priest of Nova Fannum. Wonderful times. Wonderful place."

"Does the city have a gate?" asked Jeffrey.

"Of course it does," said Thaniel. "A great city like Nova Fannum?"

"So how will we get past the guards?"

"Perhaps he will tell us," said Thaniel, looking at a rider approaching them.

Jeffrey looked up to see a richly adorned rider, with a banner on a pole attached to his saddle, gliding toward them. The horse had a cloth covering with a stylized heraldic symbol on it bearing the six pieces of the Armor of Nova Fannum and the name "Hendras" emblazoned in the center of them. Everyone prepared their weapons, but Thaniel held up a hand.

"He is an envoy," he said. "He has a message in his hand—not murder."

The envoy, about Ethan's age, bowed his head and greeted everyone. He was dressed in a black suit and had a hat with black feathers in it. Another man accompanied him and didn't say a word.

"You are Thaniel, former priest of Nova Fannum?"

"Some say I still am priest."

"And is Jeffrey Jefford among your number?"

"Some say so," Thaniel said cautiously.

"Then hear me all," he began, unrolling a scroll and reading:

To all present here in the company of Thaniel, former priest and Jeffrey Jefford, known to be the one foretold;

In as much as you have now entered this realm illegally and have cause much havoc and destruction, including the murder of a noble of the realm, Phaesus, governor of the region surrounding Caernclaw and invaluable counsel to the Authority; be it known that you and your party have been tried and sentenced to a most agonizing death. Sentence to be carried out immediately with evidence of your heads brought back to Nova Fannum this very day…

Upon these words a troop of soldiers emerged from everywhere—as if they had been invisible! They were Blackheart's elite soldiers—the Procudium—his very best. They quickly surrounded and disarmed all four before they knew what had happened. Corinth flew away and disappeared in the trees. Jeffrey swallowed hard as a large man with an ax appeared, an executioner, who stood by and awaited the signal. The messenger smiled and continued.

"However, because it is the eve of so profound a day when the Castus shall reveal the true king who shall forever reign, Hendras, the Great White Heart, has decided to extend to all of you clemency, along with lands and titles, provided that he meet with Jeffrey Jefford alone this very night to discuss terms regarding the return of Balteus to its rightful place and position…

"You were right, Thaniel," Jeffrey said. "The rat bit."

Thaniel smiled.

"Should you decide otherwise, the execution shall begin here and now without delay and the coin brought back to Nova Fannum for safekeeping.

The messenger showed the scroll to Thaniel.

"It is signed by Hendras," he said.

"I am sure," said Thaniel.

"So what will be your answer?" the messenger said, as the Procudium closed in tighter to prevent any tricks. "You have no time to discuss this. You must decide now or the girl shall be the first to die."

"Me again," Kierlin said resignedly.

"No need for that," said Thaniel. "Jeffrey will attend you. We know when we have been bested. So what shall we do?"

"The rest of you shall arrive this evening with the Procudium," he said. "You, Thaniel, priest of Nova Fannum, and you, Jeffrey Jefford, pretender and Castus, shall leave with me this very moment."

Thaniel looked at him puzzled.

"Hendras awaits us," the messenger said. "Please join me over here."

Thaniel and Jeffrey rode a few paces up the road and stood next to the messenger. What was this man up to? He grabbed an amulet around his neck and said a few words. Suddenly all three vanished—horses, riders, everything in a flash of light.

Ethan couldn't believe his eyes.

"Jeffrey?" he called out.

"They are in Nova Fannum," said a captain of the Procudium. "As we shall be shortly. Start moving."

"They certainly travel fast around here," Kierlin said, as their horses started.

Chapter 26

BLACKHEART

"WAIT here," the messenger said.

Thaniel and Jeffrey found themselves without their horses in a large, square room. The sides were decorated with enormous columns going up some 60 feet. They had ornate capitols and were as big around as some of the large tree trunks Jeffrey had heard of from the Stollweicz Forests near Edenshore. He watched Thaniel who was drinking it all in as if intoxicated.

"How did he do that?" Jeffrey asked.

"His amulet," said Thaniel. "It gives him the power to move from one place to another by merely thinking it."

"I could use one of those in Humus," Jeffrey said.

"It's forbidden and dark," said Thaniel.

They walked around the room, their footsteps echoing loudly. The room seemed both opulent and cold at the same time. There was a window high up near the ceiling that allowed some light into the room. Otherwise lamps were attached to the wall and gave an ethereal feel to it all.

"This is it, Jeffrey," Thaniel said. "This is the receiving area of the Great Temple! We're in the complex! It's been so long. Those were the very stairs I took to my quarters. They were also the last stairs I took when I left with the coin. Everything seems as before—except something..."

He nodded his head and wagged a finger.

"The colors of course," he continued. "Everything is this horrid gray. But Jeffrey, if you could see this marvelous temple in its splendor you would see white-polished marble and gold everywhere! And voices, beautiful voices, singing hymns to the greatness of our King..."

"The gold is still there, Thaniel," said Jeffrey. "It's just faded gold."

"Faded gold," Thaniel responded. "That is what Nova Fannum has become."

A man approached them from a side door, dressed in black robes and holding some scrolls in his arms. He indicated that they should follow him. He kept looking back at Thaniel as if trying to recall his face. The man, whose head was shaved, as required by the new Chief Priest, led them down a long hallway.

"We're headed toward the main corridor," Thaniel whispered. "Through that hallway is the Altar of Fatuma where the Castus must stand."

Jeffrey tried hard to recall all the twists and turns in this enormous building but found himself hopelessly lost. Suddenly they were confronted by two large doors. The man told them to wait outside and entered the room.

"This is it, Jeffrey," Thaniel said. "Hendras is on the other side of those doors."

Jeffrey was trembling. He felt for the coin. Still there.

"Don't be too quick to pull out that coin," Thaniel said. "We have to be alert in this matter."

The doors opened and the same man emerged.

"The Great White Heart shall see you now," he said with great pomp.

"Though Blackheart be his name," Thaniel muttered under his breath.

Without Thaniel as their guide, Ethan and Kierlin felt quite alone as they pressed on toward the great city that had once been their families' home. Though neither had seen Nova Fannum, having been born while their families were already in exile, they had a melancholy emotion as the tops of the great buildings began to emerge on the horizon. This was the home of their fathers, both murdered by the man who now ruled there. And it stung them both.

"Nova Fannum?" Ethan asked the captain.

The captain grunted back and nodded.

"That's a yes," Kierlin said.

"I bet that's the temple," Ethan said, pointing to a large dome that dominated the cityscape. "That's where our fathers served."

Kierlin nodded.

"And that must be the library!" Ethan continued. "Thaniel described it to me a hundred times with that pyramid roof."

"It's a beautiful city," said Kierlin. "But I think I'll like it better when I'm looking back at it instead of heading toward it."

Ethan smiled.

The doors opened to reveal another corridor that seemed to go on for miles. At the end of this was a great altar, in front of which Jeffrey could see a man in a robe. His back was to Jeffrey and Thaniel and he was facing the altar as if in prayer. The lamps on the wall were about 10 feet apart and Jeffrey counted at least 20 of these. The closer they got to the man, the more unnerved Jeffrey was becoming.

"Steady, Jeffrey," Thaniel said.

Jeffrey took little comfort in Thaniel's admonition. What was he doing here? How could he deal with a man of this immense power and ability? What was to keep him from turning the two of them into rats to join Pickworth? It was too late to run. He just hoped it would be over with quickly.

They stopped about 20 feet from the altar and waited. The man continued in his prayers for another ten minutes or so. Then he spoke, his back still turned.

"Do you have the coin?" he asked.

Jeffrey choked on the answer.

"We have," Thaniel answered, coming to Jeffrey's rescue. "But if I may speak to you, Hendras, as an old friend and partner..."

"Quiet old man," the voice said harshly. "I'll deal with you later."

"I'm afraid you must deal now," said Thaniel. "You know as well as we, that unless Jeffrey willingly gives up this particular coin, you cannot take it."

"There has been a change in plans," he answered. "I have no need for the coin. Just the Castus."

Jeffrey looked at Thaniel, his mouth agape.

"I don't understand, Hendras," said Thaniel.

"You will," said the man turning around. "Very shortly."

It was Phaesus.

The closer they got to Nova Fannum, the more people Ethan and Kierlin saw. Some gave curious stares at the young cousins who were prisoners of Hendras' special guard. Others turned away. But most—the vast majority of them—had the dull, black eyes of the Modestia—the cup that had taken their mind. They worked their fields, drove their carts, did their chores—in a stupefied state brought on by Phaesus's unholy communion.

"What good are people who cannot willingly love you?" asked Kierlin. "Look at them. Is Blackheart so desperate for their affection that he must take it by deceit?"

"It's all about controlling them," said Ethan. "Thaniel told me that. And Blackheart will do it in all the newly conquered worlds as well."

"Those poor people," Kierlin said.

She noticed a little boy in the crowd who seemed to be looking straight at her. He reminded her of a boy he she had seen whose father and mother had been killed during a running battle the Servatrix had with a Sauren raiding party. The boy's eyes were large and followed Kierlin as they rode by. For a few minutes he walked along with them. The last she saw of him was when they turned up the Grand Way to the temple. She gave a little wave and the boy waved back before disappearing in a sea of faces.

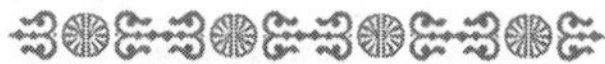

Phaesus laughed long and loud at Thaniel and Jeffrey's surprise. But it was not a cheery laugh. It was a sneering sort of chiding laugh, as when one has brought an enemy to book at long last and is thoroughly enjoying the moment. Phaesus stepped down off the altar and made a motion to an aide who hurried out some side doors.

"Please join me for a moment of refreshment," Phaesus said. "You must be very hungry after such a journey."

"Thank you," said Thaniel. "Will you join us?"

"Of course," said Phaesus. "Time is short and there is much to talk about."

They sat down at a sumptuous meal. It was then when Jeffrey noticed that the food had color. In fact, the whole interior of the Temple had its color.

"You probably are wondering many things," Phaesus said, as he drank wine from a goblet. "I shall hold nothing back, chiefly for two reasons. First, because you, Thaniel, have spent your life in pursuit of the coins of which we shall soon talk. Therefore you shall appreciate my plan more than anyone else I can think of. Second, I shall reveal all because the likelihood of your leaving here alive is quite remote."

He smiled and added.

"Eat well, gentlemen."

After several quiet, and as far as Jeffrey was concerned, uncomfortable moments, Phaesus sat back in his chair.

"You have been quite an adversary, young Jefford," he began. "I commend you. Not very many people can claim that honor."

"Thank you," Jeffrey said, confused. "Excuse me, sir. But I thought I killed you. I saw you die."

Phaesus pounded the table and laughed.

"Ah, Jeffrey. In a way you did kill me. You see, I found it necessary to create my double in order to be on mission for the coins while remaining here in Nova Fannum."

"But why?" asked Thaniel. "Surely your master, Hendras, can manage things in Nova Fannum without you."

"Can he?" Phaesus said slyly.

Thaniel looked at him for a moment and then nodded his head in quiet acknowledgment of a very capable antagonist. Jeffrey still didn't understand.

"How long?" asked Thaniel.

"Hendras?" said Phaesus. "He has been indisposed ever since we took communion together some years ago."

"The communion," Thaniel repeated.

"Hendras was brilliant but he lacked the ambition this vision called for," Phaesus said. "He was satisfied with taking the Armor. I insisted that we must have the coins as well and sent spies out for them. But Hendras ordered my men back in. I reasoned with him but to no avail. He disappointed me greatly. And so I contrived the idea of the Modestia—the communion. We drank to it. Unfortunately for him he also drank it."

Phaesus laughed.

"What did you do with him?" asked Thaniel, who lit a pipe that was offered to him by a servant.

"Hendras has been happily serving his people from one of the lower chambers," Phaesus continued. "Quite out of his mind. I immediately arrested those loyal to him and set about to find the coins that you and your brothers had taken. But events in Nova Fannum required the Great White Heart, as Hendras called himself, to be at hand. Thus I used all of my ability to create my double, which, as you pointed out Jeffrey, you succeeded in killing."

Jeffrey stared straight ahead.

"I had to give a portion of myself in order to create him," Phaesus said. "And so in a way a portion of me died. And poor Sestrin. But no worries. Soon, when the Castus, splendid in the Armor of Nova Fannum mounts the Fatuma, I shall be proclaimed the Great King."

"And suppose the true and living King returns, as the prophecy foretells?" Thaniel asked. "You will look very foolish abdicating that same day. That is if He allows you to live long enough to abdicate."

"You are a greater fool than I realized, Thaniel," said Phaesus. "What makes you believe that the true prophecy is unfolding?"

"Because the stars are in place," said Thaniel. "The twin stars have reached the Craxuz. Just as the prophecy said."

Phaesus smiled.

"Oh you mean like these," he said.

Phaesus opened his hand and little dots of light streamed out of his palm. They danced around the room a bit and then began to place themselves in distinct places, a map of the night sky. Last of all were the twin stars, which began a gradual ascent about level with the table and crossed into the Craxuz Triangle. They stopped in the exact location that the real stars found themselves now.

Jeffrey was amazed at this. He had seen something vaguely like it when a university astronomer came by the inn once in a special wagon that mapped the heavens. But these stars seemed suspended in air—as if they could be touched! Thaniel saw something much more significant in them. He looked at Phaesus, who had a satisfied grin on his silver, metallic face.

"Yes, Thaniel," Phaesus said. "I'm afraid those are phantom stars. As soon as I am proclaimed the Great King returned, they shall disappear."

"Very neatly done," Thaniel admitted. "You have fooled us all and given a great many people hope in something that is not even happening."

"Oh, it's happening," Phaesus said. "The delicious part is that when the real event occurs the people shall miss it. By then the Castus will have come and gone, the prophecy shall be spoiled, and my throne shall be secured forever!"

"But the coins responded to Jeffrey," said Thaniel. "If the time is not right, why should they do so?"

"Because, priest, the time is close," said Phaesus. "I would say that the true King would have returned sometime in Jeffrey's life. All I did was accelerate things a bit and secure my own kingdom."

"Brilliant," said Thaniel gloomily.

"I think so," said Phaesus. "Except for one delicate matter involving Jeffrey. I still need the legitimate Castus to mount the Fatuma Altar."

Jeffrey looked at Phaesus like he must be crazy.

"I know you hate me, Jeffrey," said Phaesus. "I can live with that. But my offer still stands. In a few days I shall begin the conquest of the other worlds, beginning with Humus. I will appoint you prince over that land. All you need do is bow to me here and everyone else shall bow to you. I'll even make it tolerable to you."

He held out his hand and a communion cup appeared in it.

"Drink this, Jeffrey, and we will serve together."

"Drink that and bow to you?" said Jeffrey.

He spit out a piece of meat.

"Crude, but pointed," said Phaesus, looking at the meat. "And not unexpected having spent time with Thaniel. But the communion is only for the event at Fatuma. Afterward your mind shall be free again. A short-lived dosage. It will just…take the edge off your humiliation."

“Forget it,” said Jeffrey.

“That’s right, Jeffrey,” Thaniel encouraged.

“I’ll have no more interference from you,” Phaesus said. “Guards. Take this priest where he can be alone to pray. Somewhere dark.”

The guards took Thaniel by the arms to escort him out of the room.

“Keep your nerve, Jeffrey!” was the last thing Jeffrey heard from him.

Jeffrey looked angrily at Phaesus.

“You better not hurt him,” he said.

“I’m not the one hurting him.”

“Let him go,” Jeffrey said.

“You love that old man, don’t you?” Phaesus said, standing up. “Sort of like a father to you.”

Jeffrey remained silent.

“Which reminds me. I have someone else here whom you love.”

A door opened behind Phaesus and two reptilian looking guards came in with a prisoner. The man looked up and squinted, as if even the scant light in this room was very bright to him. He had evidently not seen any light in some time. But Jeffrey had no problem with the light. He immediately recognized his father, Malcolm Jefford!

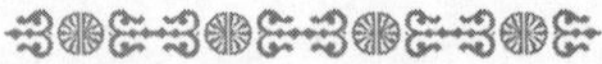

The horses stopped in front of a walled enclosure. Ethan and Kierlin were ordered off their horses. They stepped off and were immediately surrounded by a dozen or so Procudium. People in the street scattered as they formed a cordon around the two cousins.

"They must think we are pretty dangerous," said Ethan, amused at the amount of security that enveloped them.

"Yeah," said Kierlin. "I'm sure they are afraid of you."

"Well why else should they have all these guys guarding us?"

Kierlin looked into the crowd. There in the front of several men was the same little boy. She made a quick wave to him, which he acknowledged. Then she was shocked to see him discreetly pointing to a piece of paper in his other hand. He had a message for her!

"Kierlin, what are you doing?" Ethan said.

"Fight me, Ethan."

"What?"

She slapped him hard.

"What are you doing!?" Ethan said.

"Fight me!"

She slapped him again. This time Ethan responded by shoving Kierlin, who managed to fall in the crowd in front of the boy. The guards were laughing at the boy and girl fighting each other. They pulled her up and threw her back in the middle of the cordon. She dusted herself off. Ethan was still yelling at her. But she was smiling!

"Are you crazy?" he said. "What was that all about?"

Chapter 27

BEHOLD, THE CASTUS

"FATHER?" Jeffrey said, wary of one of Phaesus's tricks.

Malcolm opened his eyes.

"Jeffrey?" he said weakly.

He broke free of his guards and the two ran to each other and embraced. Phaesus held the guards back to allow their reunion. They held each other for several minutes. Malcolm was weeping aloud and repeating over and over again, "my boy, my boy." Jeffrey couldn't believe it.

In just a few minutes Jeffrey recounted the entire story for his father; how he had come after him; meeting Thaniel; the matter of the coins and the Sauren sword and...and about his mother. They cried together at the mention of Cornelia's death. For Jeffrey, this was a bitter-sweet moment—he finally found his father—and alive! They stood together for several more minutes. Finally, Phaesus spoke.

"I hate to break into such a tender moment," he said. "But now I am really pressed for time."

Malcolm shot an angry glance at Phaesus and sat down next to Ethan. He couldn't take his eyes off his son. But the reality of their predicament brought a sense of resignation to the reunion.

"What now, Phaesus?" Malcolm asked.

"The reason I had Pickworth deliver you here is because I anticipate every possibility," Phaesus said. "You were worth more alive to me than dead—at least until now. That is why you have been my guest for such a long time."

Jeffrey looked at Phaesus.

"That's right, Jeffrey," Phaesus continued. "By the time Pickworth visited you with that ridiculous letter, your father was already here—or rather at Caernclaw. Had he brought the coin with him in the first place, as instructed, none of this would be happening. But since he did not, we were forced to involve you and, unfortunately, your mother."

"Why did you kill her?" Jeffrey asked.

"Because she knew too much," Phaesus said. "And because she did not know enough. In the end, it was more convenient. And now you have a decision to make regarding preserving the rest of your family."

"What are you saying, Phaesus? What do you want?"

He held out his hand and the communion cup appeared again.

"You must drink of this cup," Phaesus said.

Jeffrey laughed.

"You expect me to drink that?"

"Drink the Modestia," he said. "It is only a short-term measure. But it's the only way I can trust you. Drink it and I assure you that your father will be spared and you will be released and can govern Humus together."

"My son will not drink your sorcerer's brew," said Malcolm.

"The alternative is to see you die before his eyes," Phaesus said calmly. "His mother was already dead when he arrived. It will be quite a different experience seeing his remaining parent slaughtered before his very eyes...just before his own death."

"In any case he will not drink."

"Think of it, Jeffrey," Phaesus said, ignoring Malcolm. "You finally have your father. You have an opportunity to live like a prince the rest of your life. You and your father can go home. You have been pulled into a conflict that doesn't concern you any further. So you may leave a prince. Or you may watch your father's throat cut like a pig in front of your eyes. And I don't mean quickly."

As he said this a man in black came in the room with a very sharp knife. He stationed himself behind Malcolm. Phaesus looked at Malcolm and suddenly he was bound to his chair by ropes that appeared out of nowhere. Phaesus was pleased with the effects his power had on people. The man raised the knife to Malcolm's throat.

"Remember, Justus," Phaesus said to the assassin. "Slowly. I want Malcolm to be aware of every drop of blood as it leaves his body."

Phaesus turned to Jeffrey.

"Well?"

Jeffrey looked at Phaesus. Could he let his father go for a second and final time? Something was telling him to take the cup. Probably Phaesus's mind game again. Still, here was a chance to save his father's life. But how could he trust Phaesus? He thought about it for several minutes and then did something that Thaniel would do. Would Thaniel try to talk his way out? Would he attempt an escape? Would he bargain? No—he would pray. And that was what he decided to do—pray to the Great King, Thaniel's Lord.

"I need a couple of minutes by myself," Jeffrey said.

"You have two minutes," Phaesus said. "New kingdoms don't wait. Keep that knife at the father's throat. If he moves—kill him."

Phaesus left the room. Jeffrey walked to the other side of the room, away from his father. Malcolm watched as his son knelt down—something he had never seen him do nor had he ever taught him. He felt very proud of Jeffrey at that moment.

"I am not very good at this," Jeffrey began silently. "You probably are not interested in the prayers of someone who is only coming because he is in trouble. And I know that I have never really believed in you. But I know Thaniel believes in you. And I believe in Thaniel. I believe his faith is sincere. He said that faith is what pleases you. So please hear me for his sake. What should I do? Should I take the cup?"

Silence.

"I don't blame you for not speaking," Jeffrey continued. "I only wish you would show me what to do…"

He began to cry.

"I just need to know. I need an answer."

"So do I," came a voice.

The door opened fully and Phaesus entered, with another aide.

"Your time is up, Jeffrey," he said. "I need an answer. What will it be?"

Jeffrey looked at his father. The knife was still at his throat. He closed his eyes and spoke.

"I'll take the cup, Phaesus."

"Jeffrey, no!" Malcolm screamed.

"I will not lose you again!" Jeffrey shouted. "I'll take the cup."

Phaesus smiled and placed his metal hand on Jeffrey's shoulder and began strolling with him toward a door. He signaled an aide to go ahead of them as if to prepare something. The aide scrambled out the door.

"Very good," said Phaesus. "You made a difficult choice. But the proper one."

"Let's just get this over with," Jeffrey said as he drank from the cup.

"Of course," Phaesus said. "At the proper time."

"And now, Jeffrey, there is something else," said Phaesus satisfied that the drug had done its work. "I must show you that which has been at the center of this quest for so long. Bring Thaniel and Malcolm to the Armor Room as well. After all, they should see what it is they are about to give their lives for."

He turned to his chief aide and pulled him over to a window. Outside was a large stone platform surrounded by colonnades. It was the Fatuma Altar.

"Prepare the Armor celebration," Phaesus said quietly. "Sound the trumpets throughout Nova Fannum for the holy assembly. I'll not wait another day."

He looked at the twin stars, neatly at the center of the Craxuz Triangle.

"It's time. Send for General On."

The aide bowed.

"As you command," he said.

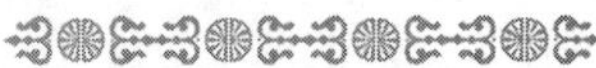

"Watch it!" Ethan shouted as the Procudium officer shoved him hard down three stone steps. He looked up and saw Kierlin being pushed through behind him.

"Look out Kierlin!"

She entered the same rough way and found herself on the ground next to Ethan. She rubbed her scraped forehead and looked at him.

"Thanks for the warning," she said.

"I tried," he answered.

Kierlin looked around them.

"What is this place?"

"Our prison, I guess," Ethan said.

They were in an open courtyard of some sort—walled in and opened to the sky. On the ground was an old, dirty straw mattress. The only door out was the one they had just come through. Ethan looked up—there was no way he could climb the smooth walls. He sat down.

"Guess we're here for a while," he said.

"Maybe not for long," Kierlin said. "The Servatrix are here. Have hope."

A long, low trumpet sounded throughout the entire city of Nova Fannum. Kierlin cocked her head and listened. It lasted for nearly a minute.

"I wonder what that was?" Ethan asked.

"Sounded like something is starting," Kierlin guessed.

Ethan looked up at the twin stars.

"I just hope it's not something ending."

Then he remembered.

"What was all that fighting business about?" Ethan asked.

She looked around and motioned for him to be quiet. Then she discreetly pulled the note out that the boy had slipped her.

"I had to do something to distract the guards," she said. "A boy gave me this."

"What? We don't have friends in Nova Fannum," Ethan said.

She motioned for him to be quiet again.

"Maybe we do," she said, slipping the paper back in her clothing. "Cren-Jaez is in Nova Fannum!"

The Armor Room, as Phaesus called it, was formerly the Room of Contemplation, where the priests gathered in the mornings to devote their day to their Great King. Phaesus had decided that once he became king, he would turn the room into a place of contemplation again—this time directed at himself. The room was elongated, at the end of which was a large, beautifully inlaid cabinet. Phaesus escorted Jeffrey through the long room.

They waited in front of the cabinet for a few minutes when Thaniel and Malcolm were brought in. Thaniel nodded at Malcolm. Jeffrey looked at the two men who were so important to him right now and wondered how this should all turn out. Phaesus greeted the two men.

"Welcome, both of you," he said. "I felt that this was too important a moment not to share it. Think of it Malcolm. Your son is about to don the greatest Armor ever and mount the Fatuma Altar as Castus, to pronounce me as the Great King returned!"

"Jeffrey?" Thaniel said quietly.

No response.

"You forced the cup on him," Thaniel said, looking angry.

"Not yet," said Jeffrey.

"Nothing so dramatic," said Phaesus. "He'll take it willingly. Just as he will wear this willingly!"

He opened the cabinet.

"Behold the Armor of Nova Fannum!"

Jeffrey really didn't know what to expect when he finally saw the armor. In his mind he had seen a beautiful suit with polished fittings and intricate engraving. What he saw, when Phaesus opened the door, was a rather plain looking armor. It wasn't even as spectacular as the armor he had seen on an Edenshore knight once. He was about to remark as much when he looked at Thaniel.

Thaniel was tearing up. He walked to the cabinet and looked over the sacred suit of armor for which his brothers had given their lives. He reached out and touched the breastplate. He shook his head in disbelief.

"It's been so long," he said. "The last time I saw this was when all of my brothers were together—so long ago."

He looked at Phaesus.

"May I…?"

Phaesus smirked and nodded. One by one, Thaniel pulled the pieces of armor out of the cabinet, handing them to Phaesus's servant who stood by.

"*Juaracas*—the sandals," he said. "They represented the authority and dominion of the Great King. That whosoever wore them take with them the good news of our King's love and compassion. *Cassis*—the helmet. This was your coin, Ethan. Allows great discernment and the ability to see and make seen. *Copis* was the coin your father bought, Malcolm. The sword of the spirit.

Copis represented the King's great ability as a warrior in overcoming his enemies."

He handed the heavy sword to Phaesus's servant.

"Ah, *Fides*! The shield of faith. Faith overcomes everything the enemy can throw at you."

He looked sharply at Jeffrey.

"Everything."

"*Lorica* is the breastplate of righteousness that lets one perceive when evil is near or when one is being false."

The servants sat the breastplate on the table with the other pieces. Thaniel reached in for a final piece—*Balteus*, the belt of truth. He held the belt. It was a finely tooled leather with six slots for the coins. They were empty.

"This, Jeffrey, is the final piece and the most important," he said. "Truth is what holds everything together. It gives meaning to the rest of the Armor. And it is the final coin—the one that cannot be taken from you without your consent."

He looked back at Phaesus.

"Without his consent."

"Careful, priest," Phaesus said. "He has already agreed to take the cup and mount the altar."

He smiled.

"He preferred his father's life to our politics."

The trumpet sounded throughout the temple area and complex. (This was the same sound that Ethan and Kierlin were hearing at that very moment.) Thaniel looked at Phaesus in amazement.

"So soon?" he asked.

"It's time," Phaesus said.

At that moment a troop of Procudium guards entered along with several officers. Among them was General On, commander of Phaesus's forces.

"The ceremony is about to start," Phaesus said. "Alert the army. The conquest of Humus begins the moment I am proclaimed king. And take these two to a more suitable place until the ceremony is over."

"As you command," General On said, and gave the order.

"And general," Phaesus said, taking him aside. "As soon as the Castus announces my authority, kill them—all of them."

The guards escorted Thaniel and Malcolm out of the room. Phaesus turned to Jeffrey and indicated the armor.

"And now Jeffrey Jefford, it is time for you to wear this armor."

Phaesus took a small leather bag out of the inside of his cloak and opened it, revealing the five coins he had. He picked up *Balteus* and, one by one, inserted the coins into the opening in the belt. Soon, five shiny coins decked the belt. He looked at Jeffrey.

Jeffrey sighed and handed him the final coin—*Balteus*, the coin of truth. When the coin was inserted, the entire armor took on a strange glow, empowered by the coins' return.

"And now, Jeffrey," Phaesus said, "Let us finish this."

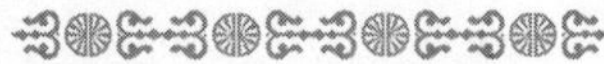

Because the trumpet had sounded, the city came alive with everyone streaming to the great Temple. The Fatuma Altar was in the center of a huge square pavilion, surrounded by enormous columns. People were not allowed on the stone platform itself, but they could watch and wait just outside. Ethan and Kierlin could hear much commotion and wondered what was happening.

"Do you think that noise has something to do with us?" he asked.

"More likely with that trumpet that sounded earlier," Kierlin said.

They heard another sound, this time outside of the door they had come through earlier. It sounded as if someone was throwing things. At one point the door actually moved as something crashed into it. Then it was silent.

"Now what?" Ethan wondered.

"Get ready," Kierlin said, as the door opened.

They saw a figure emerge hooded and looking around cautiously.

"Kierlin! Ethan!" the stranger said.

They looked at him suspiciously.

"Hurry!" the man said.

In the doorway was the unmistakable figure of Cren-Jaez, dressed in a typical Nova Fannum cloak. Several men were with him. At their feet were two Procudium guards. Cren-Jaez motioned for Ethan and Kierlin to come.

"We have to move out of here," he said. "General On is assembling his invasion force to attack Humus. And Phaesus is about to be proclaimed King."

"So what do we do?" asked Kierlin, stepping over the dead guards and into the street where several other Servatrix had gathered.

"The only way to stop the invasion force is to stop the ceremony," Cren-Jaez said. "General On won't make a move without Phaesus's authority."

"But the trumpet has sounded," said Ethan. "And look at all these people. We'll never get to the Temple on time."

"Maybe we won't," said a Servatrix officer. "But our forces are in all parts of this city. Perhaps we can still stop the proceedings."

"Or at least disrupt them," Cren-Jaez said.

"Magnificent!" Phaesus said, looking at Jeffrey.

"The armor never looked better. Especially since it is about to confirm my authority in Nova Fannum."

Jeffrey liked the feel of the armor. Since putting it on, he had felt somehow complete—as if this was something that was always intended and just now realized. Perhaps he could proclaim Phaesus and then kill him? Perhaps...

"And now Jeffrey, the cup."

Phaesus picked up the cup that he had produced earlier and held it up as if in great prayer and ceremony. Then he handed it to Jeffrey.

"This is an honorable thing you do, Jeffrey. Both for you and for your father."

Jeffrey lowered his eyes and looked inside the Modestia.

"Will you of your own free will drink of this cup, Jeffrey Jefford?"

"I will," Jeffrey said.

"Drink, Jeffrey," he said. "In the name of the Great King."

And he did.

At first nothing seemed to happen. Phaesus observed Jeffrey closely. In a few minutes his eyes clouded up and in a matter of seconds took on the dull, black color of the others who had taken the Modestia. Jeffrey stared ahead blankly.

"You will mount the Fatuma Altar at the seventh trumpet," Phaesus said. "You shall pull Copis and raise it. Then you shall say to all, "Behold your king returned!" I shall emerge and take the throne. That is all, Jeffrey. Then you and your father are free."

Jeffrey nodded vacantly. Phaesus took a step back and looked at Jeffrey.

"Behold, the Castus!" he said. "If only Hendras could see this day. He dreamed of it. But in the end he didn't have the ambition for it."

Someone entered the room.

"Excellency, all is in place," said the aide.

"Very well," Phaesus said. "Escort the Castus to his place. He has been instructed as to what he must do. And remind General On of his orders!"

"Yes, excellency."

"And now let us fulfill a prophecy."

Thaniel and Malcolm were taken down a level in the complex where a series of doors were set on either side of the hallway. The guards would give no information despite Thaniel's best efforts to get them to talk. They stopped in front of a door and the guard unlocked and opened it.

"He said 'suitable quarters,'" said Thaniel. "I'm afraid this won't do!"

The guard didn't even smile at Thaniel's attempt at humor and shoved the two of them inside the room. The room was a small cell complete with bars on the windows. Thaniel looked around.

"This is new," he said. "We didn't have need of a prison in the temple when I was here."

He shrugged.

"But those were different times."

"And look," Malcolm said, pointing to a bed in the corner. "We aren't alone."

Indeed there was a person in the small bed—a mattress really—who was covered and his back to them. They crept over to where he lay sleeping.

"Recognize him?" Malcolm asked.

"Not at all," Thaniel said. "Perhaps I can pull these back a bit."

The man woke up and Thaniel dropped the blanket. He turned and became frightened at the sight of two strangers standing over him.

"Please don't," he said, begging for his life.

"There, there," Thaniel said. "We're prisoners too."

The man relaxed a bit.

"Who are you?" he asked.

"I'm Thaniel, priest of Nova Fannum and this is Malcolm of Humus."

"Thaniel?" the man said, as if trying to remember. "Thaniel! The priest!"

"Yes," said Thaniel. "You must know me. But I don't know you."

"But you do know me," said the man sitting up. "I'm Hendras."

It took a couple of seconds for Thaniel to appreciate what was just said. He looked at Malcolm. This man was Hendras? The Great Blackheart? This broken man tucked away in the bowels of the temple was the man who once terrorized the priesthood and corrupted the office of the prophet of Nova Fannum? Thaniel examined the man as he sat up rather unsteadily.

He was much older than the last time Thaniel had seen him—his hair was nearly gone and his eyes had dark circles around them. He appeared weak and thin—but it was definitely Hendras, former chief priest of Nova Fannum. His piercing eyes still had about them that noble and priestly bearing which had been legend in Nova Fannum. Hendras sat on the side of the bed.

"Well, Thaniel, you finally returned," Hendras said. "I had given up all hope of ever seeing any of you again."

"Considering you ordered our murder I'm sure you are quite surprised," Thaniel said. "But my brothers died—every one of them."

"Hear me, Thaniel," Hendras said. "I never ordered your murder."

He looked at Malcolm.

"Who is this fellow?"

"Malcolm Jefford," Thaniel answered. "Father to the Castus, who is at this very moment about to usher Phaesus in as the king returned."

Hendras lowered his head in shame.

"Phaesus should have been dealt with early on," Hendras said. "I thought I was grooming a young priest. Instead I groomed a python."

Thaniel looked at Malcolm doubtfully.

"Are you telling us that you are innocent in this matter?"

"Not innocent," Hendras said. "I had ambitions. And ambition cannot serve in humility. And my ambition encouraged Phaesus. But when he began spending more time in the doctrine of demons and sorcery, than in his duties as priest, I confronted him."

He looked down.

"The dark knowledge got the better of him and he paid a horrible price," Hendras continued. "He was once quite handsome, you know. But he gave up outward beauty for inward corruption. I thought that the transformation which led him to wear the silver mask had humbled him, because it wasn't long after that he told me he wanted to restore our relationship. He invited me to take communion with him—the Modestia."

He laughed.

"Instead of being restored I was reduced temporarily to a servile idiot."

"But you planned with him," Thaniel said. "It was you who gave orders to take the Armor. You were the one who ordered the arrests..."

"I know that is how it appears," said Hendras. "And I am guilty. But only guilty of allowing Phaesus to seduce me. It was all so subtle. But the orders were his own."

He looked up at Thaniel and Malcolm.

"We spoke of the future of Nova Fannum and of the soon returning King," he continued. "As I said, he suggested that we introduce a new communion in honor of the great return. A communion for all the people. I believed this to be a noble gesture. And so we took the communion together as a sort of pledge. The next thing I knew I found myself conducting certain matters of state and sanctuary in a strange, trance-like state. I recall the day the Armor was brought into the council—a newly formed council hand-picked by Phaesus. By then Phaesus had complete control of my mind through his drugs and sorcery."

He looked at Thaniel.

"But when the Armor was ordered in something stirred inside of me and I began to protest. It was as if my very soul cried out in rebellion. Then it was reported that some of the priests had made off with the coins. I remember coming to my senses but was immediately arrested and tucked away down in these cells—a useful pawn for Phaesus's pleasure. I have been here ever since, dreaming that somehow you and your brothers would one day return and right the wrongs Phaesus and his council are responsible for."

"So all these years you have been a prisoner, and Phaesus has been ruling in your name?" asked Thaniel.

"Of course," said Hendras. "He only allowed me to live in case something went wrong and he needed to produce the scapegoat responsible for all of this. He keeps me updated on the latest events as to make me culpable."

He threw up his hands.

"But now it's too late. As soon as he is made king he plans to destroy the sacred texts and produce a new writing which will forever replace the old laws. Then he will export these laws to the other worlds, beginning with Humus."

"So we have heard," said Malcolm.

"What about this army of his?" asked Thaniel. "Is it as large as we have heard?"

Hendras nodded.

"Phaesus has assembled a hellish collection of creatures—human and otherwise—to subjugate and frighten Humus into capitulation," Hendras said, sipping a cup of water from a bucket in the room. "They aren't the greatest warriors, but they are loyal. And quite frightening for outsiders."

Thaniel held up his hand.

"What is that?" he asked.

A trumpet sounded a flourish. After a few seconds there was another, then another. Thaniel looked at Hendras, who nodded grimly.

"The Castus," Hendras said. "That is the assembly."

Then it's all about to begin," Thaniel said.

"You mean it's all about to end," Malcolm said, sitting down.

Chapter 28

FINAL BATTLE

KIERLIN and Ethan managed to mingle in the mass of people who were crowded around the great pavilion on which stood the Altar of Fatuma. The priests stood neatly in a row, splendidly arrayed in the garb reserved for most special occasions. The High Priest, a man appointed by Phaesus, was preparing to speak to the crowd. Kierlin wondered where the other Servatrix were—but they were so outnumbered that she wondered what good their little show of strength might do.

"If only these people would fight for themselves," Ethan said, looking around at the sea of faces with black, blank eyes. "They are like dead men."

"They might as well be," Kierlin agreed, shaking her head in compassion. "Phaesus's communion has certainly done its job."

"And now he's about to do his," Ethan said, looking at the High Priest of Nova Fannum step upon the dais. "I hope Cren-Jaez is ready."

The High Priest of Nova Fannum raised his hands to the crowd to make them quiet. Phaesus watched from a group of priests, dressed in the same costume for the occasion as the others. He didn't want to stand out from the others—not yet. His plan was to be summoned, pronounced the king returned by the Castus—called out, as it were, of the common pool of priests—and elevated by the chosen one personally.

"Citizens of this happy realm," the High Priest began. "Many years ago our Great King left us. He left us with His good word that He would one day return to usher in a golden age for Nova Fannum—an age of peace and healing and grace. And in His wisdom, He left in our care a noble suit of armor, the glorious Armor of Nova Fannum. The Armor was a symbol of His promise, and a key to His prophetic words.

"For he also promised that immediately before His return, the twin stars would rise in the Craxuz Triangle and then the Castus, the Pure One, would mount the Fatuma Altar wearing the Armor of Nova Fannum and usher in the King's return."

He looked up at the sky.

"Behold the Craxuz Triangle!"

The crowd looked up at the three stars that made a triangle. In the center were the two stars that had been on the rise for many months. The High Priest then turned to his right and spoke.

"And behold the Castus!"

Once more the crowd watched as Jeffrey, now in the Armor, walked across the pavilion. As he did, the priests broke out in glorious hymn. This was the first time the general population had ever seen the true Armor, and there was much buzz—even in their drugged state of mind. Jeffrey walked to the base of the altar and stopped. The High Priest glanced back at Phaesus who gave a subtle nod.

"And now, the Castus, chosen by the Great King himself, shall mount the holy Fatuma Altar and bring forth the Great King."

Jeffrey began climbing the six steps of the altar. The crowd was silent as he reached the top. Taking the sword from its sheath, he raised it high overhead. Phaesus waited for the words that would pronounce him king. But instead Jeffrey threw the helmet off and pointed the sword at Phaesus.

"You shall never be King in Nova Fannum, Phaesus," he shouted. "Nor anywhere else. You are a usurper and a fraud."

The crowd began murmuring.

"I never asked to be this Castus," Jeffrey continued, now addressing the crowd. "But in as much as I was chosen, my mind became clear when I took on the Armor. Don't you see? The King has returned—but not in person. His Kingdom has returned within. He lives in each of your hearts if you will only believe. Believe on Him and the darkness that has overtaken your minds will disappear."

"Heresy!" charged Phaesus. "He speaks heresy. Burn the heretic!"

Phaesus and his priests began inflaming the crowd. They began repeating the charge of heresy and called for Jeffrey's death. Phaesus gave orders to arrest Jeffrey. The captain of the guard, a huge man named Brondel, charged the altar with a squad of men. He smiled as he saw the Castus—a mere boy, he thought to himself.

"Come along boy," he said. "Make this easy on yourself."

Brondel never heard the arrow that killed him. Nor did the men with him as they died in a flurry of well-placed missiles. A horn sounded from the crowd and what seemed like hundreds of arrows flew as the Servatrix opened up on the guards around the pavilion. Priests scurried as guards trampled out—everyone trying to either save their own lives or get into the fight. Phaesus found General On.

"Order your troops in," he said. "Tear this rabble to pieces!"

"But excellency, we don't know who is friendly and who is not in this crowd," General On pleaded.

"Just kill, general," said Phaesus coldly. "Unleash those creatures and let them kill. You take care of the Servatrix. I especially want Cren-Jaez dead."

He looked to the altar where Jeffrey stood.

"And leave the Castus to me!"

Ethan smashed his ax down on a Procudium officer. The man fell with a thud. He turned to see Kierlin firing one arrow after another. Off to her right he could see Cren-Jaez and his best warriors in the thick of fighting. Most of the citizens had scattered, leaving the true number of the Servatrix exposed.

"They have us far outnumbered," Ethan yelled at Cren-Jaez.

The warrior leader didn't answer.

A growl unlike he had ever heard suddenly came from behind him. He turned to see an army of loathsome beasts—strange creatures, half-men, half-animal, coming at them with an array of axes, swords, clubs, and other crude but lethal weapons. Without even thinking Ethan brought his ax around and caught a cyclops in the neck, cutting him down. A large flying creature zoomed past him, knocking him down.

He looked up as two creatures, half-human and half-wolf, stood over him, baring their teeth. Cren-Jaez's sword took both of their heads off in one swipe, and Ethan felt himself being pulled up by some very strong arms.

"We're pulling back," said Kierlin, as they fought their way toward the pavilion. "There are too many of them."

"But we can't just quit," said Ethan, struggling to stay with the Servatrix.

"We're pulling back to the pavilion to regroup," Cren-Jaez said.

Ethan looked up at Jeffrey, who was fighting a Procudium guard.

"I'm coming, Jeffrey," he said. "At least we'll die together!"

"Jeffrey Jefford!"

Jeffrey turned to see Phaesus standing with General On. The general's army had surrounded the pavilion and what was left of the Servatrix was huddled in the middle, ready to defend themselves. The thousands of creatures that made up Phaesus's army only waited the signal for the final attack.

"As you see it's a lost cause," Phaesus said. "But I am still willing to deal with you and give you a share in this kingdom."

"You still don't get it," Jeffrey said. "You're finished. You and all liars. I drank your Modestia and you know what happened? Nothing! And you know why? Because the power of truth overcame the power of your lies. And that is why you have lost, Phaesus. The Kingdom of the Great King is within! He has already returned to those who will believe in Him. You're through!"

Phaesus was getting angrier and angrier as Jeffrey spoke. "General On, give the order to slaughter these criminals. But save Jeffrey's friends to the last. They will die on this altar—a new sacrifice to their new king!"

General On raised his hand and his army began cheering, preparing themselves for the final charge. The Servatrix—about 60 left—tightened their circle and prepared to die. Ethan looked at Jeffrey and nodded, as if to say, this is the way it needs to be. The general lowered his hand to signal the charge when he stopped with a look of horror on his face—to the west was a large army approaching! Banners and shiny swords and spears and uniforms—who were they?

A general panic began in the ranks as the unholy army of Phaesus began looking around and wondering what was happening. General On looked at Phaesus.

"Give the order, idiot!" Phaesus shouted.

"Yes, excellency," General On stammered. "Attack them now!"

Some of the creatures moved forward on the pavilion, but others found themselves engaged by this newly arrived army from the west. Phaesus even moved into the thick of the fighting to spur the troops on. But it didn't help. Within a few minutes the creatures under General On's command began to fall apart. The Servatrix on the pavilion were able to kill anything that approached them without a single loss. The rescuing army was now just a hundred yards away.

General On fought his way to the center of the huddled Servatrix. He saw Cren-Jaez, and called out to him.

"Your time is up, Cren-Jaez," General On said, his sword pointed toward the warrior.

"And yours has been up for some time, traitor," said Cren-Jaez.

"I knew you were weak when we appointed you a captain of the Procudium," On said. "Now I'll forever put an end to that mistake."

The two men's swords clashed loudly. Back and forth they parried, and Cren-Jaez felt his arm get sliced deeply. General On laughed. He charged Cren-Jaez for a final thrust, but at the last moment Cren-Jaez jumped to his side and brought his sword down, catching General On under his breastplate. The sword sunk deep into his chest. The general fell to his knees. Cren-Jaez pulled his sword out and the general dropped to the ground with a final groan.

"Jeffrey! Jeffrey! It's me!"

Jeffrey turned to see a figure approaching him with a battle uniform and insignia of the Sauren king.

"A Sauren in Nova Fannum?" Jeffrey thought to himself.

"I thought an army might come in handy," said the soldier coming up the altar steps. "I see I was right!"

"Kreelin!" Jeffrey shouted.

The two greeted each other on the altar.

"I decided it was time to take a stand in this after all," Kreelin said smiling. "When the Sauren king discovered Phaesus had been using him, and that Lorogos had died because of him, he was furious. We have been marching for days!"

"Little good it will do you!" said Phaesus.

Jeffrey and Kreelin turned to see Phaesus grasping the amulet around his neck. His silver, metallic mask took on a macabre grin, as his form began changing. Jeffrey stepped back, sword in hand as Phaesus turned himself into a large, silver dragon with iron teeth and three-inch claws. The dragon roared and laughed as he snapped Kreelin aside with one swipe of his tail.

"At least I'll have the satisfaction of killing you," he said in a hissing voice.

Jeffrey raised his sword but the dragon batted it away with his claw. He hissed as he toyed with Jeffrey, pawing him as a cat circles its prey. Jeffrey held his shield up to fend off a lunge by Phaesus, and the dragon grabbed it with his teeth and tore it away from Jeffrey's hands. He showed Jeffrey his razor talons.

"What's the matter, Castus?" the dragon sneered. "The fight not in you?"

Suddenly Phaesus lunged at Jeffrey, pinning him down on top of the Fatuma Altar. Everyone could see what was happening and the fighting stopped as if both sides awaited the outcome of the fight that would decide the day. Cren-Jaez charged the dragon and hit it with his sword—but his sword would not penetrate. It was as if the dragon was protected by invisible armor. He laughed and batted Cren-Jaez down with his head.

"You see, Jeffrey," he said. "I have armor of my own! Nothing can penetrate my protection. See what a little forbidden knowledge can get you?"

"No weapons left, Jeffrey?" said Phaesus, looking at him, his dragon teeth sharp and menacing. "Your sword is gone. Your shield."

He looked down at Jeffrey's belt.

"All you have left is the truth you hold so dear," he said hatefully. "And that you will take with you to your grave."

The dragon opened his mouth for the final attack. Jeffrey closed his eyes.

"No, Phaesus," a voice said. "*You* take it to the grave!"

Phaesus turned to see Hendras standing with *Copis*, the sword. Thaniel and Malcolm stood behind him.

"You!" the dragon hissed.

"The guards are abandoning their posts, Phaesus," Thaniel said. "Just as you abandoned the Great King."

"Stay out of this," the dragon said. "You're only making your death all the more painful."

"Not as painful as we made the lives of thousands in Nova Fannum," Hendras said. "We had honor and threw it away for personal power. We both deserve death."

"You first!" Phaesus roared.

Enraged, he lunged at Hendras, knocking the old man down. Hendras managed to toss the sword on the ground in front of Jeffrey just before the dragon broke his neck. As he lay dying he called out to Jeffrey weakly.

"Plant the truth deeply, lad."

Phaesus turned to Jeffrey.

"And now, Castus, it's your turn!"

Phaesus charged in a great silver streak.

"Watch him, Jeffrey!" Malcolm called out.

The dragon reared up for his final lunge, his red eyes blazing. Jeffrey grabbed the sword and, for the first time in his life, felt as if something or someone greater than himself was driving him—empowering him, encouraging him. He felt supremely confident as he faced the dragon's wrath.

"In the name of the true King of Nova Fannum!" Jeffrey called out.

He let the sword fly—sinking it deep into the dragon's chest. The dragon roared horribly, spitting blood and snapping at Jeffrey even as he fell to the ground.

"How did you get through my shield," Phaesus sputtered.

"Because truth overcomes in the end, Phaesus," Thaniel said.

"What is truth?" Phaesus sneered.

"A dragon killer," Jeffrey answered, looking at Thaniel.

Thaniel smiled and winked in approval.

Phaesus writhed and bled terribly for a few more minutes before he became still. He looked up at Jeffrey, raising his long neck just a bit, and with a final defiant hiss, died. With their leader dead, what was left of the army Phaesus had gathered for his intended conquest, descended back into the darkness from which he had called them.

Ethan stood next to Jeffrey, over the body of the dragon. He pulled the sword out of the beast and handed it back to Jeffrey. Thaniel and Malcolm joined them.

"You did it," Ethan said. "You actually killed him."

Jeffrey shook his head.

"I didn't do anything," Jeffrey said. "It was something inside me. In my heart. I suddenly felt a great peace. And a voice saying, 'Jeffrey I am with you. My Kingdom lives in your heart.'"

He looked at Thaniel.

"Don't you see? That was what the Great King spoke to me when I put on the belt. Phaesus's drug never had a chance. The King *has* returned—but not on a throne made by men. He lives in our hearts if we only believe!"

"But the stars," said Cren-Jaez. "The prophecy. How could He return before the stars truly came?"

Thaniel looked up. The stars—the illusion created by Phaesus—were gone. The Craxuz Triangle was empty once more.

"He is not bound by our laws or prophets," said Thaniel. "But He honored His word. And what Phaesus intended as an evil plan, the Great King used to his glory. Phaesus was too clever for himself and in the end, sealed his own fate by fulfilling the prophecy. The King honored His word. Phaesus profaned it.

Either way, the King was glorified. As Jeffrey said, truth overcomes in the end."

"I'm very proud of you," Malcolm said, hugging his son. "Your mother would be proud too. I bet she is watching all of this."

Jeffrey nodded.

SQUAWK!

"Corinth!" Jeffrey said, as the raven flew in and landed on his shoulder. "Where have you been?"

"What's this?" Malcolm said, pulling a gold stone from his beak.

Thaniel took the stone.

"This is Phaesus's amulet," Thaniel said, examining the amber charm. "His dark powers were vested in this vile thing. We must get rid of it! I'll see that it is thrown in the deepest lake in Nova Fannum!"

Thaniel placed the amulet in his cloak.

Kierlin walked over to Jeffrey and kissed him on the cheek.

"What was that for?" he asked, red-faced.

"Consider it an apology," she said. "From one fighter to another."

Ethan laughed.

"She finally says it, and the war is over!"

Jeffrey turned to his father.

"Let's go home," he said. "Ethan and I have an inn to get started."

Malcolm nodded.

"And Dad… No more maps for you."

Epilogue

A FINAL SAY

THUS ends the first grand journey of Humus's greatest hero, Jeffrey Jefford. The encroaching darkness, no longer imperiling the land of Humus, has abated, and the radiance of hope has broken through the perpetual night. Color has returned everywhere, Phaesus's evil communion no longer holds the people, and Jeffrey, while still just an innkeeper's son in Humus, was made a prince in Nova Fannum, along with Ethan and Kierlin. Thaniel was named high priest and serves to this day.

Evil remains, to be sure, in other worlds, and Jeffrey plans to make adventure there someday. But hope has returned to this ordinary place, after being turned upside down by greed and chaos.

Possibly best of all, as far as Jeffrey Jefford is concerned, business at the new Trout and Truffles has picked up. And once more in its proper place, the Sauren sword hangs proudly over the mantle.

About the Author

D. Brian Shafer is a pastor and writer. He lives in Waco, Texas, with his wife, Lori, and their three children, Kiersten, Breelin, and Ethan. He is the author of the Chronicles of the Host series, available in bookstores nationwide.

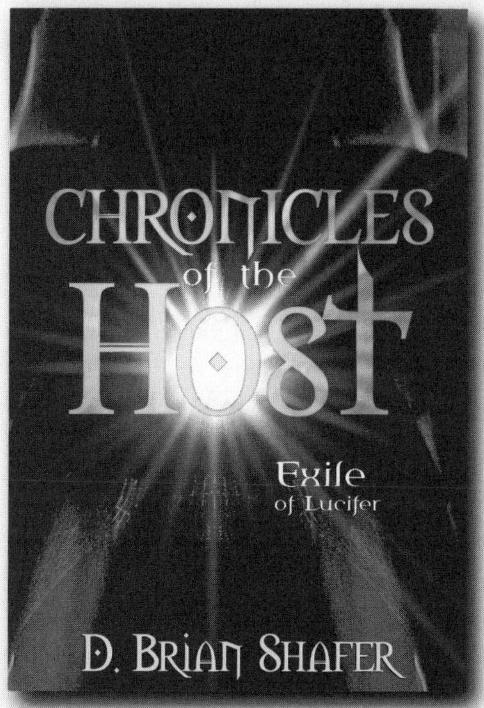

CHRONICLES OF THE HOST

By D. Brian Shafer

Lucifer, the anointed cherub, whose ministry in Heaven is devoted to the worship of the Most High God, has become pessimistic about his prospects in Heaven. Ambition inflamed, he looks to the soon-to-be-created Earth as a place where he can see his destiny realized. With a willing crew of equally ambitious angels, lucifer creates a fifth-column of malcontents under the very throne of God. Hot on their heels, however, is a group of loyalists, led by Michael and Gabriel, who are suspicious of lucifer's true motives. In detective-style fashion they slowly start to unmask the true nature of lucifer's sordid plot.

ISBN 10: 0-7684-2099-7
ISBN 13: 978-0-7684-2099-9